BELINDA BARES UP

'I'll give you a catalogue,' purred the girl. 'We find that discerning customers enjoy adding to their collection.'

Belinda had a tingly feeling that 'discerning' meant 'not actually owning a horse'.

She assured the girl she had no intention of being timid, and the girl licked her lips, with a fierce glint in her eyes. She wrapped the crop in crinkly gift paper, very carefully, and snapped the folds into place with loud cracks, like the lashing of Jan's cane. Belinda took the package, and handed over a ten-shilling note.

'Remember that for the best, that is, most painful, effect the crop should always be applied on the bare skin,' the girl said, giving Belinda a half-crown and a florin in change.

'Why, of course,' said Belinda. 'Ponies don't wear trousers.'

'It depends on your pony,' the girl murmured.

By the same author:

MEMOIRS OF A CORNISH GOVERNESS
THE GOVERNESS AT ST AGATHA'S
THE GOVERNESS ABROAD
THE HOUSE OF MALDONA
THE ISLAND OF MALDONA
THE CASTLE OF MALDONA
PRIVATE MEMOIRS OF A KENTISH HEADMISTRESS
THE CORRECTION OF AN ESSEX MAID
THE SCHOOLING OF STELLA
MISS RATTAN'S LESSON
THE DISCIPLINE OF NURSE RIDING
THE SUBMISSION OF STELLA
THE TRAINING OF AN ENGLISH GENTLEMAN
CONFESSION OF AN ENGLISH SLAVE
SANDRA'S NEW SCHOOL
POLICE LADIES
PEEPING AT PAMELA
SOLDIER GIRLS
NURSES ENSLAVED
CAGED!
THE TAMING OF TRUDI
CHERRI CHASTISED
BELLE SUBMISSION
STRAPPING SUZETTE
THE ENGLISH VICE
GIRL GOVERNESS
THE SMARTING OF SELINA
LACING LISBETH

BELINDA BARES UP

Yolanda Celbridge

This book is a work of fiction.
In real life, make sure you practise safe, sane and consensual sex.

First published in 2005 by
Nexus
Thames Wharf Studios
Rainville Road
London W6 9HA

www.nexus-books.co.uk

Typeset by TW Typesetting, Plymouth, Devon

Printed and bound in Great Britain by Clays Ltd, St Ives PLC

ISBN 0 352 33926 8

Contents

You'll notice that we have introduced a set of symbols onto our book jackets, so that you can tell at a glance what fetishes each of our brand new novels contains. Here's the key – enjoy!

1

Bare Licks

Chin on her knuckles, and long blonde tresses tickling her bare wrists, Belinda Beaucul (pronounced 'Buckle', as she had to keep telling people) gazed out of the window of her classroom in Heysham Young Ladies' Academical, towards the hazy wide bowl of the sky, a delicious mirage of pinks and blues over the shimmering waters of Morecambe Bay. Far in the distance lay the tongue of Walney Island, and the filaments of smoke rising from the factories of Barrow-in-Furness, wreathing the occasional aeroplane buzzing like a solitary bee, from the American air base at Nether Kellet. Belinda dreamed of the lithe young fliers, smiling and loose-limbed in their leather jackets. They needed no clothing coupons to look dishy. If only one of them would carry her away on silver wings, to some eastern palace, where she could be a princess, in silken robes, eating sweetmeats, and being . . . ever so beautiful!

She pressed her bare knees together, brown, from a summer's cockling on Morecambe sands, and exposed, with her short pleated blue skirt ridden up her thigh. All girls wore short skirts, due to rationing, but also because it was quite spunky for a seventeen-year-old girl to show her knees, and no one could complain, because there was the war on. The fluffy white ankle socks and canvas utility shoes made the bare legs seem girly and unthreatening, Belinda supposed. No one need know she was without knickers.

Belinda shifted her attention to the teacher, Captain Garstang, and his silky baritone, droning on about Latin verbs. Honestly! Belinda wanted to be a teacher herself, but for practical things, like cookery and sewing and handwriting, and didn't see what Latin had to do with living in modern Britain, in 1944. His lean, handsome face wore a half-smile of perpetual amusement, as if he knew that, too. She sighed, gazing at him; all the girls fancied Captain Garstang, even though he was rumoured to be almost thirty years old, which was old as . . . anyway, unthinkably old. He had a slight limp, and stories flew among the girls about his war wound, from service in Africa or the Mediterranean . . . somewhere glamorous. Yet he was undoubtedly a spunk, with a hard, muscled body, and bushy black locks, worn rakishly long over his collar.

He was a captain in the coast guard reserves . . . Belinda thought of him on the bridge, commanding, in his blue uniform, and shivered. She saw herself drifting in a stormy sea, alone in a storm-tossed lifeboat, and Captain Garstang's ship looming, to rescue her. She was in only her short summer frock, soaked by foaming waves, so that you could see right through the cotton, to her body, completely bare, with no undies at all – the extra coupons! – and Captain Garstang picked her up with a marlinspike, hoisting her on deck, but at the last moment the spike ripped her clothes clean away, and she tumbled wet and nude into the captain's strong arms, to be revived with warm, fluffy towels, and mugs of hot cocoa, and . . . ooh!

It wasn't fair to have such a spunk as a teacher, for you were enthralled, and couldn't concentrate on the dratted subject. Belinda picked up her pencil, and began to doodle, half-consciously, her gaze shifting once more to the magical palette of the sky. Beside her, Wendy Pight, her best chum, suppressed a titter, not very successfully, but Belinda was far away, and scarcely registered it. Her fingers continued to doodle, as she looked at a plane swooping low, and imagined herself parachuting, in just the white blouse and blue skirt of her school uniform, with the wind blowing her skirt up, to show her uncovered thighs and buttocks, and ripping open her blouse, to bare her breasts, with a crowd of lusty Lancashire spunks cheering her, as she billowed through the sky.

Belinda wondered what it would be like to have a proper steady boyfriend, not one with lusts that a sensible Lancashire girl learned to assuage, so as to stop things going too far. Brave boys heading for active service had to be comforted, somehow, and, if a girl could do it without surrendering her virtue, why, surely Mr Churchill would consider it a patriotic duty.

Life at the vicarage did not favour casual liaisons, unchaperoned, so Belinda felt a bit sneaky, holding hands in the Morecambe Majestic picture palace, or in some tea bar on the seafront, rather giggly, knowing what would come afterwards, when she and the boy found a deserted shelter, for some super snogging and kissing, and . . . more than snogging! She was rather jealous of Wendy, who seemed to have such an unfettered life, although it was a little bit frightening, too – not least because Belinda was afraid of being teased for her posh vicarage accent, as if it was her fault her stepfather had taught her to speak politely! Why, Captain Garstang's voice was no less polite, yet he was a male, a commander, which made all the difference.

She saw the American airmen from the base practise their parachuting, the billowing silk shrouds floating so beautifully, like big soft kisses. Parachuting seemed a thrilling idea, because boys could see her, skirts up and knickers showing, as she floated over their heads, and landed a safe distance away, to be all neat and proper, by the time they ran, panting, to her side. They wouldn't get another peek, though. It was the same tingly thrill, as when she 'forgot' to do up all the top blouse buttons, so that when she leaned over to pick up a crab or mussel, people could see her breasts, especially when it was a really hot day, and she had no bra on, which was deliciously naughty.

Nice girls were supposed to wear bras at all times, ever since William the Conqueror, Belinda supposed, otherwise they would get saggy bubs, and especially for a girl like her, whose bubbies had always been bigger than most. Yet, free of the chafing bra, her bubs did not feel saggy at all, but stood quite high and firm and bouncy, and rather liked the cool air against their bare skin. Going knickerless was the same – an easy way to save on coupons – and the cool air caressing her between her legs made her feel ever so warm and yummy down there. Knickers also rubbed on her nub, which peeped rather a long way from her orchid lips, and it was awfully nice, but sometimes too exciting. There was an extra-special thrill, if she was knickerless, allowing a gust of wind on Morecambe sands to blow her skirt right up, showing everything – just for a second – then pushing her skirt down, but dawdling just a teeny bit, so that her naked bits were fleetingly exposed.

'Ooh!' Belinda squealed, at a sudden pain in her ribs.

She looked up, blushing, at the face of Captain Garstang, inches from hers. His forefinger poked sharply into her blouse, just below her heavy 'utility' brassiere. She jumped, making her breasts bounce up, and slap heavily on her desktop, which provoked a giggle from Wendy.

'Am I boring you, Belinda?' he said, swivelling his finger in her ribs, so that she squirmed. 'Am I boring you?'

The class tittered dutifully at his oft-repeated joke, none more than Wendy. Belinda absolutely hated it when men made unfunny jokes, which they seemed to do all the time, although they weren't as cruel as girls' jokes. Belinda hated Wendy's teasing about her pash for their teacher. Why, every girl in class had a pash for Captain Garstang.

'N-no, sir,' she stammered.

'Staring out the window, were we?'

'Not really, sir.'

'War won't be won by silly girls staring out windows,' he said. 'When I was a midshipman, we got the birch for less. Tabled and strapped, for two dozen stingers. That taught us to pay attention.'

The class was suddenly silent. Belinda's blush deepened, at his careless insult. Why were girls always silly to virile men? Yet her heart thumped, at his equally casual mention of the birch. Was it true – surely such things belonged to history – that a young sailor could be birched on his bottom? His bottom would be bare, of course, and the whole ship's company would watch, as the rods swished his naked posterior, making him wriggle and squirm, as his skin turned black and blue with horrid cruel welts. Belinda knew such things happened in books, but it was beastly of Captain Garstang to mention it in front of girls, to inspire an easy terror. Of course, few Lancashire girls' bottoms were strangers to the slipper, strap or even the cane, but the birch was a dreadful, strictly masculine affair. Belinda imagined a younger Captain Garstang, naked, and strapped to a table, with his bare bum squirming under the slaps of birch twigs, and shifted guiltily, alarmed at a sudden moisture between her legs.

'And what's this?'

His bony fingers prised a piece of paper from under Belinda's elbow. He glared at the pencil drawing. Belinda glimpsed a horrid picture – a nude girl, her legs wide apart, and a monstrous hairy sex organ penetrating her nether hole. 'Captain Garstang is Belinda's best spunk' it read, with arrows pointing to 'Garstang's cock' and 'Belinda's twat'.

'This is an outrage,' he hissed.

'Sir, it wasn't – I mean, I didn't –'

Belinda looked helplessly around, and saw Wendy smirking. The minx! Of course! It was her drawing. Yet she couldn't sneak on her pal. Being a sneak was the rottenest, beastliest thing for any schoolgirl. It was simply unthinkable – and Wendy knew it.

'I must have been daydreaming, sir,' she blurted miserably. 'I didn't know what I was doing, honestly, sir.'

'That makes it worse,' he said grimly. 'To produce this filth unconsciously, like some cloggie from the slums of Wigan!'

'I'm sorry, sir,' Belinda said, wiping a tear from her eye.

'Sorry isn't enough. I shall have to make an example of you, Belinda, you realise that. The principal shall have my report, and I'm afraid having this on your file won't help your aspiration to be a teacher.'

Belinda paled. 'Oh, please sir, don't report me to Miss Tyndale,' she gasped. 'I know I deserve punishment, but not that.'

'I'm very upset with you, Belinda,' the captain said softly. 'I had such high hopes of you.'

Belinda cringed in bitter shame. 'I beg you, sir, don't be cross with me,' she pleaded. 'I didn't mean any harm.'

Belinda wasn't even sure it had been Wendy's doing – perhaps her own fingers had traced a picture of her unspeakable fantasy. If so, then she did deserve punishment. Belinda knew all about s-e-x, and what boys and girls did – but was resolved to remain pure, or as pure as possible. Flashing a glimpse of bare breast or bum, that was surely harmless teasing, although, predictably, Wendy didn't think so. She said that, although teasing was super sport, to get the spunks hot, Belinda was merely sublimating her real desires – whatever that meant.

Wendy boasted that she did it with black men, from the American base, and it was the best thing on earth, because they had such big stiff organs, and there was nothing like a stiff hot sex organ filling a girl up, ramming her orchid and making her all mushy and soaking wet, till she just exploded with ecstasy, the same as when you diddled, only miles better, because men spurted this lovely sticky hot cream inside a girl's pouch, which made her feel so happy. Belinda suspected – hoped – that Wendy was just teasing, but, all the same, Wendy's filthy talk made her hot and wet, and she diddled herself even more than usual because of it.

Doing it with a spunky chap, that wasn't unthinkable, if you really had a pash, but with – with more than one? That was shiver-making. Belinda scoffed when Wendy called her a teasing prude – she was definitely not a prude! A girl could diddle herself – which Belinda did rather a lot, frankly, as she reminded Wendy – stroking her big pink nub, down there, till she was all wet and filled with lovely, super feelings, while waiting for the right boy, who really, truly loved her. Meanwhile, she was kind to boys, in return for snogging and kisses. She admitted to Wendy that she really couldn't imagine anything sweeter than a good 'wank', as Wendy called it. Surely there were some boys who weren't . . . smutty? She looked up, to see Captain Garstang stroking his chin.

'I must punish you, Belinda,' he said.

'Yes, sir.'

'It isn't personal, despite your lewdness – but I must make an example of you to the class.'

Belinda's heart leaped. He wasn't going to report her to Miss Tyndale! 'Yes, sir,' she gasped. 'Thank you, sir.'

He smiled. 'I don't know if you'll thank me afterwards,' he murmured. 'You may come up to the front of the class, Belinda.'

She rose, automatically smoothing her school skirt, although it didn't come to her knees; that was the trouble with having such long legs, she thought, as she stepped towards the teacher's desk, the skirt caressing her bare thighs. In winter, Miss Tyndale was a stickler for proper stockings, itchy woollen things, but in summer, what with the war, was obliged to admit bare legs. It was more democratic that way. Belinda did have three pairs of real rayon stockings, with proper garters and a suspender belt, but to wear them at school would be a waste, and showing off.

As for Wendy, she had oodles of black nylon stockings from America, absolutely yummy, with seams down the back, and once let Belinda try some on, relishing Belinda's gasp of pleasure, as the smooth, silky fabric caressed her bare skin; she teased Belinda with the promise of lending them to her to go to a dance at the Morecambe Palais, but only if Belinda would promise to let her hair down and really 'jitterbug' to the swing band. It would be absolutely catastrophic for a girl to wear nylon stockings to school, for it was well known there was only one way to obtain them.

Belinda stood beside the teacher's tall desk, which smelled of ink and chalk dust. Captain Garstang looked down at her severely. Bother! He's going to make me wear a dunce's cap, and stand in the corner.

'I am going to beat you, Belinda,' he said.

A ripple went through the class of seated girls, and many crossed their thighs.

'I – I beg your pardon, sir?' she mumbled.

He held up his blackboard pointer, a long, thin stave, like a billiard cue. 'I propose to give you four strokes on the bottom,' he said.

Belinda swallowed, biting her lip and staring at the pointer, its harmless chalky bulk now transformed to a vicious cane. She opened her mouth, but no words came out.

'You do agree, of course?' said the teacher. 'It will save us the trouble of a report to the principal. Speak up, Belinda. I can't flog you without your full consent.'

A tingle shot up Belinda's spine, and she shifted her thighs, feeling a telltale spurt of wet between her legs, making the lips of her orchid suddenly mushy. She gasped – the casual way Captain Garstang had said flog, suggesting naked men, whipped at the mainmast . . .

'Flogged, sir?' she gasped. 'On my bottom?'

'It is the normal way,' said the teacher somewhat impatiently. 'I take it you've undergone corporal punishment at some stage?'

'Why, yes, sir, of course,' Belinda blurted. 'I've often been, um, spanked on my bum, like any girl; it's just that "flog" sounds so awful.'

'Flog, beat, tickle,' said Captain Garstang, wiping his rod free of chalk dust, 'it means simply that I'm going to warm your rear end with four dainty stingers, Belinda, so that you'll think twice about committing any lewdness in my class. Agreed?'

'Yes, sir.'

'Good.'

Smiling, he flexed the springy cane. 'Nice and swishy. Now, stand beside my desk, with your face to the class, and your legs braced, slightly apart, so that the girls can see your face as you're beaten. Shameful, I know, but that is part of the punishment – *pour encourager les autres* – and it'll help you be brave, and not make too much of a face. Bend over, leaning forwards, with your trunk at an angle of forty-five degrees, and place your hands on your knees to take your weight.'

Trembling, Belinda obeyed, trying to ignore the faces of her classmates, some pale and shocked, some, including Wendy, openly smirking.

'Any girl who feels unable to witness this has permission to leave the room,' the teacher said.

No one stirred.

Captain Garstang lifted his stick over Belinda's displayed bottom. 'Now, lift your skirt, Belinda, and keep it tucked at your sides,' he commanded.

'What? I beg your pardon, sir?' she blurted.

'Lift your skirt, miss,' he repeated testily. 'You don't think I'm going to beat you on that, do you? It's like cardboard! You wouldn't feel a thing. I'll beat you on your knickers. Perfectly modest, I assure you.'

'Sir,' Belinda gulped, 'I'm – I'm not wearing any knickers.'

The room was silent, but for the teacher's sharp intake of breath.

'If that's a joke, you'll pay for it, miss,' he said.

'It's no joke, sir. It's the clothing coupons, you see – I used my soft fabric to make a nice silky nightie,' Belinda replied, 'and my only good knickers are in the wash. There's a hole in my other pair that needs darning, at the gusset.'

'It's a disgrace,' hissed Captain Garstang. 'Miss Tyndale must be informed.'

'No, please, I beg you, sir!' Belinda wailed. 'It – it would only upset her.'

'Pah! You're right, you shameless, bold maid. Very well. Miss Tyndale shan't hear of it, but, for this brazen affront to decency, now you'll take eight strokes instead of four.'

'Oh, cripes! I mean, th-thank you, sir,' Belinda blurted.

'On the bare bottom.'

Belinda gulped.

'They'll be hard, I warn you. I don't want any blubbing, though.'

'N-no, sir, I promise.'

'You may raise your skirt.'

Lips pressed white, Belinda slid her skirt up and tucked it firmly at her hips, to reveal her naked bottom. She leaned as far forwards as possible, hoping to conceal her hillock from the girls' gaze, not least, because her hillock was freshly shaved that day, and gleamed, silky smooth and pale as alabaster, above the fleshy red lips of her orchid. Not all the girls shaved, although she knew Wendy did, and she feared it might seem bold, although, as Wendy said, it was a private matter, like undies – Wendy possessed black knickers! – for a girl's own satisfaction, and none of the statues in the art galleries ever had twat fur.

The air was cool, playing on her bare bottom, clean-shaven mound and the moist crevice between her thighs. Frankly, Belinda thought hairy girls were a bit grubby; body hair seemed to go with clogs and grime and headscarves. She gasped, feeling moisture ooze within her pouch, and prayed that she would not shame herself further by dripping. Her heart raced, partly in terror of her beating, and partly in longing for it to begin, and be over with. Eight strokes on my bare!

'You certainly present a well-formed pair of targets, Belinda,' said Captain Garstang, 'and splendidly big. Now, you must keep your head up. I want these maids to see what punishment does to your face. In fact, I've an idea, to stop you drooping, and keep your skirt up, too.'

He twirled a thick hank of Belinda's hair, spinning it deftly into a cord, and bunched a handful of her skirt hem, knotting the hair around it. Belinda's head was jerked back, and the taut hair-string kept her skirt lifted above her bare buttocks. Any sagging of her head would be arrested by the skirt pulled tight. Head high, she listened to the rustling of cloth, as the teacher removed his jacket, unfastened his cufflinks and rolled up his shirt sleeves.

'Nervous?' said the teacher. 'Your bottom is all goose flesh.'

'Gosh, yes, sir, a little,' she blurted.

'You wouldn't be normal, otherwise. Don't worry, Belinda, it'll sting like the very devil, but you'll feel better afterwards, for having purged your offence, and, frankly, an English girl who can't take her bare licks bravely, when she's due them, isn't worth her salt.'

Her mouth and throat were dry, her naked bottom tingling, yet her orchid was moist. Surely that was topsy-turvy? And she felt a curious, lovely tickling, where her nipples rubbed against the coarse elastic of her utility brassiere. Her nipples were stiff and erect.

'I'll try to be brave, sir,' she murmured.

'Good. We can begin,' said Captain Garstang.

Belinda took a deep breath, and screwed her eyes shut, waiting for the first stroke. Her bottom tingled with goose pimples, and she couldn't stop her fesses from trembling. Her whole body quivered, and her face was red with shame. She took a deep breath, just before the cane landed on her bare buttocks. *Vip*!

'Ooh!' Belinda gasped, the breath knocked from her by the cane's thud, and teetering on her toes.

It was worse than any cane she had known! Tears leaped from her eyes, and a dreadful choke invaded her throat, making her want to gag and scream all at the same time.

'Uhh . . . uhh . . . uhh . . .' she panted.

The pain was unbelievable, as if a red-hot poker had streaked across her naked bottom. After the wood had lashed her, the pain remained, in a dull, smarting throb. Belinda gasped hard, trying to keep the pain under control, and to stop herself trembling, although she could feel her buttocks pressing tightly together, clenching, in an effort to dissipate the pain. Spanking, slippering, or even a caning, on the bare, at the vicarage, had never been like this! She pictured Captain Garstang's rippling sailor's muscles, as he put all his manly strength into flogging her defenceless girl's bottom, and her quim couldn't help moistening. It seemed so unfair! Several seconds passed – she could not count – and her breathing eased, as the pain abated, but not fully, with her fesses still throbbing. *Vip*!

'Ahh!'

Belinda gasped, in a shrill squeal, as the second stroke sliced her. Tears coursed down her face, and her eyes wrinkled shut in agony. Her face burned red with shame, and, dimly, she thought she musn't look silly before her friends, yet that thought was a long way away; agony coursed through her flogged buttocks, in low, searing throbs, and everything else in the room faded to nothing, compared with that awful pain. The teacher's blackboard pointer seemed the most harmless tool in creation, and she had never thought a simple rod could cause such distress, with such a small noise – the tapping of the cane probably unheard outside this classroom – yet it had become the intrument of her torture.

'That's two, Belinda,' came Captain Garstang's voice from far away. 'Hurt much?'

Belinda nodded her head frantically, jerking her hair on her tethered skirt, and emitted a low, bubbling wail, with drool slithering down her chin.

'Thought so,' he said. 'Well, be brave, miss, you've only six licks to go.'

Only six! Belinda's heart spasmed, at the casual cruelty of his words. *Vip*! The third stroke lashed her without warning, following faster than the second. Her heart leaped to her throat and she wanted to scream, but all she could manage was a thin whine, as the force of the caning drove the air from her lungs.

'Ooh . . . ooh . . .' she snivelled.

'Careful, miss,' warned the teacher. 'I warned you about blubbing. You must take your licks like a proper English girl.'

Her bare bottom was red-hot, and squirming madly, as though to suck some cooling balm from the air that bathed her inflamed bare flesh; Belinda dreaded to think how abject her wriggling nates looked, but consoled herself that her classmates could not see her naked shame. *Vip*!

'Ahh! Oh! Oh!'

The fourth stroke took her slightly higher than the others, across her top buttock, which smarted even worse than her underfesse, and Belinda thought her lungs and bottom would burst with her agony. As she gasped frantically, puffing like a puppy, she knew her face, all wrinkled and crying, was a right picture to her friends, and the leering Wendy, but didn't – couldn't – care. The cane was gouging trenches in her unprotected flesh! Somehow, she must survive this torture, reassuring herself that tomorrow her naked buttocks would no longer burn with terrible welts. *Vip*! The fifth lashed her left haunch, which stung fearfully, and her legs jerked straight up, at the impact.

'Ooh! Oh, gosh, it hurts,' she squealed.

Her flogged buttocks wriggled, with her legs trembling in sympathy; as the skin of each thigh touched and rubbed, she felt a slither of hot fluid, dripping from her orchid. Her belly was fluttering, curiously excited by the awful pain, and her stiff nipples – fully erect! – rubbed, teasing and provocative, against the churning elastic of her brassiere. She hoped that she was leaning over enough for the class not to see that her nipples were stiff and swollen, as if this beating excited her.

'Yes,' said the teacher. 'You're learning your lesson, Belinda. Over halfway, now – the rest is all downhill. Don't worry, you're bearing up very well.'

Amidst her agony, these small words of praise warmed Belinda's heart. Despite his cruelty, she wanted to please her teacher; she wanted this harsh, brutal male to like her. The fluttering in her belly was joined with a more pressing need: she felt her swollen bladder demand evacuation. She desperately needed to pee! Now her loins had a second task, as well as squirming and clenching to ease her pain, she must tighten her belly, to hold in her pee. *Vip*! The sixth stroke brought fresh floods of tears to her eyes, as it landed on her other haunch.

'Ooh . . . ooh . . .' she wailed, dancing on tiptoe, with her bare bum squirming like the dickens!

What a sight, she thought, miserably. Yet, she made no effort to suppress her buttocks' clenching. Let this spunk see what he's doing to a helpless girl's bare bottom, let him enjoy the spectacle of my agony. The pressure in her bladder was overwhelming.

'Please, sir,' she moaned.

'What is it, Belinda?' he snapped. 'You've only two to go. You're doing very well – don't spoil things now.'

She didn't want his beastly sympathy! He knew she was in agony!

'Please, sir, I need to go to the lavatory,' she whimpered.

'Can't you hold it in?' he said.

'I – I don't think so, sir. The caning has made it very urgent. Girls are different from boys, sir.'

The class tittered.

'I'm quite aware of that,' he said. 'Well, if you must go, you must. But I warn you, the beating will start again from stroke one.'

'Oh, sir!' she wailed.

'Those are the rules,' he said. 'Take it or leave it. Now, do you really have to go, this instant?'

'No, sir,' she sobbed. 'I'll – I'll do my best to hold it until the end of my beating.'

'Thought so,' he murmured.

Vip!

'Urrgh!' Belinda gurgled, squirming, as her bare bum flamed with new agony, all the more terrible for the painful bursting in her bladder; yet she could feel her gash swelling, and dripping quite a lot of wet.

She wasn't trying to escape punishment! She would show him she could take it. The smarting, which seemed to envelop her entire bottom, clasping her naked buttocks in a glove of molten, white-hot pain, had seemed to become part of her, still dreadful, but somehow manageable, after overcoming the shock of her first agony, the surprise at the assault on her intimate person and the shame of nudity. Now, she had forgotten the humiliation of her naked buttocks, and no longer cared whether her face wrinkled or her bum cheeks squirmed, which helped in mastering her pain. I must smile after my beating. Feeling her buttocks automatically clenching, she thrust the bare nates up, and waggled them on purpose, to tease her caner.

'Ooh, sir,' she gasped, 'you are powerful. I've never been hurt so much before.'

'The navy gives you a lot of practice, in rough and ready

punishments,' he growled. 'A mere eight, miss, is scarcely a beating at all, on the high seas.'

'Then you've taken worse, yourself, sir,' she managed to groan, 'so I mustn't complain.'

'I have, in fact,' he replied hoarsely, licking his lips. 'Twenty-four on the bare with a rattan cane under the African sun, while strapped to an eight-inch gun. Kissing the gunner's daughter – now that was a flogging, miss. I couldn't sit down for a whole week. And it was a . . . a gel, a dratted local hussy, who – but don't distract me from your last cut.'

'Yes, sir. I mean, no, sir.'

Belinda's bladder was agony, outweighing the smarting of her bum, yet, as the teacher mentioned his ordeal, flogged naked on the gun – she imagined Captain Garstang's young bottom, firm and bare and muscled, covered in dreadful purple stripes from the cane – her orchid overflowed with hot oily juice, mingling with the first drips of pee, from her bursting belly. She struggled to clench her belly, and hold back her flood, wondering if she could manage to sprint to the lavatory, in time to squat and pour. *Vip*!

'Ooh!' she gurgled, and could hold on no longer.

As her flogged bottom writhed, striped and burning in agony, a massive torrent of hot pee burst from her orchid, and hissed all over the classroom floor. Grimly, despite her seared bottom, which she longed to rub, she held position, sobbing, as the piss flowed from her hole, streaking her thighs, and dripping into her shoes. Captain Garstang merely clicked his tongue, untied her hair and ordered her to kneel and clean up her mess.

'Oh! I'm sorry, sir,' she snuffled, 'but with what?'

As her flood of pee hissed, steaming, to conclusion, the class began to giggle. The teacher rapped his cane for silence.

'It's not possible to use your knickers, obviously,' he said, 'so I suggest your socks – they look absorbent enough – unless you want to take off your skirt, and use that.'

There were hoots of laughter. Belinda stooped, took off her shoes and socks, then balled her socks in her hands.

Because her buttocks were so sore, and her thighs wet with pee, she kept her skirt tucked up, oblivious of her bare bottom's shaming spectacle, as she squatted on all fours to wipe up her lake of steaming, acrid piss. She wiped heartily, wrinkling her nose, and occasionally wringing her sopping socks into the tin wastebasket, with her wealed buttocks bobbing in view of the class. She could not resist rubbing them, kneading the welted flesh, and gasping at the hardness of the caned ridges. The rubbing spread her bum cheeks, showing her gash lips and shaven mound, which stilled the laughter somewhat, as girls gazed in awe at the full wet slice, swollen and red, tipped by the pearl-white shaven hillock, and the lips dripping with seeped juice.

Belinda felt the eyes on her bare, and spread wider, until she knew every girl was feasting her eyes on her welted buttocks and boldly dripping slit. Her heart thumped at this new naughtiness, and her seep of juice quickened, the droplets splattering on the floor, beside her wrists. Wilfully, she exposed herself – showing my doings on purpose, and not even the teacher can touch me, for I've already been punished.

She continued mopping, even after the floor was wet only with the exudations from her bare orchid, until the bell went, and she was jostled by a throng of girls wanting to feel her bum. Somehow, she got her piss-wet socks on, and grabbed her schoolbag, leaving the room among excited chatterers, with a shy smile to Captain Garstang. The chatter ceased outside the door, when the girls collided with the immobile figure of Miss Tyndale, arms folded and smiling icily at Belinda.

Belinda quaked.

'Good girl,' was all the principal said. 'You took your licks like a sailor. You may spend the rest of the day knickerless – privilege of a licked girl. I'm sure you will make a very good teacher, Belinda.'

Flushed with pride, Belinda curtsied, and thanked the principal, then dashed for the lavvy. Once locked, gasping, inside the cubicle, she squatted, lifted her skirt and parted the lips of her orchid. Her clitoris was up and bobbing, poking stiffly erect through her orchid flaps, and sending shocks of tingling pleasure up her spine, as she began to rub. With the awful smarting of her flogged bum, her wet pink orchid seemed unusually alive, the outsize clitoris bursting with electric pleasure. She masturbated, imagining her bare bum, wealed, and shamefully exposed to an ogling audience of muscular, whip-wielding seadogs, with their sluttish girls, looking like Wendy, clad in black nylons and knickers . . . then, Captain Garstang, naked and strapped, with his croup shivering under her cane, purpling the naked buttocks with vicious welts, as he screamed and begged for mercy. Her revenge was sweet – a helpless, virile spunk, whipped at Belinda's pitiless whim. It took only a few strokes to bring herself off, with her belly fluttering, and slit copiously juicing, in an orgasm that had her moaning aloud.

Trembling, she left the cubicle, and found Wendy waiting for her.

'Hurry up, or you'll be late for maths,' Wendy said. 'Whatever were you doing? Blubbing about your sore bottom, I suppose.'

'Actually,' said Belinda, 'I was playing with myself. That was a beastly trick you played, with your horrid drawing, but I'm glad you did. Being beaten by my favourite spunk got me all hot, and I've just had the most delicious wank.'

2

Fruity to Burst

The two girls waited, sucking on a shared Woodbine, under the lime tree outside Mrs Mimm's sweetshop, a few yards from Lancaster Castle, until Belinda saw a young man leave, on his way to the Waggonload of Monkeys. She nodded to her companion, and a bell tinkled as they entered the shop. The handful of customers idly eyed the racks of pennants and royal souvenirs, while Belinda and her hockey league chum Jan Suckling, now a nurse at the Royal Lancashire Infirmary, marched to the sweets counter. With Jan in her nursing blue and white, both girls attracted lustful glances from the male customers, and envious, or disapproving, ones from the females. A bright September sun illumined the dusty jars of boiled sweets, as Mrs Mimm fiddled with piles of ration coupons.

Belinda wore a short skirt in red tartan, and a white cotton short-sleeved blouse, rather tight, and loosely knotted with a striped tie of the Royal Army Education Corps, with her breasts, bouncing in their casing of white elastic, plainly visible through the thin fabric, and its low cut exposing a generous amount of bare breast skin. Her black school jacket and handbag were tossed carelessly over her shoulder. The summer of 1947 had been mercifully warm, after the cruel winter, and Belinda's bare arms were golden, the skin gleaming smooth and shaved of down. Her long tresses were piled in a bun, with locks dangling below her earlobes, while her legs shimmered in white rayon stockings, above brown lace-up shoes with a two-inch heel and pointed brogue toes. Jan would rib her for looking more schoolgirl than schoolteacher.

'I shan't be a jiffy,' Belinda said to Jan. 'Must stock up with bull's balls. Then we can go to the Prince Albert for a glass of beer and a sandwich.'

Jan laughed. 'You mean those gigantic treacly gobstoppers, from Wigan or somewhere? I haven't heard of those since before the war,' she said. 'Cripes, they're as big as apples, and take ages to melt.'

'Which is why they're so yummy. I suspect Mrs Mimm's stock dates from before the war,' Belinda said. 'Anyway, they're off ration – I think I'm her only customer, and she keeps them away, up on the top shelf. Her son's gone for his lunch, so I'll probably have to climb the ladder, and fetch them myself.'

'So that's why we paused for a fag,' mused Jan.

'You'll see,' Belinda murmured, with a wink. 'It could be fun.'

Mrs Mimm greeted Belinda warmly, but moaned about climbing the steps, and gratefully accepted Belinda's offer of help.

'You are keen on your bull's balls, Miss Beaucul,' she said.

'I eat them all the time,' Belinda said, 'especially when I'm teaching a class of rowdy boys. I think it frightens them when I chew one of those whoppers, very slowly.'

Even with the help of the stepladder, and despite her five feet nine, she would have to stretch hard to reach the jar of gobstoppers. She gave her jacket and bag to Jan, then clambered up, bottom and thighs wobbling, with deliberate clumsiness, and, by the time she perched herself at the top, all eyes in the shop scanned her. Her bottom quivered under its clinging skirtlet, a good three feet above the watching eyes.

'Here goes,' she said, and, smoothing her skirt down, sprang upwards, shaking the ladder and sending her tartan skirtlet flurrying up, to reveal her stocking tops and garter straps.

'Oops, missed,' she cried.

She ascended further, and placed a foot on the next rung, so that her skirt slipped sideways, showing not only her stocking tops, but a sliver of white silk panties.

'Gosh, I hope my shorties aren't showing,' she said, giggling.

Another jump revealed her whole knickers, the white parachute silk of the square-cut shorties clinging wetly to her quivering buttocks. Her hands grasped the jar of gobstoppers, but slipped off. Frowning, Belinda smoothed her skirt down once more, fussing with the crease of her buttocks, so that no eye failed to pay attention, then climbed to the top of the stepladder, and, with one foot on its platform, extended her other leg onto the lower shelf, wedging her toecap between two jars of sweets. She looked down, checking her foothold, while her hands groped among the jars on the top shelf. Her skirt rode up to the top of her buttocks, and flapped slightly, now with her entire knickers, suspender belt, garter straps and stocking tops on full show to the goggling spectators.

Belinda's arse cleft was above their heads, and showed her silken panties clenched between her thighs, with the naked skin of her lower buttocks extruded from the tight silk, and the gusset of the panties passing in a ribbon between the lips of her cooze, which were fully exposed, with just a hint of pink pouch flesh beneath the tight strap of the panties gusset. Her fingers fastened on a jar.

'Is this it?' she said.

'No,' replied Mrs Mimm, 'two jars to your left.'

Belinda grasped the next jar. 'This one?'

'No, the next.'

Belinda pretended to stumble, which sent her skirt fluttering even higher, with a wiggle of her panties, and grasped the jar on the far side of the bull's balls.

'Gosh, I'm so clumsy,' she cooed.

After three more attempts, she brought the right jar triumphantly to earth, dawdling on her descent and showing her swaying bottom to the full. She grinned brightly at the ogling males, who quickly turned their faces downwards. All were young, and all had bulges in their crotch, which Belinda scanned, with a lick of her lips, and a wink at the giggling Jan.

'Well!' she said. 'You see what a girl will do for bull's balls. Half a pound, please, Mrs Mimm.'

She popped the package of sweets into her bag, and followed Jan out of the shop, with a cheeky waggle of her bottom, letting the skirt flounce up, to show a farewell flash of knickers and stocking tops. She turned abruptly, beamed at the goggling males and eyed their bulging crotches, licking her lips at their crimson faces. Once outside the shop, the two girls exploded in giggles.

'That was fun,' said Jan. 'Did you see those bulges? Showing your shorties – you did expose yourself on purpose, didn't you? Of course, a nurse's uniform gets its fair share of bulges anyway. If I was a bloke, I'd have a stonker, watching your lush bum in those undies. Gosh, it must be wonderful to have a prick and lovely juicy ballocks, and get all hard and spurt cream whenever you sniffed a girl. But how cruel, getting them all excited, and having to suffer the frustration! I suppose they'll go and . . . you know, relieve themselves.'

'Mm, yes, I suppose they will,' said Belinda, licking her lips. 'Pity we can't watch. It is lovely and cruel doing that to boys.'

'You're a dark horse, Belinda.'

'Want to know more?' murmured Belinda.

'You bet.'

'Then the light ales are on you,' said Belinda. 'In fact, it's my half day off, so we can have more than one.'

They entered the lounge bar of the pub, and clinked glasses, before swallowing the foaming ale.

'I mustn't get stinko,' Jan said, 'as I have to be back on duty at eleven.'

Their roast beef sandwiches arrived; both girls applied generous blobs of horse radish sauce, and took big bites.

'You must have a bit of a grudge against men,' Jan said, through becrumbed lips. 'Teasing them like that. Is that why you teach squaddies? Must be a thrill, knowing all those spunky young cocks are stirring, as they watch teacher.'

'Not a grudge, exactly,' Belinda murmured.
'Current boyfriend?'
Belinda reddened slightly. 'Oh, no one special.'
'Meaning no. I wonder why not. You're quite a dish, Belinda.'
'I suppose that's what worries me. I'm wary of boys liking me for the wrong reasons, purely for lust.
I do have dates with boys, and I love dancing at the Morecambe Palais, and I've had some fabulous snogging and kisses, but I – I make it clear I won't go all the way.'
'Boys never believe that. They take it as a challenge. Especially from a girl with such a gorgeous bod.'
'I know they can't help liking girls with big bubs and bums, and long legs and everything, but – but I'm not a racehorse. However –' Belinda pouted, blushing '– I have my own way of disarming them. Can you keep a secret?'
'Hope to die, Bel,' Jan trilled.
Belinda began to whisper conspiratorially. 'Well, when I'm having a super snog, and a boy is feeling my bubbies – I let them do that – or gets his fingers into my orchid, and tickles my bum, under my knickers, I get under his underpants. Then, I, um, do him. Tickle his ballocks and sex organ, and rub him, till he spurts. I love the feel of a naked organ, all stiff and trembling as I rub the tip, or the bell end, or the little neck just beneath, or the crinkly bit behind. They go wild when I do that, and I get some super kisses, and my orchid gets all wet. Sometimes a boy's fingers on my nub will get me to come, and that's a plus, only a lot of boys aren't sure how to hit the spot. It doesn't matter though, they are so grateful when I make them squirt in my hand, and it makes me happy.'
'That's absolutely terrific,' Jan cooed. 'But I still feel you've more to tell.'
'What girl hasn't?' Belinda retorted hotly.
Jan put her fingers on Belinda's stockinged thigh, and stroked the muscle beneath. 'I bet, if you do bare up – show that lovely big bottom without your knickers – it'll drive a bloke wild. It would drive me wild, if I were a

bloke. I couldn't get enough of that bum. I'd want to biff you from behind.'

'Mm! That sounds awfully naughty.' Belinda smiled, as Jan's palm rested on her thigh, and shifted in her chair, so that her tartan skirt rode up, to show her garter straps, and a parcel of naked thigh skin. 'There are other things a girl can do besides biffing,' she murmured. 'Why do you think I buy all these bull's balls?'

'To eat, of course,' said Jan, with a sly smile. 'Or . . .?'

'They're a lovely fit, down there,' Belinda whispered, 'and they take ever so long to melt. Four bull's balls in your pouch, and you can have the most delicious wank.'

Jan exploded in a peal of delighted laughter. 'Why, that's super! I frig a lot, and I use things – a cucumber, a carrot, even a stethoscope – but I'd never thought of sweets. It must be really swoony, all those big balls rolling around inside your twat.'

'Would you like to try?' Belinda murmured, her thigh shivering under Jan's touch. 'I know it sounds a bit naughty, but I wouldn't look, if you didn't want me to. Would you? Say you would, please.'

'You bet. I'd like you to look. It's always more yummy, wanking off with a chum.'

'It does sound naughty. What you nurses get up to! Well, we both have the afternoon off.'

'Lead the way. Gosh, I'm getting all wet in my knickers, just thinking about it.'

'Not,' Belinda said regally, 'until we've had a few more light ales. You're paying, remember?'

Jan's fingers slipped up Belinda's stocking, and pinched the bare thigh flesh beside her garter strap. 'It'd better be worth it,' she said, licking her lips. 'We can go to my flat, if you like. It's a nice walk along the canal.'

'You've a flat?'

'Yes . . . it's, um, paid for.'

'I thought nurses had to live in the hospital.'

'We do, sometimes,' said Jan, before going to the bar to procure two more light ales. When she came back, Jan began, 'As I was saying to Wendy the other day –'

'Not Wendy Pight?' Belinda interrupted.

'Why, yes. How did you guess?'

'I sort of imagined you two would be friends.'

Jan swallowed a mouthfull of ale, then licked her lips and smiled. 'We've been friends for a long time,' she said. 'I was at Lancaster Girls', but used to know a few girls at Heysham, and Wendy was one. I only knew you from a distance, and I'm glad we've met. We seem to have so much in common.'

'We do?' said Belinda.

'For one thing,' whispered Jan, 'we like to wank off.'

'That's hardly original. What girl doesn't diddle?'

Both girls enjoyed a suppressed titter.

'And your love of teasing men,' Jan went on, 'it's so exciting. I'd like to know more. I've never been very good at teasing boys – more the cut and thrust of a rapier, or else the blunt instrument, if you know what I mean.'

'I suppose you've known lots.'

'I have, rather. You do, as a nurse.' Jan's hand returned to Belinda's thigh. 'One more light ale?' she said, stroking Belinda's bare skin. 'Or we could go straight back to my place. I've got some wine – the really good stuff, two shillings the bottle.'

Belinda smoothed down her tartan skirt, and clamped Jan's hand to her thigh, letting the nurse's knuckles brush the swelling of her mound, under the silk knickers. Jan's fist made a squishy sound under the skirt – Belinda's knickers were moist.

'Yes, let's go,' Belinda said.

They walked along the canal to a quiet, leafy suburban street of spacious terraced houses, and soon ascended the stairs to Jan's room, whose door was painted red.

'I call it the red room,' she said, as she opened up. 'I'm the only permanent resident, although I'm not here all the time, of course. The other rooms are for . . . for research. The Royal Lancs owns the whole house, you see. I'm attached to a special therapeutic unit, and a lot of my work is done in what we call controlled surroundings.'

Inside, the flat was cosy, with a bed, table, armchairs,

sofa, gas fire, and an adjoining kitchenette and bathroom, just the sort of place Belinda would expect a modern girl to have, including a big walnut Pye wireless set, except that the walls, ceiling and bare floorboards were painted red.

'That's for professional reasons,' Jan said, smirking. 'Psychiatrists say that red is an aggressive colour. My patients are mostly young males, who suffer from an excess of aggression. Some of them were in the war, and had to be aggressive, but have difficulty in curbing their, um, passions, in civvy street. Dr Warrior, our unit psychiatrist, says I have a very high success rate, and I'll soon be promoted to Sister. Well, let's have a glass of wine, and then –' she patted the crack of Belinda's skirted bum '– we can make ourselves comfortable. I do love that tartan skirt of yours.'

'Why, thank you.'

'Perhaps because I'm keen to see it off,' Jan murmured, licking her lips.

'You're the tease,' Belinda said, pouting.

Jan uncorked a bottle of claret, and poured two glasses, then sat down beside Belinda on the sofa. She reached for Belinda's sweets, but Belinda swished them out of her reach, sticking her tongue out.

'In due course, young lady,' she said, with mock solemnity. 'I'm dying for a wank, as much as you are, but waiting till you are absolutely fruity to burst makes it all the more yummy.' She sipped her wine. 'Mm! This is delicious.'

'One of the perks of the job,' said Jan casually. 'From a grateful patient. Same as these.' She produced a fresh packet of Gold Flake, opened it, smelled the aroma and passed one to Belinda. A single match lit both their smokes. 'Now,' Jan said, puffing luxuriously, 'I'm really intrigued by that little bit of teasing you did in the sweetshop. So cool, so casual and effortless! I bet you've had lots of practice.'

'A bit,' Belinda admitted.

'Do tell.'

Belinda sucked on her cigarette. 'It's pretty easy,' she said, blowing smoke. 'These soldiers I teach are quite innocent mostly, despite two years of national service. That's why the army makes them attend classes, to prepare them for civilian life. They don't get their demob gratuity unless they have the right number of passes. Other teachers do literature, and politics and things, but I have to teach them how to boil an egg or make a cup of tea, or cook sausage and mash – they are so used to having everything done for them. Honestly!' She sighed. 'The poor lambs are always ogling and leering at me, not nastily, but in a sheepish, frustrated way. Sometimes I think boys like being frustrated.'

'I would agree,' said Jan, pouring more wine. 'It's good for them.'

'Exactly. So, when I finally . . . do it – have my first biff – I'll know it's with the right boy, and he's been saving his juice just for me,' Belinda blurted. 'A modern girl doesn't need to let a boy stroke her, if she has her fingers to wank him with.'

'If you like baring up,' Jan said, 'there are other variations. You could try wanking him between your bare breasts, called a titwank, or jellying. A goosing is where you rub your bare thighs on his organ, and make him spurt over your skin, but without penetrating you. I like nesting – that's doing his cock in your armpit. Or there's pygisma – squashing the boy's cocktip between your naked buttocks, with his peehole touching your arse cleft, to bring him off, also without penetration. Those lush big bum puds of yours could easily do it.'

Belinda shivered. 'I'd be tempted to let him go too far,' she said. 'I prefer sort of acting up. Not exactly flirting, but letting myself be caught unawares – a glimpse of bubbies, or stockings, or knickers, as I bend over, completely innocent. That's the whole point; I can do it at a bus stop, in the park, or anywhere. Sometimes I'm walking by the canal, and pop into the bushes for a pee. I squat, with my knickers at my ankles, and make sure I'm not too hidden, then stand up, and flash my bare bum or cooze as I pull my knickers up, but all the time pretending I think I'm alone. I do the same, out winkling on Morecambe strand

– if you get far enough away from everybody, but still in view, you can squat and lower your knickers, and it's pretty obvious what you're doing. Sometimes I even finger myself – have a quick wank – because there is something so shiver-making and beautiful about Morecambe Bay. It's a lovely feeling of power, and such a thrill, to see the bulge of a watching boy's pego, and sometimes I get so fruity that my knickers are positively drenched, and I can't wait to get home and strip off, to frig myself really hard.'

She blushed. 'A bit like today, really. Except it's nice to have a wanking chum. Wendy used to ask me to diddle with her, but I was a bit scared – she's so experienced, and awfully mysterious about it.'

'I know,' said Jan, nodding sympathetically. 'Wendy can be a bit overpowering.'

'But I can understand why boys get excited by a glimpse of our bodies,' Belinda blurted. 'Girls' bodies are so beautiful. Doesn't it feel so yummy when you run your hands up and down your body, in the bare? I mean, caress yourself – belly, titties, especially your bottom . . .'

'And your twat.'

'Yes, of course, but even tickling your own toes, and stroking your soles is nice.'

'Or licking them,' purred Jan. 'I do that – lick myself all over, where I can reach, take my toes inside my mouth, and tickle and suck them, and sniff myself too. A girl's body smells so sweet; if you open your thighs, and bend your head right down, holding the lips of your cooze wide, then you get a lovely smell of yourself, especially if you are all wet inside your slit. And if you wank off, it's super to hold your head as close to your twat as you can, while you diddle your nubbin, and just gaze at your lovely wet pink, all streaming with juice, and your nub swelling as you flick. You can see yourself come; your cooze lips pulsing and gaping like a big shiny mouth. Wouldn't it be super to be able to lick your own twat?'

The girls stared at each other, Belinda blushing, and flushed with wine, while Jan licked her lips.

'You've got me all hot,' Belinda murmured.

'Time for those bull's balls, then,' replied Jan. 'Let's drink our wine in the bare.'

'You first,' gasped Belinda.

'No, you.'

'Beast. I'll need another gasper.'

Accepting a fresh Gold Flake, Belinda parked the cigarette in the corner of her mouth. She put down her wineglass, and undid the first two buttons of her blouse, showing her bare breast flesh, cupped and swelling in her tight elastic brassiere.

Jan licked her lips. 'Mm,' she said, 'I can't wait for more. You're making me very wet in my twat.'

'Jan,' Belinda said, 'you're not . . . funny, or anything like that, are you?'

Jan threw her head back, and her throat rippled with laughter. 'Of course not,' she said. 'You are a goose. All girls like to masturbate together. We're going to be lovely wanking chums, Belinda.'

'Oh, I'm sorry,' Belinda blurted. 'I must sound awfully silly.'

'You do want to be naked with me, don't you?'

Belinda blushed. 'Yes, I do,' she whispered.

'Then let's get that kit off.'

Taking a deep drag on her cigarette, Belinda unbuttoned her blouse, and let it fall from her shoulders. She reached behind her and smartly unhooked her brassiere, clutching it to her breasts for a moment with a teasing grin, before letting her bare bubs spring free.

Jan gasped. 'They are super jellies,' she murmured.

Belinda extracted the last smoke from her dogend, then stubbed it out, and drained her glass, while Jan, cigarette drooping from her lips, went to fetch a second bottle of wine. When she returned, Belinda stood in just her shorties, suspenders and stockings. Jan made no secret of her lustful enjoyment, as Belinda put on a teasing show, coquettishly playing with each garter strap, before snapping it open, and wiggling provocatively in her lacy suspender belt, before sliding it down the shiny surface of her rayon stockings, over her rippling thighs. She caressed her cooze hillock, swelling tightly under her shorties, mimicking wanking.

'You should have been on the stage,' breathed Jan, and her nostrils flared. 'If I were a bloke, I'd be stiff as a pole, at that display.'

Belinda simpered. 'Why, thank you,' she trilled, then snapped the waistband of her knickers against her bare belly, and smoothly rolled the panties down her thighs.

Gaping at the satin mound of her shaven cunt hillock, Jan whistled, dropping her cigarette end from her mouth. 'What a beauty,' she gasped. 'The lips so full, the clitty peeping, everything shaven to purity; it's all so perfect. Now, let me see that bottom.'

Belinda waved a finger. Stockings off first,' she said.

Slowly, she peeled the rayon hose from her legs, inching the fabric down the silky smoothness of her thighs and calves.

'You're a beast for making me wait,' said Jan, sipping wine.

'I'm a tease, remember?'

Finally, with a flourish, the completely nude Belinda swivelled, and stuck out her bare buttocks. 'Ta-daa!' she cried.

'Oh, Belinda, I've never seen such a lovely croup,' Jan panted. 'It's a real gluteus superbus – that's the medical term. And your nubbin looks deliciously big, the way it peeps from your twat.'

'You don't think my nub's too big?' said Belinda anxiously.

'A girl's clitoris can never be too big,' Jan replied solemnly.

She kneeled, and made to press her nose and lips into Belinda's bum cleft, but Belinda dodged her, with a giggle.

'Naughty,' she said. 'Not till we're both in the bare. Your turn.' She poked the bag of sweets beside her haunches. 'When you're nude, nurse Jan, you get your bull's balls.'

Jan rose, smiling, and lifted her starched nurse's skirt. She pulled it right up to reveal her bare lower back and bottom, its twin globes trembling in tight blue satin knickers, which were cut surprisingly high, with a few inches of bare flesh on the outer face of each firm buttock, and the elastic of the knickers biting gently into the flesh, giving the buttocks the look of two jellies wobbling, only barely restrained, in silken cups. Dark blue latex garter straps snaked across the buttocks to the taut stocking tops, from a lace suspender belt that enclosed her elfin waist to a thinness so surprising that Belinda's breath was taken away.

Jan's body was lithe, smooth and hard with muscle, her spine curling like a snake, down to the startling wide ripeness of the two arse globes that seemed to spring from the dimpled nubbin of Jan's spine like giant fruits, suddenly swollen, and almost menacing in their size – either weapons or promises. The long, silky legs trembled, rigid in their shiny stockings, as Jan snapped off her garter straps, then unhooked her suspender belt, and let them fall swishily to the floor; she then rolled down her panties, to expose her naked buttocks.

'You minx,' said Belinda. 'That bum puts mine to shame.'

'Liar,' said Jan. 'Yours has perfect proportion.'

Her stockings came off, then her blouse, peeled from her supple torso, until the nurse wore only her bra. She turned, showing Belinda her full mound, while she unhooked her bra, and tossed it aside; her hard, conic breasts sprang to attention, their red nipple domes tautly erect. Between her thighs, a massive pubic forest trailed its tendrils up almost as far as her navel, and dangling low between her parted thighs, with the hairs caressing the open lips of her quim, and framing the wet pink pouch meat. She put her hands on her hips, the fingertips almost touching across her belly.

'Like what you see?' she trilled. 'Don't gape, you goose.'

'I've . . . I've never seen such a big twat thatch before,' Belinda blurted. 'Doesn't it get too hot?'

'In the Lancashire climate? You are silly. Here, give me a hug, and then we can shove in those naughty bull's balls.'

Standing, the two girls embraced. Belinda felt Jan's fingers running up and down her spine, across her bare buttocks and into the cleft of her bum, the fingers dappling gently, like a butterfly's wings. Gasping, she returned the caress, marvelling at the tautness of Jan's massive buttocks, the soft skin shielding hard muscle, yet round and firm, two ripe pears indeed. Jan rubbed her naked breasts against Belinda's, bringing Belinda's nipples to full erection, and swished her naked belly against Belinda's. Their quims met, Jan thrusting her hairy mound forwards, and swaying, to caress Belinda's satin-smooth hillock, until Belinda yelped, giggling. 'Gosh! That tickles.'

'Then let's get our bull's balls in, and masturbate.'

'Masturbate?' said Belinda. 'That sounds awfully clinical.'

'It's what it is,' Jan replied.

They sat, thighs pressed, on the sofa, and Belinda apportioned four of the sweets each.

'Gosh,' said Jan, 'they are monstrous. I'm not sure if I can fit four in.'

She opened her thighs wide, exposing her swollen vulva. She squeezed a ball into her wet cooze flaps, but it slipped in the copious come oozing from her gash, and fell, with Belinda catching it.

'Butterfingers! Let me do it for you,' Belinda said, pressing the sweet to Jan's cooze, while Jan held the lips wide with forefinger and thumb. It made a sticky plop, as the wet pouch engulfed it, and Belinda's finger rammed it right to Jan's wombneck.

'Steady on,' Jan gasped. 'That's almost too nice. You'll have me coming before I've even started my wank.'

'Just think of me as a nurse, all right?'

Belinda inserted the second, then the last two, with Jan groaning, and her cunt basin writhing, as streams of come openly coursed down her quivering inner thighs.

'That's lovely,' she panted. 'Look at my nubbin. It's ever so stiff.'

'I'd noticed,' said Belinda, wiping her slimy fingers on Jan's thigh. 'Now, hold your slice tight shut, and then wank off at your nub, that's the best way. If you squirm a bit, and roll the sweets around in your pouch, it's awfully thrill-making. Watch.'

Quickly, Belinda popped the four bull's balls into her slit, held her lips shut, and began to gyrate, rubbing her naked clitty, with little gasps, as the balls clacked together inside her. Jan did the same, and soon the two girls sat with spread thighs and crimson faces, frigging their clits, and watching each other wank. Mingled come and brown juice from the melting confections trickled down their quaking thighs.

'Gosh, what a lovely masturbate,' Belinda gasped.

'Mm . . .' Jan panted, 'this is the best wank ever. Wait till I tell Wendy.'

'You mean, you and Wendy . . .?' Belinda blurted.

'Well, yes, Wendy and I masturbate quite regularly. It's harmless fun, Belinda. '

'I suppose so. As long as it isn't anything more.'

'And what if it were? Didn't we all diddle each other in the lav, as smutty schoolgirls? Heavens. Belinda, after your telling me about wanking off boys . . .'

Belinda laughed. 'I suppose I mustn't be hypocritical,' she gasped. 'I'm just curious how much more there could be.' Her fingers dived inside her pouch, jangling the bull's balls, with spurts of come and brown juice sliming her quivering thighs. 'Gosh, this is good. Are you coming yet? I love watching you wank, Jan. I'm making mine last as long as possible.'

'I'm holding back too. And I adore looking at your diddled twat, Belinda, and that huge clitty.'

'I suppose I'm a bit different,' said Belinda coyly.

'Lucky you. Bigger clit, bigger joy.'

Jan's lush pubic foliage was soaked in dripping come, while her taut belly tensed and throbbed. 'I have the feeling you aren't telling me everything about your teasing and exhibitionism, though,' said Jan thoughtfully, as she rubbed her swollen red clitty, with slopping, squelchy noises gurgling from her wanked cunt. 'Isn't there a desire to punish those poor boys with their stiff pricks? Revenge for some humiliation at a male's hands?'

'You really are a psychiatrist,' said Belinda. 'Well, all right, there was something. It happened in my final year at school, when I was beaten in front of the whole class, for something I didn't do. It was Wendy's fault, but I couldn't sneak on her. That would have been rotten.'

'Quite so,' said Jan. 'Who beat you?'

'Captain Garstang.'

'On the bare?'

'Yes. That's what was so shameful, because that part was my own fault – I wasn't wearing knickers, you see.'

'I'd love to hear the details,' Jan purred, sliding her hand down her belly to cover her gash lips. 'A beating from a spunk could be thrill-making.'

Belinda blurted out the whole story, not omitting her excitement at the beating, the wetness in her cooze and her need to masturbate afterwards. As she spoke, Jan rhythmically caressed her glistening gash flaps, and the bright red thumb of her clitty, poking between the swollen fleshy slices.

'What was it like?' she asked, her breath rapid. 'The pain, I mean.'

'Well, it was sore,' said Belinda. 'It hurt dreadfully, a horrid, smarting, stinging, thuddy sort of pain. I don't think you can really describe the pain of bare licks. Each stroke felt like a red-hot sword, and sent shock waves all through my bare bum-puddings, with my gorge rising, and tears in my eyes, and my heart racing, thump-thump-thump. Just when I thought I could bear it, another stroke landed, even harder. Such shame, that your private flesh is exposed and bruised, all red and squirming, with your quim and bumhole on show, as your buttocks sort of clench and wriggle. You tighten your bottom muscles to try and squeeze away the pain, but you can't; it just keeps smarting and throbbing. You feel so helpless. Like being a slave, in Africa, or somewhere, paraded naked, all trussed in ropes, and helpless to stop cruel men from thrashing you with their whips.'

'Mm ... I can imagine,' panted Jan. 'I'm not sure it wouldn't be rather exciting.' Jan's cooze lips squelched stickily, with brown candied juice flowing from her tightly shut slit, as her fingers manipulated her swollen clitty, and stroked the pink pouch flesh, glistening with come. Her belly quivered, tensing, and her engorged conic nipples were pointed and stiff. 'Exposing yourself, teasing, is a form of revenge,' Jan said. 'You like getting boys stiff, seeing the bulging rods in their trousers.'

'Yes, I admit I do,' said Belinda.

'Their rods are ready for action, but powerless to move. The cane that whipped you was free and powerful, so you are exorcising that memory by summoning up rods that won't hurt you, and taunting their owners with their own helplessness.'

'Gosh, you're wizard! A real psychiatrist,' Belinda blurted. 'How do you know so much?'

'I'm paid to,' panted Jan, masturbating, her quim opened wide, with her thighs casually spread and one knee resting on the sofa arm. 'I suppose I'd better tell you about my very special kind of nursing. Who knows, it might make our wanks even fruitier.'

3

Spanked Rotten

Jan swivelled, raised her legs and clasped her toes together, with her back curled, while her head swooped down between her outstretched thighs. Her face inches from her gushing cooze, she continued to masturbate, flicking her erect clitty, with joyful little yelps.

'How do you do that?' cried Belinda.

'It's easy,' Jan gasped, raising her head. 'Go on, try. But keep wanking – the view is lovely.'

Gasping, Belinda did the same, feeling her soles and toes pressed together, and swung her head between her thighs. She gazed on her open cunt, with her fingers working at the engorged clitoris, and rivulets of brown oily juice spurting from the wanked hole. If only I could take my clitty in my mouth . . . She squeezed her cunt sphincter, making the bull's balls clink inside her pouch, and gasped, as tingling pleasure flooded her belly and quim. Flushed, she looked up, to see Jan licking her ankles and soles, then taking the toes of her right foot into her mouth, and sucking them, with her eyes twinkling at Belinda.

'Mm,' Jan said, releasing her toes, 'a bit cheesy, but fun.'

Belinda began to lick her own calves, then her ankles and soles. 'It tickles,' she gasped, before taking both sets of toes into her mouth, and slurping, her jaws agape.

'That's good,' said Jan. 'It's all about getting in touch with your inner self; that's what modern psychiatry teaches. All of us, especially girls, misunderstand or repress our intimate feelings. My work is to help young males –

some females too, though – suffering from uncontrollable sex drive and aggression. In blokes, it's due to excess testosterone – the stuff that gives men cream in their balls. Chemical therapy produces peculiar side effects, so Dr Warrior teaches that it is better to deal with these urges by psychology, and that's where I come in. You see, males aggressive towards women secretly want their aggression tamed by a woman. What they need, and really desire – you mustn't be shocked – is a good thrashing on the bare behind, and, well, that is just what I give them.'

Belinda squealed, as a sudden spurt of come tickled her thighs. 'You – you whip men, and they want you to?' she gasped. 'That's so wet-making.'

Jan sprang to her feet, with the bull's balls rattling inside her quim, and opened a cabinet, where a row of shiny whips and canes hung on display. Belinda gasped, but wanked her cunt even harder, as she stared at the oiled wood, rubber and leather of the rods, single tongues and quirts.

'What I do is excite them, then teach them to control their urges, by controlling them – making myself the dominant figure. It's perfectly safe, because hidden microphones transmit the proceedings to male orderlies in the next room, and I haven't had one unseemly incident yet.'

Jan returned to the couch, to resume her masturbation, thighs well parted, with one knee up, and lazily frotting, as she showed her wet pink to Belinda. 'Depending on the patient, I'll administer his therapy while wearing my nurse's uniform, which men find sexy, or else strip to the bare. Sometimes they need a powerful purgative enema, while I give them relief massage – wank them off – before the special treatment, which I'll explain; or I might put on a show – masturbate in front of them – and sometimes a double show, what some call a lesbian act, with both me and my partner in the bare, or wearing only sexy skimpies.'

'So that's where Wendy comes in,' gasped Belinda.

'Correct. Wendy, like myself, is a girl who can take pleasure with another girl. It's not the same thing as being a lesbo, and Dr Warrior says that most, if not all girls, are basically girl-friendly.'

'But what do you actually do?' said Belinda, her thighs and belly writhing, as her hand squelched her come-slimed cunt.

'Same as we are doing now, only we do it to each other. Or, we suck each other's twat . . . oh, whatever fancy takes us. The point is, the male gets all excited and aggressive and, at the right moment for his special treatment, I assume my sternest persona and order him to bend over and bare his bum. Then I thrash him with a cane, or whip him. I really hurt him –' Jan licked her lips, and masturbated harder '– so that he comes to equate aggressive desire, in a red room of passion, with pretty awful corporal punishment, and is able to put a lid on it.'

'Girls, too?'

'Some. Mostly aggressive lesbians. We try to cure them of lesbianism, with a hard whipping on the bare – much like the one Garstang gave you,' Jan said, smiling crookedly.

'I'm not a lesbian,' cried Belinda hotly. 'Girl-friendly – it sounds so sweet; how could I not be, when diddling is such fun, and girls' bodies so beautiful, but –' Her hand flew to her lips. 'Gosh,' she gasped.

'Don't be ashamed,' purred Jan. 'It's much better to face, and enjoy, the truth – that all girls like the feel of other girls. That's why –' she reached behind Belinda's cunt basin, and cupped her two bare buttocks, like ripe fruits, one in each palm '– we girls should pleasure each other. Trust me, I'm a nurse.'

Her hands moved up Belinda's back, kneading and stroking, then passed to her breasts, which she cupped, pinching the nipples between her fingers.

'Oh, that's nice,' Belinda sighed, wanking faster.

'Such lovely jellies, your bubs, I mean, so big and soft and firm. And your nips, why, they're stiff already, like big pink strawberries. May I touch?'

'Yes. Oh . . .' Belinda moaned, as Jan's fingernail circled her left areola. 'Ooh!'

Jan stroked the nipple bud with her fingertip. 'Like it?' she whispered.

'Mm . . . you know I do. It goes all the way down to my nubbin, a gorgeous electric tingly feeling.'

'You do have a lot of clit! I've never seen one like it. In the medical bizney, we call such an enlarged clit a priapiscus. Wish I had one.'

'How many have you seen . . . or touched, Jan?'

'Trade secret.'

Jan extended her fingers, and rubbed both Belinda's erect nipples with long, sweeping caresses of her palm and fingertips.

'Ooh . . . ooh . . .' gasped Belinda. 'You're making me so wet.'

Jan slid her hand down Belinda's quaking belly to her shaven cunt mound and plunged two fingers inside the wet slit, cramming the bull's balls tightly to one side of the cunt pouch, to press from the inside on Belinda's pubic bone. Her other hand caressed the nubbin of Belinda's spine, making her moan, before entering the deep valley of the bum cleft, and coming to rest on Belinda's anus. Jan pushed a fingertip inside the anus bud, and began to ream Belinda's anal elastic.

'That tickles so!' squealed Belinda.

Pushing aside Belinda's wank finger, Jan began to rub her clitty with her thumb, while plunging two, then three, fingers deep into her juicing slit, stroking Belinda's hard wombneck with her fingernails, and reaming it several times with the bull's balls, before withdrawing for a fresh poke. She alternated this slow penetration with a rapid jerking motion, pummelling the root of Belinda's cunt in quickfire, which had Belinda's crotch writhing and her gash, clattering with bull's balls, spraying copious come over Jan's fingers. She guided Belinda's hand towards her own open pouch, and, moaning, Belinda began to masturbate her friend, plunging her fingers into the gaping wet slit, and swirling the bull's balls from side to side, while kneading Jan's massively engorged clitty with her thumbnail.

'Mm . . . that's so good,' rasped Jan.

'Oh, gosh, I'm sure I'm going to come,' Belinda panted.

Jan slipped to the floor, and kneeled, with her face between Belinda's thighs. Her mouth plunged to Belinda's cunt, and her tongue penetrated the sopping hole, to begin a fierce flickering caress, darting in and out of the slit, while licking the raw red erection of the clitoris.

'I love this clit,' she gasped. 'It's so sweet and full and juicy, like some African girl's, grown big under the hot sun. I must suck it.'

She took Belinda's throbbing nubbin between her lips, and sucked, with her tongue flicking the glans of the clitty.

'Oh! Gosh! Stop! I'm going to come!' whimpered Belinda. 'I mean, don't stop . . .'

As she gamahuched the writhing nude Belinda, Jan sank two fingers fully inside her anus, penetrating the rectal pouch, and began to jab Belinda's arse root. Squirming, Belinda thrust her cunt against Jan's come-soaked face. Jan gurgled, swallowing Belinda's gushing come, and the brown juice from the melting bull's balls.

'Oh! Oh!' Belinda whimpered. 'That's so lovely. I'm going to come any second, really.'

Panting, Jan withdrew her fingers and tongue. 'Then it's time to teach you a lesson, you naughty bitch,' she murmured, through lips dripping with Belinda's come.

'Oh! Don't stop! What – what do you mean, lesson?'

Jan removed Belinda's fingers from her own cunt, and licked her come from them. 'When Garstang flogged you, all that time ago, you submitted, didn't you?'

'I had no choice.'

'Of course, you had a choice. You chose to bare up for a whipping, by a spunky male. After your beating, you went to the lav and wanked off. Since then, you've been exposing yourself, however innocently and coyly, because you are really demanding a repeat of the same treatment – daring your audience to rip your knickers off, bare your bum and give you the whipping you crave.'

'That's absurd! It hurt dreadfully. How could any girl want – ooh! Stop! What are you doing?'

Jan grasped Belinda by the hips, and swivelled her, sliding on her drooled come, with her belly across Jan's thighs, and her buttocks upthrust. She pinioned Belinda by her hair, and held her head down. Belinda's legs threshed, with her exposed buttocks wriggling, as Jan lowered her head, with her fist in Belinda's cunt, lifting the buttocks up towards her mouth. Jan began to bite Belinda's bottom, licking and drooling over the writhing buttocks, and leaving garish pink teeth marks in the quivering bare flesh. She pushed her nose into Belinda's anus, and sniffed deeply, then covered the pucker with licks and kisses, getting her tongue an inch into the girl's anus, and darting in and out, with pauses for fierce bites to the buttock walls surrounding the anal bud, while Belinda shrieked, her bitten bum squirming. Panting, Jan raised her head. 'Giving that gluteus superbus what it begs for, girl. It's too beautiful to go unspanked, so I'm going to spank you something rotten. Any girl would be jealous of an arse like that! I'm freeing my healthy instinct to punish you.'

Jan's palm cracked on the bare buttocks. Smack! Smack! Smack!

'Ouch! Ooh! That hurts!'

'Consider it your punishment for teasing.'

Smack! Smack! Smack!

'Stop it, Jan! It really does hurt.'

Smack! Smack! Smack!

'Oh! Oh! I don't deserve this.'

Belinda's spanked bottom glowed crimson at the nurse's heavy slaps. Jan continued to spank the bare croup, while Belinda's cries of protest softened to snuffling whimpers, and her buttocks writhed, squirming on Jan's legs, with her cunt hillock sliding in a pool of her own come, pouring faster and faster from her slit. Her cunt basin squelched Jan's thigh, rubbing her distended clit against her spanker's skin.

'Ohh . . . ooh . . . don't,' she moaned, as her squirming bottom glowed crimson with bruises. 'Maybe I do deserve to be punished, but please, not so hard.'

After a dozen more spanks, Jan lowered her hand. Belinda's bottom continued to writhe.

'Are you sure you've been punished enough?' Jan murmured.

'You're the nurse,' Belinda whimpered. 'It's up to you. Ouch!'

Jan wrenched her head up by her hair. 'On your feet, bitch, and bring me a suitable instrument from my cabinet,' she ordered lazily, her thumb squelching her distended clitoris, a bright pink tube between her come-slimed, parted thighs.

'Oh, you are too cruel,' sobbed Belinda, wiping the tears from her eyes, and rubbing her bruised crimson bottom, as she shuffled barefoot to the punishment cabinet.

Come and brown juice sluiced from her twitching cooze flaps, down her thighs, splattering her feet. Jan resumed her masturbation, as she watched Belinda sort through the canes and whips, finally choosing a bright yellow willow wood, with a crook handle, three feet long. Head bowed, and face crimson, she handed it to Jan without a word and flung herself over the sofa back, with her face buried in the come-soaked cushions and her bottom high in the air. Still masturbating her clitoris, Jan rose, flexed the cane and lashed the cushion beside Belinda's head, with a loud whistling rush.

'Oh, no,' Belinda whimpered, shuddering, her voice muffled by the cushion.

Jan took her caning stance, behind the rosy red buttocks of the spanked girl. Belinda's legs were shivering, rigid and parted wide, showing the red, swollen cunt lips and the twitching anus pucker, enlarged by Jan's fingers. Jan licked her lips, as she lifted the cane over Belinda's quivering fesses. 'You are a wise girl, Belinda,' she purred. 'You know a spanking isn't enough.'

Her fingertips stroked the shivering crimson jellies of Belinda's spanked bare. 'What a luscious bum you have, Belinda,' she whispered. 'This is going to be so nice.'

Vip!

'Ooh!' Belinda howled, her buttocks twitching frantically, as the cane lashed a thick red stripe squarely across the mid-fesses.

'Remember, this is therapy,' Jan panted. 'And I am a nurse.'

Vip!

'Oh, no . . .'

Vip!

'Ahh!'

'Less of the blubbing, bitch,' Jan snarled.

Belinda's legs shuddered, with her striped nates clenching and squirming violently. Her breath rasped in harsh pants. Belinda did not cry out, but groaned, in a long choked sob, her bubbies heaving and slamming against the sofa back. A long, slender drip of come plopped from her cunt onto the floor between her knotted toes.

'Uhh . . .' Belinda whined, thumping the sofa with her fists.

Vip!

'Urrgh!'

Belinda pulled the cushion over her head, and held it down tightly.

Vip!

'Mm! Mm!' came her squeals, muffled by the cushion, as her buttocks glowed redder and redder with deep, criss-crossed cane weals, and her legs shot rigid, beneath her squirming bottom.

'My, you're a frisky mare, for a virgin,' Jan panted. 'I've never seen a bum wriggle so much.'

'Mmph! Mmph!' moaned Belinda, followed by a muffled squeal, which Jan demanded she repeat clearly.

Belinda lifted her cushion a fraction. 'I thought you were my friend,' she sobbed, before tugging the cushion down again, as if for protection.

While Belinda snivelled under her cushion, Jan reached into her punishment cabinet, and removed, from under the rack of flagellant implements, a massive, very long black cylinder, sculpted in rubber and covered in gnarled ridges and striations. It was slightly curved, in the form of a double male sex organ, with a swollen knob at each end. Jan drained her wineglass, then lit a Gold Flake, which she parked at the corner of her lips. Sucking then exhaling fragrant blue smoke, she parted the lips of her quim between finger and thumb, then, pausing in the caning, rammed one end of the rubber tube into her wet cunt, with a gurgling plop, as one of the two cockshafts disappeared inside her. The tube had a central grip, with indentations for the fingers, and rings, through which Jan eased her index and forefinger. A brief flick sent the shaft pounding in and out of her slit, while its other end reared, waggling between her thighs. Masturbating her cunt, with loud squelches of the dildo, Jan lifted her cane again.

The cane streaked Belinda's crimson welted bare, with the flogged girl's howl muffled by her cushion. As she beat Belinda, Jan licked her lips, masturbating hard, with the black rubber tube, slimed with copious come, mechanically ramming her slit, and the extended shaft poking back and forth from her cooze lips, like a massive black clitty. Her thumb tweaked her stiff nubbin, and, as the slapping rubber tube churned her cooze, her cunt basin and bum began to writhe sensuously, in counterpoint to the frenzied squirms of Belinda's bare. A chunk of cigarette ash fell into Belinda's bumcleft, and dissolved in the sweat which lathered her buttocks.

'Ooh, ooh, ooh . . .' wailed Belinda, her crimson bare dancing, and tiptoes drumming the floor.

Jan panted hard, as she caned the wriggling croup, her own breasts bouncing in time with the strokes. Come poured down her rippling bare thighs, as the cocktube slammed in and out of her gushing cooze, and her thumb kept up its relentless mashing of her stiff, extruded clitoris. When the cane had striped Belinda's bare over thirty strokes, Jan put it down, and, holding the dildo inside her cooze, darted to her cabinet. Still masturbating, she selected a quirt of five braided leather thongs, an inch thick and two feet long, and returned to pinion Belinda's cushioned neck with her foot.

'Oomph! Urrgh!' Belinda squealed, bum and spine wriggling, as Jan lifted the quirt over her bottom.

The heavy tongues lashed her buttocks from above, Jan laying her stroke deep towards the thighs, so that two of the tongues whipped inside Belinda's bumcleft, stroking her anus bud and the pendant lips of her cooze. A fan pattern of five crimson weals overlaid the deep bruising of the cane.

'Urrgh! Agghh!' Belinda screamed, her buttocks flailing, and her feet bouncing up and down, pattering the floor in a dance of agony.

Thwap!

'Ooh!'

Thwap!

'Ahh! Ahh! Ahh!'

As the quirt slapped Belinda's squirming bare, Jan thrust her cocktube harder and harder inside her slit. Come poured from her quivering gash flaps, and her belly fluttered, as she panted, then whimpered, her face scarlet, in a shuddering orgasm. Her whipping did not falter, and, as her gasps gave way to satisfied mewls of pleasure, her cunt clamped the tube inside her, while she continued to lash Belinda's helpless bare, wriggling and red on the chair. She switched the dildo round, and, with only the power of her tense, knotted belly and sucking cunt, drew the unslimed portion inside her slit, to expel it, catch it and suck it in again. She switched the dildo round again, both of its knobs now dripping with her come, and clasped the quirt handle with both hands.

The whip tongues entered Belinda's bumcleft at every stroke, nipping her anus and quim lips, with the whipped girl's moans of agony pulsing beneath her cushion. A steady drip of Belinda's come plopped on the floorboards, beneath her cunt. Her cries grew softer, turning to a high-pitched, moaning wail – 'Uhhh!' – punctuated by sharp gasps for breath – 'Ah! Ah! Ah!' – until, at a vicious cut, slapping the tongues right between her threshing naked buttocks, Belinda shrieked, and went on shrieking, as her cunt spurted come – 'Ooh! Ooh! Ooh! Yes!' – and her spine writhed in a sinuous dance of orgasm.

As Belinda's cries of coming softened, Jan rewarded her with an extra-hard stroke of the leather; Belinda shrieked, then lifted the cushion and poked her head out to stare at

Jan's dripping minge and cunt lips, with the cocktube sliding smoothly in and out of her gash, under her rippling belly.

'Please, Jan,' she whimpered. 'I need to pee.'

'Hold it in, bitch,' Jan snarled. 'You are a pervert – you came under whipping.'

'Oh, no . . .' Belinda wailed. 'Please let me pee, Jan.'

With a thick rubber cord, Jan strapped the dripping cocktube firmly around her waist, buttocks and quim; one knob of the dildo filled her slit, squashing her extruded clitty, and the other reared from her gash like a monstrous male sex organ. She ripped aside Belinda's cushion, and pulled the girl's head up by her hair. Belinda's face was flushed crimson, wrinkled in pain and glazed with tears.

'Suck on this, bitch,' Jan ordered, thrusting her cunt at Belinda's face, with her false cock dripping her come an inch from Belinda's lips.

'What? Ugh! No – urrgh!' Belinda gasped, as, with a savage wrench of her hair, and a jerk of her buttocks, Jan plunged the rubber tube deep into Belinda's throat.

'Suck it dry, bitch,' Jan commanded, thrusting her buttocks in the motions of fucking, and ramming the tube to the back of Belinda's palate.

As Belinda slurped on the hard rubber cocktube, Jan poured herself more wine and lit a fresh Gold Flake. Clasping her cigarette, she dabbled her fingers at her clitty, rubbing the stiff nubbin. As she sipped, smoked and masturbated, her pumping buttocks kept up a rhythmic thrust of the dildo in Belinda's mouth, while Belinda gagged on its coruscated, come-slimed hardness, licking off Jan's come and swallowing, with gurgling whimpers and sobs. As the other end of the dildo poked Jan's own cunt, her come poured, with little squelches, with her gash flaps squeezing the penetrating shaft. Belinda opened her mouth and bit the rubber to stop Jan's thrusts.

'It's dry,' she mumbled. 'I've swallowed all your beastly juice.'

'I expect you'd like a drink,' Jan murmured, jerking the dildo from Belinda's mouth.

'Yes, please,' Belinda gasped. 'Then, may I pee?'

'We'll see. '

Jan emptied her wineglass over her own breasts. The wine trickled down her belly into her cunt bush.

'Lick me dry, bitch,' she hissed.

'Oh ... oh ...' Belinda sobbed, as she applied her tongue to Jan's breasts, licking the erect nipples and slurping wine from the hard, quivering teat cones. Suddenly, Jan wrenched Belinda's hair, pulling her up; her face swooped and pressed against Belinda's quivering bubbies. She opened her jaws wide and bit savagely on Belinda's erect left nipple. Jan chewed and bit Belinda's bubs, until the breast flesh was raw with teethmarks.

'Oh, no, don't ...' Belinda wailed.

After a minute's vicious chewing of Belinda's breasts, the flesh was livid with crimson bites. Jan pushed Belinda's face back to her own teats, and ordered her to suck her nipples. Belinda took the hard domes into her mouth, and, with her nose squashed against Jan's naked breasts, sucked and licked the stiff nipples. When Jan pronounced herself satisfied, Belinda's face slid down Jan's belly, licking up the wine, and her nose and lips entered Jan's pubic forest, where Belinda took mouthfuls of hair, wringing the tufts dry, and swallowing the squeezed liquid. Jan rammed Belinda's face against her open gash flaps, with her nose pressing against Jan's clitoris and her chin on the dildo, extruded from Jan's come-slimed vulva.

'Do me, bitch,' Jan commanded, pouring herself fresh wine. 'Suck my nubbin till I spasm, and drink up the juices, till my twat's clean.'

Belinda got her lips around the clit, and began to suck, her face sopping with Jan's come. Jan slid her spent cigarette under Belinda's cunt, where it sizzled to extinction, then lit another. She writhed her hips, slopping her wet cunt into Belinda's face, with Belinda chewing hard on her clitty, swallowing the mingling of come and sweet brown juice, only pausing to spit out pubic hairs tangled in her mouth.

'Yes, you're not bad for a fucking virgin,' Jan gasped. 'Let's do something about that.'

As Belinda sucked, Jan's belly tightened and knotted, until she pressed hard on Belinda's head, smothering her in pubic hair, and let her cunt spurt a flood of come into Belinda's mouth, while her nubbin squashed Belinda's nose.

'Yes, that's good,' Jan gasped. 'Oh, yes . . . suck me, bitch; chew my clit. Make me spurt come all over your bitch virgin's face.'

Belinda opened her mouth wide, and took the clitty firmly between her lips, beginning a new, fierce sucking.

'Mm . . . mm . . . don't stop . . . yes! Ahh! Yes . . .' Jan moaned, spasming.

Her come drenched the quivering rubber cocktube. Panting, she pushed Belinda's face back into her cushion, with a drool of come and brown juice fouling the seat fabric. Jan moved behind Belinda, and seized her hips. Parting the wealed buttocks, she positioned her strapped-on dildo at the entrance to Belinda's sopping cunt, and nuzzled her erect clitty, making her groan with pleasure, before plunging the tube into her slit, right to the wombneck.

'What? No! No! Ahh . . .' Belinda shrieked, as Jan began to fuck her cunt from behind, her hips and buttocks pumping hard.

As she fucked, her arse muscles clenching and jerking, her portion of the double dildo reamed her own cunt, with slopping noises of come, and the gnarled striations rasping her stiff clitty. Belinda's head was buried in her cushion. Her bottom wriggled and swayed under Jan's vigorous tupping, and her legs shuddered, as come from her fucked gash flowed down her quivering thighs.

'Oh! Oh! Oh!' Belinda gasped. 'It's so good . . .'

Jan's belly slapped Belinda's squirming buttocks, as the tube slammed inside the wriggling girl's slit, spraying oily cunt juice over her legs.

'Oh, Jan, wank me please,' panted Belinda. 'I want to come.'

'You don't need to wank, when you're twat-fucked,' said Jan. 'A good ramming makes any girl spurt.'

'Please.'

'Oh, very well. Bitches like you are so bloody demanding.'

Jan transferred her cigarette and wineglass to her right hand, and thrust her left under Belinda's quaking belly. She grasped the girl's clitty between two fingers, and began to knead the swollen nubbin of pink wet flesh. Belinda groaned, shivering, as Jan continued to ram her cooze with the rubber shaft.

'Yes, yes!' she moaned. 'I'm going to come.'

The cocktube squelched loudly in the spurts of come gushing from her fucked gash. Jan, too, gasped, as the tube pummelled her clitty, and her own cunt poured come.

'Uhh . . . uhh . . .' the naked girls panted, both their bodies heaving, as one fucked and the other writhed in submission.

'Oh . . . oh . . .'

'Yes!'

'Ooh! '

'Oh, yes!'

Jan and Belinda ejaculated copious glistening come, as their slippery nude bodies shuddered in mutual orgasm.

'Oh, gosh, that was good,' panted Belinda.

'Same here,' said Jan, leaning on Belinda's back, puffing her smoke and gurgling from her wineglass. The rubber cocktube remained, tightly filling Belinda's cunt.

'Oh, gosh,' said Belinda, 'I need to pee awfully badly.'

'Fucking bedwetter,' snapped Jan. 'You wait till I say so.'

'I can't. I'm bursting. It's going to come. I can't stop it,' Belinda wailed. 'Ooh . . .'

A stream of piss sprayed from her blocked cunt all over Jan's thighs and belly, then onto the floor, where it formed a wide, steaming puddle.

'I'm sorry, I'm sorry,' Belinda sobbed, as the aromatic golden piss flowed from her.

When the heavy flow abated to a few drips, Jan withdrew the dildo from Belinda's slit with a loud squelch, put aside her glass and took Belinda by the hair. She unstrapped her dildo, plopped it from her cunt and spanked Belinda's buttocks with several smacks of the come-slimed rubber tube.

'Ooh . . .' Belinda moaned.

'You dirty little slut,' Jan snarled.

She pushed her cigarette between Belinda's gash flaps, where it sizzled and went out. Forcing Belinda to kneel, Jan mopped her piss-soaked body with Belinda's hair, then wrung out the soaking mane into the waste bin.

'Now the floor,' she ordered. 'Wipe up every drop with your hair, and any you miss you can lick up.'

'Oh, Jan, I said I was sorry,' Belinda sobbed. 'How can you be so cruel?'

Jan kicked Belinda in the open gash; Belinda squealed and bent down, crouching to mop the floor with her blonde mane. After several minutes, and after wringing her mane three times, only a few scattered droplets of her piss remained on the floor. Putting her foot on Belinda's neck, Jan forced her head down, until she had licked up the drops. Then, she had to lick Jan's feet of piss, taking each toe into her mouth and sucking it dry. Her flogged bottom glowed dark with weals, and bobbed, in time with her head, as she attended Jan's smelly wet feet.

'Gosh, you pong,' Jan said, wrinkling her nose. 'There's a bucket in the bathroom. I suggest you give youreself a good drenching.'

Belinda stumbled to the bathroom, which contained a tin bath, single cold tap and bucket. The tap emitted a spew of rusty water, and, when Belinda had finished showering her body, streaks of brown remained on her skin. She looked in the grimy mirror, turning to see her bottom, and ran her fingers up and down the deep purple ridges of her flogging; she examined the overlaid patterns of cane, handspanks, whip and teethmarks, and she smiled, licking her lips. She padded back to the red room, where Jan had a glass of wine and a freshly lit Gold Flake waiting for her.

'Well!' Jan said brightly, pulling Belinda down beside her on the sofa. 'How do you feel?'

'My bum's awfully sore,' said Belinda, squirming in her seat. 'It's the most painful wanking session I've ever had.'

She sucked smoke and gulped wine.

'But this wine is so delicious,' she said giggling, 'it might just have been worth it. Even that dreadful rubber thing. I can't believe I had it inside me. Tell me, do you use it on your girl patients?'

'Certainly. Males, too – anal penetration, of course.'

'Up their bums?'

'Some patients need extreme therapy,' said Jan. 'Aren't you one? You didn't make any serious attempt to stop your flogging, or get away, did you?'

'N-no,' blurted Belinda. 'But that's not really fair. I was in your power, Jan.'

'You chose to be in my power. You are a bit of a pickle, Belinda – coming when I whipped you, then wetting yourself.'

'You came too.'

'Nurse's privilege. Here, let me rub some zinc ointment on that flayed bum. The smarting will ease, and you'll be right as rain in no time, although the bruises will firm up, and it'll feel like corrugated cardboard for a while.'

'Gosh,' Belinda blurted, 'I'm getting used to the smarting, you know. My bum's all throbby and stingy, but it's warm, too, and the throbbing seems part of me.'

She rolled over and showed her bare to Jan whose expert fingers kneaded the bruised flesh, rubbing cold zinc ointment up and down her weals.

'Ooh! That hurts more.'

'Shall I stop?'

'No, don't.'

The nurse's fingers probed Belinda's bruised anus and cooze.

'Mm, that is nice. Almost worth a whipping. No, on seconds thoughts, leave out the "almost". Jan, what did you mean, bitches like me? You said we were so bloody demanding.'

'You'll find out . . . if you're lucky.'

'Don't be so beastly mysterious. I'm quite normal, you know.'

'Nobody's quite normal,' Jan retorted, plopping her fingers from Belinda, before licking them, with an impish grin. 'Some of my males keep coming back for further treatment. A good course of bare-beating should cure them of urges, but most of them demand repeat treatment to stay cured. I think they actually like having their bare bums flogged. Perhaps that's normal. And it is yummy, whipping a juicy male bum, wealed red under my lashes, and squirming in shame – I feel so deliciously in control. You like my rubbing your bottom, don't you? Well, lashes are just an extra-hard caress, for more sensation, rather like pepper in your soup. I say, Belinda, Dr Warrior would be thrilled to meet you. She could tell you more about yourself than I can. You could be her case history du jour.'

'I am not a case history,' blurted Belinda, flushing. 'I am a perfectly normal Lancashire girl.'

'Who likes exposing her body to strangers, and being caned and whipped on her bare bottom by her wanking chum, and who won't hold in her pee, because she knows she'll have to endure the humiliation of wiping up after herself? I wish I had been a fly on the wall when you took your flogging from spunky Captain Garstang. I think that might explain, or reveal, a lot. Why not come to Dr Warrior's regular gathering next Sunday afternoon, at home in Morecambe? Dr Warrior moves in quite an amusing set; there will be plenty of free drink, lots of nurses and spunks and broad-minded people, who like playing games.'

'Free drink?'

'Oodles. Dr Warrior has contacts.'

'Just as long as I won't be made to do anything I don't want.'

Jan laughed, a silky, smoky rippling of her throat. 'Darling Belinda, that's the whole point. Dr Warrior wants girls to do what they do want.'

Jan tweaked both her nipples, then pinched the buds, tightening her fingernails, until her nipples were white, and her face creased in pain. 'See?' she gasped, smiling, as she freed her nipples.

'Well, all right. But I'm not going to be some sort of exhibit.'

Jan laughed, and placed her hand on Belinda's still-wet cunt. 'Belinda, to a learned lady like Dr Warrior, everybody is an exhibit. She's studied a lot in Africa, and is awfully experienced. That's what makes her so fascinating.'

'Dr Warrior is a she? Then it's all right, I suppose. Thank you for the wine, by the way.'

'Thank you for the bull's balls. I'll meet you outside the castle at two, and we can get the Morecambe bus. And I promise you I won't mention your absolutely appalling behaviour this afternoon.'

'Me?' Belinda spluttered. 'Appalling behaviour? Why, I've been spanked rotten, poked in my orchid with a horrid huge rubber thing, been shamed into wiping my own piss, and I've been wanked off, and *I'm* the appalling one?'

'Don't pretend you didn't like it.'

Belinda blushed, smiling. 'I didn't say I didn't like it,' she murmured, patting Jan's cooze lips. 'I did like it. That's why I'm so peeved with myself.'

4

Expert Bitch

'Uhh . . . uhh . . .'

Belinda's gasps filled her bedsitting room, as she stroked her wealed bare bottom, with her nude body sandwiched between two mirrors. The remains of her breakfast tea and toast lay on her tablecloth beside her packed school bag; her three inches of tepid water, in her cracked enamel bath, from Shanks of Barrhead, were cooling rapidly; the sun was risen and the market clock tolled ten. Belinda wiped a sticky hair from her brow, watching in the glass while her fingers squelched inside her open naked cunt. As she masturbated, groaning and panting, her free hand caressed the powerful bruises which striped her buttocks, writhing in the glass behind her.

I've lost count of my wanks, looking at my poor smarting bum! I can't keep my fingers from my nub. Was Jan right, that a big clit is good? Gosh, I mustn't be late for class.

Belinda's rigid fingers stroked her belly, taut and trembling; her nails scored pink blossoms on her shaven smooth cooze hillock, as her fingers descended into the wet valley of her quim lips to tweak and pummel the erect, throbbing nubbin, glistening in the come that spurted from the folds of her fleshy pink orchid. *So sweet, my body's opening.* Come poured from her wanked gash, as her belly began to flutter in approaching orgasm. Her fingernails clawed the stiff ridges of her cane welts, framed prettily by Jan's bitemarks, faded to mauve, and her buttocks wriggled, as if under flogging. Her hand slid from her croup to her bubbies, where she pinched and rubbed her nipples, and squashed her teats against her ribcage, panting hard, at the electric tingle surging down her spine to her clitty. Her hand returned to the wealed buttocks; Belinda gazed at the tapestry of welts, laid across every inch of her naked bottom.

That bitch Jan was expert.

Now, someone was going to suffer for those welts. Not Jan, of course – it was hardly her fault, for it wasn't really her friend Jan whipping Belinda, but Jan the therapist. In an hour, she would be teaching the men of 2 Platoon, C Company, Royal Lancs Light Horse and facing a squad of truculent, swaggering males, bursting with sap. This time, she would tame them, curb their leers and take the lustful twinkles from their eyes.

It was all the more shiver-making, because their spunky maleness did arouse Belinda. Luckily, it was not done to 'fraternise' with her students, but she still found her cooze wetting, at the thought, if only. L/Cpl Tiepolo was the worst. The beast knew that his muscled body and silky dark hair, combed in an insolent duckbill, would excite any girl. And he always sat in front of the class, gazing saucily, and making her blush, as she tried to concentrate on her home economics lesson. She was sure he had a sex organ bigger than Jan's dildo – what would he look like, nude and stiff?

'Ooh, yes . . .' Belinda gasped, masturbating faster, and cupping her palm to catch the come flowing from her flapping gash mouth. Her thumb pummelled her raw, extruded clitty, swollen massively between the red slit lips, and her belly quaked, with her knees buckling, as orgasm flooded her.

'Oh, oh, yes . . .' she whimpered, licking her lips frantically, as she saw her welted bare buttocks writhe in the glass. How gorgeous, if onlt I could lick my own bum . . .

Panting, and with sweat dripping from her quivering titties, Belinda wiped her gash of come, with a paper tissue, then slipped into her bath, shivering, as she splashed, sponging herself in the cold water, and rubbing herself with her remaining transparent sliver of Pear's soap. Dried, and sparingly powdered with precious talc – fivepence a tin, when you could get it – she rummaged in her knickers pile, holding each garment to her nose and making a face. They were all smelly. Shrugging, she decided that it would have to be bare bum, under a long skirt, of course.

She snapped herself in a plain white suspender belt, and rolled up her – rather smelly, but it couldn't be helped – second-best pair of cream rayon stockings to fasten the dangling garter straps on the frilly stocking tops. Next, she slipped on a shiny white petticoat of real American parachute silk with an elasticated waist that bit her tummy. It was scarcely more than an apron, which came only halfway down her thighs, but was better than nothing, in her absence of panties. Selecting a chalk pinstripe skirt in blue wool – although it was gorgeously sunny, for autumn – which swirled just below her knees, she stepped into it, relishing the airy freedom of her unsheathed bottom and quim. A white utility bra enclasped her breasts, topped by a crisp cream blouse.

Lacing up her shoes, Belinda glanced nervously at the cloth bag containing her squash raquet and things. She had no intention of playing squash, but it was a useful cover for the instrument, whose pointed tip peeped from a loose buttonhole. It was bought in a fury, but the deed was done, and now the gleaming riding crop of braided leather on a whalebone frame lay there, daring her to use it.

After hobbling, bow-legged with pain, from Jan's flat, and clutching her smarting bottom over her tartan skirt, she had passed the saddler's shop in St Leonard's Gate, and there they were, a rack of shiny leather crops, amid the stirrups, boots and hunting hats.

Furious at her throbbing weals, Jan's deceit and her own humiliation, she simply had to possess the means of punishing another. The bell tinkled as she entered the shop, musty with rich perfumes of leather. Behind the counter was a girl of Belinda's age, with straight ash-blonde hair combed over massive bubs, jutting in a tight crimson blouse, with a bow tie; white jodhpurs clung to her ripe bum peach and muscled, rippling thighs, and were tucked into lustrous black kneeboots. Her kit was so tight it seemed painted on, with every crevice and curve of her body in sensuous relief. Belinda stammered that she wanted a riding crop, sure that the haughty shopgirl could see through her skirt to her blistered bum! Belinda murmured something about a stallion, then, blushing, changed it to a pony, adding that he was almost grown up.

'So the whip is for a grown-up male,' the girl drawled, scarcely trying to hide her contempt for this obviously bootless and unhorsed customer.

However, when Belinda stroked the loveliest, whippiest, hardest crop, nearly three feet long – which, at five shillings and sixpence, was also the most expensive – and said that she wanted one that really hurt, the girl's eyes softened.

'That's rather expensive, but absolutely the best, for all-purpose work,' she purred.

'It's not the price,' Belinda blurted. 'I just want it to do the job. I get pretty good pay, actually, and, what with rationing and shortages, what else can a girl spend her money on but treats?'

'Treats, eh? I see you are a discerning customer,' the girl said, licking her lips and casually stroking her thigh, just beside the ripe swelling of her twat hillock, 'and you won't be displeased – unless you are timid, and fail to lay it on hard enough.'

The girl picked up the crop, and poised it over her own bottom. With a sudden flick, she lashed her left buttock – *Vip*! – then the right, then lowered her arm, and dealt herself a strong backhand stroke across both fesses. Belinda gasped at the force of the strokes; yet, all the time, the girl's buttocks did not flinch or clench, and she licked her lips, creased in a faint, almost mocking smile, while her deep-green eyes stared Belinda full in the face.

'You see?' she said breathily. 'Splendid sting, and remarkably good thud, too. It's from Crupper's of Kirkudbright; they have been making whips, canes, tawse, saddles, straps and harnesses since the seventeenth century, and have a lovely range of luxury products. I can show you some very fine canes and tawse, if you like, for general-purpose discipline. The Scots have such a way with leather, haven't they?'

'I imagine I'll just want the one,' Belinda blurted.

'I'll give you a catalogue,' purred the girl, rubbing her bottom with the palm of her hand in a long, circular motion. 'We find that discerning customers enjoy adding to their collection.'

Belinda had a tingly feeling that 'discerning' meant 'not actually owning a horse'. She assured the girl she had no intention of being timid, and the girl licked her lips, with a fierce glint in her eyes. She wrapped the crop in crinkly gift paper, very carefully, and snapped the folds into place with loud cracks, like the lashing of Jan's cane. Belinda took the package, and handed over a ten-shilling note.

'Remember that for the best, that is, most painful, effect the crop should always be applied on the bare skin,' the girl said, giving Belinda a half-crown and a florin in change.

'Why, of course,' said Belinda. 'Ponies don't wear trousers.'

'It depends on your pony,' the girl murmured.

At home, Belinda scanned Crupper's catalogue, printed on wartime paper, but with clear enough photos of the items for sale. It was, as the shopgirl said, a cornucopia of disciplinary instruments, in leather or wood: crisp-looking quirts of several tongues; canes, long or short, with or without school crook handle; leather tawse, the vicious double-tongued Scots straps; wooden paddles, like cricket bats with holes; harnesses, bridles and bits, for rather small horses. Curiously, the text did not mention horses, but spoke of 'sting', 'thud' and 'bite' on 'miscreants', suffering 'maximum pain, shame and remorse'.

Gingerly, she unwrapped her new riding crop, and stroked the supple braided leather, feeling the strong whalebone shaft within. It was a handsome thing; how strange that instruments of pain should be beautiful. She touched her bottom, and winced; Jan's weals were far too fresh for her to test the crop there. Biting her lip, she lifted her skirt, cracked the crop gently on her stockinged thigh, and gasped at the pain. Closing her eyes, she lashed her other thigh and gasped again, with a tear springing to her eye – a thrashing of six or eight strokes, even a dozen, on meaty male buttocks must surely be uncomfortable. That decided, she put the crop away, and gave herself to a day of heavy masturbation, spurred on by the smarting in her whipped buttocks.

Now, on Monday morning, she wondered if she really could use the crop.

As she walked the half mile to the barracks, her spirits rose. It was a lovely sunny day, and her step was light. If people knew I had a riding crop in my bag! By the time she signed in at the barracks, she was brimming with confidence. The classroom was an ancient Nissen hut, in what the squaddies called the 'arse end' of the camp, deserted most of the time. Having gathered her cookery supplies from the stores – signed for in quadruplicate, under the leering eye of a warrant officer – she strode past drilling soldiers, across cracked concrete and weeds, to her hut. She opened the door, feeling satisfaction, as the squad of lusty young spunks in uniform rose smartly to their feet, and cried, 'Good morning, Miss Beaucul.' They were cheerful, all due to be demobbed in a week or two, and, Belinda realised, less likely than ever to attend to her lessons on simple cookery.

Below her classroom blackboard, she had a long trestle table, equipped with Bunsen burners and cooking utensils.

'Pay attention, for you'll have to look after yourselves when you're demobbed, boys,' she said, to smirks and winks.

For the umpteenth time, she illustrated the subtleties of boiling an egg and making a pot of tea; invited volunteers (everybody volunteered, except L/Cpl Tiepolo) to stand beside her and repeat the experiment; and proceeded to fry some sausages, after making them herself and binding the meat in skins – so much cheaper than buying shop ones.

The lesson was going smoothly – too smoothly, for nobody had done anything to merit correction, not even the svelte L/Cpl Tiepolo, who was yawning or staring out of the window, neither of them really a beating offence. Curse him, he is dishy, in his sluttish way.

'And, as you see,' she said, 'you can make them to your own size. I like them extra large.'

She sat on a high stool, her skirt drawn up over her stockinged knees, and put a steaming sausage between her teeth. She nuzzled the greasy skin with her lips, then slid it to the back of her throat, rolling it inside her mouth, and making smacking, slurping noises. Her lips fastened hard on the sausage, and she sucked loudly, before withdrawing it from her mouth. The class was agog.

'You see?' she said brightly. 'Home cooking can be fun, boys. More important, you won't get your twelve ounces of demob tobacco unless you pass.'

She looked at the clock, and saw there were only minutes to go before the end of class.

Damn! I'll have to leave it to another day – or perhaps forget it. The idea that a grown-up boy would lower his pants and let me beat him! I was being a bit silly . . .

She was almost relieved, when, suddenly, she saw L/Cpl Tiepolo doodling on a scrap of paper, with a nasty leer on his face, and his neighbours staring over at him, leering also, with furtive glances at Belinda.

'Mr Tiepolo!' she snapped. 'Will you please share your work with me? Come up here at the double, sir.'

Blushing – Belinda noted proudly – the lance-corporal swaggered up to her table, and nonchalantly placed the paper before her.

'I found it, miss,' he drawled. 'Reminded me of things I saw in Port Said, don't you know. No harm meant, miss.'

His blue eyes twinkled, daring her. Belinda flushed. The drawing depicted a male, and a female, both naked, with the male seated in a throne, and the female crouching below him, sucking his monstrously erect sex organ. Her teats hung below her ribs, and her huge buttocks jutted into the air. Her hair was blonde. Her thighs were parted, and the enormous clit and quim lips were pendant, almost to her knees.

Do I dare? Should I? Can I get away with it?

'The author of this filthy smut must be punished, of course,' she said, her voice trembling. 'Not least, for his appalling ignorance of human anatomy.'

'Can't remember where I found it, miss,' said Tiepolo cockily.

'Then, as its owner, you must be punished,' Belinda said, meeting his gaze and staring him down, 'for failing to destroy it, hand it in or report it.'

The buzzer sounded, signalling the end of class and luncheon parade.

'Scarcely a jankers offence, miss,' he said less confidently. 'You don't want to bother the sergeant with it, surely?'

'You're right, I don't,' Belinda said. 'You will remain after class to discuss how you are to be punished, Lance-Corporal Tiepolo. Class dismissed!'

The soldiers filed out, grinning at Tiepolo.

'Egyptian women do not tend to have blonde hair, I believe,' Belinda said, when they were alone.

'No, miss.'

'Then I think we understand each other, Tiepolo,' she said. 'You made this filthy thing, didn't you? Tell the truth, and we can settle this matter between ourselves; otherwise, a formal charge, and a demob in disgrace, might not look good for your job prospects. '

Tiepolo smiled. 'Be a sport, miss,' he drawled. 'I couldn't help it. You're much too beautiful and tempting to be a schoolteacher.'

'Watch your lip, boy, or it will go worse for you,' she blurted, blushing hotly.

'Aw, miss, you're too pretty to threaten me,' he drawled. 'Anyway, I'll be working for my dad when I get out. Don't you know Tiepolo's ice-cream parlours? Blackpool, Barrow, Bury, Oldham, Preston, Lytham St Annes? You can eat free at any of our places, miss, I promise.'

'Bribery won't get you out of it,' she snapped. 'You'll be punished, and take it like a man. We've a good three hours before this hut is used again, and, in that time, I intend to give you –' Her heart was thumping.

'Yes, miss?' he said innocently.

Oh gosh, my cooze is wet. 'Tiepolo, I understand you are a young man, with a young man's . . . urges . . . so I can forgive you just a little, but only if you've paid for your beastliness, in a way we can both understand.'

He nodded sheepishly.

So,' Belinda said, taking a deep breath, 'I am going to thrash you.'

My orchid is positively dripping! And no panties to absorb my naughty wet stuff.

'Thrash me, miss?'

His jaw dropped, but his eyes glittered. Quickly, she delved into her squash bag, and withdrew her riding crop.

'I keep this for just such eventualities,' she blurted, blushing, for she knew her lie was transparent. 'You're not the only naughty boy in the regiment, you know. A quick thrashing, and we'll forget the whole incident, for both our benefits.'

He pursed his lips. 'I suppose I deserve it, miss. You mean here and now?'

'Yes. There's no one around to bother us, or hear you, if you squeal.'

That stung him. 'I never squeal, miss,' he sneered.

'Then you may bend over this table, after lowering your trousers and pants. I'm sure you are no stranger to a sound beating on your bare buttocks.'

'Miss?' he gasped rather shyly, licking his lips.

'You heard. I am going to whip you on the bare. A doz – two dozen stingers should teach you your lesson.'

'Cripes, miss, you're harsh,' he murmured, but with a smile, straight to her face, that was half devilish, half angelic. 'I haven't had that sort of treatment since my sister Gina whopped me for spilling a whole gallon of strawberry ripple over her party frock. Made me drop them, in front of my other sisters, and licked me three dozen, bare-bum, with the long spoon –' he sighed '– but an Italian bloke can't disobey a woman.'

Belinda was panting hard, feeling the seep of come from her tingling cunt ooze into her silken petticoat.

'I assure you this will be more painful than a spoon,' she said. 'You may take the position for your punishment.'

She swiftly bolted the classroom door, then watched him unfasten his belt, lower the coarse khaki trousers and slip down his panties. He stood a moment, before turning to bare his buttocks, and, in that instant, she saw his monstrously huge sex organ, trembling in half stiffness. His lewd drawing had not exaggerated.

'I suppose you do this to lots of fellows,' he said, bending over the table.

'Lots,' said Belinda, trembling.

His bottom was a delicate olive colour, smooth and tautly muscled. Belinda put her hand to her unpantied crotch, feeling the squelchy come oozing from the pouch and slopping her petticoat. Outside, the barracks was silent.

'I'll get you done quickly,' she said, 'and then you won't miss your luncheon.'

'Miss,' he said indignantly, 'I don't eat army slop. I have my own food. Gina sends it in.'

'In that case, we can take our time,' she said. 'I think it's better if you take off all your kit below the waist, then knot your shirt at your ribs. That way, I'll get a nice clear shot at your rear end.'

'You are an expert, miss,' he muttered, and complied, stripping off, to bend over, fully bare below the waist, and his sex organ insolently erect.

Belinda's mouth was dry, as she gazed at his almost hairless body, the legs and bum as smooth as a girl's, yet with that enormous organ standing stiff, way up across his belly, with the huge olive balls tight in their sac. It was so much bigger than any boy's organ she'd touched before, and she trembled, thinking how much creamy stuff those massive balls must contain. Her breasts heaved, nipples tingling stiff, as she breathed heavily.

To whip that bum black and blue with luscious crusty welts, until he squeals and wriggles and begs for mercy. Oh, lovely revenge.

His face wore a smug grin.

'I see you have an erection, Tiepolo. Did you have one when your sister whipped you, or is it just for my benefit? I assure you, I've seen plenty of – I mean, I don't shock so easily.'

'I can't help it, miss,' he protested, still grinning. 'A swell dame does that to me. If you've seen plenty, you should know that.'

Belinda blushed. 'I didn't say – oh, you are a bally nuisance. Let's see if a few stingers can't soften you up,' she said, lifting her riding crop.

She struck him full across the bare buttocks, and was pleased to see the nates clench, with a small shiver of his legs, and a gasp of 'Oof!'. A second stroke took his bottom aslant. A third completed a crisscross pattern. His bum was quivering nicely, clenching before and after each cut.

'Ooh . . .' he moaned. 'You really know how to hurt, miss.'

'Thank you for the compliment.'

His bare bum squirmed quite violently, and did not cease to wriggle, as she lathered the boy with heavy strokes, not the timid taps she had practised on her own thigh, but full-force stingers, as her own bottom had taken from Jan.

'Ooh! Ouch!' he panted, his buttocks flaming with livid welts, and jerking up and down, while the cheeks clenched and his pendant ball sac wobbled.

'Chin up,' she said. 'You're taking it quite well. You're obviously no stranger to beating.'

'Nor you, miss, more's the pity,' he gasped. 'I've never been thrashed so hard.'

Slipping her hand beneath her skirts, Belinda touched her bare quim, and her fingers came away sloppy. Her cooze was really juicing. It was a mistake to go knickerless – surely she was by now as smelly as even her oldest pair of knickers? She touched herself again, felt her throbbing clitty and stifled a gasp of pleasure, as she rubbed the swollen nub. Her skirt and petticoat rustled softly, and her stockinged thighs slithered together, as she began to masturbate, eyes fixed on the shivering naked bottom of the male, helpless under her crop. Belinda lashed the wriggling buttocks a savage backhand and forehand.

'Oh! Ooh!' he squealed, dancing on tiptoe, with his flogged bare bum squirming. 'Oh, you bitch!'

'What?' Belinda thundered.

'I'm sorry, miss – I didn't mean it. I'm really sorry,' he whimpered. 'I couldn't help it – you're so expert.'

'You will be sorry, after the extra dozen cuts you've earned.'

Her cunt spurted come.

'Ohh . . . ohh . . . no, please,' he gasped, sobbing. 'Not an extra dozen!'

'Shall I give up, and report you to your captain?'

'No, miss. Please. I'll take your punishment. Oh, cripes.'

'You're darn right you will, sir,' she hissed. 'You're in my power, remember. Even that beastly insolent erection, which you seem in no hurry to lose.'

She clasped his ball sac, cupping the stiff orbs in her palm, and squeezed very gently. His whole body went rigid.

'Oh, miss . . .' he groaned.

She stroked his balls, slicing a fingernail in the cleft between the orbs. His erect cock bucked, slapping his bulging crimson helmet against his belly.

'Not quite like Port Said, eh?' she murmured. 'Tell me, do the girls there really do those things?'

'That's not a fair question, miss,' he whimpered, as she felt his balls.

Gasping, she withdrew, and raised her crop.

His flogged buttocks writhed. Belinda slid two fingers into her sopping wet pouch, and began to frig her slit, with her thumb mashing her clitty.

'I decide what's fair, you whelp. Answer.'

'Yes, miss, they do. They're foreign, miss.'

'And are they good at it? Do they swallow your horrid spunk?'

'Ahh! Yes, miss, yes. They have girls from all over Africa and Arabia, and they are good at all sorts of things, belly-dancing, bumming, jellying, nesting, goosing, shrimping –'

'What on earth is that?'

'Making a fellow spurt with her toes, miss.'

'And those other disgusting things?'

'Nesting is doing it in her armpit, miss, goosing, between her thighs, without entering her hole, and jellying is . . . you know, a wank between the bubbies.'

'Bumming – surely no Englishman would stoop to something so vile?'

'I'm Italian, miss,' he said. 'I must admit I have. It's quite normal in Africa, and ever so sweet. There is such a tight, sucking silkiness to an African girl's bumhole –'

'Ugh! You're disgusting! What sensible girl would submit to such shame, and such discomfort?'

'Girls out there prefer bumming, miss. Most girls do, if you want my opinion.'

'I certainly don't. You filthy boy, you deserve to have your balls . . . um –'

With Belinda's cunt gushing come, she flicked her finger against his ball sac, before cupping the whole balls in her palm and rubbing the tight skin.

'Ooh! That's nice, miss.'

Belinda's fingers made slurping squelches, as she wanked her wet cunt. 'It's not meant to be nice,' she gasped faintly.

She released his balls, and he made a disappointed moan.

Two stingers to the left haunch, and Tiepolo's legs shot rigid behind him, the shudder of his spine matching the frenzied squirm of his naked buttocks. Belinda licked her lips, as she wanked off, scrutinising the tapestry of crop weals on the boy's helpless arse.

Does it help when you squeal like that?' she panted. 'It's rather girly, don't you think?'

'I'll try not to, miss.'

'It'll be over before you know it,' she said. 'See if you can keep a stiff upper lip, and take the rest without too much blubbing. I know time seems to stop when your bare bottom's whipped, but, if you blubbed, what would your girlfriend think?'

Vip! Vip!

'Ooh!' he gasped. 'I haven't got a regular girlfriend, miss. It's hard for a squaddy to keep one. Just, sometimes . . . casual pickups, in the palais.'

Belinda's fingers slapped the engorged lips of her gash, with come pouring from her slit, and pooling in her palm.

'And what sort of girls do you like, Tiepolo?'

'Ooh, busty girls with big bottoms . . . and blonde, and . . . like you, miss.'

Three hard slices deepened the same livid weal.

'Ahh! Ohh!'

His buttocks squirmed frenziedly.

'Cheeky boy.'

Belinda's belly was fluttering, as her wanked cunt approached orgasm. Reaching to the cookery table, she grabbed the giant homemade sausage, still warm from the pan, and slipped it between her cooze flaps, thrust it in and out of her slit several times, until the sausage dripped with fat and come, then jammed it right to the root of her cunt. She rolled her thighs, squeezing the hot tube inside her wet pouch flesh, and groaning. Her wet petticoat stuck to her cunt and thighs, making a squishy noise, as her legs quivered at each rub of her nubbin, and her cooze soaked the petticoat with fresh, flowing come.

Tiepolo's head hung low, with his breath a hoarse, rasping pant; yet his cock still reared untamed. Staring at the hard balls, and the massive cockshaft above, Belinda lifted her entire skirt and petticoat, baring her cunt and belly, and gave her forearm a free field of approach to her clit and cooze, over her bare tummy. Her hand crept across her haunches, to stroke her bottom, ridged with Jan's welts, and soon her buttocks wore an oily glaze of come and sausage fat. She wanked faster and faster, as she thrashed the quivering boy, his breath now punctuated with choking sobs, and his whipped bare nates a mass of crimson welts, darkening to puffy purple.

'Oh, miss,' he sobbed. 'You're enjoying this!'

'I certainly am,' she panted, masturbating vigorously. 'If you could see how lovely your bum looks, Tiepolo, all red and purple – an artwork.'

'Is that why you're wanking off, miss?'
'What?'
'I can see your reflection, miss, in the window.'
Belinda stared. Facing her, in the window, was a distorted image of her naked cunt.
'Why, you –'
Scarcely pausing for breath, she took the thrashing past two dozen, with Tiepolo squirming and squealing that he didn't mean any harm, honestly. His balls jiggled, as the crop relentlessly deepened the weals on his madly clenching buttocks, with pauses of ten or twelve seconds, so that she could feast on the spectacle of those wriggling nates. How it must hurt him. Will he hate me for it? When Belinda, pouring with sweat, lowered her riding crop, there was a pool of come on the floor, between her feet.
'That's it,' she gasped, looking at the clock; the flogging of three dozen had taken seven minutes.
'Ooh . . .' moaned Tiepolo. 'Permission to rub my bum, miss?'
'Denied. Hold position, soldier.'
'What if I disobey?'
'You wear the king's uniform, and may not disobey.'
'I'm not wearing it now, miss.'
'Damn you for a cheeky devil,' she gasped. 'Even a thrashing can't tame you. And your sex organ is still so hard and mighty! I've never seen one so insolent.'
Panting, Belinda took hold of his swollen glans between finger and thumb. He shivered, but said nothing. She began to rub his helmet, while wanking her own slit and clitty. She shifted behind his buttocks, and pressed her naked belly to his flogged bum, rising on tiptoe, until her wet cooze was pressed against his ridged welts. She got her clitty against the hardest and puffiest welt, and began to rub her cunt basin up and down his bruised bare bottom.
'You poor boy,' she whispered. 'I'm sorry I had to hurt you so much.'
All the while, she applied delicate pressure to his glans, rubbing his peehole and making him gasp, then slid her fingers down his cockshaft in a tight embrace, to clasp and

squeeze his balls, before returning to her massage of the bulging helmet.

'Oh, miss,' he gasped. 'If you tease me like that, I'm going to spurt.'

'Hold still and be quiet, soldier. This is for hygienic relief, nothing more.'

His cock began to tremble and buck; deftly, Belinda pulled her silken petticoat away from her waist elastic, and sheathed his bell end in the soft fabric. She continued to grind her clitty against his hard buttock weals, while gently pulling at his cock, through the petticoat silk. Belinda's come, gushing from her cunt, trickled through his bum-welts, and dripped onto his balls. With a groan, Tiepolo shivered and began to pant rapidly.

'You really know how to do a fellow,' he panted. 'How many have you done?'

'No! No!' Belinda moaned. 'I'm not like that.'

'You are an expert bitch,' he said, as his cock trembled in her fingers.

'Ooh ...' she gasped, 'yes, come on, soldier, give me your cream, your whole load from those balls.'

His breath quickened, and his cock bucked; Belinda's hand was drenched in hot creamy spunk, soaking the petticoat silk.

'Uhh ... uhh ... ahh!' Belinda panted, as her own orgasm engulfed her, and come spurted from her cooze, spraying the boy's flogged buttocks.

Her cunt hillock slapped his wealed bare, with a sticky, squelchy slurp, as her cooze gushed come over his bruises and her clitty writhed against the hard cane ridges. The sausage inside her cunt burst, filling her pouch with sticky hot sausage meat.

'Oh ... ohh ...' she gasped, sliding from his come-slimed arse. 'Let that be a lesson to you, soldier.'

L/Cpl Tiepolo stood up, rubbing his arse and wincing. He removed his fingers, wet with Belinda's come, and made loud slurping noises, as he licked his fingers of the come.

'Mm,' he murmured. 'You're the sweetest doll I've ever tasted, miss. How about a date?'

'I beg your pardon?'

Belinda paused in smoothing her sticky wet petticoat over her thighs. Tiepolo stood cockily, hands on hips, waving his sex organ at her. The beastly thing had hardly softened!

'You know, come out with me, on a proper date. I'll be out in civvy street in a week. Look at my cock, miss. It's ready to eat you up.'

'I shall do no such thing, you insolent brute. Get your kit on at once.'

He made a moue, and began to dress. Belinda pretended to pack her kitchen things.

'We could go up to Derwent Water, or the seaside, in my roadster, and have a picnic. Gina makes a luscious pizza – that's an Italian delicacy – and we could have red wine. Or, if you like, beer, and all the veal and ham pie you can eat.'

Veal and ham pie!

'You have a car?' she said.

'Triumph two-litre open-top two-seater, this year's model,' he said.

Belinda's eyes widened, and he slid closer to her.

'I can get you nylons. Real American ones. I know a few people.'

Real American nylons!

'No! it's unthinkable,' she blurted. 'I forbid you to say such things. You're under military discipline, remember.'

'I shan't be in a fortnight. Pick you up here, after class, one day?'

'No, I forbid it. Damn you, Tiepolo, you're teasing me.'

'It's a date, then,' he said, opening the door.

'No!'

'Come on, miss, you know you're begging for it. By the way, I'd love some of that sausage from your twat.'

Belinda blushed a fiery crimson. 'Oh, you –' she squealed, lifting the frying pan to throw it at him, and spilling grease all down her skirt.

She scooped a wad of the meat, slimed with her come, and threw it at him. Catching it, he popped it in his mouth, sucked and swallowed.

'Bellissima,' he murmured, licking his lips of her come. 'Remember, Miss Beaucul, all girls mean yes when they say no.'

He ducked out the door, as, quivering with rage, Belinda began to extract mushy sausage meat from her cooze.

Do we? she wondered.

5

Blistered Bum

'How nice, Belinda, that you are chums with Jan,' said Dr Emily Warrior. 'She's quite my most inventive nurse.'

Jan blew smoke from her Gold Flake, smiled and sipped wine. 'Belinda is also inventive,' she said. 'In fact, she's a really modern girl. She's a teacher, with the army.'

'How ripping,' said Dr Warrior. 'As you see, I myself try to set a modern example. Some might find it daring but, in Africa, one rather gets used to it.'

Dr Warrior was nude, save for her rings and Grecian sandals: a lithe, muscular, ash-blonde, with sleek, close-cropped hair, pert breasts, like twin golden apples, and firmly protruding buttocks. She was, Belinda guessed, in her late thirties. Her quim hillock gleamed, completely shaven, like Belinda's. The long, coltish legs, the hard thighs taut with muscle, were slightly curved and apart, as if she was permanently on horseback, which, with her all-over suntan, gave her the look of the veldt. From each nipple dangled a golden hoop, bigger than a half-crown, and pierced right through the nipple bud; a single gold hoop hung from the pendant, hairless lips of her cooze, the ring pierced through each quim gash flap, dangling free in the space between her parted thighs. Dr Warrior's fingers played with her cunt ring as she spoke, twirling it, to spin between her thighs.

'I dare say we'll find out how modern you are, Belinda,' she purred. 'What are you smoking? Woodbines? Heavens, I know, a young teacher's salary . . . how brave of you to be a teacher.'

'Actually, the army pays quite well,' Belinda said. 'That's why I don't have to live at home with stepfather at the vicarage, in Bolton-le-Sands.'

'Have one of mine anyway. You don't mind Player's Navy Cut?'

Belinda accepted the cigarette, and expelled fragrant smoke into the sun-dappled air. It was a bright, sunny afternoon, and Belinda breathed deeply of the sea breeze, wafted from Morecambe sands, far below Dr Warrior's snug clifftop villa. Her guests drank wine in the sloping garden, chatting animatedly among roses and honeysuckle, and feasting from a buffet table.

'Morecambe gels are quite the liveliest spanks, the sea air, don't you know.'

'Fleetwood gels are fresh, too.'

'Sheila from the NAAFI used to bare up for four dozen on the runway, between scrambles, absolutely wizard for morale.'

'Algerian bints really know how to wriggle their arses, specially over the hot bonnet of an armoured car.'

'Sulky, pouting Normandy milkmaids, a pleasure to make them squeal, with a clog-whopping on the slit trench.'

'She chased me starkers through the streets of Naples, then whopped me with my own swagger stick, the saucy minx.'

In the driveway gleamed Dr Warrior's Austin Ten tourer; on the trudge from the bus stop, Jan and Belinda had passed the parked Humbers and Rileys of the doctor's evidently well-heeled guests. Dr Warrior followed Belinda's gaze.

'Do you drive?' she said.

Belinda shook her head.

'Nor I. The Austin is a modest enough banger, although a Ford Anglia is cheaper, but my daughter Clarice is frightfully snobbish. I can't think what's keeping her, putting on her face, I suppose. She'll have to learn punctuality when she becomes a nurse! Well, let's go and feed, and you must taste a vanilla pod, all the way from

Africa. They're awfully expensive, but heavenly to suck. I expect you know everybody already, Belinda.'

Belinda didn't. The company was youngish, with the ease of affluence: Mr and Mrs Ludbotham, Mr and Mrs Granett, Dr and Mrs Stove, Professor and Mrs Fazackerley . . . Belinda couldn't remember all their names, nor the names of the unattached girls who wafted around the garden, refilling wineglasses, and who, she supposed, were nurses. They all wore white, pink or beige shorts, like the khaki ones of wartime Land Girls, but cut daringly high to show lots of thigh flesh, with skimpy, short-sleeved blouses, knotted at the waist, exposing their tummies and belly buttons. Some were innocently barefoot, while others wore tennis shoes and fluffy ankle socks. At least she had dressed correctly, in her light cotton, flowery frock, with string straps over her bare shoulders, and showing most of her legs, though without Dr Warrior's toffee-coloured African tan, she thought enviously.

For the occasion, Belinda wore a special brassiere, which was very skimpy, actually a utility bra with half the cups cut off, a bit oopsily, so that it didn't even cover her nipples – still, it showed she was wearing a bra, which was the main thing – although, obviously, she could be a nudist like Dr Warrior, if she wanted. She tried to imagine a society where everyone was nude, under the African sun, their smooth young bodies all black and brown, with gorgeous bums and firm titties and big long cocks; it made her orchid feel tingly and moist. Belinda's shorties were the same silken ones she had showed in the sweetshop, so smooth that, from behind, you would scarcely know she had any panties on, which gave Belinda a super, secret thrill.

Jan and Belinda accepted refills of wine, from a girl Belinda recognised – Heather Todmorden, from Heysham.

'Heather,' cried Belinda, 'how nice –'

'Belinda! Super! Your first time?'

'Why, yes.'

'Lucky girl. I expect the doc will go easy on you.'

Heather was barefoot, and her breasts, almost as big as Belinda's own, were absolutely uncased by any bra at all!

Her blouse was drawn up right over her ribs, cupping her large quivering teat jellies, and her shorts were cut so high that – honestly! – she might as well have been nude.

'I don't understand,' Belinda said, while Jan smirked, meeting Heather's eye.

'Oh, I see,' murmured Heather vaguely, while giving Belinda's body quite a lascivious look up and down. 'Dr Warrior certainly likes you, giving you one of her Player's, and all. You certainly pass her bottom test – your globes are too jealous-making. Just make sure you don't mention Mr Warrior – rather a sore point. Speaking of sore points, I don't want to take any more than I must, so I'd better circulate.'

She tapped her bottom, with a wink, and padded away, over the grass.

'Dr Warrior lives alone with Clarice,' Jan whispered. 'They say that Mr Warrior deserted her, in Somaliland, or somewhere. They were studying a tribe where the girls have absolutely the most enormous bottoms, and Professor Warrior went off with one of them, or several, for serious biffing.'

Belinda remarked that all the girls present had very generous buttocks.

'But of course,' Jan said, over the braying of a dark-haired young man nearby, named Rodney Heckmondthwaite, who was swilling wine, with his hand on his wife Bettina's large, quivering bum flans, and punctuated his pronouncements on mares, fillies and stallions by jangling his Jaguar car keys over his port-wine belly or smacking his wife's bottom. The sloe-eyed brunette Bettina, in a fluttering summer frock, sipped wine, smiling at her husband's emphatic slaps to her generous croup.

'Bareback riding, that's the ticket,' Rodney chortled. 'Taking a mare out for a canter, of a summer's morn, with her flesh between your legs.'

'Isn't it awfully uncomfortable without a saddle, though?' a woman said.

'Not a bit!' Rodney said, leering. 'Here, I'll show you – Bettina, my filly, bare up, now. All fours, girl, chop chop!'

'What? Here, Rodney?' simpered his wife. 'It'll spoil my frock.'

'Then frock off, my dear. You do have knickers on, I suppose?'

'Why, of course, Rodney,' Bettina said pouting. 'You are awful.'

She slipped her frock over her head, and stood only in her cream silk bra and matching panties, only they weren't really panties at all. Bettina's knickers were scarcely more than a thong wound around her waist and baring her buttocks fully, except for a string that vanished into her bum cleft and came up the other side to broaden into a thin silk triangle that only just shielded her swelling, shaven cunt hillock. At the bottom of the triangle hung a fringe of silken cords, just like that yummy John Wayne's shirts in the cowboy films, which Belinda thought very fetching.

'Why, she's almost bare-bum,' she hissed to Jan.

'That's a G-string,' Jan murmured. 'Rodney was in Cairo in the war, and must have brought back oodles of naughty things. Isn't he a spunk?'

Bettina preened and cooed, obeying her husband's order to take off her shoes, and seeming to enjoy the guests' attention.

'Isn't she a fine wench?' he bellowed, slapping her bare buttocks. 'Look at that arse.'

'Rodney, please,' protested Bettina, beaming.

'Down you go, girl,' ordered Rodney, and his wife dropped to a crouch.

Rodney mounted the small of her back, and flicked her left buttock with the sole of her shoe, making a loud tap. 'Giddy-up!'

Bettina neighed, and began to shuffle across the grass, carrying him, while he spanked her bare bottom, on alternate fesses, with the shoe raising big pink blossoms, and making her whinny at each spank. The crowd clapped, as the equine pair made a circuit of the lawn, with Rodney pausing to accept glasses of wine and allowing his steed to take her mouthful. After three circuits, Bettina's bum was glowing from her spanks, and, with a flourishing whap-whap-whap to her croup, Rodney permitted her to rise, to enthusiastic applause. Bettina made a great fuss of rubbing her spanked bottom, proudly displayed.

Heather brought a basin and sponge, kneeled, and mopped the grass stains from Bettina's elbows and knees, before helping her into her sundress. She also mopped Bettina's inner thighs beside her crotch of the glaze of oily fluid bathing her skin and wetting the bottom of her G-string. Heather lifted up the fringe and revealed that Bettina's silken mons triangle did not fully cover her vulva; the cooze lips were bare under the fringe and each lip wore a row of rings, pierced, like earrings, into the flesh of the cunt itself. The narrow thong of the panties passed between the cunt lips, pressing her raw pink pouch flesh and trapping the clitty, which swelled quite visibly stiff beneath the string. Belinda gaped, thinking of the dreadful pain of having the orchid pierced, and gasped at a sudden seep of moisture in her own gash.

'Wasn't that super?' Jan cooed.

'It was rather quaint,' replied Belinda. 'How quickly her bum reddened!'

'I'm sure he uses more than a slipper when they're at home,' mused Jan. 'I wouldn't mind him riding me, and giving me a proper lathering.'

'I thought you only dished it out,' said Belinda.

'Nothing's written in stone, girl. Sometimes it's fun to feel things from the other end.'

'Well, my bum's still tingly from . . . you know, and I've a jolly good mind to have my revenge on yours,' Belinda said, pouting. 'But it would be no good if you actually enjoyed it.'

They helped themselves to plates of cold cuts and salady things, with real potted shrimps, meatpaste sandwiches and the curiously sweet vanilla pods, when a cool, sultry girl's voice said, 'You must be Miss Beaucul, the famous disciplinarian.'

Belinda turned, to see a tall, raven-haired girl, balanced on impossibly high black heels. Her scarlet silk tube dress, scarcely halfway down her thighs, clung to her shamelessly braless and knickerless body, the breasts and buttocks swelling like pears under the silk, ruffled against her rippling muscles by the sea breeze. She looked ever so tiddly! Her smooth olive skin suggested she was in her late twenties.

'I'm sorry?' Belinda blurted.

'I'm Vergina Tiepolo,' said the girl, smiling. 'Gina for short. The naughty lance-corporal's sister.'

'Oh! Miss Tiepolo,' Belinda blurted, with a potted shrimp dropping from her lips. 'I – yes – um, you see –'

'No need to explain,' Gina purred, lighting an oval Balkan Sobranie. 'I was thrilled when the whelp snivelled to me what you'd done. I made him bare up – by gosh, you did a good job, miss. His croup was a proper painting. I felt tempted to add some stripes of my own – Alberto is always guilty of something – but I couldn't spoil a masterpiece.'

'I say, Belinda, keeping secrets, like a naughty girl?' said Jan. 'You know what happens to naughty girls.'

'It's no secret,' retorted Belinda.

'Then spill it,' said Jan.

Jan blurted the story of L/Cpl Tiepolo, and noticed that several of the guests were earwigging, not very discreetly, with the ladies' smiles the widest.

'You dark horse, Belinda,' Jan said. 'Thrashing fellows on the sly.'

'It was only one,' said Belinda, 'and he deserved it.'

'Of course the smutty pup deserved it,' Gina agreed. 'But only three dozen? A slipper doesn't do much damage.'

'Oh, well, it wasn't a slipper,' Belinda admitted. 'I used a riding crop.'

Gina clapped her hands. 'Three dozzies with the crop,' she said, chortling. 'Wonderful! I'd have given anything to see his smutty bare bum wriggle. It was on the bare, I take it?'

'Of course,' said Belinda, feeling bolder.

'Capital,' said Gina. 'Pity the brat's out of the army now. Of course, I whip him when he needs it, but he's so rarely home, with that beastly new car of his.'

'I didn't know you possessed a riding crop, Belinda,' murmured Jan. 'Wherever did you get it?'

'Why, from me,' said a girl's voice.

Beside them stood Dr Warrior, with her arm casually draped around the buttocks of a pouting ash-blonde, with piercing green eyes, dressed in white jodhpurs, boots and a clinging crimson blouse, and her mouth flaming in crimson lipstick. Her blouse was unbuttoned to the third button, which strained to contain the heavy jutting teats, plainly naked under the silk, and with big nipple plums plainly stiffened. Belinda gasped, for it was the snooty shopgirl from the saddler's in St Leonard's Gate.

'At last, my daughter, Clarice,' said Dr Warrior. 'If we've finished feeding, perhaps we'd all like to move into my playroom?'

Belinda walked behind Clarice, watching the girl wiggle her – admittedly gorgeous – bum in an unabashed, snooty tease. We're both blonde, she thought, and both big-bummed, though mine is surely bigger, both with long legs, but mine certainly longer, and both with big bubbies, though I think I win that contest too. Clarice's arse globes, full and ripe and firm, bobbing under the clinging white cotton, were to die for. If she wants a silly girly feud, she can jolly well have one.

Mrs Ludbotham, a trim young woman in her mid-twenties, with bobbed hair, full, upturned breasts and a bottom almost embarrassingly big for her slender frame, was beside Belinda.

'Have you been here before?' she asked rather timidly.

'Why, no,' said Belinda.

'Me neither. I'm – I'm not sure what to expect. That is, I am, but I'm not sure if I can take it. These nurses all look so experienced. I do so want to please my husband – it's a wife's duty, isn't it?' She smiled ruefully. 'Sometimes, I think he only married me for my bottom.'

'You do have a super bottom, and I'm sure it'll be tremendous fun,' said Belinda, uncertainly.

'Yours is much lovelier,' said Mrs Ludbotham coyly. 'It'll be fun to compare them in the bare.'

She entered the shady coolness of the house, without asking Mrs Ludbotham what she did expect or why they should be in the bare for it. Dr Warrior led them to an unusually large back room – she explained she had 'knocked through' – painted in lemon yellow, with a stone-flagged floor, comfortable chaises and armchairs. French windows looked out onto the extensive lawns, secluded by a tall yew hedge. The walls were hung with African paintings and objects: whips, belts, buckles, clamps and canes. The paintings showed these instruments in use on the naked bodies of African or European girls, all sumptuously crouped, with mouths gaping and faces contorted in agony, as they were flogged, bound with cords, thumb-clamped or had their nipples and quims pinched with metal pincers. Belinda shivered.

The torturess of the African girls was a trim European, naked but for high boots, who looked like a more youthful Dr Warrior, whereas the European girls were whipped and tormented by nude, sombre African girls, their swollen croups and hard, conic titties glazed with red mud. In the corners of the room stood frames or tables, festooned with straps, chains and cuffs, with black wooden sculptures beside or above them, depicting nude young men whose shamelessly erect cocks Belinda found ridiculously big, though utterly fascinating. Could such members exist? Belinda's eyes switched, mesmerised, from the massive sculpted cocks to the instruments of discipline.

Heather and the other nurses circulated with glasses of wine. The air was plumed with curling blue smoke, as the guests, expectantly sprawled in their easy chairs, lit up their Gold Flake, Churchman's or Player's, snapped from silver cigarette cases. Belinda gratefully accepted one of Jan's Gold Flakes, and puffed nervously, as she warmed herself with another glass of wine.

'I prefer to call this playroom my dungeon for you first-timers,' said Dr Warrior brightly, perched in a high-backed padded chair, like a throne. 'Just my conceit! As you see, it contains mementos of my African sojourn.'

She held, snugly clasped in her arms, a long cane in braided leather, like Belinda's riding crop. Seeing Belinda pale at the word 'dungeon', Dr Warrior said that a dungeon was not to be feared, but was a place of useful correction. Belinda's heart thumped and her quim moistened.

'And which of us does not require correction, for our misdeeds?' the doctor continued.

Cynthia Padden, a leggy, big-breasted blonde (although Belinda was sure she dyed), all the way from Carlisle, put up her hand.

'I rather think I do,' she drawled.

'Would a husband care to volunteer?' said Dr warrior.

Cynthia lifted her dress and lowered her knickers, then touched her toes to take a vigorous spanking of twenty slaps on her bare bum from Mr Throate of Accrington, which Mrs Throate and Mr Padden applauded. Her shaven pubis gave Belinda no clue to her real hair colour.

'Hard enough, Cynthia?' said her spanker.

'Ooh, yes,' said the red-faced Cynthia, rubbing her bum, 'that feels better. Thanks awfully.'

Next for spanking was Mrs Headwell from Bury, her wet Player's bobbing at the corner of her lips, emitting nervous plumes of smoke, as she was spanked by Mr Ludbotham; then, Mrs Poole, from Oldham, spanked by Mr Leadbitter, of Lancaster. In all, six young wives received sound spankings on their bare buttocks, with the guests heartily applauding, as the girls' bum puddings quivered under spanks. Each spanked wife thanked her chastiser and regained her chair, smiling ruefully, while wiggling her pink bottom, as she dawdled over pulling up her panties.

'Clarice,' said Dr Warrior, 'as if your sluttish lipstick isn't enough, you are dreadfully unpunctual.'

Clarice stood up, smoothing her jodhpurs over her bottom. 'Yes, Mummy,' she said meekly.

'I think you should make amends, don't you?'

'Of course, Mummy.'

Clarice bent over the back of an unoccupied armchair, and lowered her jodhpurs to mid-thigh. She wore no panties, and quickly exposed two quivering, delicately tan arse melons in the bare. Belinda wetted her dry lips, feeling her cooze seep come. The girl's bottom was gorgeous.

'Get 'em off!' cried Rodney Heckmondthwaite, clapping his hands.

Clarice rolled her trousers down a few more inches, until halted by a reproving glance from Dr Warrior. She raised her blouse, showing the golden down glinting on the small of her back, and knotted the ends under her bubbies. Biting her lip, she clasped the arms of the chair, with her upthrust golden buttocks trembling like jellies, washed by the warm afternoon sunlight.

'What do you require, Clarice?' asked Dr Warrior pleasantly.

'A spanking, please, Mummy.'

'Dr Stove, would you care to oblige?' said Dr Warrior.

The doctor sprang to his feet, licked his lips and took his position above Clarice's upthrust bottom.

'How many should the doctor spank you, Clarice?'

'A score, if you please.'

Dr Warrior nodded; the male raised his arm and slapped the girl's naked buttocks with full force. Smack! Clarice's bottom trembled a little, and she gasped, but made no sound of pain or protest. Smack! Smack! Her buttocks began to redden, glowing with the imprint of her spanker's palm. Clarice's face was flushed, her cheeks bulging, as she held her breath, with her eyes screwed shut. Belinda shifted in her chair, trying not to stain the cushion with the come seeping faster from her tingling twat, as she gazed at the girl's lovely bare bum globes, twitching under the male's loud, cracking spanks. She saw that most of the ladies watched with flushed faces, skirts raised indecently high, and, in some cases, a hand discreetly rubbing under the dress, between the legs. Smack! Smack!

'Ooh!' Clarice gasped, exhaling dramatically.

'Do try not to make silly noises, Clarice,' murmured Dr Warrior.

Smack! Smack! Clarice's reddened buttocks clenched and began to squirm. Smack! Smack! The spanking concluded.

'Phwooh!' Clarice panted, pouting and shaking her head, as her spanker regained his chair.

Her naked bottom continued to wriggle and clench, as she rubbed the glowing red skin.

'And what do we say, when obliged, Clarice?' snapped Dr Warrior.

'Thank you, sir,' mumbled the spanked girl.

'Manners forgotten! I fear another spanking is necessary. You may lower your things right to the ankles, girl. Professor Fazackerley – another score?'

'Ooh, Mummy . . .'

Pouting, Clarice rolled her jodhpurs down over her boots, and stood with her legs and bottom fully bared. The professor took position. Smack! He landed a heavy spank on her bare, and Clarice gasped, her buttocks straight away squirming and clenching. Smack! The bruises glowed a deeper red, darkening to crimson, with the professor's palm prints blotching over the previous spankmarks. Smack!

'Ooh . . .' whined Clarice, panting, through gritted teeth, with a teardop shining at her eye.

As her buttocks writhed, her heavy, dangling titties shook at each spank, wobbling violently in their thin, clinging silk. Smack! Smack!

'Uhh . . .' Clarice groaned, bubs and bum heaving.

The professor spanked hard, jolting Clarice's legs rigid at each smack, and, by the end of his score, her buttocks flamed crimson, streaked in mauve, with Clarice's face wrinkled in pain and her teeth bared in a rictus. A low, gurgling whine bubbled from her throat, as she panted hoarsely. As Dr Warrior invited a third male to spank her daughter, Clarice threshed her legs, kicking off her trousers completely, then removed her boots, so that she stood naked, but for her knotted blouse.

Clarice positioned her legs wide apart, exposing her pendant cooze flaps, gleaming wet. Her inner thighs glistened with the trickle of moisture oozing from her swollen gash, and Belinda was able to see her hillock, nude as her own. Some of the others were openly masturbating, especially Heather, who sprawled, eyes glazed, and rubbed her cunt under her shorts with dancing fingers, and a telltale stream of come staining her twitching bare thigh. Belinda's fingers crept to her gash, pulsing under her thin sundress and come-soaked shorties.

'I hope you modern ladies are masturbating comfortably,' said Dr Warrior, stroking her braided training cane. 'Do, please, lift your dresses, or remove them. An exposed wank is so much more satisfying.'

Mr Ludbotham was next, and spanked Clarice without bothering to conceal the erection, bulging at his crotch. Belinda thought Clarice must have been exceptionally naughty. Several ladies, including Rodney's wife, had their dresses tucked up to their titties, and their panties spanning their thighs, with their fingers slurping and squelching at naked cunts, open, pink and wet. Half the ladies were shaven, half thickly fleeced like Jan. Belinda looked round, and saw Jan masturbating enthusiastically, with her hairy cunt fully exposed.

She gulped, and raised her own dress to her belly, then began to tweak her throbbing clitty, while trying to cup her flowing come in her hand, although she had no idea where to put it, if not in an empty wineglass. Fixing on this solution, she drained her glass and poured her palmful of come into it, before resuming her wank, as spanker after spanker took his place to smack Clarice's quivering dark bum globes. Smack! Smack! Smack!

'Ooh! Ahh!'

Clarice's bruised buttocks squirmed vigorously and without pause; her gasps and sobs mingled with the sighs of pleasure from the masturbatresses, all with dresses up, and twitching wet cunts exposed. Rodney Heckmondthwaite swigged wine, rather sullen at being pointedly overlooked as a spanker.

'Poor Clarice! It's scarcely her fault. A girl's big bum provokes and teases,' said Dr Warrior, above her daughter's sobs and squeals. 'Our modern psychology calls the bubbies and buttocks secondary sex organs, signposts to the primary one, the vulva. My experiences in the field suggest that the buttocks are the primary sex organs, symbolising the warmth and mystery of the female, without which the male would have no urge to despunk. A twat is easy of access, helpfully juicing, at the slightest sniff of cock – a bottom less so, and only after vigorous softening, so to speak. The coy, yet devilishly provocative female bottom is the challenge that all males seek. Some desire to punish that which arouses for its cheekiness.'

That drew nervous giggles, and a flushed grimace from the clearly tumescent Rodney, as Dr Warrior smiled, caressing her rod. Belinda gasped, as Jan slipped her hand under Belinda's dress and touched her bottom on her shorties; then pried open her waistband, and caressed her naked flesh. Belinda did not resist, as Jan's hand stroked her bare bum cleft, and come spurted over Belinda's wanking fingers onto her thighs.

'You've the biggest bum here,' whispered Jan, with a titter. 'Watch out.'

'I readily admit,' the doctor said, smiling, 'that my daughter's croup surpasses my own. Lest she respond too boldly to the spunk-filled male, she must learn that her big buttocks are a vessel of painful correction as well as lustful pleasure.'

Clarice, her crimson face glazed with tears, sobbed and gasped, as her bottom wriggled, and her belly slapped the armchair's back, at each spank to her bare.

'Oh, Mummy,' she groaned. 'I – I . . . ooh . . .'

Come slimed her quivering bare thighs, dripping to the floor in a puddle.

'Why don't you take her, Rodney?' purred Dr Warrior. She proffered her braided trainer. 'Please,' she said. 'Give the brat's bum a proper blistering. Twelve should do the trick.'

'That's more like it,' hissed Rodney. 'Ha!' Rodney sprang to the trembling girl, and flexed the cane, lashing the air with a whistle.

'Mummy, no!' shrieked Clarice. 'Not the cane, please, not that!'

'It's for your own good, Clarice,' said Dr Warrior, pursing her lips.

Three vicious strokes, in quick succession, raised dark, puce welts on Clarice's spanked bare, and had the girl convulsing, her flogged buttocks clenching and squirming quite uncontrollably. Come squirted from her gash; her torso writhed, breaking her strained blouse button; and her braless titties burst naked from the clinging silk. Her bare bubs banged on the chair back, as her bum jerked above legs straining rigid. The buttock flesh was a mass of livid dark welts and bruises. Belinda and Jan wanked passionately, gasping, with all the other ladies doing likwise; Bettina Heckmondthwaite had her dress off and her bra undone, showing her naked bubbies, which she tweaked and pinched, as she wanked her cunt, gushing over her slender G-string.

Vip!

'Ooh!' Clarice wailed. 'You rotten beast!'

Vip!

'Ahh! You bastard!'

Vip!

'Oh! Ooh! Ouch! Gosh, it hurts, you fucking shit!'

'I think I'm comng,' Jan panted, wanking herself.

'Me, too,' panted Belinda.

Her wineglass brimmed with come.

Moans and yelps around the room indicated that many of the womenfolk were bringing themselves off. Clarice's mottled bare squirmed helplessly, her rigid legs dancing on tiptoe, at Rodney's vicious caning. *Vip*! *Vip*!

'Ooh! Gosh! Ahh! You fucking bastard!'

Vip!

'Ooh! You shit!

Vip!

'Ahh! You dirty fucker!'

Her quivering bare was furrowed with livid blisters, nestling beside the purple slashes of welts. The final stroke took Clarice on the vertical, with the cane slapping up her bum cleft, to strike her anus, cunt flaps and perineum. *Vip*!

'Ahh! Ooh! Ooh! You bloody fucking shit bastard wanker bugger!' shrieked Clarice, bum writhing, as come squirted from her squelching cunt flaps.

Dr Warrior looked pained. 'Such language,' she murmured, then nodded to Rodney.

Snarling, Rodney handed her the cane, and unfastened his belt. He lowered his trousers, letting his stiff cock spring naked. He thrust his hand between Clarice's legs, and brought his fingers up, dripping with her come, to oil his tool.

'The floozie's wet as bloody Windermere,' he hissed, before parting her buttocks, and, to squeals of delight from the masturbating wives, thrust his cock tip into Clarice's anus.

'Oh! No! Not that!' squealed the girl, impaled and wriggling on his cock.

'Oh, no,' gasped Belinda. 'It can't be –'

'It is,' hissed Jan. 'What do you think girls really like, even if they won't admit it?'

The cock sank into her rectum, right to Rodney's balls, and he began a vigorous buggery.

'You love it, don't you, Clarrie?' he gasped.

'No! Never!' sobbed the buggered girl, her speared arse writhing and slapping against his balls.

'Never is an awfully long time, girl,' said Dr Warrior, eyes glinting, as she watched her daughter bum-fucked. 'You must learn the hard way that males can never resist bumming girls whose big bottoms invite them.'

Rodney's cock made a greasy, slurping sound, as he slid it fully out of Clarice's anus, leaving only the peehole inside, before plunging the shaft fully into her rectum once more, reducing her to paroxysms of squeals and wriggles, as his bell end stabbed her colon. The assembled ladies eagerly masturbated, with Jan's fingers drumming on Belinda's bare arse, and both girls powerfully wanking off, agog at the spectacle of shameless, brutal buggery.

Initially astounded at the readiness of the women to bare their quims and wank openly, Belinda now thrilled to the electric pleasure of exposing herself in this communal masturbation. It was so liberating to share an experience most girls thought they had to keep private – an admission, and celebration, of all girls' animal need to wank off. Yes, wanking together, flaunting quims, was so much fun, and Belinda was astonised how various the different slits were, some like tulips or roses or lupins, some squat, some thin, some bulging and fat. I wonder what I look like – is my twat too big or too tight?

'Urrgh!' Clarice shrieked. 'I don't invite him . . . I don't want – it hurts so. It's too horrible and shameful . . . oh, please stop!'

Rodney held her clamped by the hips, pulling her thighs and bottom towards him to meet his thrusts; after several minutes, Clarice's buttocks began to thrust of their own accord, slapping Rodney's balls and belly, as she moaned and gurgled, sobbing all the while, but with her breath rasping in increasingly hoarse pants. Her quivering thighs were slopped with come, flowing from her gash.

'Mummy . . . please . . . may I have a cigarette?' Clarice gasped.

'Why, of course,' said Dr Warrior.

Quickly, Jan lit a Gold Flake, and stuck it between the girl's lips. As Jan resumed her wank, Dr Warrior nodded thanks.

Clarice held the tube in the corner of her mouth, puffing luxurious clouds of smoke, as her naked breasts thumped the chair, with each slam of Rodney's cock to her colon. Her buggered arse swayed, writhing and squeezing the impaling cock, so that Rodney had to pull hard to withdraw from her rectum's clinging embrace.

'Oh, yes,' Clarice snuffled, blowing fumes, 'do me, fuck my bum hard, fill me with spunk, you bastard. I'm going to come.'

Rodney grunted, and a bead of white cream bubbled at Clarice's anus lip. It became a frothing, bubbling torrent, as he spurted his spunk at her colon.

'Yes!' Clarice howled. 'Oh, yes, I want it! Do me, bugger me, spunk in my hole, yes, oh do me . . . ahh! You fucking shit, I'm coming. Oh, gosh! Ahh . . . Oh! Oh! Yes!'

Belinda and Jan both moaned, as they wanked themselves off, in time with Clarice's heaving, come-spurting orgasm; Belinda gazed at the gnarled monstrosity of the male's cock and the delicate creamy fountain of bubbling spunk from the writhing girl's anus. Dr Warrior noticed her gaze.

'Surprised, Belinda?' she said.

Belinda decided a modern girl should not be surprised. 'Why, no, doctor,' she blurted, 'though I admit the practice is new to me.'

'Quite right, for a well-brought-up vicarage girl,' purred the doctor. 'In Africa, it is widespread. African girls consider bumming both normal and desirable, so as to satisfy their carnal urges, and need for submission to a male, while preserving their bride price intact. I want only the best for my daughter, and Rodney has quite the biggest cock in the company. For that insolence, of course, he must be punished. Don't laugh, Belinda, you have quite the biggest bottom.'

There was a plop, as Rodney withdrew his cock, and tucked the dripping organ into his pants.

'By gum,' he gasped, 'I need a bloody drink.'

He groped, rubbing sweat from his eyes, until his hand lighted on Belinda's table. He grasped the wineglass, filled with her come, brought it to his lips and drained it in one gulp.

'That's the stuff,' he said. 'Best bloody *Gewürztraminer* I've ever tasted. I could do another bitch right away.'

'Rodney, I'd prefer you not to call my daughter a bitch,' said Dr Warrior icily.

'Emily,' said Mr Ludbotham, 'the other girls need a tickling.'

'Of course they do,' said Dr Warrior. 'Every girl with a provocative bottom must have her bum blistered, punished for her big ripe arse melons, like those filthy Nubian whores who seduced my husb –' She paused, panting, then resumed. 'Who would like to do Mrs Ludbotham?'

6

Dirt Whipping

What a beastly idea, having to take turns, like prizes in a lottery. But Jan and Gina are modern girls, and so am I. I feel so confused.

Belinda shivered, watching Mrs Ludbotham strip to the bare, and, disdaining Clarice's chair back, meekly bend over, touching her toes. The males stood in a solemn row behind her. Belinda clutched her slip of paper, distributed by Heather, smiling coyly with her big eyes. Belinda was number eight, with Jan number six. She hoped the males' spanking arms would be well exhausted by that time.

'Jan,' she whispered, 'I can take a spanking, I think, but –'

'You took much more from me, remember?' Jan interrupted.

'That was different. I couldn't take the cane from a fellow. And as for bumming . . .' Belinda shuddered.

'I do hope we have to,' Jan whispered. 'Don't you?'

Smack! Smack! Professor Fazackerley began Mrs Ludbotham's spanking, with rapid, powerful spanks to her big bare bottom, quivering and pinking almost at once. A low moan escaped the woman's lips, with a sparkling teardrop in her eye. Her compact apple-shaped breasts shook, as her bum clenched at each spank. Smack! Smack! His palm cracked wetly on the quivering arse jellies. Mr Ludbotham, standing beside Dr Warrior, to scrutinise his wife's arse, rubbed his hands gleefully.

'Give it to her hard, professor,' he said, with a chortle.

Mrs Ludbotham took her score with only a little gasping, although when she rubbed her glowing red bottom after the spanks Dr Warrior told her to stop. Next to spank was Mr Granett, who delivered his score leering rather nastily, Belinda thought. However, Mrs Ludbotham's arse squirmed so prettily that Belinda's cunt moistened anew, and she wondered if Jan was ready for another mutual frig. Jan was already busy at her own clit, masturbating, and licking her lips.

'A girl's bum,' she murmured, 'is never so beautiful as when it's spanked.'

Smack! Smack! Another male had taken over the spanking, and Mrs Ludbotham's buttocks were deeply reddened, with her head swinging from side to side, her fesses clenching and jerking at the pain, and choked sobs coming from her throat as she gasped hard at each impact.

'Oh . . . oh . . .' the spanked woman moaned.

She cast an imploring gaze at her husband, who leered. The next spanker was Vergina Tiepolo, who dealt a score of the hardest, smiling cruelly, and with her thighs squeezed together, wriggling, as she spanked. Gina's face was flushed, and her nostrils flared with heavy breathing. Belinda started, as she felt Jan's fingers on her cooze, then sat back, letting her friend masturbate her. Her cunt spurted juice, as she saw a bare-bum Clarice Warrior take over from Gina, the buggered girl brandishing a heavy, bifurcated strap, which Jan said were Scots tawse.

Clarice remained bare from the waist down, save that she had donned her boots, and strutted smugly, wiggling her flogged bare, a mass of mingled dark bruises and pale blisters. Her heavy teats bobbed up and down in the slender constraint of her blouse, carelessly fastened, as though daring the bubbies to burst out once more. Hearing the slither of leather, Mrs Ludbotham raised her crimson, tear-stained face and gaped in dismay.

'Oh, Nigel, not the tawse. I simply couldn't bear it! Clarice is so cruel! Haven't I been spanked enough?'

'Not yet, darling,' said her husband.

The twin tongues lashed two cruel welts across the full

mid-fesse. Mrs Ludbotham's bum jerked, her white knuckles clutching her trembling knees, and she squealed.

'Ooh! Ouch, that hurts! Oh, Nigel, please –'

Thwap!

'Ooh! Ahh! Oh! Nigel, I can't take it! I really don't like being whipped! I hate the pain! Please, I want to go home.'

Clarice's tawse lashed her bum cleft, slapping the bare cunt flaps and anus bud.

'Ahh!'

A heavy stream of piss burst from Mrs Ludbotham's cunt, splattering her thighs and feet, before pooling in a steaming puddle on the flagstones.

'Ooh ... ooh ...' she moaned. 'I've never been so shamed.'

'You've shamed me, you fucking bitch,' snarled Nigel.

Snatching the tawse from Clarice, he grabbed his wife by the hair, whipping her savagely on the tops of her thighs and between the legs. His wife wriggled and spluttered, as the leather snaked between her heaving buttocks and whipped her bumhole and cooze lips, dripping piss. After several strokes of the tawse, Nigel dragged her to the armchair and pinned her head down, with her whipped bum flailing helplessly over the chair back.

'Who wants to have a go, gentlemen?' he growled. 'The cheeky slut has it coming.'

'Noo ... no, please, Nigel, I'll do anything!' his wife moaned. 'Not that –'

'Be quiet, bitch,' snarled Clarice. 'If I can take it , so can you.'

'Ooh!'

Mrs Ludbotham howled, as Clarice's boot flashed and kicked her right between the cunt flaps.

'Ouch! Oh, you fucking bitch!' shrieked Mrs Ludbotham. 'Dr Warrior, that wasn't fair.'

'You have been a bit gabby, girl,' murmured Dr Warrior.

'Oh! Oh!' moaned Mrs Ludbotham, hopping and wriggling, as Clarice kicked her again three further times, the leather toecap thudding wetly in Mrs Ludbotham's drenched cooze.

Clarice secured Mrs Ludbotham's discarded knickers, threw them in the pool of piss and mopped up the piss with her boot. She flicked up the sodden knickers, caught them and stuffed them into the groaning woman's mouth.

'Mm! Urrgh!' Mrs Ludbotham whimpered.

She continued to gurgle through her gag, as Clarice took her whipping to over thirty strokes of the tawse. Her husband held her tightly by the hair, wrenched taut, so that, despite the violent squirming of her flogged bare, his wife was helpless to escape the leather tongues. Panting, Clarice lowered her tawse, and Mr Granett mounted the whimpering woman, his naked tool bobbing erect.

'Make the bitch squeal,' snarled Nigel.

Mr Granett pushed his crimson bell end into Mrs Ludbotham's anus, heaved and sank his cock in her rectum, right to the balls. He began to bugger her vigorously, with her cries of pain filling the room.

'No, stop,' she sobbed. 'It hurts so. Oh, please, sir, don't bugger me.'

'I've a low number, but I can't wait,' gasped Bettina Heckmondthwaite, waving her slip. 'Isn't someone going to spank me?'

Nude, but for her G-string, she bent over, touching her toes, with her firm buttocks exposed and parted. A male – not her husband, who ogled her bum through his wineglass – sprang behind her and began to lather her bare with spanks. Smack!

'Ouch! Ooh, that's good,' Bettina gasped.

Mrs Ludbotham's thighs dripped with Mr Granett's creamy ejaculate; he plopped his cock from her squirming anus and playfully slapped her bum, before Dr Stove at once took his place, sinking his cock fully to her colon, and buggering her hard. Her wriggling was less intense, and her cries less shrill; holding tightly to the chair back, she writhed softly, moaning, as her husband held her wrenched tresses, and her buttocks began to slap against her buggerer's hips, meeting his thrusts. Dr Stove spurted his spunk inside her rectum, and a fresh dribble of creamy fluid appeared on her quivering bare thighs. A third male leaped on top of her bruised bum, and Mrs Ludbotham moved her hands to her buttocks. She pulled the cheeks wide, and he rammed his cock into her gaping bumhole.

'Mm ... mm ...' she moaned, her buttocks tightening on his cock to squeeze the shaft deeper inside her.

As he buggered her, Mrs Ludbotham heaved her bum to slap loudly on his balls, with his cock withdrawing slowly from her squeezing anus.

'Mmm ...' she sighed, as his cream filled her rectum, then bubbled over his balls to trickle on her thighs.

Her thighs slithered together, mashing her skin in the glaze of spunk, and, as his softening cock plopped from her rectum, Mrs Ludbotham stretched her buttocks wider to welcome a new buggerer. Bettina Heckmondthwaite gazed, licking her lips, at Mrs Ludbotham's stretched and penetrated anus, inches from Bettina's face. As her bottom wriggled under spanks, come seeped from Bettina's pulsing cooze, and she tweaked her bulging clitty, with shudders of pleasure.

'Damn filly's wanking off!' snorted her husband. 'Spank the girl harder; you chaps.'

Another wife, giggling, bared herself, and took position, bare bum raised for punishment; then another, and another, until the dungeon was a sea of upthrust bare buttocks, quivering under the spanks of compliant husbands, eager to spank wives not their own.

'Here goes,' said Jan.

She lifted her dress over her head, folded it and, nude, bent over with bum bared and thighs well parted to show her swollen quim lips and thick cunt hairs dangling between her arse cheeks. Hair trailing the floor, and knuckles white on her ankles, she wiggled her buttocks provocatively.

'I need spanking, gentlemen! Come on, Belinda. You too.'

'Just a mo,' Belinda said. 'I'm number eight, you know.'

'Who cares, when we're having fun? Ouch!' Jan gasped, as a spanker's hand cracked on her bare.

'Please, doctor,' said Heather, curtsying to Dr Warrior, 'I know I've a low number, but mayn't I get my beating over with? I need punishment, for I've been a very naughty nurse.'

'My number system seems all topsy-turvy,' sighed Dr Warrior. 'Very well, Heather. Get those shorts off – everything, in fact – and go into the garden. I want you to take an earth bath, and come back nude, with a good wad of earth in your mouth and pouch. No swallowing, just yet.'

Making a rueful moue, Heather curtsied and scampered through the French windows, across the lawn, to a freshly dug but unplanted flowerbed. She stripped to bare, and lay down in the dirt. Rolling her nude body luxuriantly, she slapped handfuls of earth onto her skin and kneaded the muck into her quivering titties. She packed a huge fistful of soil into her cunt, then buried her face in the dirt, grinding her nose and lips in the earth, scooping muck over her hair, and came up with her cheeks bulging, and dark earth seeping through her clenched lips. Her hair plastered, and body entirely smeared with shiny muck, she padded back into the dungeon. Dr Warrior wrinkled her nose, and ordered Adela Ardsley, another nurse, to attend to Heather. Nude, but for skimpy, crotch-stained panties – Belinda was sure she had immodestly cut them away – Adela bound Heather's wrists and ankles in leather cords, then bent the girl forwards, and hogtied her.

'Shy, Belinda?' said Dr Warrior.

'Not shy, doctor. I'm waiting my turn,' Belinda blurted. 'I've never been to such a modern party.'

'Perhaps you'd like to chastise Heather. I'm sure you'll want to when I tell you how naughty Heather has been. You don't mind, do you, Heather?'

'Mm . . .' Heather moaned, dribbling earth.

'Heather has been giving relief to male patients,' Dr Warrior said, raising her voice over the spanking slaps, and Mrs Ludbotham's groans of buggered pleasure. 'Wanking them off, to put it bluntly. That is, of course, the duty of any thoughtful nurse, but Heather was demanding payment for her services – a packet of Woodbines for relief massage. Woodbines, indeed!'

'Please, doctor,' said Adela slyly, 'she was doing the girl patients too. Licking their clitties, and sucking their quims and bubbies, or letting them do her – you know, gamahuching.'

Dr Warrior made a moue. 'The girl must be hanged,' she said. 'Clarice!'

Her daughter paused in spanking Mrs Witherspoon, of Barrow, and fetched a heavy rope, which she slung through a pulley in an oaken ceiling beam. Adela helped her wind the rope around Heather's belly, and the shivering nurse was hoisted to spanking height, with her bum upthrust. Muck dripped from her filled cunt.

Nigel Ludbotham released his wife's hair, as she climaxed under Mr Witherspoon's buggery, and plunged his tool into the squirming arse of Mrs Heckmondthwaite.

'Ooh! Ooh! Yes!' cried Bettina.

'Good lad, Nigel,' said her husband Rodney, chuckling. 'Bugger the bitch hard.'

Rodney's drool-slimed tool was sucked by Jan, crouching, with her bare bum writhing, under spanks from Professor Fazackerley. Copious come squirted from her cunt, as the male's hand reddened her quivering bare. Jan's face was as red as her spanked bottom, and her lips clamped on the cock, with her cheeks sucking in and out, as she fervently fellated the panting Rodney. Gwenda Broach, an elfin, bony nurse, with big bullet breasts and cropped auburn hair, had her face poked between Rodney's thighs, and his balls in her mouth, with Jan's naked titties squashed in her eyes, as she sucked hard on the ball sac.

'You vicious minx, Jan,' Rodney gasped, 'you really know how to suck cock, don't you? I bet you've sucked scores of fellows.'

'Mm, mm,' Jan gurgled, nodding her head.

'I'm going to fill that cheeky throat with spunk, and you'll swallow every drop, won't you?'

Jan smiled, her lips on his peehole, and nodded assent, then yelped, as Professor Fazackerley impaled her anus with his cock, and began a bum-fuck.

'Oh! Gosh, yes,' shrilled Bettina, squirming under Nigel's buggering tool. 'It's so good. You're going to split my bum in two, with that fabulous hard cock. It's right up my rectum. Watch me, Rodney, and see how to bum a girl properly.'

Rodney glowered.

'Unghh . . .' groaned Heather, as Adela affixed mousetraps to each of her quim lips, and each nipple, pinching the flesh to white bulbs.

Clarice tied a London brick to each mousetrap, and Heather dangled, groaning, with her teats and gash flaps grotesquely stretched by the suspended weights. Dr Warrior proffered Belinda her cane.

'Care to do the honours?' she said. 'Vergina tells me you're quite a thrasher.'

Belinda blushed. The spectacle of the trussed and tortured nude girl made her slit gush with come. 'Only naughty boys,' she blurted. 'I – I don't think I could whip a girl. It would seem wrong, somehow.'

'But you've been thrashed.'

'Yes – yes, I have.'

'What's the difference?'

'I felt I deserved it.'

'And you don't mind watching a girl whipped.'

Dr Warrior's cunt ring, shiny with juice, whirled round and round, as her fingers played between her legs. As she spoke, her breasts quivered and her nipple hoops tinkled together.

'No, I don't mind.'

'You're quite wet, you know.'

Belinda's blush deepened.

'Watch me spin Heather like a top. I expect you'd like another wank. That nubbin of yours is peeping through your gash folds – it's lovely and stiff, quite a corker. With proper clitoral exercise, you could be as well endowed as some of my African girls.'

Dr Warrior raised her cane over Heather's spread buttocks.

'I'd never thought of myself that way,' blurted Belinda. 'You mean, a big nubbin isn't abnormal?'

'The bigger, the better,' said Dr Warrior. 'Allow me a doctor's guess – you have always masturbated excessively.'

'How did you know?' gasped Belinda. 'I admit it, but all girls diddle, don't they?'

'A mature clit requires more stimulus, that's all. Like ripened buttocks, which you also possess.'

The cane fell hard on Heather's upturned buttocks, rocking the trussed girl in her suspension. A second stroke sliced the same weal.

'Mm!' Heather gurgled, gobbets of earth dribbling from her filled mouth and cunt.

'Hold it in, Heather, my sweet,' purred Dr Warrior.

A brown liquid of come mixed with soil drooled from her flapping cooze. Two strokes lashed her haunches, and Heather gurgled in her throat, her body spinning on its cord, and the bare buttocks clenching. Dr Warrior played with her cunt rings and nipple hoops, as she flogged the bound nurse, with the doctor's breasts bouncing and buttocks clenching firmly at each stroke, while her powerful thigh muscles rippled.

Belinda watched the lithe grace of the nude whipper, and the convulsing agony of the beaten girl, and, gasping, touched her clitty. It was rock hard, and come instantly bathed Belinda's fingers, as she began to masturbate. Beside her, Gina writhed, hands clutching her cunt, and, winking at Belinda, she briefly lifted her dress to show her naked cooze. Inside her slit was a giant rubber tool, like the one Jan had used on Belinda's own gash. Gina pumped it in and out of her gushing twat, ramming its tip to her cunt root, and flicking her swollen clitty with her thumb.

'Isn't it wonderful to wank off at a beaten bum?' she gasped. 'That's why I wear my best dildo to all of Emily's dos. The sight of bare whipped buttocks is the loveliest in creation. Didn't you masturbate while flogging Alberto?'

Wanking hard, Belinda blurted that she may have done. The heavy lashing of the cane on Heather's squirming bare was mesmerising. Come drenched her frigging hand; she looked aside to see Jan's bum scarlet with spanks, and her throat convulsing, as she swallowed the load of spunk spurted by Rodney, gasping heavily as he orgasmed, while the panting Professor Fazackerley's cream bubbled from Jan's buggered anus.

Rodney's spunk spurted so powerfully that gobbets splashed over Jan's lips and chin, and trickled down the shaft of Rodney's cock to wet his balls in white creamy fluid, which Gwenda eagerly lapped. Gwenda smeared Rodney's residue from her lips into her erect nipples, while Professor Fazackerley withdrew his cock from Jan's bum-hole, and shoved it into Gwenda's mouth for her to lick it clean of his spunk and Jan's arse grease.

'You clumsy bitch,' Rodney snarled, as his wet cock plopped from Jan's lips. 'I told you to swallow every drop.'

'You're too hard a comer, sir,' Jan moaned.

'Straddle the horse, bitch, at once.'

Sullenly, Jan slapped her body over a leather flogging frame, a steeply pointed pyramid, whose summit bit her waist, with her torso and legs draped over the slopes, and her bottom upthrust at the top. Rodney seized a rubber quirt, with six square thongs, and began to whip her bottom, already red from her spanks. Jan's eyes met Belinda's, and the whipped girl's teeth bared in a rictus. *Thwap*! *Thwap*! The thongs danced, thrashing Jan's squirming bum globes, and the girl's breath rasped hoarsely. Gwenda squatted, holding Jan's ankles, and masturbating her slimy cunt on Jan's twitching big toe, while Mr Granett kneeled, to spank Gwenda's muscular bare bottom.

'Uhh . . . ohh . . . you're so cruel,' Jan hissed. 'Go on then, whip my arse raw, you bastard.'

Jan wanted to be whipped! Judging from the spinning Heather's gurgles of pain and pleasure, her bright eyes and flaring nostrils, and the soiled come gushing from her dirt-packed cunt, so did Heather.

'You haven't bared up, have you, Belinda?' said Dr Warrior pleasantly. 'I fear I'll be quite long with naughty Heather, so perhaps Vergina will be so kind as to service you.'

'Oh,' Belinda blurted, pausing in her wank. 'I'm not sure – that is, I'm not ready . . .'

Dr Warrior's eyes flashed, and her nipple rings clanged. 'That sort of talk is the sure sign of a deceitful slut, whose bottom needs thorough scourging at once.'

Gina wheeled a second horse into position beside Jan's, and ordered Belinda to take position.

'Obey, or you'll regret it,' purred Dr Warrior.

Gingerly, Belinda lowered her naked body onto the clammy leather, squashing her titties, and with the sharp pinnacle thrusting her bum high.

'I say, look at that arse.'

'Ripe for strokes.

'Choice filly.'

Belinda's heart thudded as she spread her thighs, showing herself to the guests.

Exposed, my naked bum ready for stripes . . . shamed! And I'm so wet!

Thwap! *Thwap*! Beside her, Jan's reddened bare jerked and wriggled, with the flogged girl gasping hoarsely.

'Bare up and take it, Belinda,' Jan gasped. 'You know you can.'

'Go easy, please, Gina,' Belinda whimpered.

Gina laughed cruelly. She flexed a horrid four-foot cane of sullenly gleaming dark wood, and whipped it suddenly – *Vip*! – across Belinda's bare buttocks. The pain was searing; Belinda's gorge rose, and tears sprang to her eyes.

'Ahh!' she moaned. 'Oh, gosh, not so hard, Gina. What is that fearful thing?'

'It's a Sudanese rattan,' said Gina. 'The sort they use on criminals. Emily's told me all about it – mm, all those luscious brown bodies, stark naked, lined up, men and women, for their buttocks to be whipped raw.'

'Tough luck, Belinda,' Jan gasped. 'I'm taking Rodney's quirt.' *Vip*! 'Ooh . . . it's dashed painful, but not so bad, really. It leaves a nice pretty pattern, as the welts crust.' *Vip*! 'Ahh . . . you'll have trenches from that bloody rattan.'

'No,' Belinda whimpered, her buttocks aquiver with goose pimples, awaiting her canestroke.

'Ooh! Ouch!' cried Belinda, her flaming bottom squirming madly on the leather, already slithery with her gushing come.

'Flog my little brother, would you, you stuck-up madam!' Gina hissed.

The long, snakelike rattan tongue whipped Belinda over every portion of her bum, with Gina paying special attention to the tender haunches and upper nates, the soft underfesses and even the thigh tops. The cane lashed right across those, inches below her squirming bare buttocks, and Belinda sobbed in a paroxysm of agonised wriggles.

'Oh, Gina, please,' she moaned, 'thighs are really too much.'

'Wait for what's coming,' Gina snarled, nodding at Bettina and Mrs Ludbotham, squirming, as fresh cocks anally impaled them, amid wives gamahuching wives, or fellating husbands, while their arses were thrashed or buggered.

Mrs Ludbotham groaned and snivelled, her face wet with tears, as her arse was whipped before each buggery; even the lustful Bettina grimaced in pain, as tool after tool penetrated her rectum. Adela Ardsley squealed, as Mr Throate thrust her head down to suck his erect cock, while Mr Witherspoon ripped off Adela's skimpy panties and tawsed her naked croup. The flagstones glistened with come and piss, for several ladies could not take stripes on the bare without wetting themselves. Mrs Ludbotham bitterly wailed at her shame, as her piss flowed over the cock and balls of her buggerer.

Heather's cunt bubbled with a fountain of mud-slimed piss, sprayed in an arc, as she whirled, under Dr Warrior's expert caning of her squirming bum puddings, now with livid weals glowing under the mudstains. Her brick danglers swayed, wrenching her distended breasts and cooze flaps to pale envelopes of tortured flesh. Jan and Belinda jerked, writhing, as they took their punishment on their leather horses.

'Ahh . . .' Belinda whimpered. 'But why, Jan? Why must a girl's bum suffer so?'

'Because it's there,' gasped Jan.

Gina parted Belinda's thighs to reveal her shaven bum cleft. Licking her lips, she began to cane the girl right in the perineum, with the rattan lashing her anus and cunt flaps, as well as the tender skin of her inner thighs, next to the arse crack. *Vip*! *Vip*!'

'Ooh!' Belinda squealed, her flogged cunt threshing, and slithering in her lake of spurted come. 'That isn't fair.'

'Your cunt's wet, you filthy slut,' said Gina. 'You want it – the pain, the shame.'

'Ooh! Ahh! No, no, no!'

Belinda's flogged bum was a mass of heavy red welts, deepening to purple trenches and pale blisters; her arse cleft glowed crimson with weals.

'When a girl says "no", she really means "yes" – right, Belinda?'

'Not this girl,' sobbed Belinda, lurching from her flogging horse. 'You've hurt me too much, and now you're going to get a licking.'

'Wait! What are you doing?' blurted Gina, as Belinda grabbed her. 'Stop this, you silly bitch, or –'

'Or what?' snarled Belinda through her tears. 'You'll thrash my bum?'

She snatched the cane from Gina, who stumbled, snagging the hem of her dress on a splinter of the flogging horse.

'Drat,' she cried.

Belinda raised the cane, and lashed Gina's skirted bottom. *Vip*! The stroke crackled on her seat.

'Oh! Ouch! That's not fair!' Gina wailed.

Belinda lifted the cane for a second stroke and Gina took to her heels, hobbling out the French windows into the garden, with Belinda in pursuit, and her dress unravelling from the snagged thread. Hampered by her rapidly disappearing dress and teetering high heels, Gina could not evade the nude Belinda, who lashed her on the bum, breasts and thighs. '*Vip*! *Vip*!' echoed through the stillness of the garden.

'Oh! Ooh!' Gina wailed, panting, as she stumbled. 'My dress is ruined!'

Still caning the wriggling, suspended Heather, Dr Warrior watched, her lips curled in amusement, while her daughter glowered. Gina's ripped dress turned to a memory of tangled threads, exposing her thighs, bum and cunt, belly and teats. The naked, sobbing girl was felled by a vicious stroke between her legs, the cane clattering on the dildo wedged in her slit. Whimpering, Gina toppled into the flowerbed, where Belinda kicked her cunt and bottom, rolling her in the muck, until Gina's body was slathered black with earth.

'Eat it, you bitch,' hissed Belinda.

'All right, all right, please don't cane me any more,' babbled the muddy girl, as she sank her face into the muck, and began to swallow.

Vip! *Vip*! With her foot on Gina's neck, Belinda began to whip her mucky bottom.

'Urrgh,' Gina squealed, frantically chewing dirt.

Belinda continued to cane Gina's squirming fesses, until the buttocks were flensed with livid gashes. Gina sobbed and wriggled, her writhing hips pushing her cunt into the dirt. Panting, after a dozen further strokes, Belinda lowered her cane, stared at the dirty flogged arse globes, scooped a palmful of mud and began to masturbate her gushing cunt, rubbing the slimy mud all over her wet pink slitmeat and engorged clitty. Still mud-wanking, she squatted over Gina, thighs apart, and pissed on her bottom.

A hissing muddy stream splattered the dirt-eating girl, who continued her mucky repast, even when her bum was freed of canestrokes, rubbing her titties in the muck and tweaking her nipples. As Belinda's piss bathed her, Gina's hand slid through the dirt to her cunt, and she writhed, splashing in piss, as she masturbated, pushing her dildo in and out of her muddy cunt. Belinda grabbed the dildo, and extracted it with a plop from Gina's twat, then rammed the giant rubber shaft into Gina's anus, where she sank it to the hilt against the girl's arse root, and began a vigorous bum-fucking.

'Ooh ... no, no ...' Gina moaned, her arse writhing against the penetrating dildo.

'No means yes, eh, Gina?' panted Belinda. 'You deserved your punishment, didn't you?'

'Yes!' moaned Gina, gasping, as she wanked. 'I mean, no . . . ooh, yes. Oh! Ah, I'm coming! Ohh . . .'

Her naked cunt writhed in the mud, wetting it with her spuming come, as she shuddered in climax. Belinda wanked her own clitty harder, with two fingers pummelling her slit, as come sluiced down her rippling thighs. Her belly fluttered, and she began to moan, stroking the vicious welts on Gina's bare.

'You poor thing,' she moaned, 'ooh, I'm coming too . . . ouch! Ooh!'

Belinda squealed, as Clarice, eyes bright with fury, wrenched her hair, toppling her from her crouching position. The dildo squelched from Gina's anus, and fell on the ground.

With her cunt in the grass, Belinda was dragged back to the dungeon, by Clarice, quivering with rage.

'You beastly bitch, to give my best chum a dirt whipping,' she snarled. 'See what you get, bitch.'

Clarice secured Belinda's left ankle, and twisted savagely, flipping Belinda onto her belly, with her leg held high, at Clarice's breast. Her right leg flapped helplessly on the flagstones, with her dripping cooze and bumhole fully exposed. Clarice lifted her boot, and with a thud, the toecap kicked Belinda between the cunt flaps.

'Ooh!' Belinda howled, squirming and wriggling, but unable to escape the wrestling hold.

Thwap! *Thwap*! Clarice began a methodical kicking of Belinda's anus and gash, landing her toecap alternately on the anal pucker, and squarely in the pink wet flesh of Belinda's squirming pouch.

'Clarice, don't be a brute,' gasped Heather, wincing in suspension, under Dr Warrior's thrashing.

'Give her what for,' said Rodney, chortling and bouncing Jan, with her back to him, in his lap; his cock squelched in and out of her anus, as her wealed buttocks slapped his pot belly.

'Stop, stop,' sobbed Belinda, writhing under the savage kicks between her thighs.

Suddenly, Clarice cried out, her boot slipping in a pool

of piss and come. She toppled on her belly, aided by a stabbing kick from Belinda, who, panting, rolled on top of her. Face to Clarice's churning buttocks, Belinda ripped off the girl's boots, and grasped her ankles, twisting hard, so that Clarice thumped the floor in pain. She was helpess to move, with both her ankles in Belinda's lock. Belinda's head dived between Clarice's spread buttocks, and she bit savagely on the pinioned girl's quim lips.

'Ahh!' screamed Clarice.

Belinda bit her again and again, fastening her teeth on the clitty, and grinding hard, until Clarice's sobs drowned the whimpers of pleasure from the several buggeries, and even Heather's groans, as her flogged bottom purpled with Dr Warrior's canewelts.

'Oh, gosh,' wailed Clarice, as a fountain of piss squirted from her bitten cunt, splashing Belinda's face with the acrid, steaming liquid.

Belinda's head rose, dripping with Clarice's piss and come, and she began to cover the writhing girl's bare buttocks in bitemarks.

'Oh! Ouch! No!' Clarice begged, her bitten bum shuddering between Belinda's teeth.

Gina's shadow covered Belinda. The muddy naked girl proffered her muck-slimed rubber dildo.

'This might come in useful, Belinda,' Gina said shyly.

Belinda took it; after releasing one of Clarice's ankles, she thrust the tube into her anus. Well greased by its coating of mud, the dildo slid easily to Clarice's colon, and Belinda began a vigorous pumping, while Clarice squealed and wriggled, her buttocks threshing, and anus cruelly distended by the huge dildo.

Holding Jan by her hips, Rodney was slamming her down on his cock, so that her bottom slapped his thighs. Jan was masturbating her cunt with dripping fingers and rubbing her come into Rodney's balls. He smacked her buggered bare bum in applause, as his cock slid slimily in and out of her sucking anus.

'Splendid catspat,' he panted. 'Like a pair of Port Said belly dancers. Tarts are the bloody same everywhere.'

'I say, girls,' Jan said, 'I don't think we ought to put up with that sort of rudeness.'

'Absolutely not,' gasped Bettina, squirming under a cock.

Chewing earth, hogtied Heather frowned angrily.

'It's outrageous,' said Mrs Ludbotham.

'Absolutely beastly,' panted Clarice, her bottom writhing on Belinda's impaling dildo.

There was a loud plop, as Jan's withdrawal of her anus left Rodney's stiff cock dripping arse grease in thin air.

'What the –' he gasped, as several female hands grabbed him. 'I haven't spunked in that fucking bitch's arse yet! Let me go!'

Belinda rose, releasing Clarice, who clutched her dildo, rammed in her bumhole, as she joined the girls in securing Rodney's person. The struggling male was slapped face down in a pool of piss and come, with Clarice's foot on his neck, and Belinda's under his balls. Belinda leaned back, allowing Jan, Bettina, Adela and the others a clear target of his bare buttocks. Jan lashed his bottom with the rattan cane.

'Ooh,' Rodney squealed.

'Take that, you pig,' cried his wife, whipping him with the quirt.

'Ahh . . .'

Vap! Adela flogged him with the tawse.

'Oh! Ooh! Please . . .'

His balls trapped by Belinda's toes, Rodney wriggled, bleating in anguish, as his squirming bare darkened with weals beneath the lustful bright eyes of his female chastisers, all masturbating, with fingers squelching cunts slimed in squirted come. There was a clatter, as Heather's brick danglers fell to the floor. Swallowing her mouthful of earth, the whipped nurse was released, seized Dr Warrior's cane and, teeth bared in a rictus of fury, added her own strokes to Rodney's beating. Her grotesquely stretched titties and cunt lips flapped wildly, as she whipped. Earth sprayed from her filled cunt, while she masturbated, with her nubbin poking stiff and red through the slime of muck dripping from her slit.

'I bet you he's rampant,' panted Bettina, her tasselled G-string swaying, as she beat her groaning husband. 'He's beastly like that.'

'Oh! Ladies, please,' whimpered Rodney. 'Have mercy –'

Belinda slipped her clasping toes from his balls up the shaft of his cock, and found his swollen glans She clamped the neck of his glans between her toes, and began to frig his erect cock.

'Ooh . . .' Rodney gurgled.

Belinda's toe slid to his peehole, rubbing it, then moved down the corona of the glans and back to the neck, with her toes sliding and slithering all over the bell end, then pausing for strong strokes at the glans neck, stretching the prepuce fully back. Her toes were slimy with Jan's arse grease coating his cock. As Rodney's flogged arse wriggled, Belinda's big toe caressed his peehole and felt a hot oily spurt of liquid.

'Ooh . . . Ooh . . .' Rodney whimpered. 'Don't stop. Yes . . . yes . . .'

Vip! *Thwap*! *Vap*!

'Yes,' Rodney gasped, and a jet of spunk flooded Belinda's wanking toes.

Bettina, Mrs Ludbotham, Jan, Adela, Heather, Clarice and the other girls joined in a chorus of gasps and whimpers, as they wanked themselves to gushing orgasms. Come spurted from quims bare and shaven alike, slopping over fingers and thighs. Panting, they laid aside their instruments, and Rodney rose, rubbing his bottom.

'Whew! Splendid fillies, all of you,' he gasped. 'What spirit, what British spunk.'

'Thank you, Dr Warrior, for a lovely party,' said Mrs Ludbotham, blushing. 'I've never had so much fun, although I'm afraid Nigel will spank me for my naughtiness when we get home.'

'Wizard thrash, Emily,' drawled Bettina, blowing smoke over her husband.

Chattering happily, the guests gushed thanks, exchanged telephone numbers and prepared to leave.

'You, Jan and Gina may stay, Belinda,' Dr Warrior said. 'I shortly have to see a private patient, who would love to meet you. Besides –' she held up her slip of paper '– we must do things by the rules. I'm number seventeen, and I haven't had my turn yet.'

7

Barecock

Bustling, Clarice served a light tea of hot buttered scones, with steaming darjeeling. The four girls sat, sipping tea, as the light waned, with Jan and Gina casually nude, Belinda having opted for her bra and shorties, and Clarice's bum and teats swelling in a fetching mauve set of high-cut panties and uplift bra. The tray held one empty cup. Belinda fiddled with her cut-down bra, her bubbies thrust high and the tops of her nipple domes just peeping from their cups, which she thought was far more teasing than Jan's total nudity. Her shorties would ride up, with the panties getting all wrinkled and stuck in her crotch, showing quite a spread of naked quim flap, and the soft bits at her thigh tops, even though she kept pulling them down. Clarice proffered her packet of cigarettes; the girls helped themselves and lit up.

'Gosh! Real American Chesterfields,' Jan said. 'Mm . . . where did you get those?'

'No wonder her bum pucker's so wide,' observed Gina. 'All those spunky yank airmen.'

Clarice blushed.

'You have been naughty,' said Dr Warrior.

'I've already been punished, Mummy,' said Clarice. 'It's your turn.'

'I know. Belinda can do me while I await my patient. Clarice, would you be a darling, and prepare the x-frame? And bring something strong – the whalebone switch, bound in catgut.'

Clarice whistled. 'Are you absolutely sure, Mummy?' she said. 'You haven't used that for ages.'

'Yes,' said Dr Warrior. 'This is a little therapy for our new friend. '

'I – I don't understand,' Belinda blurted.

Clarice wheeled in a sturdy wooden stand, with a top consisting of two six-foot bars in a cross shape. At the intersection and tips of the crossbars dangled buckled rubber straps, fixed to an adjustable slide. The entire apparatus swivelled in a circular motion, or from horizontal to vertical, by a lockable ratchet. Dr Warrior lay face down on the crossbars, her legs and arms stretched apart, and Clarice fastened her waist with the rubber strap, while Gina cuffed her wrists and Jan her ankles. The rubber made a horrid slapping noise on the doctor's skin, and Belinda shivered.

'You will please thrash my bare bottom, Belinda,' she said.

'I've never done anything, um, pervy, before,' Belinda blurted.

'Liar,' hissed Jan.

'I mean, this is my first time at – at a spanking party.'

'You were pervy enough before an audience,' said Dr Warrior, straining against her straps. 'Mm, good, nice and tight. I shan't be able to wriggle too much when doughty Belinda thrashes me. Most girls like an audience, which is the reason for my little get-togethers, and Belinda enjoys exposing herself, eh, Belinda?'

Belinda blushed.

'You've shown you can whip in a fine frenzy, Belinda, and now you must whip me in calm detachment. Pretend I'm a male, and flog me the way you flogged Gina's brother.'

'It wasn't all that calm,' Gina said, giggling. 'She wanked him off afterwards, and wanked herself.'

Belinda blushed furiously – Alberto, the sneak! – but accepted the vicious whalebone flogger from Clarice.

'You have exposed yourself, Belinda, haven't you?' said Dr Warrior. 'Shown your titties or private parts in public?'

'Go on, own up,' said Jan with a smirk. 'Your show in the sweetshop? Peeing and wanking on Morecambe sands?'

'Jan, you rotter,' Belinda hissed.

'No need to be embarrassed, Belinda,' said Dr Warrior. 'Exhibitionism is perfectly healthy for a modern girl.'

'So I like to tease,' retorted Belinda, rising and flexing her flogger. 'But it's only in fun. I'm not sure I like being talked about behind my back.'

She stood above Dr Warrior's trimly swelling naked buttocks and her slender back, rippling with muscle, the skin a uniform tan and satin smooth. Viewed from above, the buttocks were revealed asymmetrically large, thrusting as a hard rounded outcrop on the soft plain of her back and thighs. The parting of her thighs showed her anus pucker, a little larger than normal, and the big pendant lips of her bare cunt, hanging down, pierced with their hoop. Belinda licked her lips.

'Why, Belinda, to a psychologist, there is no –'

Belinda lashed Dr Warrior's bare with the switch, full across the mid-fesse, and was pleased at the violent jerk of her buttocks.

'Ooh!' gasped Dr Warrior.

'I'm sick of psychology, and being told I'm normal. I am beginning to feel angry at you, doctor,' Belinda spat.

'Good, good! It's healthy to feel –'

Vip! Vip!

'Ooh! Ouch! Those were tight,' gasped Dr Warrior, as two livid red weals puffed on her whipped bottom. 'I like that; I'm due for some. Make them pretty hard.'

The smiling girls crowded Belinda, watching the doctor's beaten buttocks and rubbing their quims.

'By the way, Belinda, I expect you'll want to masturbate, as you see my bum squirm,' panted the doctor, 'so feel free. It's quite normal.'

'And I'm sick of being given orders,' hissed Belinda, 'and told to be normal. I'm perfectly normal.'

Vip!

'Ahh! Ooh! Yes, I rather think you are. That was so tight.'

Vip!

'Ohh! That really hurts. You're an expert whipper, my girl.'

Belinda did want to masturbate, for the sight of the muscled bare bum wriggling and the body of the naked woman straining at her rubber thongs made her slit flow with come. She tickled her clitty under her wet panties, shuddering, to find it already stiff and throbbing and bathed in spurting oily come from her pulsing gash. The other girls smiled at the come-soaked panties clinging to her quivering bum, and outlining her cunt hillock.

'I'm not anybody's girl,' Belinda snarled.

She snapped open the ratchet and tilted the x-frame, until Dr Warrior hung upside down, bottom and back facing the girls, with her weight taken by her ankle cuffs, and the tight rubber corset strapping her waist. *Vip*! She lashed the woman's thigh backs.

'Uhh . . .' whimpered Dr Warrior, her whole body twisting and squirming in her bonds. 'You haven't said how many I'm to take. Please, not too many. You're so strong.'

'I'll do you till I feel weak, then,' sneered Belinda.

'Ooh! I was afraid of that. It's the way Amur's people used to whip me. Nude, tied hanging upside down beneath the biggest palm tree in the oasis, for an unlimited flogging. I had to take it – for my work, you know.'

'I'm just an ordinary girl from Lancashire,' Belinda blurted. 'I'm not part of your work.'

She lashed the tender haunches, which at once darkened with deep crimson welts.

'Ahh!' Dr Warrior gasped, wriggling in her bonds. 'Everybody is part of my work, Belinda.'

As she flogged the suspended woman, Belinda masturbated hard, filled with exultation at her brute power over a helpless female body, shamefully naked under her lashes. The legs, spread upside-down, offered a tempting juicy target, in the parted lips of the woman's cunt, with the slit flesh shining pink and wet. The shaven mound of Dr Warrior's upside down cunt hillock glistened with seeped come from her gash, where her clitoris stood hard and erect between the swollen fleshy folds. Jan and Gina wanked their naked cunts, Gina's undildoed gash allowing her vigorous finger penetration, while Clarice busied herself in the kitchen, loudly urging Belinda to 'lay it on hard'.

'Ahh!' Dr Warrior shrilled, as Belinda whipped her hard between the cunt lips.

Vip! She lashed the arse cleft, striking the whorl of the abnormally large anal pucker.

'Ohh! That's too much!' the flogged woman moaned. 'It hurts so much more, upside down. Amur's people believe upside-down whipping enhances a girl's bum.'

'That's awful!' Belinda gasped. 'When did this happen to you?'

'Why, most days,' gasped the doctor. 'I stayed several months – my research included the task of taking young men's virginity, and the whipping was to increase my sensuous power.'

The flogged woman's body shivered, as spurts of come dribbled down her belly, and over her breasts, bathing her rock-hard nipples in the oily liquid. Belinda began a methodical lashing of her full croup, making sure that no portion of skin was left unwealed. Dr Warrior's flogged buttocks squirmed, and she moaned incessantly, with hoarse gasps, as the rod sliced her wriggling bumflesh.

'Ooh . . . ooh . . . ooh . . .'

Come flowed copiously from the flogged woman's cunt, sliming her whole belly and teats in her gash juice, with drips trickling off her chin into her mouth. Belinda delivered every fourth or fifth stroke to the cunt, sending Dr Warrior into a paroxysm of squirming, with her mouth hanging open, spraying drool, and whimpering in anguished gurgles. Belinda masturbated her own cunt through her wet shorties, feeling the hot come flow down her rippling thighs, and beside her the other girls cooed in their vigorous wanks. As the flogged woman's bottom jerked, her teat rings jangled, and her cunt ring bounced up and down, striking her massively erect clitoris, extruded from the gash folds.

'Ooh! I've never been hurt so much, since – since Africa,' Dr Warrior whimpered. 'It's so good, to be in another's power, to squirm naked, shamed and exposed. It's what all girls want. Belinda, my bum is big, isn't it?'

'It is, rather,' Belinda murmured.

'Ooh! Ah! Thank you – you're big, too, with that gorgeous arse and heavenly outsize clit. You'd be worth a lot in Africa.'

'How dare you make me sound like some slave girl? Take that!'

Vip!

'Ooh!'

'And that!'

Vip! *Vip*!

'Ooh! Ahh! Ouch! Oh!'

Come spumed from Dr Warrior's cunt, as her flogged bottom purpled with welts. The taut buttocks clenched frantically, pumping in and out, a bellows of naked bumflesh.

'More, Belinda,' she gasped, through drooling lips. 'Harder, more, girl . . . I'm going to –'

Vip! *Vip*!

'Ahh! Yes! I'm coming.'

'Shameless bitch,' Belinda snarled.

'*Vip*! *Vip*!

'Oh! Oh! Yes . . . ahh . . .' gasped the doctor, as come sprayed from her writhing cooze, and her belly convulsed in orgasm.

Belinda flicked her own clitty with the handle of the switch, then lowered her panties and poked the tip, hot from the woman's bottom, into her gushing slit. She, too, gasped, coming at once, as she watched the bare buttocks squirming before her. The sweating girls beside her shuddered, as they wanked to orgasm.

'That was gorgeous,' gasped Dr Warrior. 'I counted to forty-three strokes. I haven't had such a good whipping, nor such an intense come, in ages.'

Groaning, she let herself be released from her bonds. Clarice bustled in, with fresh tea things; the wanked girls, crimson and smiling, sat down to finish their tea, with Belinda pulling up her come-drenched shorties. Dr Warrior rubbed her bum, wincing, before gingerly sitting down to join them.

'Don't you feel better, Belinda?' she said.

Mouth full of scone, Belinda nodded shyly.

'We girls must toughen our bottoms to be thrashed, and our minds to thrash,' the doctor said. 'Learn to show off our bodies, to make males drool, and develop our choicest parts – our bottoms and clits – for female power and pleasure. I explore this theme in my occasional pieces for the *Manchester Guardian*, although not quite so explicitly.'

There was a jingle of bells, and Dr Warrior bade entrance. Through the French windows stepped a tall young African, wearing a black blazer with razor-creased pinstripe trousers, white shirt, pearl-grey waistcoat and striped tie, and a homburg hat. He bowed to Dr Warrior, then to the girls, before removing his hat and calfskin gloves. He jingled as he walked, with music from his bulging crotch.

'What a spunk,' whispered Jan to Belinda. 'You know about black men – awfully big down there.'

'Girls, this is my patient, Amur,' said Dr Warrior, 'a student of economics at Bolton Technical College. He is a real Nubian prince, a royal highness.'

'One prefers not to make a fuss about it,' he drawled.

He sat down, and Clarice served him tea. Belinda studied his face, with its lustrous long lashes, slender, sensuous face and wide lips, then – curse Jan! – eyed his crotch. She stifled a gasp, at the bulge perceptible within his yummy pinstripe trousers, a bulge which seemed to be growing, as his eyes lazily scanned the girls' bodies. Well, he's a fruity young spunk, scarcely nineteen, and his organ would swell, wouldn't it, seeing naked girls. As if guessing Belinda's thought, and with his stiffened cock straining unconcealed in his trousers, he said casually that their nudity made no difference to his condition – the mere scent of female meat would 'set him off'. He looked awfully strong – Belinda shivered, wondering if he was going to . . . to ravage them all.

'So, your Highness, how do you like Lancashire?' she said.

'Very much. There is a freshness and vitality here –' he positively ogled Belinda's breasts '– which is lacking in the metropolis, although I do keep a small flat in Curzon Street. In particular, I like the cuisine – the hotpot, the fish and chips, the mushy peas. Our diet in Africa is somewhat restricted, and one tires of roast gazelle, partridge wings and the eternal dates and pomegranates.'

'You seem awfully young to be a prince, sir,' Belinda blurted.

He smiled graciously, his dark eyes piercing hers. 'Actually, I have been a prince since birth, miss. One doesn't have much choice in the matter.'

How the others laughed, even Dr Warrior, and how Belinda blushed, her quim so moist with come she feared she had wet herself.

Gosh, he certainly is a spunk.

Amur flicked open a gold cigarette case, and the girls pounced on the fragrant oval tubes, gleaming white.

'I hope you don't mind Balkan Sobranie,' he drawled.

'Ooh!'

'Super!'

'Charmed, I'm sure.'

The girls daintily puffed the scented smoke. Belinda's gash flowed and her heart pounded, because, after previous doings, she guessed Amur's therapy involved young, naked girls. His cock bulged like a mountain, and he made no attempt to conceal the erection, which seemed at odds with his exquisite politeness. Neither did the girls pretend to avert their gaze from his swollen organ. Jan and Gina openly licked their lips, while Clarice blushed, her mauve knickers wet at the crotch. Belinda squeezed her thighs, to stem the seep of come at her gash, and her gesture drew Amur's attention to her hillock, swelling under her moist shorties. Jan – the minx! – had the advantage of nudity, and casually raked her jungly minge with her fingernails, her thighs open, to show her wet pink cooze flesh.

'So, you've known Dr Warrior a long time?' said Gina, crossing her naked thighs, with a wet slither.

'Absolutely,' he purred. 'It was the doctor who relieved me of my virginity.'

The girls ogled his cock.

'That must have been ecstasy for her,' breathed Jan.

'It was, rather,' said Amur, with a shrug.

Dr Warrior blushed.

'Is it true you regularly whipped her?' said Belinda.

'Not personally,' he replied, licking his lips, as his eyes devoured her bared flesh, 'save for one or two private occasions. Whipping is usually women's work. I ordered it done, of course. The female is best flogged upside down, for her planet energy to flow from her feet, which absorb it from the earth, into her buttocks and vulva. During pauses for refreshment, the males worship those parts in the manner of our nation. In particular, we hold sacred the rite of buggery, penetrating the chamber of earth, rather than the chamber of water. Our females have the sacred duty of constant masturbation in order to nourish the earth with their juices, and we especially esteem the practice you call cunnilingus, with the drinking of those juices.'

'Whatever's that?' whispered Belinda to Jan.

'When a chap licks your twat and nub,' said Jan, fingering herself between the legs. 'It's ever so come-making.'

'And do you have a girlfriend, your Highness?' asked Belinda, blushing.

'Heavens no, I should say not,' he said, chuckling. 'There would be the dickens to pay.'

'But, sir, a handsome man like you, if I dare say so –' Gina began.

'I am husband to fourteen concubines, at my last count. They would all take a very dim view if I had a girlfriend. I'd be in no end of a pickle.'

Jan licked her teeth, parted her thighs wider and quite openly stroked her swelling cunt lips, glistening with come. 'But don't you whip them, sir, to keep them obedient?' she murmured.

'Yes, of course. Royal females must be whipped every day, by our custom. I mostly whip them myself – one must set an example – but sometimes delegate to the women themselves, or have a male servant do it, which saves me the bother. Royal females are rather demanding.'

'It sounds awfully cruel,' Clarice said, eyes wide and panties stained moist.

'I suppose it is. But my females would take umbrage if they weren't whipped, and they do take a perverse delight in whipping each other.'

'Are they very beautiful?' blurted Belinda, eyes fastened on his monstrously erect cock.

'They must be the nation's choicest, by law,' he said. 'I myself have no say in the matter. The females most blessed of buttock and quim become the prince's concubines. I am permitted to choose the choicest female as my prime concubine.' He smiled shyly. 'May I say that, if one of the beautiful ladies present here were my subject, it would be my pleasant duty to enslave her as my prime concubine.'

The girls cooed and twitched. Belinda's shorties were so sopping with come she longed to strip them off and show her wet cooze to the prince.

'Enslave?' she blurted. 'That sounds ever so glamorous – a hareem slave, swathed in filmy robes and scented with exotic perfumes, eating marshmallow and drinking sherbet by a fountain.'

'Alas, my concubines are obliged by law to remain naked, save for adornments of precious metal,' he said. 'It accords with their duties, which are to service their master at all hours.'

'You mean, you just snap your fingers, and a slave girl comes rushing, to open her legs, and . . . you know . . . do it?' Belinda gasped.

'Again, I don't have much say in the matter. Concubines tend to be . . . aggressive. I scarcely have time to snap my fingers.'

Belinda unhooked her bra. 'I hope you don't mind, your Highness,' she gasped, 'but I'm awfully hot, and, if you are used to nude girls, why –'

She ripped off her bra and slithered out of her come-soaked shorties; impishly, she squeezed the panties gusset and drips of come splattered her bare feet.

'Well, if you're going to –' Clarice exclaimed, defiantly stripping off.

The four girls sat, quivering in the full bare, bubbies quivering and quims oozing limpid shiny come.

'Delicious tea,' said Amur, shifting slightly, so that his trousers ballooned round his massive pole. 'I absolutely live on tea.'

'Oh, so do I,' chorused four girls.

'Another pot, your Highness? said Clarice.

'Well, if it's not too much trouble.'

'Shan't be a jiffy.'

As her bare bum wiggled into the kitchen, Dr Warrior snapped her fingers. 'If you girls have finished shamelessly exciting my patient,' she said, 'it's time for business. Amur, get them off this instant.'

Amur rose and padded to the bathroom, with that curious jingling of bells. Breathlessly, jaws dropping, the girls cocked their ears, to the sound of clothes sliding to the floor, water splashing and the slap of soap and sponge.

'He's too shy to boast,' she continued, helping herself to a Balkan Sobranie, 'but a prince is traditionally revered for his excellence of sex organ – size, and in particular, stamina. We all know that with skilful, frequent masturbation girls may achieve limitless orgasm – you may consult my pieces in the *Manchester Guardian* – but it is less well known that certain males are also thus endowed. They may pleasure a female, and in instants harden again, ready with a fresh load of spunk. Amur is one such heavy creamer. Excessive virility makes him priapic, with his organ perpetually stiff. The task of royal concubines is to drain their master of spunk, by demanding sexplay day and night, just as his duty is to whip and enhance their bottoms. Here in Lancashire, Amur's virility is a condition, rather than a virtue, and so I regularly milk him of spunk to normalise him. The music from his sex organ is due to gold balls inserted under noble cockskins by a benign surgical procedure.'

Amur returned in the nude, his sex pole erect, slapping his belly, with the black glans shining well above his navel, and the massive ball sac like rocks beneath his gleaming shaft. His body gleamed completely hairless, the cock and balls shaven smooth as satin. All the girls gasped, and clasped fingers to mouth.

'A bare cock,' panted Jan. 'Oh, I'm going to come, just looking.'

'Amur is going to fuck me, perhaps several times, and then we shall play other sex games. May I have volunteers to assist me?' purred Dr Warrior.

Belinda was the first to put her hand up, followed like lightning by Jan and Gina.

'Me!' cried Clarice from the kitchen.

She bustled back, almost dropping her tea things when she saw Amur's massive cock, knobbed with the gold balls, swaying beneath the ebony skin. Without being aware of moving, Belinda was on her knees at his feet, beside Jan and Gina, their lips inches from his swollen balls. The naked girls whined, gasping and drooling, titties heaving and spreading their cooze lips with eager, inviting fingers. Amur stood over them, his arms folded.

'There will be enough for all of you,' he said. 'Your delicious bottoms make my orbs brim with spunk.'

Impishly, Belinda swivelled, and crouched with her bum high and spread, so that, instead of her quim, she presented her anus bud. She prised her buttocks fully apart, and wriggled her cunt basin, exposing her pendant, come-slimed gash flaps and her crinkling, pouting anus pucker, its brown whorl opening and closing. Amur's nostrils flared, as his cock jingled loudly.

'I must spunk in this one, first,' he hissed, seizing Belinda, who shuddered, as his massive glans nudged her anus bud.

'Oh, your Highness,' she gasped. 'I've never – I'm a bit frightened.'

'The prince must have his way,' Dr Warrior said, placing her fingers on her clitoris, and licking her lips. 'You are going to be modern about this, Belinda?'

'Ooh . . .' Belinda moaned, as her bum writhed, with the stiff tool poking in a savage thrust into her anus, and the gold jingle balls raking her anal elastic. 'Ahh! Gosh, it hurts.'

Tears sprang to her eyes.

A second thrust penetrated her rectum, and Belinda squirmed, gasping for breath, as his huge bell end slammed her sigmoid colon.

'Oh! Oh! Oh! I can't take it, you're so big!'

'You asked for it, you slut,' snarled Jan.

Amur began a vigorous buggery, grasping her hips and slapping her buttocks against his balls, as he thrust the massive knobbed cock through her rectum. Come spurted from Belinda's cooze, as she threshed beneath the male's powerful buggery, with her titties bouncing helplessly. His cock slid from her rectum, with just the peehole nuzzling her anus bud, then slammed back vigorously to fill her chamber, and pound her colon.

'Ooh!' Belinda panted. 'It hurts so much. Oh, yes! Fuck my bum, shame me, hurt me! Watch me squirm for you. Fill me with that huge awful cock . . .'

He buggered her for over three minutes, with the watching girls at a crouch, discreetly wanking off. Dr Warrior made no secret of her voluptuous masturbation, squelching her fingers deep into her slit and pummelling her extruded stiff clitty, while tweaking her hard nipples with little excited gasps.

'Ooh! Oh! Yes!' Belinda groaned. 'I'm bursting! Split me! Give me your cock! Squirt your hot spunk in my bum! Fuck me, fuck me . . . oh, I'm going to come . . . yes, yes, yes!'

Her body shook, and come sprayed from her twitching cooze flaps, as her belly heaved in orgasm, with little choked yelps of pleasure gurgling in her throat. Amur made no sound, save for a slight rapidity of breath, as his cock spurted cream to her arse root so copiously that spunk bubbled from the lips of Belinda's cruelly stretched anus. His cock, half stiff, made a loud plopping sound, as he pulled it from the girl's clinging rectum. Belinda grabbed his bum and clasped his wet cock to her face. She took his balls, dripping with spunk and her own arse grease, into her gaping mouth and sucked and licked them, then slid her lips up his tumescent shaft to his glans, which she enclosed in her mouth, and began to play her tongue across his peehole. The cock stiffened almost at once to full rigidity.

There were hisses from the other girls, until Dr Warrior said that Amur was a prince, and it was most important for his therapy that he command at all times. Her eyes were glazed, her belly trembling, as she masturbated.

'Go on, Belinda,' she gasped. 'I'm having a lovely wank.'

The kneeling Belinda's head bobbed up and down like a pigeon's, as her lips sucked Amur's slimy cock, descending to press the balls, before rising to the glans, filling her mouth with the massive helmet, while she licked his peehole. Gasping, she released his cock and clasped his balls, pulling him down towards her, as she lay back on the floor, with her thighs open, and her wet pink cunt winking at his tool.

'Amur, your Highness, please fuck my twat,' she gasped. 'I'm pretty much a virgin. I so want yours to be the first cock spurting in my pouch.'

Amur sank on top of her, pushing her legs almost straight, thigh backs flat, and ankles in her hair. He grasped her titties, and began to squeeze them viciously, tweaking and flicking the stiff nipples with his nails, and grabbing the whole teats to roll them up and down, almost wrenching the bruised bubs from her rib cage.

'It's so good,' Belinda moaned. 'Hurt me, spank my titties!'

Her clitty stood stiffly erect, between her soaking cunt folds; jerking his hips, Amur began to flick the clit with his peehole. He fucked her clitoris for nearly a minute, with his gold cock balls jingling, until Belinda exploded in a second orgasm, and, as she gasped and wailed, writhing in pleasure, her buttocks slithering in the pool of come from her cunt, Amur penetrated her slit with his whole tool; he rammed in a single thrust, until her cunt was filled and his glans reamed her wombneck.

'Ohh . . . I need it . . . yes!' Belinda drooled, threshing beneath him.

He pinioned her by her calves, with her thighs pressed against her belly, and placed his whole weight on her as he fucked her cunt.

'Ooh! Ahh! Yes, fuck me, fuck me hard,' she gasped.

Her buttocks banged with loud slaps on the flagstones, rising from the floor to meet his bucking balls, as his cock slammed her. Come squirted from her fucked cunt, bubbling from the mashed cooze flaps, to slime her belly and drip down her perineum to her cock-bruised anus pucker. She thrust her loins up, to smack his belly at each cock plunge, with her trembling erect clitty smacked by his pubic bone.

'Ooh! I don't believe it,' she whimpered. 'I'm coming . . . again . . . oh! . . . oh! Oh!'

Come poured from her cunt, as Dr Warrior flicked her own nubbin in the approach of climax; the wanking girls gasped, rolling their eyes and drooling, as they watched the massive cock and balls plunge, squelching, into Belinda's spread gash, the ebony cockshaft hammering the wet pink flesh of the open cooze. Amur's breath quickened, and his fucking became a blur, with his bell end pounding the wombneck and his cream spurting into Belinda's wet cunt. The doctor and girls wanked themselves to gasping comes, while Belinda's loins squirmed, her bum slapping the floor in a frenzy, with Amur's spunk frothing from her cunt lips, and sliming her thighs and arse cleft with spunk and girl come.

'Yes! Yes! Yes . . . Ahh!' she moaned, spasming once more.

Amur withdrew his slimy cock from her cunt lips, still pulsing and spurting come. He sat rather daintily, reached for his teacup and drained it, then snapped his fingers. Dr Warrior sprang to light him a cigarette, then mopped his cock with her perfumed hankie. Clarice promptly poured him fresh tea. Flushed with orgasm, the girls kneeled, cooing, at his feet, with their own teacups shaking in their fingers and fresh cigarettes wet between their lips. Belinda slurped her own tea, scrabbling for one of Jan's Gold Flake, then lighting it. They smoked with deep drags and luxuriant puffs and drank tea, gazing at Amur's face, solemn and – Belinda thought, her cunt tingling – deliciously contemptuous. Girls must be sluts to please a male, and must relish his disdain for their sluttishness.

After less than a minute, his cock trembled, swelled and began to rise. Instantly, Dr Warrior had his bell end enveloped in her scented hankie, and was gently rubbing the glans through the cloth. She caressed the neck and corona of the glans, and ran her fingertip up and down his frenulum. His balls shivered, and his cock trembled to massive hardness.

'Why, doctor, you certainly know how to place a chap in your power,' he gasped. 'When you touched me there – you remember – with your – oh, a woman's perfumed cloth on my organ, it's ecstasy. I can refuse you nothing.'

'Then I shall organise the rest of your therapy,' said Dr Warrior. 'Belinda's been done – Clarice, will you suck and swallow?'

'I'd prefer bum.'

'Right-ho. You, Gina?'

'Yum, sucking that! Lovely.'

'Then who's for twat?'

'I'll spread,' Jan volunteered.

'Me, first, though,' said Dr Warrior. 'You don't mind my juices on his tool?'

'No, doctor,' Jan said, 'but how – I mean, your quim hoop –'

Dr Warrior coyly twirled the golden cunt ring. 'It's made just for him,' she confided.

Clarice spread cushions on the floor; Belinda sat, smoking and watching, dazed, with her slit and rectum glowing from the fullness of the African's cock, and her bum quite sore from stone burn, as the therapist girls coupled with the priapic prince. First was Dr Warrior, who made Amur lie on his back, with his cock towering above his belly. She played with his balls, stroking the sac with dainty fingertips, then stroked the shaft, tickling and teasing, but without rubbing or stimulating his bulging black glans, while masturbating her own quim, until her cunt ring dripped with come.

'I love the feel of cock and balls,' she purred, 'so adorable and soft, like a bottom, then swelling and stiffening to a huge hard knob, all fierce and terrifying and yummy, and so come-making, when everything's shaven completely bare. All girls would really like to have a cock and balls, just to play with, like a fluffy toy. We must make do with our clitties and train them to be big, as the African girls do.'

Thighs split, she straddled Amur, lubricating his cock with her come, before sliding it deftly through her cunt ring, and into her slit. The cunt ring clamped Amur's cock just at his balls and Dr Warrior began to bounce up and down, rising, to let his cock slide fully out, and the peehole tickle her erect clit, before thudding down with a gasp, as his organ penetrated her to the balls. She fucked him for several minutes, while masturbating her nubbin, and brought herself off three times, her pulsing quim lips squeezing his cock, until he grunted softly, and a flood of spunk erupted from her gash to wash his pumping balls. Belinda was hot and wet, and could not resist a new wank, rubbing her throbbing clitty, as she squirmed in her chair.

She paused in her wank, as Amur joined the girls for more cups of tea, before resuming position for Gina to fellate him. Gina crouched over his stiff cock, taking the glans in her lips, then swooping to plunge the tool right to her throat. Masturbating vigorously, and twice gasping in climax, she sucked his cock for over five minutes, before Amur made his delightful little grunt, and Gina's throat bobbed, as she swallowed his copious jet of spunk.

Next up was Clarice, who crouched, buttocks spread, on the cushions, wiggling her bottom, until she gasped, as Amur's cock cleaved her anus. Her face contorted in pain, but with a leer at Belinda, she began to buck her bum to meet the slaps of his hips and the gurgling squelch of his cock, ramming her colon. It did not take long for Clarice to orgasm under buggery, and Amur bummed her to two more spasms, before ejaculating his load of creamy white spunk, which dribbled from her pouting anus down her shuddering thighs.

After more tea, Jan took Clarice's place, opening her cunt to Amur's throbbing, grease-slimed cock, and wrapping her legs around his neck, as he bucked her. Jan heaved with so much gurgling, moaning and gasping that it was hard to spot her climaxes, but Belinda was sure she had at least three. All the girls wanked off, including Dr Warrior, advising on various subtle caresses to prolong the pleasure of a slow wank. Amur signalled his completion, and Jan's cunt flowed with mingled spunk and girl come, her juice flowing in torrents from her bright pink cooze flesh.

Gina insisted on masturbating the prince to new stiffness, with her lips and fingertips playing on his glans, until she clamped his stiff, jingling cock in her armpit. Masturbating her clit, she pumped her biceps, while squelching his glans in her sweaty crevice, until he spurted copious spunk all over her naked breasts. Beaming, Gina rubbed the spunk into her nipples, as she wanked off to climax.

After a tea break, Dr Warrior demonstrated 'goosing'. She lay on her back, thighs up, and Amur mounted her, sandwiching his member between her thighs, inches from her cooze. Dr Warrior's thighs pumped as if riding a bicycle, squeezing and pulling his cock, until he spurted all over her belly, with drops splashing her titties. Like Gina, she maassaged her teats with his spunk.

'So much cream in those balls,' she purred, tickling his scrotum. 'Someone must queen him – you, Belinda.'

'Queen?'

'Sit on his face, of course,' said Jan. 'Make him lick your cooze and clitty. It's ever so lush!'

8

Dogging Girl

'I'll – I'll do my best,' Belinda blurted.

Amur lay prone, his huge ribbed cock beckoning her. He parted his lips; she squatted over his face, in dunging position.

'Oops, sorry,' she gasped, as come plopped onto his nose.

'Ahh . . .' he sighed.

He drew her hips down to his face, until Belinda's cunt and buttocks squashed him. She felt his tongue exploring her slit, and his nose wriggling inside her anus. Balancing over his face, with her feet braced on the flagstones, she adjusted to his directions, as he steered her by the hips, her cunt basin sliding up and down on his nose, eyes and lips, with come spurting copiously from her twitching gash flaps.

'Lift your feet off the floor, and put the full weight of your bum on him,' urged Jan.

'All of it? I'm rather afraid.'

'He wants you to.'

Gingerly, Belinda obeyed, raising her thighs and calves, with her feet balanced on Amur's chest. He sighed, a long gurgle of pleasure, and Belinda gasped, as his tongue probed her pouchmeat, penetrating and stabbing her gushing cooze, almost to the wombneck, then rolling out, to slurp at her tingling clitty. Belinda blurted that she was unsteady, and didn't know what to do with her feet.

'Shrimp him,' said Jan. 'You haven't your total weight on him yet. Stretch your legs, and wank his cock with your feet. Crush his face with that big meaty bum. It's what fellows like.'

Belinda clasped the huge cock between her bare feet, squashing his face with her buttocks. His whimpers and tongue-fucking were frenzied, as she began to roll his cockflesh between her toes. His bum thumped on the ground, and he moaned, as she caressed his glans with her sole, then the peehole with her big toes, sliding down to frig his balls, legs pumping, with her sweaty thighs rubbing his chin. His frigged cock rang with bells, as her cunt gushed come all over his bum-crushed face, and she could feel his throat heaving, as he swallowed her juice.

His cock began to buck, and she knew his spurt was coming after only a couple of minutes' shrimping; Clarice was glowering jealously. Belinda panted, sweat pouring from her bouncing bubbies and armpits and mingling with the come sluicing from her tongue-fucked cunt. Her belly heaved and fluttered. Amur's lips enfolded her whole gash flaps, and sucked them like a lollipop, with his stiff tongue reaming her nubbin, as her cunt squelched loudly.

'Ooh . . . yes . . . ooh . . .' she moaned, at the first drop of cream from his peehole.

She tickled and squeezed the neck of his glans, his peehole and frenulum, and a fountain of creamy spunk splattered her wanking toes.

'Yes . . . Ahh! Ah! Ah!' Belinda whimpered, as her cunt spurted come and orgasm convulsed her.

Amur's cock spurted jet after jet of hot spunk, until Belinda's bare feet were bathed in the sticky cream. With a last sucking kiss to her cunt, Amur lifted her bottom and sat up, his face glazed with her come.

'I am perfectly drained,' he pronounced. 'Such pretty feet! How fortunate you are in Lancashire, girl, and not Africa! Otherwise, I fear I should be your slave.'

'So,' said Jan, 'you're no longer a virgin. Happy?'

'Yes,' said Belinda. 'I feel dreamy.'

The girls walked to the bus stop, in the rays of the sun setting over Morecambe Bay.

'And both holes,' Jan murmured. 'What a cock!'

'Jan, don't be crude,' said Belinda, blushing. 'It was so lovely. I'm still hot, from his fabulous . . . you know. My toes are still sticky from all his cream. I don't think I'll ever wash my feet.'

Lights sparkled in Dr Warrior's house, and a rhythmic tap-tap-tap drifted through the fragrant evening air, with faint female groans wafting like sighs.

'Dr Warrior seems to like being flogged,' Belinda said.

'Doesn't any girl crave whipping? I bet you'd come and come if Amur thrashed you.'

'So would you,' Belinda retorted.

'We could have used a ride home in his super Lagonda.'

'Don't be so selfish.'

'We could have paid for it by despunking him, sucking that super cock, while he drove.'

'That wouldn't be safe. He'd spurt all over the windscreen, same as he did all over my feet. Gosh, shrimping and queening him was so wonderful! He whimpered, under my bum, as if he was worshipping me!'

'He was,' said Jan. 'Men worship girls' beautiful bottoms, and like being thrashed for their crime of not possessing one.'

'My bottom's awfully sore.'

'But in a nice way.'

'Yes.'

They giggled.

'I can't believe my poor little bummy took that enormous thing, right inside,' Belinda murmured coyly. 'It hurt so, but after a while it was lovely, like being filled up with chocolate cake.'

'And no need for ration coupons,' replied Jan. 'Those knobs on his cock! To come and come!'

'I did.'

'Which did you prefer, twat or bumhole?'

'What a rude question!'

'Then give me a rude answer.'

'I'm not sure,' Belinda murmured. 'Bumhole, perhaps. It was so exciting to be filled, where you'd least expect such gorgeous pleasure. I felt pierced, impaled . . . deliciously helpless.'

'He must have oodles of naked girl slaves,' Jan blurted, 'to whip and bugger. Too shiver-making.'

'A slave? Ugh,' Belinda said. 'Imagine being paraded nude in the African sun, by brutal men, pawing you like a piece of meat, lashing your bottom, to see if you winced, poking into your every orifice, feeling your bubs and twat . . . then being sold, like an animal.'

'I wouldn't mind being his slave. Neither would Clarice. I don't think she's forgiven you, Belinda, for thrashing her – and toe-frotting Amur. She's the jealous type.'

Belinda shrugged. 'You know,' she said, frowning, 'I can't help feeling I've been used for pleasure.'

'How else do you want to be used?' Jan retorted. 'You've a well-blistered bum and filled holes. What else could a girl want?'

'Nothing else,' said Belinda. 'I just want more.'

During the next week, Belinda was obliged to chastise Pte Harry Turp and Pte Ron Prewitt, two of her cheekiest classroom spunks. Beforehand, she revisited Clarice's shop, and enjoyed seeing her face flush, when Belinda coolly drawled, 'Good afternoon, miss, I'd like a pair of your strongest leather tawse, as whippy as possible, for a very naughty boy's bottom.'

The other customers looked shocked or lustful, especially when she flipped up her skirt, just enough to show her shorties, started to pull down the pants and whop her own bare bum, then smiled, and said, 'Oops, not in public,' finally testing the tawse on her stockinged thigh, with a dramatic wince. As the sullen Clarice wrapped her package, she added, 'Boys are so mischievous these days you simply have to whop them on the bare – don't you agree?'

It was worth the three shillings and elevenpence to hear Clarice forced to mutter, 'I surely wouldn't know, miss.'

It certainly did the trick on the two smarmy privates that she whipped in front of the class for insolence. The first licks of the tawse wiped the smirks from their faces. Each took thirty on the bare, while Belinda loudly regretted the good old days, when soldiers were flogged two hundred lashes. By the end of their sets, the titters from the class had given way to silent fidgeting, and the two tawsed boys were fighting to restrain their tears. Their bottoms quivered like hot red jellies, puffed and blistered, yet their cocks were stiff! As Jan had said, Belinda felt deliciously in control. After those beatings, Belinda suffered no more indiscipline, to her relief: each beating rather inconveniently made her quim sopping wet, and she couldn't wait to get to the lav and masturbate.

After her easy afternoon class on Saturday, she left the camp, tripping merrily, and full of vim for the weekend. Would Jan like to see the new Clark Gable film at the Majestic? Should she part her hair high, like Veronica Lake? Did she dare write a note to Amur, at his college in Bolton, telling him – well, hinting – that she missed him and, in particular, his cock, and that she wanked herself to sleep every night thinking of it? A car horn broke her reverie.

She turned and gasped at a Triumph two-litre, two-door roadster, gleaming in silver and scarlet. She had never seen such a gorgeous car, so sleek and powerful. The male behind the wheel wore aviator sunglasses, a brown leather jacket and a red silk cravat. He waved – he was hooting at her! From the gate, soldiers winked, with low whistles – she approached, preparing an angry challenge, when the driver sprang over the side and opened the passenger door for her. It was Alberto Tiepolo.

'Why, lance-corporal!' she blurted.

'Not any longer,' he said. 'Demobbed last week, and free as a bird. Call me Al, by the way, miss. Isn't it a lovely afternoon? Thought you might fancy a spin to Morecambe, dip in the sea, then a nice tea at the Midland Grand Hotel, and a dance at the palais, with a drink or two. They have some really tiddly swing bands there.'

'Oh, I'm not sure . . . I think I have something on,' she said.

'No, you haven't,' he replied.

'How do you know? Anyway, bathing is out of the question. I haven't got my cossie.'

'We'll go to your place and pick it up.'

'Now just a minute! This is an infernal cheek, coming here like this, and assuming – oh, thank you.' She accepted his hand, helping her into the low car seat, fragrant with new leather. 'Gosh,' she said, nestling against the leather. 'Is this yours? Isn't it awfully expensive?'

'Paid cash. Not much change from a thousand nicker. Told you I had a posh roadster, miss, didn't I?'

'I suppose you did. But you mustn't be cross if I didn't believe you.'

'Perhaps I won't. Perhaps. Aye, squaddies do tell fearful fibs.' He gunned the engine, making it roar, and grinned at her. 'I thought of getting a Wolseley, but the Triumph's much spunkier – like you, miss.'

'I say, Al, you are awfully sure of yourself, aren't you?' she said, then gasped, as the car's acceleration squeezed her to her seat. With an involuntary motion, she hitched her pleated blue skirt up, showing her petticoat and stockinged thighs, with a sliver of shiny knickers at the vee of her crotch.

'You bet.'

Alberto's eyes flicked on her exposed legs, and she blushed, ruffling her skirts, but, despite her fussing, there seemed more of her legs on display, with her knickered cooze well exposed. The parachute silk of her shorties tended to crinkle in her quim folds, and she bit her lip, hoping that her naked flaps weren't showing – the gusset would ride up right into her slit – but thankful that she was freshly shaved that morning. Her hair blew in the breeze, and she decided she didn't mind if she was showing, so parted her thighs a teeny bit and felt the wind in her cunt, so knew her gash was visible. She glanced at his crotch, and smiled at his unmistakable bulge. The beast is already stiff! Not quite Amur's, but it will do. Thinking of Alberto's copious spunk cascading into her hand, with his bum reddened by her thrashing, she felt her knicker silk moisten.

'I'm friends with your sister Vergina, you know,' she shouted, in a warning tone.

'I know you know Gina,' he replied, with a wink. 'And I know she knows you.'

'Oh. Um, I see.'

'Gina tells me everything, Belinda. It's all right if I call you Belinda?'

'You already have.' Belinda gulped nervously, then slowly raised her leg and hugged her knee, in mock coyness, showing her top stockings and sussies and baring her whole knickers, the wet gusset snaking inside her bare cunt-lips, between her opened thighs. 'And what has she said about me?'

'Not a lot, except that you were the prettiest girl I'd ever gone with.'

'But I haven't gone with you.'

He flashed his perfect white teeth, his tongue flickering on the uppers. 'That's what we're here to fix, isn't it?'

'Oh, you!' she said crossly. 'You've an answer for everything, haven't you?'

They drove to her home, and he sat with the engine running while she scampered up the stairs. After stripping off, she smoked a cigarette in the nude, while lengthily scanning her wardrobe. Let him wait. When she returned, bare-legged, she wore tennis shoes and white fluffy socks, with a white pleated gym skirt, swaying at mid-thigh, and a green blouse, tucked into her skirt. She vaulted into the Triumph, dumping a kitbag on the floor.

'I've got my cossie on under my dress, and my tiddly frock and shoes and everything, in there,' she explained, smirking, as she noted his still rampant erection.

As he drove into the Morecambe Road, Belinda said she had an idea. 'Let's go a bit further,' she said. 'It's Botts Cove, just down from Bolton-le-Sands, where I grew up. I often used to go there to bathe. It's a bit of a hike over a hilly track, so it's never too crowded.'

They passed Morecambe, and turned into a rutted track, leading across hillocks of beach grass, until they emerged at Botts Cove, a horseshoe of sandy beach, around the mouth of a freshwater stream, and flanked by two secluding rocky outcrops. Barrow-in-Furness shimmered across the sea in the distance, wreathed by warm pink sunlight. Another car, a black Morris Eight, was parked, sloping awkwardly on the dunes, with a couple sitting inside, behind steamed windows. The silhouettes were male and female, writhing in romantic embrace. The Triumph bumped to a halt on the sand, just beside the stream.

'Isn't it lovely?' she said, when they stood on the sand.

'Happen it's not bad,' he admitted. 'Fancy a light ale? I've got some in the boot.'

'Let's bathe first,' Belinda said, 'unless you're the type that rolls his trousers up, with a knotted hankie on his head.'

'Am I heck,' he said, and swiftly stripped to bathing trunks.

Belinda extracted a rubber bathing cap and dark goggles from her bag; she scooped her hair under the cap, knotting the strap at her chin, before snapping the goggles on her head by its rubber band, just like Rita Hayworth in – oh, what was the film? She unbuttoned her blouse, letting her bare breasts spring free, then shed the garment. It was followed by her skirt, under which she was knickerless. Naked, she stood before Alberto, with her hands on her hips.

'Told you I had my cossie on under my dress,' she said, extending her foot. 'Here, unlace me.'

'You, a raw-bather? You bold minx,' gasped Alberto, his erection straining against his trunks, as he unfastened both her shoes. 'What about those people?'

'They won't mind,' she said airily. 'They're too busy snogging. Anyway, who cares if they see?'

She waggled her feet in his face, and he rolled down her socks, pausing to sniff them, with a satisfied smile.

'Lovely pong,' he murmured.

When she was fully nude, she scampered into the sea, followed by Alberto. He followed the bobbing orbs of her foam-slapped buttocks, as she swam far out, then paused, panting and treading water, with her titties bouncing in the lapping wavelets. Behind her, colliers and ferry boats crawled across the horizon.

'People come to Botts Cove to snog,' she panted. 'It's secluded, and you can be as naughty as you like. I haven't been here for years – but isn't that what you had in mind, Alberto?'

'Happen it was, miss – I mean, Belinda.'

'You're a little overdressed, though,' she said, and plunged beneath the water.

'What the heck!' Alberto gasped, as Belinda grabbed his trunks, hoisted the waistband over his stiff cock and pulled them down to his ankles.

A final jerk and the trunks came away. Belinda floated to the surface, broke water and flung the trunks out into the sea, where they sank.

'Don't tell me you're shy,' she trilled. 'Remember, I've seen your beastly bum before.'

She clasped his bare bum, and ran her index finger up and down his arse cleft, until she was stroking his tight balls, with her other hand rubbing his peehole.

'Those trunks cost four and eightpence,' he gasped.

'Then I deserve spanking, don't I?'

She broke away, swimming powerfully in circles, ever nearing the shore, but eluding him. At last, she ran onto the beach and sank to her knees in the surf. Alberto lumbered after her, his stiff cock bobbing at his belly. Grabbing her unresisting waist, he squatted and pushed her over his knee. His hand rose over her wet bare. Smack! Smack! Smack!

'Take that – and that –' he cried, spanking her bottom, with sizzling wet slaps, until her bumflesh glowed pink.

'Ouch! Ooh!' she cried.

Smack! Smack!

'Oh! It hurts! You utter beast.'

Her naked buttocks squirmed under the spanking, with her breasts slapping the sand. He spanked her to fifty, until he rolled her off his thigh, to fall with a wet thump onto the beach.

'Bloody hurts, and all,' he said, shaking his fingers.

Belinda stood up, her ankles washed by surf, and with her reddened bottom facing the parked Morris. She rubbed it very slowly, making a face at Alberto, with the sun glinting in her goggles.

'Not much of a spanking,' she mocked. 'I'd have thought you wanted real revenge for your beating, Lance-Corporal Tiepolo.'

'Come here, baby,' he said, leering.

She moved close, and clasped his balls, squeezing slightly.

'Ooh . . .' he moaned.

'Not so fast, soldier. Get some towels and light ales, while I rinse in the stream.'

Belinda splashed in the fresh water, before returning to rub herself briskly, letting Alberto see her breasts flap as she towelled. He rinsed off too, and they sat naked in the car, swallowing bubbly ale and puffing cigs, with Belinda still wearing her rubber cap and sun goggles.

'That's better,' she said, finishing her bottle. 'Now we can snog.'

'Now you're talking, baby,' he panted, clasping her in a tight embrace, and pressing his lips to hers, with his tongue probing her mouth. His fingers pressed between her locked thighs. 'Come on, baby,' he moaned, 'you know I want only you.'

Belinda's thighs were slippery with the come trickling from her cooze. He forced a passage into the rippling flesh, and reached the lips of her gash.

'Oh, yeah,' he drooled, tonguing her mouth. 'You're the one for me, baby.'

He grasped her breasts, squashing them together and squeezing them hard against her ribcage, with his thumb flicking and slicing her erect nipples. His fingers slipped inside her wet cunt, and began to poke her. Belinda gasped, and her cunt basin and buttocks began to writhe on the leather, slippery with her come.

'Mm!' he whimpered, as her palm cupped his balls, and pressed. His erection twitched against her belly.

'Just a snog, soldier,' she panted, rubbing his balls.

'Don't tease me, baby,' he moaned. 'I've got to go all the way.'

Belinda moved her fingers from his balls to his cocktip. She took his glans between her finger and thumb, and ribbed its swollen stiffness. 'My, you are throbbing,' she gasped, her naked breasts squirming against him.

'Let me inside you, Belinda baby,' he cooed. 'I'll make you the happiest girl in Lancashire.'

'Like all the others, I suppose,' she said, pouting.

'No! Honestly! Other girls were nothing compared to you.'

'Well, go on, then,' she said.

She spread her thighs wide, and guided his cocktip between her gash flaps.

'Oh, yeah, baby!'

Belinda's feet straddled the steering wheel, with the gear lever sticking into her haunch, as Alberto rolled on top of her. Her ankles clasped the small of his back, and she pressed his loins to hers, gasping, as she felt his cock penetrate her right to the wombneck. Buttocks squirming, she raised her cunt to slap against his belly, and meet his vigorous thrusts, while, crushed by his pumping groin, her fingers masturbated her throbbing clitty. The car rocked back and forth as they fucked.

'Gosh, soldier,' she whispered, licking his earlobe, 'you're the biggest ever! Do me with that big soldier's cock.'

'You mean it, baby?'

'Oh, yes,' she panted, wanking hard, as he fucked her.

His cock slammed in and out of her sucking cunt, with loud squelches from her slit, as her come slopped his tool and balls. Belinda glowed with electric pleasure, and her body seemed to float in starlight, as the sweating male pounded her writhing wet slit. This is fabulous; I'm being fucked and filled. Alberto's body passed into shadow; behind him, two figures stood, embracing, as they watched. It was the couple from the Morris, a boy and girl, both nude. She was busily frotting his erect cock, while he wanked her clitty, and played with her bubs. Come dribbled from her cunt.

'Oh, baby,' Belinda shrilled, 'it's the biggest cock I've ever had.'

The masturbating couple panted excitedly. Belinda's belly fluttered, as she neared her come, and, from Alberto's urgent pounding, she sensed his spurt.

'Come on, baby,' she panted, 'give me your load of hot spunk. Fuck me with that big tool. Fill me up.'

That's what Jan would have said. The two spectators, silhouetted against the sun, wanked harder, with little gurgles of delight; abruptly, the girl disengaged, sank to her knees and pressed her face to the male's belly. She took his cock into her mouth and slid it into her throat to begin a vigorous fellation, while tickling his balls and wanking herself with her free hand. Belinda watched, as the male trembled, and his sucked cock bucked, spurting its load of spunk into the girl's mouth, with her throat bobbing, as she swallowed. Driblets of spunk drooled from her sucking lips, down her chin and onto her breasts, where she rubbed the cream into her erect nipples, while squealing in her own spasm.

'Yes, baby,' whimpered Belinda, writhing under Alberto's stabbing cock. 'Do me, split me. Fill me with your spunk . . . oh . . . oh . . . yes!'

Her belly shuddered and her cunt sprayed come over Alberto's balls, while his hot spunk squirted massively to her wombneck. Gasping, Belinda removed her swim cap and goggles, then sat up, wiping her come-slimed cunt with her fingers, and casually rubbing the fluids into her belly.

'Gosh, Belinda, you dirty dogger,' cried the girl. 'I didn't recognise you in your goggles. We saw you spanked – so exciting – and what a lovely fuck from your bloke. Such a big cock – so wet-making. He's a regular – I'd know that super car anywhere.'

Belinda frowned at Alberto, who leered.

'How super you're a Botts Cover,' the girl continued. 'It's the best dogging spot for miles. You've certainly blossomed, Belinda. Jan told me you liked teasing and flashing, so it's logical to go all the way, isn't it? Saturday's the best day for action, especially after dark.'

'Hello, Wendy,' blurted Belinda, to the grinning face and pert breasts and bum of Wendy Pight. 'What on earth is dogging?'

'That's obvious – doing it, for others to watch . . . or join in?'

Her words dangled in the air.

'Yes,' said Belinda, licking her lips, 'why don't you join in?'

'Oh, goody,' chirped Wendy. 'My bloke – I don't know his name – is a really heavy creamer, and I like to despunk him by hand or mouth to get him ready for a long, hard fuck. That's the dogging way; it's so much fun, when you don't know your spunk's name. Yours looks fit, so we can use both of them.'

'Agreed,' said Belinda. 'But on one condition, Wendy. Remember back in 1944, at school, when Captain Garstang thrashed me, and it was your fault?'

Wendy nodded, blushing.

'You'll have to take my spanking, in revenge.'

'Mm . . .' said Wendy, clapping and waggling her trim bare bum. 'I'd love you to spank me, Belinda. Actually, ever since that day, it's been one of my fantasies.'

'Agreed, then?'

'Agreed.'

Belinda delved in her bag, and produced the shining, oiled tawse. Wendy paled.

'Wait a minute,' she gasped.

'You agreed to take my spanking, Wendy,' said Belinda.

'Yes, but –'

'Even though I didn't specify what with.'

'Want me to hold the cheeky minx, baby?' sneered Alberto.

'Yes, please.'

He sprang from the car, and pinioned Wendy across the bonnet, while her bloke secured her ankles. Wendy threshed and squirmed helplessly. Belinda stood behind her with the tawse, and caressed the girl's bare buttocks.

'Such a lovely bottom, Wendy,' Belinda purred. 'And such a shame to mark it. But shame is what you deserve.'

The tongues flashed in the pink sunlight, whipping Wendy squarely across her buttocks, which clenched tight.

'Ooh,' Wendy gasped. 'Oh! That hurts.'

'Of course it hurts.'

Wendy's squirming bottom assumed a vivid, blotchy red, as the tawse weals mingled.

'Oh! Ah! Steady on, Belinda, that's awfully tight.'

'I suppose Jan doesn't whip you as hard,' Belinda sneered.

Thwap!

'Ooh! How do you know . . .?'

Thwap!

'Ahh!'

'I know lots of things. That's not all you do, is it?'

Wendy's ankles strained against the fists restraining her, and, as her flogged buttocks clenched and squirmed, her breasts thumped the car bonnet. The males, holding her fast, smiled, as her lithe nude body wriggled on the hot metal.

'Urrgh! So we play games, what of it?'

'What sort of games?'

'You know, kissing and cuddling, and wanking off. We go dogging if we have a bloke with a car, and put on a lesbo show, each of us sucking the other's twat, and drinking the come. But it's just in fun. Surely you're not jealous? That's so old-fashioned.'

Thwap!

'Ahh! That's enough, Bel, honestly.'

'Not even twenty. Not enough. You're jolly well right, I'm jealous,' Belinda spat.

Another car, a silver-grey Humber, glided to a halt and parked several yards away on the other side of the stream, and Belinda saw the glint of binoculars. Sweat pouring from her, and her bubbies bouncing high, with each stroke of the tawse, Belinda continued Wendy's flogging to well past thirty strokes.

'Ooh . . . no . . . no . . .' Wendy wailed, squirming, as the bruises on her whipped bum turned to deep purple trenches.

At the thirty-seventh stroke, she pissed herself, a long fountain of steaming golden fluid splashing down the bonnet of the Triumph.

'My car!' growled Alberto. 'Make the bitch pay, baby.'

Belinda flogged the sobbing, squirming girl over sixty lashes, until Wendy's bum was purple with welts, and she banged her head on the bonnet, arching her back in agony, at each cut of the leather to her bare, with her cunt and belly slithering in a pool of her own come. Belinda's gash oozed come, which trickled down her thighs, as her stiff clitty throbbed. She put her fingers to her clit, and began to wank. Both males licked their lips. At last, Wendy sobbed, 'Please, Belinda . . .'

'Please what, you slut?' Belinda snarled.

'Please, my bum's so hot. I need tooling. Please, someone fuck me in the bumhole,' she whimpered.

The males released Wendy, who fell to her knees, clasped Belinda's bottom and pressed her face to Belinda's cunt.

'Wendy! What the –' Belinda gasped. 'I'm not a lesbo.'

'Neither am I, so we can have fun, while I'm buggered,' Wendy panted. 'Thank you for my gorgeous whipping.'

She began to kiss and suck Belinda's dripping cooze and engorged clitty. The males grabbed Belinda by her wrists and ankles, and draped her on her back across the car bonnet, with her thighs spread wide, while Belinda moaned in protest, yet engulfed by the electric thrill in her wet cunt from Wendy's artful tonguing. Wendy continued gamahuching her come-slimed slit, while her bloke wrenched Belinda's hair, so that her head drooped backwards over the far side of the bonnet. Face buried in Belinda's cunt, Wendy presented her spread buttocks, and squealed, as Alberto's erect cock penetrated her anus. Her nose and jaw slammed against Belinda's cooze, as her body jolted under the force of his buggery. Belinda's mouth hung open, dripping drool, as her head, upside down, swayed back and forth against the metal.

'Urrgh,' she gurgled, as Wendy's bloke thrust the swollen glans of his cock, right between her lips.

'Suck me, miss,' he murmured, 'and make sure you swallow every drop of my cream.'

Stretched over the car bonnet, Belinda wriggled wildly, as the giant tool rammed her throat. Her thighs and buttocks threshed, as the buggered Wendy tongued her gushing cooze, and she began to suck the stiff cock penetrating her mouth. She got her tongue to the peehole, licked it, then raised her head and engorged the cock right to his balls, where she began to nibble with her teeth, before sliding her mouth up to the neck of his glans and pressing hard with her lips. Between her caresses, the bloked fucked her mouth, as if it was a cunt.

'Nngh! Nngh!' she squealed, as he wrenched her hair really hard, hurting her.

Her come flowed in torrents, as Wendy chewed and sucked her distended clitty, with Wendy herself gurgling, as she was buggered. Belinda's belly fluttered; she felt the bloke's cock start to tremble, and knew he was near spurt, while her own orgasm swelled in her gamahuched cunt. She tasted the first drop of spunk at the peehole, got her tongue on his frenulum and licked hard, squeezing the knob with her lips, as a jet of spunk filled her mouth so copiously that it sprayed from her lips and dripped into her nose and eyes, before soaking her hair in the sticky hot cream.

'Mm . . . mm . . . urrgh!' she groaned, swallowing his torrent of spunk, as her body shuddered in orgasm, and she heard her cries joined by Wendy's staccato moans, as Alberto buggered her to her own climax.

'Ooh!' she shrieked, as the bloke wrenched her spunk-smeared face up by her hair.

'I told you to swallow every drop, slut,' he snarled. 'Now see what you get.'

Wendy helped them roll and pinion Belinda, face down, over the bonnet.

'No – no . . .' Belinda whimpered. 'I did what you want. This isn't fair. Alberto, do something.'

'I'll do something,' grunted Alberto.

He lifted her tawse high above her naked bottom. *Thwap*! The tongues lashed Belinda's bare.

'Ooh! No!' she squealed.

Thwap! *Thwap*!

'Ahh!'

Thwap! *Thwap*!

'Oh! Oh!'

Her cries were muffled by Wendy's cunt pressed to her lips. Head up, Belinda tongued the girl's wet slit, her teeth round the engorged nubbin, and chewing hard, while Wendy's loins writhed, her cunt gushing come, and the girl emitted little mewling squeaks of pleasure.

'Do me, Bel, suck my twat hard,' she gasped.

As Alberto thrashed her, Belinda sucked and swallowed copious come from Wendy's writhing slit. *Thwap*!

'Ahh!' she moaned into Wendy's cooze flaps, as Alberto whipped her wet gash and arse cleft.

Thwap! The tawse sliced her anus.

'Mm! No . . .' she groaned.

Thwap! The leather bit her throbbing nubbin.

'Oh! Oh! No . . .'

A long jet of piss hissed from Belinda's flogged cunt lips.

'Thought you could disrespect a soldier of the king, eh?' hissed Alberto.

Thwap! *Thwap*!

'Uh . . . ooh . . . ahh . . .' Belinda sobbed.

Her tawsing continued until her bottom throbbed with smarts, and she knew it would look a right picture, all red and black and purple, just like Wendy's. She tongued Wendy to orgasm, with Wendy's cunt juice filling her throat, and then shrieked, as she felt a cock enter her anus.

'No, please . . .' she gasped, but felt her buttocks writhe, thrusting to meet her buggerer's thrusts, as his cock filled her rectum and the tip slammed her sigmoid colon. She wasn't sure whose cock it was, and her come spurted at the naughtiness. 'Urrgh,' she spluttered, as Wendy's cunt splashed a stream of piss in Belinda's face, washing away her bloke's crusted spunk.

Belinda bucked powerfully, meeting the buggerer's thrusts, and slammed her erect clitty on the car bonnet, bringing her to orgasm once more, before she felt her rectum fill with hot spunk, and the cock soften and leave her arse with a plop, to be replaced at once by another cock, which recommenced her buggery. Her belly slithered, heaving and squirming on the car bonnet, slimed with her spurting come. The cock buggered her for several minutes, before it too squirted its load of hot cream inside her glowing hot arsehole, to be replaced by a third cock. Another bloke – from the Humber!

Writhing and groaning under a really quite savage bum-fucking, Belinda glanced round, and saw, through her tears, Wendy fucked from behind by Alberto, with her bloke fucking a slender slip of a girl wearing glasses, with short brown hair, a huge bum and small, boyish titties, while the two girls' mouths locked in a sucking French kiss. She orgasmed, as her bum was filled with spunk, and kneeled, to take her buggerer's come-slimed cock and balls into her mouth to lick him stiff again.

Darkness was falling, and more cars purred into Botts Cove. Shadowy figures of girls and boys watched, then joined in. By starlight, Belinda opened her legs for cock after cock, with Wendy squirming and groaning beside her, and occasional pauses for light ale. Writhing under buggery, she howled, her cunt spewing juice, at teeth biting her bottom, belly and bubbies, and yelped repeatedly in super orgasms, as lips sucked her throbbing, distended clitty, while she drank come from cunts squashed on her face. As an eager tongue poked her juicing slit, she felt something smooth sliding on her shaven cunt hillock – the slender girl's glasses.

Her rectum ached; her buttocks smarted dreadfully, and she couldn't wait to see how puffy her bruises looked in the glass and enjoy a super wank, as she stroked her wealed bumflesh. Wendy was right – a modern girl shouldn't be jealous, when there was so much pleasure to be had. It was such a shivery, nameless thrill to be fucked by unknown blokes and tongue cunts of unknown girls! At last, panting, they disengaged, and prepared for the drive home.

'That was super, Bel,' cried Wendy, glowing. 'Thank you so much for . . . you know, doing me.'

'Thank you for doing me,' Belinda murmured.

'So you'll be a regular at Botts Cove?'

'I'd love to. We could ask Jan to make a threesome. And we girls can all whip our blokes.'

'Hey up,' said Alberto. 'What if the blokes object?'

'Blokes?' sneered Wendy. 'A dogging girl is never short of blokes, baby.'

9

Thrashed Nude

'Put your hand on my bottom, Al. I mean, really on my bottom.'

'What, here?'

'Go on.'

They were dancing cheek to cheek to a slow tune from Ronaldo Rimini's Accrington Swing Band. Al slid his hand over Belinda's croup to her arse cleft and gasped, touching bare skin.

'You've no knickers,' he blurted. 'And your skirt's unfastened.'

'Thought I'd make it easy for you,' she purred, grinding her crotch against his erection.

'Everybody'll see.'

'We're doggers!'

'But this isn't Botts Cove.'

'Afraid to grope a girl's bare bum? Go on, they'll be so jealous.'

Belinda's unpinned frock fell away from her stockinged thighs, revealing her naked bottom, black American nylons – dear Wendy! – and scarlet sussies. In the smoky, perfumed dimness of the dance floor, Belinda's gleaming moons flashed amid the couples shuffling to a slow smooch. Just below the bandstand, Belinda spied Clarice Warrior dancing with a tall, good-looking spunk and she knew Clarice saw her, by her jealous glare. Al cupped each fesse and rubbed her bum, then slid his finger up and down her crack, caressing the spinal nubbin, and the soft perineum just before her anus.

'Ooh, that tickles,' she whispered, nibbling his ear. 'Don't stop.'

She lowered her hand, pressed his balls, then got his stiff bell end between her fingers, and began to rub.

'You'll have me spurting in my bloody pants,' he gasped.

'Then I'll spank you for being a mucky boy.'

'You've a cheek.'

'Two, actually. Ooh!'

Al's fingers penetrated her wet cunt, and jabbed in and out, while his free hand rubbed her bottom. Snogging couples noticed Belinda's bare, and snogged harder. Clarice writhed, heels off the floor, in a clinch with her spunk. Belinda unbuttoned Al's fly, and took out his naked cock. Her fingers glided over his peehole, as his hand squelched her streaming cooze.

'You'll wet my nylons,' she murmured, frigging his throbbing bare glans, with caresses to the neck and corona, and little slicing jabs with her nails.

Ronaldo Rimini's band concluded the slow smooch, jumping seamlessly into a fast jitterbug. Couples began to whirl, with skirts flying, to show knickers and sussies. The more athletic swains lifted their partners off the floor, even onto their shoulders, whirling the girls like hoops. Belinda leaped up to clasp Al's neck with her hands and his bottom with her ankles.

'Do me,' she hissed.

'You've a right sauce,' he gasped, as she pushed his stiff cock into her cunt, clamping the small of his back with her legs.

They began to whirl, Belinda's body spinning like a top, while she jerked her buttocks and cunt up and down on his impaling cock, with loud sucking slurps, as her come sprayed his balls. Her titties bounced under her strapless black frock – for really bold girls, whose titties needed absolutely no support – until the left bub spilled from its slender satin mooring and shone naked, with the big strawberry nipple fully erect.

'Tuck me in, baby,' Belinda panted, as nearby couples gaped.

Al popped her breast back under the cloth, leaving his hand to squeeze the naked teat. Belinda's bum lunged back and forth at his groin, as his cock stabbed her wombneck and come gushed from her fucked cooze to dribble down her thighs and bum onto the dance floor. Goody, with my legs up, my nylons won't get wet. Ronaldo Rimini, leering from the stage, waved his conductor's baton faster, and Belinda's bum bounced in the jitterbug rhythm, the squelching noises from her twat growing louder beneath the swirling frock. Al wiggled his hips, plunging his cock into her.

'Isn't this dogging?' she gasped. 'I'm going to come ever so soon. Ooh . . . yes, feel my juice spurting. Yes, here it is . . . oh! Oh! Ohh!'

As Belinda orgasmed, her head twirling, eyes rolling and jaw drooping, both breasts popped from her cleavage, but she let them bounce bare. Al grunted in his own spurt, his cock bucking, his balls caressed by her silky dress, as he filled her cunt with spunk. With a squelchy plop, as her cunt slid from his cock, Belinda dropped to the floor, and tucked her bubbies in. Covering his bare cock with her dress, she exposed her own bum and thighs, while she slapped the slimy tool back into his trousers.

She continued to dance, twirling, with her skirt flying over her waist, revealing her naked bottom, and thighs glistening with come and spunk. As Ronaldo Rimini flourished a deafening finale, there was scattered but hearty applause from the dancers, smiling at Al and Belinda. Panting, they reached the bar, where Al ordered a benny sour – Benedictine liqueur and sarsparilla – for Belinda, with light ale for himself.

'Have one yourself, darling,' he said to the buxom barmaid, a sloe-eyed, twentyish brunette with bulging cleavage, wearing a slinky sequinned dress, slit high over her thighs.

'Mind if I make it a stiff one, cowboy?' she murmured, licking her lips, while unashamedly ogling his crotch. 'I'd love something long and wet.' She opted for a benny sour, like most of the girls at the bar, putting a candy-striped pink straw into her glass, then sucking noisily. 'That's better,' she said, wiping her lips. 'I'd love to dance like you two.'

'Anyone can, if you know how,' Belinda said.

'I know how – just can't get enough of it. That's why I'm a regular at Botts Cove.'

Her mascara-laden eyelid flicked a wink. Belinda spotted Clarice at the end of the bar with her spunk, but Clarice didn't say hello. Snotty bitch.

'Why, so are we,' Belinda coolly replied. 'We must have seen you.'

'I've certainly seen you,' said the girl, licking her lips. 'My boyfriend drives a blue Riley. Bit chilly to get out and play, with winter here, but it's hot in the car. Do you know what Ron does?' Her voice lowered to a whisper, for Belinda. 'He takes a pair of bicycle clips, and shoves them in my twat, backwards. Holds me open ever so wide, like those doctor's things. Then he fills me up with mushy peas, and eats them.'

'Gosh, that's sounds fun,' Belinda said. 'Once, we did it – you know – in the one-and-ninepennies at the Majestic, with absolutely everybody looking on, and my feet over the seat, so that I could hardly see the screen. It was *Double Indemnity* with Edward G. Robinson – isn't he dishy? The last time it was warm enough to bathe, we brought a couple of my girlfriends, Jan and Wendy, and we put on a show for the watching blokes, cuddling and wanking off and everything. That really got them going, and they biffed each of us in turn. It was super, being done by spunks with no name.'

The girl's nostrils flared. 'You're getting me all steamed up,' she said. 'I'll need a wank soon. But wasn't your twat all sore after so many pokes?'

'No, because I like it in the bum,' Belinda whispered.

'Mm . . . I do need a wank,' the girl gasped.

Ronaldo Rimini joined them, planting a smoochy kiss on the barmaid's lips. Belinda looked at his pencil moustache, and frowned.

'Hey up, Marlene,' he said.

'I was just complimenting the folks on their dancing,' Marlene said, pouting, as she poured him a Worthington's.

'Yeah, it was swell,' said Ronaldo, leering at Belinda, who blushed.

'They're regulars at Botts Cove,' said Marlene.

'Well, well,' said the bandleader, fingering his moustache. 'I thought I recognised you, miss – your bottom, at any rate.'

'Ron, don't be crude,' said Marlene.

'I'm sure I know you, Ron,' Belinda said.

He smiled. 'Wondered when you'd twig, miss. Private Ron Prewitt, as was – demobbed a month ago. "Ronaldo Rimini" gives the band a bit of class, see? Marlene, Miss Beaucul here gave my bare arse the most almighty licking, in the army. I deserved it, of course.'

'So that's where you got those bruises,' Marlene said smirking. 'I do wish I'd been there, to cheer.'

'That geezer up there –' Ron gestured to Clarice's beau '– that's Harry Turp. Couple of weeks to his demob, she thrashed him and all, and he's still got the hump.'

'Gosh,' Marlene said, 'these benny sours go right through me. I have to go to the powder room, or I'll wet myself, if I haven't already.' She smiled at Belinda. 'Coming, Miss Beaucul?'

Belinda followed Marlene's big bum, waggling, on her impossibly high stiletto heels. They passed Clarice, who saw Harry Turp give Belinda a nod of recognition, and glared icily at Belinda. The powder room had two spacious lavatory cubicles, each with its own washbasin, with cracked tiles and rusty pipes spottily daubed in pink paint.

'Isn't it posh?' said Marlene. 'Which cubicle do you want?'

'Oh, after you,' said Belinda.

Marlene was already lifting her dress. 'Scarcely fair to occupy both bogs, when there's room enough for both of us,' she panted.

Trembling, Belinda followed Marlene into the second cubicle. With the door locked, both girls speedily stripped to the bare, but for sussies and stockings. Marlene's eyes widened, seeing Belinda was knickerless. With Belinda nude, Marlene's huge titties burst from her bra, and quivered, jutting unsupported. She rolled down her panties, to reveal a shorn pubis.

'You shave too,' she cooed. 'May I touch?'

Belinda parted her legs, and the girl's fingers stroked her bare hillock before penetrating the quimcrack. Her fingers slurped in the come oozing from Belinda's slit. Belinda stroked Marlene's bare bottom, feeling the gooseflesh pimple the smooth, firm globes. Her hand slipped round the haunch to Marlene's gushing cunt, which soon slimed Belinda's fingers.

'I couldn't wait to diddle,' Marlene gasped. 'See how wet you make me, miss? I've always wanted to try a lesbo. Oh, do me, please?'

Belinda thrust three fingers into Marlene's cunt, and began to poke her wombneck, while thumbing her erect clitty. 'I'm not a lesbo,' she murmured. 'I just like to play games.'

'That's so good,' Marlene moaned. 'Yes, tweak my clitty, fingerfuck me.'

Her fingers probing Belinda's wet slit, she pushed her face to Belinda's titties, and began to lick and chew her nipples. Belinda stiffened her fingers, and spanked Marlene's breasts, slapping the big pink cones of her nipples. Marlene gasped, and her cooze spurted juice over Belinda's wanking hand.

'Harder,' she panted. 'I do love a tit-spank! Ooh, I'm coming off.'

Belinda delivered a vicious breast-spanking, while stabbing Marlene's pouch, and the girl's belly quaked, with come gushing down her thighs.

'Ooh! Ooh!'

As Marlene panted loudly in orgasm, Belinda wrenched her hair and forced her to her knees. 'Now lick me off,' she hissed.

The girl's tongue penetrated Belinda's gash folds, and found her clit. 'What a gorgeous big nub you have,' Marlene cried.

Alternately probing her quim with the tongue, then withdrawing to lick the stiff, throbbing nubbin, Marlene made Belinda gasp in long moans of pleasure and buckle at the knees.

'Drink me,' Belinda ordered.

Marlene's throat bobbed, as she swallowed Belinda's copious cooze slime. Belinda pressed the girl's face to her cunt, and began to pant, as her own climax approached. 'Yes . . . yes . . . I'm almost there,' she gasped, to the gamahuching girl, who wanked off her own clitty, as she tongued Belinda's. 'Yes . . . yes! Ah! Ah! Ah!'

'Won't you give me a spank, Miss Beaucul?' whimpered Marlene, drooling Belinda's come. 'Make my bum red as my bubs?'

Her titties glowed with bruises from Belinda's breast-spanking. Belinda thrust her, crouching, over the lavatory bowl, then squatted and began to spank the quivering fesses. Smack! Smack!

'Ooh!' yelped Marlene.

Smack! Smack!

'Oh! Ouch!'

Smack! Smack!

'Ahh, miss! Harder.'

'Cheeky madam,' Belinda hissed.

Belinda spanked Marlene's squirming bare bottom until the buttocks glowed red with bruises. She forced the clenched nates wide apart, so as to spank directly in the bum cleft and on the streaming cooze, with several spanks reaching deep to slap Marlene's clitty, making the girl squeal. As she spanked, she masturbated her own cunt, with her come dripping copiously, until the tiles were a pool of her fluid. After three minutes' hard spanking, Marlene's quivering arse globes were a blotchy mass of livid puce bruises. Marlene moaned, and suddenly a torrent of piss splashed Belinda, spraying all over the floor and filling the lavatory bowl.

'Ooh! I'm sorry,' Marlene wailed.

'Mucky slut,' snarled Belinda, and spanked harder.

Slap! Slap!

'Ooh, yes, miss, I'm going to come again,' Marlene whimpered, and began to writhe and gasp. 'Ooh, yes! Harder! Spank me to pieces! I'm there! Ahh . . .'

Wanking her own throbbing nubbin, Belinda bent down, and savagely bit Marlene's wriggling croup.

'Yes! Oh, gosh, it's good. Oh, oh . . .' shrieked the orgasming girl, as Belinda's livid red teethmarks joined the spanked bruises on her squirming bare.

Leg up, Belinda jabbed two fingers to her wombneck, with her thumb reaming her clitty, and her gash pouring come, until she, too, moaned in orgasm.

There was a rap on the cubicle door.

'Marlene? I came to see if you are all right. What's going on?' came Ron's voice. He wrenched at the door, and the flimsy fastening gave way. 'What the –' he gasped, then fixed Belinda with a leer. 'So,' he drawled. 'Playing lesbo games, you dirty sow? Nobody spanks my Marlene except me.'

He slammed the door shut, then grabbed Belinda by the hair, kicking Marlene's bottom, so that she toppled, with her breasts squashed in the pool of piss and come.

'Wait,' Belinda pleaded. 'I can explain –'

'Say hello to Shanks of Barrhead,' he sneered.

'Ooh! Urrgh!' Belinda gurgled, as Ron thrust her head into the lavatory bowl, under the yellow water, and held her there, kicking and spluttering, for several seconds.

He pulled her up, and she gasped, liquid spuling from her mouth.

'Please don't hurt me,' she whimpered.

He pushed her head under once more, and she gurgled, swallowing Marlene's piss. He held her for almost a minute, before wrenching her soaked head up, piss dripping from her eyes.

'You going to be quiet, bitch?' he snarled.

'Yes, yes, I promise,' she spluttered. 'I'll do anything –'

Marlene scrambled to her feet, and seized Belinda's hair, forcing her head down. Her face lapping the water, Belinda crouched over the bowl, with her bottom up, and thighs spread wide. She groaned, hearing a belt unbuckled, studs rattling, and slapped into a double thong.

'No, please,' she gasped. 'It was only a playful spanking.'

'Like the one you gave me in class?' Ron spat. 'I haven't forgotten, Miss Beaucul.'

'Ahh!' Belinda cried, as the heavy leather belt lashed her croup, with the studs stinging cruelly on her naked skin.

'Oh! It hurts! You'll ruin my nylons!'

Marlene thrust Belinda's head into the water.

'Urrgh!' Bubbles squirted from Belinda's mouth, as her whipped bum writhed frantically.

'Nngh!'

Marlene wrenched her head up.

'Oh, please, Marlene!' Belinda sobbed. 'I know I deserve a thrashing, but please don't duck me.'

'Shut up, you lesbo cow,' said Marlene.

Vap!

'Ah! Ouch!'

Vap!

'Ooh! Oh, Ron, it hurts dreadfully,' whimpered Belinda. 'I can't take it. I've never been flogged like this.'

'Good,' he said, licking his lips.

The beating continued, with Belinda's squirming bare lathered in vicious stripes, pinpointed with welts from the belt studs. When her squeals became too loud, Marlene immersed her head for several seconds, before letting her emerge, sobbing and spluttering.

'Ooh! It's not fair,' Belinda moaned. 'My hair is soaked in pee.'

Marlene's fingers squeezed Belinda's gash flaps. 'Hey up,' said the girl. 'The bitch is all wet with twat juice. She likes it, Ron.'

'No!' Belinda shrieked. 'It's awful. Please don't whip me any more.'

Vap! *Vap*!

'Ahh!'

Marlene whispered to Ron, and Belinda heard the slither of doffed clothing.

'No!' she whimpered, as the hard bulb of Ron's bare cock nuzzled her anus bud. 'No, not that –'

'Al said you were anybody's dogger,' sneered Ron.

'You said you liked it up the bum, bitch,' Marlene hissed, ducking Belinda's head.

Squirming and spluttering, Belinda shuddered, as Ron's erect cock penetrated her anus and filled her rectum. He buggered her hard, his cocktip slamming her colon, while her face writhed under piss. After a minute, Marlene wrenched her head up; drooling and sobbing, Belinda gasped hoarsely, as her cooze sluiced come, and her fucked bottom thrust against her buggerer's hips with loud wet slaps.

'Oh, you bastard. Yes, do me, do me hard,' she moaned. 'Split me with your cock!'

Ron panted, his naked body dripping sweat on Belinda's back and bum, as his tool cleaved her bumhole. There were moans and grunts from the adjacent cubicle, but it hardly mattered. Belinda's arse was on fire, seared by the stiff cock splitting her rectum. Come poured from Belinda's gash, as she felt Marlene's face under her belly, sucking up her come, and licking Ron's balls as he bum-fucked.

'Ooh! Ooh! I'm there. Fuck my bum! Oh, yes . . . ah! Ah! Ahh . . .'

Her belly heaved and, as the cock issued its first hot drops of spunk to her sigmoid colon, Belinda whimpered and gasped in orgasm. Her buggerer tooled hard, his cock spurting copious spunk to fill her rectum and dribble down her bucking thighs, where Marlene licked up his cream, tickling Belinda.

'Ooh, gosh,' Belinda gasped, raising her dripping hair from the bowl.

Ron's cock was still stiff in her rectum, and she squeezed him with her sphincter, playfully waggling her bottom and trapping his cock inside her.

'A teacher! What an example,' said a girl's acid voice. 'You steal my Alberto – we were to be engaged! – and now disgrace yourself in public.'

'Hey up, miss, the jakes is private,' said Marlene.

Belinda looked up to see Clarice, face red with anger, skirt up, baring her bottom and cunt, and her breasts spilling from her undone blouse. Behind her, leering, stood her beau, Harry Turp, buttoning his fly. Ron nodded amiably, and said he had to get back to the band.

'You've no business interfering, miss,' blurted Marlene. 'Ouch!'

Clarice's palm cracked across her nipples, leaving a livid bruise. 'Be quiet, slut,' snapped Clarice.

'Why, you fucking cow,' Marlene spat, and sprang at Clarice, pulling her hair and kneeing her between the legs.

'Ooh! You bitch,' Clarice gasped, swinging her fist to Marlene's titties.

Marlene drew back, and kicked Clarice hard in the cunt. Her face wrinkled in agony, Clarice slumped to the floor, where Marlene threw herself on top of her and began to pummel her face and teats, with her knee slamming her groin.

'Ouch! Bitch!'

'Ooh! Cunt!'

'Ah! Ah! Slut!'

Suddenly, Clarice squirmed in the lake of piss and come, toppling Marlene on her belly, and allowing the spluttering Clarice to straddle her, with Marlene's face and breasts squashed in the fluid. Smack! Smack! Clarice began a vigorous spanking of Marlene's naked buttocks, sliding around in come and pee.

'Ooh! Ooh!'

The spanked girl's cries filled the lavatory. Clarice continued the spanking for over a minute, blistering Marlene's bare with livid bruises. Marlene's thighs were spread, kicking and wriggling.

'Will you be still, slut,' hissed Clarice.

She poked two fingers brutally into Marlene's anus, following them with a third, and thrust right to her knuckles.

'Ooh!' Marlene wailed, her impaled arse squirming.

Clarice began to jab Marlene's rectum, in a hard fingerfucking; she added a fourth finger, stretching Marlene's anus wide, and balled her fist, getting four fingers and a thumb into the rectum, up to her wrist. Marlene wriggled in agony, as Clarice fisted her bum. Her fingers on her stiff nubbin, Belinda panted, wanking off at the girl's humiliation.

'Uhh . . .' Marlene whimpered, as come spurted over her threshing thighs. 'Oh, miss, frig me, please.'

'Frig yourself, slut,' sneered Clarice.

Marlene's hand darted to her cunt; wriggling and whimpering, she masturbated to a violent orgasm, her wriggling arse impaled on Clarice's fist.

'Let that be a lesson on speaking to your betters,' snarled Clarice, withdrawing her fist with a plop, and leaving Marlene's anus gaping as wide as a sovereign.

The door opened, and Al entered. He scanned the dishevelled girls, and Belinda masturbating, her thighs slopped with spurting come.

'Al, baby,' cried Belinda, embracing him, 'I've been cruelly abused, but I'm so hot and wet. Fuck me, Al, please fuck me.'

'Not on your nelly,' snarled Clarice. 'Alberto's mine. Prove it, Alberto, and fuck me.'

Al dropped his trousers, and stood with a huge erection. He scanned Belinda's spunk-smeared thighs. 'Seems you've had a go already, Belinda, baby,' he said, pulling Clarice's bum towards him.

His jaws gaped, and he sank his teeth into Clarice's bare, taking several bites, which left glowing red toothmarks.

'Oh, Al, how could you?' Belinda moaned.

'Yes!' gasped Clarice. 'Do me, do me hard.'

Balancing on fingertips and toes, Clarice spread her arse cheeks, and Al entered her anus, plunging his cock to her arse root, for a vigorous buggery.

'No . . .' Belinda wailed, yet vigorously wanked off, as she watched his glistening cock pound the girl's toothmarked arse, his hips and balls slapping her twitching bare buttocks. I'm so wet, watching them fuck. Why does my twat overrule my heart?

Belinda wanked herself to a shivering come, when Al's vigorous buggery brought the whimpering Clarice to orgasm, as his spunk dribbled from her squirming anus.

He withdrew, and Clarice squatted, red-faced and triumphant. Her cunt spurted a steaming jet of piss to form a glistening lake on the tiles, obliging Belinda to sidestep.

'That's cleared one thing up, Belinda,' she panted, 'but there is still the matter of your disgrace to HM Forces.'

'Clarice,' blurted Belinda, 'I can explain –'

'No need,' spat Clarice. 'I expect Harry will give his commanding officer full information, Miss Beaucul, if he wants to enjoy my favours.'

'Of course, Clarry,' he blurted. 'You're the boss.'

Disciplinary tribunal. Belinda wasn't to appear before Major Burleigh until Friday, after a whole shivery week of teaching, unsure if her classes knew about her misadventure at the palais. Every leer or smirk, every lewd glance, seemed ominous, yet, to her relief, no one challenged her with a canable offence. Who was Major Burleigh anyway? Undoubtedly some top military policeman from Catterick. At last, on Friday afternoon, her last class dismissed, Belinda popped into the lav for a quick Woodbine and a tidy-up – she wore her most demure blue skirt and white blouse, with white stockings, bra and sussies – before timidly entering the interview room to see a uniformed man and woman seated at a desk, both smoking. There was a packet of Churchman's on the desk, but Belinda was not offered one.

'I'm Major Dr Burleigh,' said the female, a slender ash-blonde, her hair in a neat, shiny bob, with her tailored uniform clinging to her pert breasts and muscled thighs, 'and this is Captain Dicks of the Military Police.'

She smiled, and ordered Belinda to stand at ease before their desk. Dicks was lanky, with sandy hair and a lopsided grin, not at all like an MP, Belinda thought, in fact, rather dishy. Neither officer was much older than Belinda. Major Burleigh said that she was a doctor of psychiatric medicine, and wished to know if Belinda understood the charge against her, of gross moral turpitude in a public place, bringing disgrace to the king's uniform.

'I'm not uniformed, ma'am,' Belinda blurted.

'You certainly weren't on the night in question,' said Captain Dicks, chuckling.

'That affects the penalty, but not the offence,' said Major Burleigh. 'We have written witness testimony from Private Turp and Miss Clarice Warrior.' She scanned the charge sheet, and sucked breath. 'Need I go on, miss?' she said. 'You've read the charges and statements, and know what you were doing – caught red-handed, it seems.'

'Or red-bottomed,' said Captain Dicks, sniggering and lighting another Churchman's.

'The written evidence of both parties would tend to condemn you,' said the major, 'except that I understand you harshly disciplined Private Turp, which may strike out his testimony as prejudiced. Perhaps you can give some details.'

'Well, ma'am, Turp is a cheeky spunk, and I had to thrash him in front of the class. I thrashed another boy, Private Prewitt, who was also involved in this affair, yet he hasn't testified against me.'

'Perhaps because he was buggering you,' said Major Burleigh drily. 'Can you describe these soldiers' punishments?'

'Well, I made them lower their pants, and I tawsed them.'

'On the bare buttocks?'

'Yes, ma'am. It's the only way.'

Major Burleigh smiled. 'I dare say. Were the tawse army issue?'

'No, ma'am. I bought them privately.'

'Suggesting malice aforethought. How many strokes did you apply?'

'Thirty, ma'am.'

'Were Turp's buttocks severely bruised or coloured?'

'Not severely – I mean, thirty is scarcely harsh – but quite crimson, with some purple welts, yes, I admit.'

'And you consider that bare-bottom discipline is the best way to keep males in line.'

Belinda blushed. 'Yes, ma'am.'

'And girls?'

'As a modern girl, I'd have to say the same.'

'So, you yourself might be deterred from deviant conduct by a bare-bottom flogging.'

Belinda blushed furiously, as Major Burleigh lit another cigarette.

'Did you gain pleasure from the punishments?' she murmured.

'More like satisfaction,' said Belinda.

'But the sight of a young man's bare buttocks squirming, as you whipped him, must surely have aroused you.'

'It wasn't unpleasant.'

'Did you observe erection of their sex organs under whipping?'

'Yes, ma'am.'

'Surely that excited you?'

'Yes, ma'am, I admit it did,' whispered Belinda, her face crimson.

Exhaling a plume of smoke, Major Burleigh fidgeted with the hem of her khaki skirt, and showed a flash of her matching stockings and panties.

'We may discount Turp, but Miss Warrior is an impeccable witness, her mother, Dr Warrior, being an esteemed colleague of mine. Her statement will be read into court, but you may plead mitigating circumstances.'

'The statement is correct, ma'am – I was buggered, with my head in the lav, but Marlene was holding me down.'

'Did you attempt to free yourself?'

'I don't know. I was so confused from my whipping. Ron thrashed me with his belt, and it hurt so dreadfully, I couldn't think. You don't know what a belting on the bare can do to a girl.'

'Don't I?' said Major Burleigh, fidgeting with her skirt, again briefly flashing her matching stockings, sussies and panties. 'I believe you were brought up at Bolton-le-Sands vicarage.'

'Yes, ma'am, by my stepfather.'

'And were you spanked when naughty?'

'Why, yes. I was often naughty.'

'On the bare?'

'No, ma'am. On panties, or pyjama bottoms.'

'Caned?'

'Only after my sixteenth birthday – light caning, no more than six strokes.'

'Also on cloth?'

'No, ma'am, on the bare.'

'That must have hurt.'

'Yes, of course.'

'But you didn't complain.'

'Certainly not – I deserved it.'

'And did your vulva moisten when you were caned?'

'Oh, ma'am, must I answer that?' Belinda blurted.

'No, not really,' said the major, with a thin smile. 'Hmm. The incident was a week ago, so I think we should still see the welts of your alleged whipping. You may bare up, Miss Beaucul. Lean over the desk, and lower your panties, please.'

Belinda obeyed, feeling the cool air on her naked fesses, as she bent over and bared up. Major Burleigh's fingertips brushed her corrugated weals, and she winced.

'You certainly have been whipped recently, Miss Beaucul,' said the major, 'but there are traces of previous – I assume – pleasure beatings. Most girls enjoy bare-bottom chastisement, but you also display a dominant tendency. Possibly, by thrashing males, you are subconsciously daring them to thrash you.'

Belinda held position, bum cheeks spread, as the major's fingers caressed her anus bud.

'Quite distended,' she said, 'indicating frequent anal penetration. You are holding your buttocks apart, exposing yourself, Miss Beaucul – flagellance and anality often accompany exhibitionism. Now, would a brisk barebeating allow us to clear this matter up?'

'Why, yes, ma'am,' Belinda blurted.

'All girls have two sides: the submissive and the dominant, the demure and the exhibitionist. You seem a fascinating mixture of the two.'

'It's so confusing being a girl,' Belinda blurted. 'I – I don't really know which I am.'

'A good flogging is worth any amount of psychiatry,' said Major Burleigh. 'You will please strip naked.'

'Surely not to the full bare, ma'am?' Belinda said.

'Yes. Everything off, including stockings and sussies.'

Belinda began to undo her things, feeling the captain's gaze, as she exposed her bare breasts, then unfastened her skirt and sussies, and rolled down her stockings. Captain Dicks unbuckled his studded leather belt. Sliding down her panties, Belinda gasped, as, cigarette drooping at her lips, Major Burleigh began coolly stepping out of her own uniform. When both girls were nude, Major Burleigh ordered Belinda to don her uniform. Belinda did so, with a shiver of excitement at donning another woman's panties; then her stockings, shoes and sussies, heavy khaki bra, and crisp army skirt and blouse. Everything was too small, chafing and tight, the panties and shoes horridly so, and her titties were almost bursting from the bra and straining blouse buttons. Captain Dicks handed Belinda his belt, folded, with studs out.

'As a test,' Major Burleigh said, bending nude over her desk, with her legs splayed, and pert bare fesses raised, 'you are going to beat me, Miss Beaucul.'

Parting her buttocks, she lit a fresh cigarette, and stuck the white tube into her anus, where, with a wriggle of her bottom, she puffed smoke.

'You may thrash me, until my cigarette is finished,' she said.

Belinda's twat oozed come, as she raised the belt above the trembling arse globes.

'Hard as you like, miss,' said the naked major, blowing blue smoke from her anus. 'Pretend I'm a squaddie.'

Vap! The buttocks clenched, as Belinda's belt lashed a jagged streak of weals across the full bare jellies, and Major Burleigh gasped, her knuckles white on the desk rim. *Vap*! Belinda whipped a second. *Vap*! A third. Belinda had to avoid the cigarette, so aimed her cuts at top buttock and thigh backs. *Vap*! At the fourth, Major Burleigh's bare began to squirm, smoke puffing agitatedly from her anus.

'Ooh . . .' she gasped.

Vap! *Vap*!

'Ouch! That's tight.'

Vap!

'Oh! Oh! You whip a damned hard lash, girl.'

Vap!

'Ooh! Ah!'

Major Burleigh danced on her tiptoes, with her wealed buttocks wriggling.

Vap!

'Ahh!'

Belinda continued the whipping, very fast, with the woman's bare arse blistering and striping in ugly crimson welts, which rapidly puffed to jagged ridges, pricked by the belt studs. Her gasps grew louder and more anguished, and the squirming of her buttocks quite violent, until the cigarette was burned down to an inch. Still, Belinda whipped, until the fag end was a mere stub and, panting, she lowered the belt.

'Ooh!' gasped Major Burleigh, expelling the cigarette end from her anus. 'That was damned close, miss. My prune's jolly well singed!'

Major Burleigh rose, her scarlet face grimacing, and put her fingers to her flogged arse, wincing, as she touched her blisters. Tears moistened her eyes, and seeped come glazed the lips of her shaven cunt, where her clitty peeped stiff amid the flesh folds.

'My panties, please, Miss Beaucul,' she blurted.

Belinda rolled the knickers down, with a squelchy sound. The major squeezed them, and Belinda's come squirted from the cloth.

'As I thought,' she said. 'You are excited by beating, especially when in uniform. In flogging bottoms, you secretly invite penetration of your own. Skirt up, please.'

She inserted her forefinger into Belinda's anus, and began to poke her bumhole. Belinda's thighs parted, allowing the major to ream her rectum.

'Now clench.'

Belinda squeezed her anus on the probing finger. 'I don't understand,' she gasped, as her knickerless cunt spewed come.

'Your clitoris is abnormally huge,' said Major Burleigh, 'and your anus most elastic, the signs of a constant masturbatress and submissive analist.'

She wrenched Belinda's hair, slamming her face to the desk.

'No!' Belinda squealed, her legs threshing, as Captain Dick thrust his naked cock between her quivering bare bum cheeks.

'When a pervert says no,' snapped the major, 'she means yes.'

'Ahh,' Belinda whimpered, as the male plunged his stiff organ into her anus, thrust again and filled her rectum.

He began a vigorous buggery, with the major holding Belinda's hair, and, through tear-blurred eyes, Belinda saw the major masturbating her come-slimed cunt.

'Consider this your punishment,' she said, wanking off, with come squirting from her mashed cooze flaps. 'Of course, you are dismissed from your post, as we cannot tolerate a pervert on our staff. However, we shall provide another.'

'Ooh,' Belinda whimpered. 'Bugger me harder. It's so good, up my bum, damn you, sir.'

'The army needs spunky girls,' said Major Burleigh. 'There's a job as assistant mistress, in St Cloud's College of Higher Education.'

'Where?' Belinda gasped, legs jerking, and bare bum slapping her buggerer's balls, as come spewed from her cunt. 'Oh, yes! Fuck my bum! Split me, sir!'

'In Berbera, British Somaliland,' the major said. 'The mixed student body requires strict traditional discipline, and you will be in uniform. You'll enjoy Somaliland – a girl learns all sorts of tricks in Africa, and your clit is already an African priapiscus. If you accept, SS *Mesopotamia* leaves Liverpool for Berbera this day week. You've time to pack, and pay a sentimental visit to Botts Cove.'

'Ooh! Ahh! I'm almost there . . .' Belinda whimpered. 'Oh! Ohh!'

Spraying come, her cunt writhed, as her belly heaved, in the onset of spasm.

'What?' she gasped. 'You know about –'

'Did you never spy a big Triumph Renown, in olive drab?' said Major Burleigh. 'The captain and I are army doggers.'

She raised her foot to the desk, fully exposing her wanked cunt, and pushed the wet folds inches from Belinda's face. Panting, the major wanked herself to a groaning come, her juices spraying Belinda's lips. Belinda's belly fluttered, at the electric thrill of her bum-pounding, and the captain's cock spurted its first drops of hot spunk at her arse root. The major drew back, and a jet of liquid arched from her cunt, straight up in the air, splattering Belinda's face.

'Oh! Yes! Bugger me! Fill me with your spunk!' Belinda cried. 'I'm coming! Yes! Ooh . . .'

Her cunt spurted come over the captain's balls. He grunted, as his spunk filled Belinda's rectum and dribbled from her anal lips onto the khaki army stockings.

'You peed upwards,' Belinda gurgled, swallowing the major's scented ejaculate. 'How on earth . . .?'

'Not exactly peed – a twat trick one learns in Somaliland,' said the major, lighting two cigarettes, and passing one to Belinda. 'Do you want the job?'

'Yes,' said Belinda, sucking smoke. 'I'd like to be in uniform.'

'You'll love it,' said Major Burleigh, cigarette drooping at her lips, as she wiped her slimy cunt on Belinda's hair. 'A uniform is so thrilling when you take it off.'

10

Filled Panties

Lancashire seemed ever so far away, as Belinda puffed on a tax-free du Maurier, with the moonlight glinting on the ocean, beneath the deck of the SS *Mesopotamia*, and the lights of Berbera twinkling in the distance. Belinda's bare shoulders gleamed above her black cocktail dress, with shiny seamed black nylons swooping to her patent leather high heels, seven shillings and sixpence from Clitheroe's in Heysham. Her braless breasts jutted, jellies quivering, under thin satin. Her fesses rolled together, in her clinging short shorties made from parachute silk she had bought from Wendy, then dyed black, only it came out more a sort of purply colour. She wasn't so comfortable in the too-tight panties, pinching her cheeks and quim crack – the gusset would ride up, right between her quimfolds! – but being braless and knickerless seemed a little too daring, on the posh *Mesopotamia*. Gazing up at the stars, she started from her reverie at a young man's voice.

'Awfully pretty, isn't it?' he murmured.

He was tall, handsome – a right spunk! – and wore a navy blue blazer, cravat and white trousers.

'I've seen you before, miss, but was too shy to approach. Now it's our last night –' He sighed.

'I'm glad you have,' she murmured. 'I haven't really made acquaintances, beyond Lady Pickell, Mrs Forward, Mr Anstruther – but even they're a bit stuffy. I'm just a schoolteacher, you see. Other chaps tend to be, well, a bit bold.'

He nodded sympathetically. Belinda flung her cigarette end into the sea, and, after an interval of silence, he snapped open a gold cigarette case.

'Care for a Camel?' he said. 'From the American PX.'

'Why, thank you.'

They smoked, looking at the velvet sky.

'It is pretty,' she said.

'Yes. You are going to Somaliland to teach? Please forgive me for being intrigued.'

'I'm flattered.'

Shyly, Belinda explained her new and former jobs.

'How exciting,' he said. 'An army school – will you be in uniform?'

'Oh, yes,' Belinda swanked.

'Mm, I can just picture you, awfully stern and strict. I'm Jeremy Quince, by the way.'

'Belinda Beaucul.'

'What a lovely name,' he said.

'Thank you. It's my first time away from England – from Lancashire, really. What takes you so far from home?'

'My yacht is my home, and she's laid up in Berbera – bit of a typhoon in the Indian Ocean, and I was lucky to get her back in one piece. Several months for repair, damnably slow, so I took a holiday back in Blighty.'

'It sounds ever so romantic,' Belinda said.

'Travelling's just what I do. I skippered a motor gunboat during the recent flap and, last year, the Admiralty wanted to sell them off, so I bought the old girl, made her habitable . . . actually, I plan to see an old Corsican friend of mine, Count Scazza, from the Free French Navy. We were on patrol in the Med together. Now he's a high-up in the Foreign Legion, in Djibouti. But enough of me, tell me more about you.'

'Oh, there's not much to tell.'

He looked deep into her eyes. 'Every beautiful woman has much to tell,' he murmured. 'I have . . . a certain acquaintance with Lancashire.'

Belinda blushed, her heart thumping. He was a dish. 'Did you know a Captain Garstang?' she blurted. 'He was our teacher, at Heysham Academical – he was in the navy.'

Jeremy smiled. 'The navy's a big place,' he said, 'but, funnily enough, I did know a Captain Garstang. He was in torpedo boats, very brave chap, lots of gongs, and sent home wounded, I believe, rather hush-hush. Was he a special friend?'

'Not a friend,' Belinda said, shivering. 'He was a teacher . . . quite strict.'

Jeremy nodded to a passing steward.

'Naval chaps do tend to be disciplinarians,' he said. 'I expect you'll have to, in a school like St Cloud's.'

'That's true,' said Belinda, 'so I suppose it was useful experience.'

A bottle of champagne in an ice bucket appeared.

'Frightfully rude of me,' Jeremy said, pouring each of them a flute. 'I didn't ask if you like champagne.'

'Why, every girl does,' said Belinda.

'That's what I dared to assume. What exactly was useful experience?'

'Well – you know –' Belinda blushed '— corporal punishment.'

'Captain Garstang used the strap?'

'And worse. Naval discipline! I expect to use the cane quite a bit on those unruly bottoms in Berbera. It's what I did to keep squaddies in order in my classroom in Lancaster. Pants down for a licking.' She giggled. 'I expect I sound like an ogress, but I'm really a very modern girl.'

'So, you were . . . ah . . . disciplined, at your girls' school?'

'Lancashire folk believe beating does a girl no harm. Don't tell me you weren't caned at school.'

'Yes, we were, at Gishington. Rather a lot.'

'What was it like?'

'It's awfully embarrassing.'

'But why? It's quite normal for boys to take the cane. Go on.'

'For shame, we were caned by the matron, a rather attractive young lady. It was dreadfully humiliating, baring up for a dozen cuts from a woman, especially since there were sometimes . . . embarrassing physical results. I won't insult you by presuming you know what I mean.'

'But I think I do,' Belinda said, eyes glistening. 'You mean that boys got excited when caned by a lady on their naked bottoms?'

'Well, yes,' he said.

'And did you get excited, Jeremy?'

'Invariably,' he stammered. 'She was beautiful – not half as much as you, miss.'

'Thank you. I imagine it does excite a boy to bare up for a lady. I don't mind telling you – out here, it doesn't seem to matter – that girls get a thrill out of showing themselves, too. It's called "exhibitionism". I was a terror for exposing my bubbies or my bum, as a prank. It excited me to know that chaps stiffened, looking at me. I imagine your matron was excited too, when you got hard, as she caned you.'

'Yes, but they made such a dashed ceremony out of it! A boy to be flogged would parade through the school, wearing only his pyjama bottoms, carrying the cane, behind matron in her best blues. One felt such a booby, especially if one got excited, even before the caning, and everyone saw. I always did, and so, when I had to step out of my pyjamas and bare up, I was convinced I deserved my beating, if only for impertinence. That was the most awful moment, when I felt my pyjamas slithering down, leaving me exposed, with my excitement plain to see.'

'So the lady would cane you in the full bare?'

'Yes. Naked, and with a panel of "monitors" looking on to ensure I took it like a man – masters, prefects, but always some ladies. I had to bend over and touch my toes, unless matron preferred to take me bending over an armchair. She liked to take a run-up. That was awful – the pounding of her feet and the swish of the cane before it lashed me. The sting was indescribable – a chap couldn't help squirming and clenching like a girl – begging your pardon, miss. And so on for another eleven! And as the dreadful cane sliced my bare, and my gorge rose, I had to keep my head up, choking back my tears, with my bare bum all red and wealed and wriggling – that was real shame.'

'Did it cure you of . . . embarrassment?' Belinda said coyly.

'Not often. I shouldn't really say this, but –'

'Do go on.'

'Well, matron, being quite young, and not a bad stick, really, if she saw a chap was still, you know, excited, after a bare-beating, she would order him to surgery, and take him in hand, to, um, relieve him. Some boys earned the cane on purpose.'

'Did you, Jeremy?'

His blush glowed fiery, under the pale moonlight. 'Maybe once or twice,' he murmured. 'But I was still left with the shame of dreadful welts on my bare bottom, all hard and ribbed like old leather, and at scrub-up, where we were all in the nude, everyone could see.'

'I know what you mean,' Belinda said. 'Girls can take it too, you know. Except that Captain Garstang could be a bit unfair. About three years ago – gosh, this champagne is super – he flogged me for something he knew I didn't do. It was my best friend, but I couldn't blab on her, so I had to bare up and take it.'

'Really bare up?'

'Of course. It smarted dreadfully, and I've never forgotten.'

'Bare-beating – I thought it was just for chaps.'

'Not in Lancashire.'

'It's an English tradition, I suppose. Sometimes, I would cane a refractory swab, aboard my wartime barge. No messy paperwork, got it out of the way quickly and the hands appreciated it. A swift dozen, and no hard feelings.'

'Gosh,' Belinda said, licking her lips. 'You look strong – you must cane awfully hard. I wish I could have been there.'

Jeremy refilled her glass, and lit two cigarettes, then passed one to her.

'It wasn't pleasant duty,' he murmured. 'Your presence, Miss Belinda, might have made it gentler. A lady sees a man's stripes with understanding. I learned that in Lancashire – where I grew to appreciate the women of your fair county – no, it's too painful, and I mustn't impose on you.'

'Oh, but do, please,' Belina cried. 'Was it a sweetheart? Was she cruel to you? Did she break your heart?'

He turned away; Belinda took a deep drag on her Camel.

'Something like that,' he murmured. 'At first, it was blissful, for we never argued – Wendy understood me, you see. When I was awkward, she knew the best thing was – well, matron's treatment, a sound whopping of my naked bottom. Do I shock you?'

'Not at all, Jeremy,' Belinda blurted, her thighs slithering together, as a seep of juice trickled from her gash.

'Wendy was awfully good at it,' he continued dreamily. 'Her cane kept me shipshape . . . until she left me . . .'

'Oh, gosh. For another fellow? How sad.'

He laughed bitterly. 'It wasn't for another chap. It was for another girl, or girls. Lots of them. Wendy was lesbian. How humiliating! I asked if it was my fault, offered to take any punishment she desired, and she agreed to that – made me bare up and bend over, and I took the hardest caning of my life, fifty stingers on my naked buttocks. I was in tears – I thought my pain would soften her heart – until I looked round, and saw that she hadn't beaten me, but Jan, her paramour, had. How they laughed!'

Belinda's hand flew to her lips. 'Was her name Wendy Pight?'

'Why, yes. Do you know her?'

'Oh, very slightly. We were at school together,' Belinda blurted. 'Poor Jeremy, how you've suffered.'

He waited until she had removed her cigarette, and exhaled a blue plume of smoke, before swiftly embracing her, his hands on her bare back, and her breasts pressed to his chest; Belinda trembled, as his lips met hers, in a passionate kiss. Her arm snaked round his shoulders, and drew him close. Belinda's tongue darted into his mouth, and flicked his own. She rubbed her stiff nipples through her flimsy dress against his shirt buttons. Locked in a French kiss, they swayed on the deck, until he released her.

'Forgive me, Miss Belinda,' he gasped. 'I've behaved unpardonably.'

'No, Jeremy, don't say that.'

'We've scarcely met – it's just that you are so dashed beautiful –'

She clasped him, and stuck her tongue once more into his mouth, while guiding his hand under her dress to caress her naked breast. Her crotch pressed against his throbbing erection. She removed his champagne glass, and slipped his other hand under her dress and panties, to her bare bum. He moaned, stroking her buttocks, with his finger sliding in her arse cleft.

'Mm . . .' purred Belinda.

Suddenly, he took his hands away. 'I'm a beast,' he gasped. 'An Englishman shouldn't treat an English lady like some cheap – oh, I deserve punishment for my insolence.'

'You don't mean that,' she murmured.

'But I do! As an officer –'

'I can accommodate you, officer,' she whispered, with her tongue licking his ear. She grasped his massive bulge. 'That does deserve punishment,' she said. 'I think a spanking is in order.'

'Oh, yes,' he gasped.

'But where?'

'My cabin's a bit small,' he blurted, 'but should have enough room – you're serious? I mean, you'd spank me?'

Licking her lips, Belinda nodded. 'More than "would",' she murmured. 'Will.'

'Gosh, I've never done anything like this before. That is, not with a –'

'I'd like to do more than spank. This talk of discipline has made me hot. You see, Jeremy, I – I like corporal punishment. I love the sight of a male's bare bum wriggling, as I thrash him.'

'I'd certainly feel better if I atoned for my rudeness.'

'You silly,' she said, goosing his balls. 'It is I who shall feel better.'

She followed him below decks, to his door, where he fumbled with his key, while Belinda stroked his buttocks.

'You must obey me, Jeremy,' she whispered. 'I'm going to spank your naughty bottom raw.'

'Of course. You are my officer commanding.'

The door clicked shut behind them. The room was tiny, but luxurious, with an open porthole admitting the breeze. On the table stood another ice bucket, with a bottle of champagne. Jeremy opened it, and poured.

'First class! How super,' Belinda said, clinking glasses.

'A favour. We naval chaps stick together, and the skipper – actually, he was my sub-lieutenant, and I've thrashed his arse a few times.'

'Speaking of which,' Belina said briskly, 'let's to business. You know what you're here for, sir.'

'Oh . . . yes,' he said, blushing, with his erection bursting his trousers.

'So strip, completely. I shall take you in the full bare, over the table, if you please.'

'For a spanking?' he blurted. 'I thought, over your knee –'

'It's more than spanking you require, sir,' she drawled. 'Frankly, I don't have much time for your sort of sniveller. Worms need proper lashing on bare.'

Jeremy goggled, smiling and licking his lips.

'Get them off,' Belinda snapped.

He stripped coyly, and stood before her, shielding his erect cock.

'I intend to thrash you until that ceases to offend me,' she said, scowling. 'You may take position, sir.'

Trembling, he leaned over the table, with his buttocks upthrust. 'Please be kind, Miss Belinda,' he whimpered.

'Kind?' she snapped. 'You've come to the wrong girl for kindness, sir.'

'Ooh . . .' he moaned.

She kicked off her shoes, and, her nyloned toes clenching the carpet, lifted the left shoe high over his croup. The sole slapped a pink mark on his arse. *Vap*! Another bum blossom pinked, and his cheeks quivered.

'Oh!' he gasped. 'It hurts, miss.'

'So it's supposed to,' she rasped.

Vap! *Vap*! Belinda's naked breasts bounced in her skimpy top, and she was worried the teats would spill out.

'Ouch! Ooh!' he groaned.

'Will you desist from those girly noises?'

Vap! *Vap*!

'Oh! Oh! I'll try, miss, but you spank awfully hard,' he panted.

Vap! *Vap*! His cheeks jerked, clenching and wriggling, but he bit his lip and, with his face as crimson as his arse, took his punishment in gasping silence. As she spanked, Belinda felt a growing trickle of wet coursing down her thighs, and into her stocking tops, making the nylon all wet and mushy against her skin. Her dress flapped up at each spank, baring her glistening knickers, and her fingers flew down to smooth the dress, but brushed her clitty, throbbing and extruded under the knickers.

An electric tingle shot up her spine, and she began to wank off, rubbing her clit under the wet silk panties gusset. Her panties squelched so loudly, as her thighs quivered, that she felt the panties must be filling up with come. *Vap*! *Vap*! Masturbating vigorously, she spanked the squirming male, until his whole bare arse was flaming crimson, with the skin puffing to fiery blisters. She espied an officer's cane, with a silver knob, laid on his bed.

'What's that?' she gasped, smoothing down her skirt, which stained deeply, where her cunt gushed.

He looked round. 'Oh, my swagger stick from the navy – I keep it as a memento.'

'Bring it to me. Fingers off your arse, mind – no rubbing.'

Groaning, he obeyed, and, as Belinda flexed the supple cane, he resumed position.

'You're not going to –' he blurted.

'What do you think?' she hissed, lifting the cane. 'Slippering won't punish you, sir. Only –'

Vip!

'Ooh!'

'– a proper –'

Vip!

'Ahh!'

'– caning.'

Vip! *Vip*!

'Oh! Oh! Ohh . . .'

The baton made a supple cane, and Belinda wanked harder, as she was rewarded by a lattice of livid crimson stripes on his croup, darker than the puffy red mass of spanked flesh. His buttocks squirmed violently, and she heard his gasps punctuated with choking sobs. *Vip*!

'Ooh!'

'Hard enough for you, Quince?' she snapped.

'Devilish hard, thank you, miss,' he sobbed.

Vip!

'Ouch! Oh! Ahh . . .'

As she masturbated through her sopping panties, Belinda gazed at his squirming bruised buttocks, then at the erect cock bobbing at each canestroke.

'We haven't managed to thrash your erection away,' she said.

'No, miss. I'm sorry.'

'You will be. I'm less tolerant than your beloved matron. Tell me, what did you think about when she wanked you off?'

Vip!

'Ahh! About her, miss,' he groaned. 'I had to kneel on a chair, with thighs apart, while she sat facing me. While she was . . . uh . . . stroking me, I had to look her in the eyes, with a straight face, and not look into the cleft of her breasts, although I couldn't help thinking about kissing and touching those big soft melons, with their bewitching perfume.'

'Go on, you smutty worm.'

Vip!

'Uhh! She didn't look down, but stared me straight in the eyes. She began by wanking my naked organ, but, when I began to gasp and tremble a bit, she put on a sort of sheath. I had to spurt into a square of satin, from one of her old nighties she had cut up. It was awfully exciting when I got the bra part.'

'You disgust me. Continue.'

Vip!

'Ooh! She made the satin into a purse, and fitted it entirely over my organ and ballocks, and then she rubbed my glans, while her other hand stroked my ballocks underneath. She was very good at wanking me off, and used to pull my prepuce all the way down, which was almost painful, and awfully thrilling, then tickle my bare bell end, so I usually spurted quite soon. She made sure to drain me of spunk, by rubbing my balls as I spurted, which is so very lovely, miss.'

'Filthy beast.'

Three stingers striped the tender haunches, which blossomed at once with deep crimson welts.

'Ooh! Ahh! Please, miss! That's cruel!'

Vip! A cut took him in the arse cleft, the cane tip a hair's breadth from his balls.

'Ooh! Ahh! Please stop,' he sobbed, his flogged bum wriggling violently.

Vip! A stripe at top buttock, just below his spinal nubbin.

'Oh, miss . . .' he whimpered, blubbing helplessly. 'You are the cruellest lady in the world.'

'Thank you,' she panted. 'Poor boy, your cock is still stiff. You do need relief. Get up on the table, and kneel, bending backwards, with your thighs apart.'

He obeyed, and squatted, crying, with his erect cock poised over his belly.

'Ooh,' he gasped. 'My bum hurts so.'

Belinda slipped off her come-drenched panties, and held them up, dripping on his balls.

'These cost me two and elevenpence,' she said solemnly, with her fingers crossed behind her back. 'Will you reimburse me?'

'Of course, miss. In my jacket pocket –'

Belinda counted out two shillings and two sixpences. 'I'll owe you the penny,' she said.

'It's all right.'

'Sure?'

Grimacing, he nodded.

'Well, thank you.'

Belinda tucked the coins into her deep cunt, then placed the panties on the table, beneath his balls, and grasped his glans between her finger and thumb, massaging the swollen organ around the glans neck and corona. Her fingertip darted up the smooth, hard surface to the peehole, which she brushed briefly, making him shudder and groan. She rubbed the delicate frenulum, and Jeremy's bum bucked.

'Gosh, miss, that's so good,' he gasped. 'Wherever did you learn to do it?'

Her free hand cupped his balls, and stroked the tight sac. Caressing the balls, she let her palm and fingers clutch his cockshaft, at the neck of the glans, and began to squeeze, rubbing up and down, then pulling his prepuce fully back to expose his glans with each downward stroke, before tugging it up over his peehole again. She applied this motion for several seconds, before reverting to the nimble flicking of his frenulum and peehole, and tracing a spiral around the glans wall with her fingernail, until she poked it between the lips of the peehole. All the time, she played with his balls, and his gasps became frantic.

'Oh . . . oh . . . oh . . .' he moaned.

The cock was trembling, as she squeezed harder on his glans neck, and drew her hand right to the balls, stretching his prepuce to a pale ribbon of skin.

'Oh, gosh, Miss Belinda,' he whimpered. 'I'm completely in your power.'

Belinda's cunt dripped come into her dress, as she massaged Jeremy's throbbing cock; she could feel her rock-hard, elongated clitty brush against the dress, as her thighs swayed, with a gentle, liquid susurration of her come-soaked nylons.

'Are you going to spurt?' she panted, frotting him. 'I can feel your cock trembling. And your balls are so tight. They're going to fill my panties with a lovely big load of hot spunk, aren't they?'

Deftly, she fashioned a purse from the silken panties, and sheathed Jeremy's cock and balls, continuing to massage him through the silk, sopping with her oozed come. Still clasping his balls, she cupped his corona in her palm and fingers, slowing her milking, but squeezing alternately tightly and gently, and still drawing his prepuce fully back with each stroke. The panties stretched tightly over his peehole, as she pulled his prepuce down, then the silk ballooned again, as her fingers rubbed his frenulum.

He gasped, writhing, then sobbed, as the panties darkened with his first jet of spunk. Belinda did not relax her squeezing, but applied a firm, slow pressure, as his panting grew shrill, and his breath hoarse and rapid, as the cock bucked, filling her panties with his spunk. Both Belinda's hands were occupied, so she squeezed her thighs together, gasping, as she frotted her erect throbbing clitty, with come sluicing from her swollen cunt lips.

'Uhh . . .' he gasped. 'You are so beautiful, Miss Belinda.'

She squeezed the sopping panties up and over his glans, and swung them, with his copious ejaculate balling the gusset.

'You are a heavy creamer,' she purred, 'one of the heaviest I've known.'

'There have been others?' he gasped.

'Why, of course, silly. How do think I learned to . . . you know?'

'I might have guessed.'

'Still, you feel relieved.'

'Wonderfully. But looking at you, miss, I'll want another quite soon.'

'Naughty boy! It's girls who are supposed to be inexhaustible. At least, Wendy always was.'

'Wendy . . .?'

'Well, we were more than just friends, weren't we?' she said, smirking.

'You . . . a lesbo! With Wendy . . . you absolute bitch! You slut!'

He leaped to the floor and wrenched her hair, pinioning her to the come-slimed table, with her bottom in the air.

'Wait, Jeremy! What –'

He ripped her dress up to her shoulders, fully exposing her naked back and buttocks, then seized his cane. Holding her face pressed in his pool of come, he lifted the cane and lashed her quivering bare.

'Ouch! Ooh! Stop! Oh! That hurts!'

The cane laid vivid red weals on her squirming arse globes, and Belinda's kicking legs could not deflect his merciless flogging.

'Ahh! No! please!'

'Shut up, you slut,' he snarled.

'Ooh!'

'Right! That does it.'

He grabbed her filled panties and jammed them into her mouth, gagging her. Trickles of come and spunk glazed Belinda's chin, as her face was thrust down. His cane whipped every inch of her naked bumflesh, with Belinda moaning and wriggling, as her arse blistered in a mottled patchwork of puffy crimson weals.

'Urrgh! Urrgh!' she gurgled, twisting her head to see Jeremy's cock newly erect.

Belinda shook her head violently, wrenching her hair roots, and banged her titties on the table, while her caned bottom squirmed. Jeremy caned viciously, as come sprayed from Belinda's squirming crevice, and her bubs squelched in a pool of her tears. Her flogged buttocks glowed crimson and purple, with puffy pink blisters swelling above the jagged gashes of her welts. Her thighs were wet with spuming come, sluiced from her cunt flaps.

'Juicing, you bitch?' Jeremy snarled. 'I'll teach you.'

Vip!

'Urrgh!'

The cane cut Belinda in the crevice, its tip slapping her cunt lips and clitty with a squelch, as the hissing rod splashed in her mushed pink cooze flesh. *Vip*! Her bum jerked, as he caned her on the wrinkled arse pucker, and she shuddered, sobbing, in a gush of tears. After several minutes' caning, he laid down the cane, leaving Belinda's bruised bare body flopping on the table, her face splattered with the shreds of her gag, quite bitten through. With a cry of disgust, he ripped the ruined panties from her mouth.

'Oh!' she gasped, as he wiped the come-slimed gag on her hair and titties. 'I'm so sore, Jeremy. I've never had such a caning – you're so cruel.'

He clutched her hot flogged bum, pressing the cheeks together, over the tip of his cock, nuzzled at her arse crack. With his cockshaft and glans sandwiched between her wealed buttocks, he began to rub the arse flesh against his cocktip.

'Aren't you going to fuck my cunt, Jeremy?' she whimpered. 'Or my bum – I've been a naughty girl, and deserve really hard, painful bumming.'

'Tool a lady's orchid?' he sneered. 'That's rude. I prefer it between the thighs, or this – pygisma, what they do in Africa, where the bitches have big arses like yours.'

'You mean a bum-wank?' she gasped, clenching her buttocks to knead his stiff cock. 'Why not bum me properly, Jeremy? Oh, please. You've made me so hot! Tup my bumhole, like a real man, and I'll milk you with my rectum – I know how.'

'You filthy whore,' he snarled. 'Oh, damn your arse, slut, it's too beautiful to leave unpoked.'

His hand slapped her cunt, cupping a palmful of her come to oil his cock.

'Mm!' Belinda squealed, as his peehole nuzzled her anus.

The slimy cock penetrated her anus in a powerful thrust, then, at a second, plunged into her rectum, with his glans slammed on her colon. He began to fuck her arse vigorously, his hips slapping against her blistered bum, and making her cry out, squirming, as he hurt her weals. Belinda's bum bucked hard, with her rectum squeezing his cock, to milk the penetrating tool, and make him gasp at the elastic pressure, as he painfully withdrew the shaft for each new thrust.

''You're an expert at this, too, you Lancashire cow,' he hissed, as his cock squelched in her arse grease.

'Oh, I'm such a naughty girl. Bugger me hard, Jeremy. Hurt me. Split my bum in two,' she whimpered. 'It's so good, your tool in my hole. I'm going to come . . . yes, I'm coming . . .'

He lunged hard, slamming his cock to her arse root, and grunted, as his spunk began its spurt into her sigmoid colon.

'Yes, yes, yes . . . oh! Ohh!' she squealed, come squirting from her gash, as her clitty throbbed in orgasm.

Spunk filled her rectum, and spilled from her anal lips to dribble down her bucking thighs. There was a knock on the door.

'Your champagne, sir?' said a male voice.

'Cripes,' said Jeremy, 'you'd better hide.'

'But where? There's no room.'

'Out the porthole.'

'What?'

'You can stand on the runnel below. It's only for a moment, girl. I can't let scandal get round –'

The knock was repeated.

'Shall I enter, sir?'

'Just a moment,' Jeremy blurted, clambering into his trousers.

He lifted Belinda's bottom, and shoved her head-first through the porthole, with a struggle to force her breasts, until she jammed at her waist.

'Ooh! I'm stuck,' she hissed.

'Your blasted bum's too big,' he snarled, heaving her.

'Ouch! You're hurting me,' she wailed, her titties swaying over the Indian Ocean.

The door opened, and Belinda heard male voices, Jeremy's far from apologetic.

'An English lady, sir?' purred the steward. 'Sir does like a varied diet. Perhaps a restful change after those Egyptian mots in Port Said, who were so demanding.'

'Sluts are the same, anywhere,' said Jeremy, with a chuckle. 'All begging for it.'

'The usual, sir?'

'If you please.'

'Ooh!' Belinda squealed, as she felt something hard, cold and wet thrust into her anus.

The glass shook, for several seconds, before a muffled pop. Belinda squealed, as the champagne cork thudded painfully into her colon, and sticky bubbling wine frothed in her rectum.

'It's not fair,' she moaned. 'Help me, someone.'

Jeremy's lips were at her anus, slurping the champagne. Belinda pushed and pushed, but the dratted cork wouldn't come out, until with an extra hard shove, it shot from her bumhole like a bullet, ripping her anal elastic.

'Ooh, the bitch hit my knob,' the steward complained.

'Mm,' Jeremy said. 'Have your usual tip, steward.'

'Thank you kindly, sir.'

'Oh! What? Noo!' Belinda wailed to the ocean, as her buttocks were parted, and a hot, stiff cock penetrated her anus.

Her legs threshed, kicking the bulkhead, until strong hands pinioned her ankles, and left her bottom helplessly squirming, as the steward buggered her. His tool reamed her rectum, slamming hard at her sigmoid colon, while Belinda sobbed and wriggled, her titties flailing the ship's hull, until a jet of hot spunk filled her arsehole.

'Jeremy, you vile beast,' she sobbed. 'You've had your pleasure, now please release me.'

The door opened again, and Belinda heard other laughing male voices.

'No,' she pleaded. 'No . . .'

Her titties flapping wildly, she squirmed to extricate herself, and wailed, as another stiff cock entered her rectum. Belinda began to spit copiously on her palms and titties, wiping the spittle as lubricant on her belly and hips. The unseen male buggered her to his spunk, and then, almost at once, his cock was replaced by another. She could not help her buttocks from thrusting upwards and towards her buggerers, squeezing their cocks with her anal elastic and milking them to spunk, while come sprayed from her jerking cunt.

'She's a ripping biff, sir,' said a sailor's voice. 'Look how she juices! Our English sluts are the best for bumming.'

'Pity we can't have a titwank,' said another. 'Still, doing arsers means we don't have to look at her damn face.'

Arsers! I'm nothing but a bare bum, a bit of girlflesh, for male brutes to lust over. Why, oh why, is my orchid so wet?

'Wank the girl off,' said Jeremy. 'It's only fair.'

Belinda gasped, as gnarled fingers tweaked her throbbing clitty, and she climaxed after only seconds of frotting. Cock after cock filled her rectum with spunk, as she came at each load of hot cream washing her tripes, sending electric twitches of pleasure through her wanked clitty. Spasming, she tweaked her stiff nipples hard, slicing the fleshy buds with her fingernails, until her cunt shuddered and spewed in orgasm.

'Ooh . . . ooh . . .' she sobbed, tears streaming over her bouncing bare teats, as she lubricated her heaving body with spittle.

When her arsehole ached enough to split, Belinda's torso was glazed with her drool. Furiously, she wriggled; the porthole scraped her cunt hillock, and she plopped from her trap to plummet into the sea. She plunged deep, righted herself, then swam powerfully to the surface.

'Help!'

The ship's passengers were gathered on the foredeck, in evening dress, sipping their cocktails in the balmy night air. A matelot threw her a lifebelt and a rope and, in a few seconds, she was hauled, dripping, onto the deck. Another matelot hurried with a blanket, but she refused it.

'The night's quite warm,' she said. 'I'll dry off nicely.'

The passengers gaped at her nude body, draped in seaweed and crustaceans. Belinda smiled brightly, and began to slap her titties and bum to shake off the water droplets. She thrust her buttocks at the watchers, showing the blisters from her spanking, and parted her thighs to extricate a wriggling crab from her quim.

'Cheeky bugger!' she said, holding it up, before tossing it back into the ocean. 'I wondered who was fiddling with my twat! Why, hello, Lady Pickell, Mr Anstruther, Mrs Forward – how nice to see you.'

She grabbed a cocktail from a waiter, and sipped. 'Mm!' just the ticket, after a dip in the briny, eh?' she trilled. 'Jeremy Quince not here? Pity – I've just had the most wonderful time in his cabin.'

She tapped her bottom again, tweaking her blisters and weals – though it hurt awfully – and was gratified to see every male crotch bulge. When she had finished her cocktail, she had another, and stood chatting to eager spunks for fifteen minutes, before swishing through the throng, bum waggling, to regain her own cabin. She extracted Jeremy's three shillings from her quim, and giggled. After taking from her suitcase a handful of the bull's balls she kept for emergency wanks, she pushed half into her quim and half into her anus; then, looking at her wealed bum in the mirror, she opened her thighs, squeezed her bum cheeks and wanked herself off to a heaving, groaning come.

I'm such a clever clogs. Three shillings for my panties, when I only gave Wendy ninepence for the silk!

11

Whop Shop

'Lancashire? Hmph!' said Miss Selma Harrod, headmistress of HM Forces St Cloud's School, Berbera. 'I'm a Durham lass, myself – Daddy has a few acres near Hexham – and I'd say, for holiday fun, our Seaton Carew has your beastly Blackpool beaten.'

'I wouldn't disagree, miss.'

'You are settled in all right? Know your timetable? Accommodation and uniform sorted out?'

'Yes, miss, everyone has been very helpful,' said Belinda, tugging the hem of her army skirt over her cream rayon stockings, permitted by regulation.

'Good,' said Miss Harrod. 'Berbera's a genial place, and you mustn't believe silly rumours about English girls being kidnapped by lustful tribesmen. More tea?'

'Yes, please,' Belinda replied.

'I'll call Sally for a fresh pot. We English girls all like a nice cup of tea,' said Miss Harrod, ringing a silver bell.

'Oh, I agree,' Belinda replied.

Miss Harrod, slender, long-legged and thirtyish, shifted her pert buttocks, tightly skirted in dark green cotton, crossed her thighs – firm and rippling, under super red nylon stockings! – patted her blonde Betty Grable bob, gazed at Belinda over her horn-rimmed spectacles and pursed her lips. Her cannonball breasts rippled under their clinging green blouse, casually open to the third button to reveal tan breast flesh under a golden necklace. Her blonde tresses danced in the cooling blast of two huge electric fans.

'You agree? I hope you're not a yes-monkey,' she said. 'In Durham, we consider Lancashire folk soft. You're not soft, are you?'

'I hope not, Miss Harrod.'

'Good. A girl in Somaliland needs British spunk, and a mind of her own. Your reports say you are something of a martinet, used to whopping unruly squaddies. I like that.'

'Martinet, miss?'

'A stickler for discipline – oddly, it also means a girl who's not afraid to bare up and take discipline. We both know what we mean by discipline, don't we?' Her hand suddenly slapped her left haunch, with a loud crack. 'Teaching at St Cloud's means keeping the buggers in order,' she drawled. 'Forget any hifalutin notions. We thrash the three Rs into their lazy behinds, and get them their diplomas. That applies to Europeans and Africans alike, and, if anything, the Africans are less trouble. The girls look awfully sweet when crammed into a proper English school uniform but, at home, they run around in the nude, jingling with metal doodads, and smeared with red earth and camel fat! We don't take anyone under seventeen, but, nonetheless, the lash is their daily diet, so your first duty is to know your straps. The purser's given you a copy of the school rules, I trust.'

'Not yet, miss. You mean, I may have to apply corporal punishment?' Belinda said timidly, her heart thumping.

'May? Must, girl. If I'm on the prowl, and don't hear the whack of wood or leather from my classrooms on disobedient bare bums, there'll be merry hell to pay. I might even thrash you on the bare. I dare say you wouldn't appreciate that.' Miss Harrod smiled puckishly. 'I do occasionally thrash junior staff,' she drawled, crossing her thighs to show bare skin, white garter straps and a flash of green silk knickers. 'In this heat, they can be quite juvenile, flirting with the students, and suchlike. I find a quick whopping on the bare saves an awful lot of paperwork.'

'Like any Lancashire girl, I'm no stranger to corporal punishment,' said Belinda coolly. 'If I deserved punishment, miss, I would expect to take it, with a stiff upper lip.'

'Bravely spoken. Only, after a St Cloud's thrashing, the upper lip is the only thing not squirming. They don't call my school the "whop shop" for nothing.' Crack! Pouting, Miss Harrod slapped her other haunch, and daintily wriggled her buttocks. 'Cane, tawse, strap and sjambok,' she said briskly. 'You must know how to apply them all. Beatings are always on the bare, and preferably public, before the class or at morning assembly, which I call my morning thrash. No prayer books, or any of that tommy rot, just whops. Classes are girls or boys only, but assembly is mixed, and the shame of a public thrashing works wonders.'

She lowered her voice to a whisper, and leaned forwards, showing bare breastflesh, snuggling in a tight green bra. 'You might witness, or administer, a full whipping. That is for the most beastly cheek, cribbing or snogging – really serious offences. The miscreant, boy or girl, is in the full bare, not a stitch, and strung up by the fingers, navy fashion, for a flogging with the sjambok, on buttocks and back.'

She sat back, licking her lips, and fiddled with her skirt, hoisting the hem and fanning her thighs.

'You mean, I must discipline girls as well as boys?' Belinda asked.

'Of course. Girls are far naughtier than boys. The boys will fall in love with you, beastly little tykes – quite sickening – and that's when you must thrash them the hardest, especially when they promise to abduct you on camelback. The Europeans are a mixed bunch, but the Africans are all pukka, from high-up families, and the parents cry murder if their blasted offspring go home with no weals to show for their education. It's the only lingo they understand. Carry a suitable instrument at all times, and don't hesitate to use it. A cane is useful for general purposes, but the tawse makes quite a delicious ceremony, and of course the sjambok is agreeably terrifying, for flagellance royale. It's up to you. How's your Latin?'

'It's – well, um –'

'Good. You'll be taking advanced Latin – just open *Caeasar's Gallic Wars* and use the crib – along with cookery, history, maths, French, geography and English. Any oik who raises nose from book, out in front, bare up and bum-whop. The girls wear proper English uniform, so they lift skirts and lower knickers, but the males insist on wearing tribal robes and other ghastly nonsense. Luckily, they are naked underneath, so whopping their derrières is easy. Where is that blasted maid with our tea?'

There was a tinkling of bells and a dark-skinned African slipped into the room. Eighteen or nineteen years old, 'Sally' was most definitely a boy, his sleek ebony body nude, save for a frilly girlmaid's black skirtlet, with a flounced white apron. He carried a teapot, as he approached the ladies, his lips solemn and his long-lashed eyes hooded. Belinda's eyes were fixed on his skirtlet, bulging unmistakably with an erect cock, and she pressed her thighs together over a trickle of juice from her cunt lips. Sally scanned Belinda's body, and she shivered, blushing slightly, as his lazy eyes devoured her titties, crotch and thighs. His groin swayed at her, rather lustfully, and, as he poured their tea, some liquid dripped to the floor.

'Clumsy girl,' snapped Miss Harrod. 'I call him Sally to shame him – his real name is Sali-something, far too long – but I don't think he knows the bally difference. The girly skirt is to make him soppy, and diminish that –' she scowled at his erect cock – 'but I'm not sure he doesn't rather like it. A lot of African boys display – priapism – it's the heat, d'you see. I call it bally cheek! When I was matron of Gishington College, I used to make cheeky boys plunge their horrid things in an ice bucket. Unfortunately, ice is at a premium in Somaliland.'

'He's rather pretty,' Belinda murmured.

'Dangerously so,' said Miss Harrod. 'An arrogant brute – desert royalty – and wears these blasted jingle balls, like several others. When they reach manhood, nobles have a doings, apparently painless, where these – these balls are inserted – under the, ah, skin of the pego, to indicate wealth and nobility. Pure showing off! A bit of a cock robin, our Sally – his papa's rather generous dosh means we must tolerate the son's eccentricities. I reckon that priapic pego of his has pleasured half the girls in school – and half the mistresses.'

'Really,' purred Belinda. 'Is it – I don't dare inspect – is it fully agitated just now?'

'Scarcely halfway up,' snorted Miss Harrod. 'Behind that silky smile is the devil of a tease.'

Sally put down the teapot, spilling liquid onto Miss Harrod's red nylons.

'That is the limit,' she said crossly. 'Insolent sloppiness! Girl, bring me my best cane – you know, the long, whippy one.'

The boymaid looked at her with smouldering eyes, as his frilly skirtlet stretched to breaking, from the massive erect pole stiffened within. Sally padded to Miss Harrod's cane rack and, contemptuously, drew down a three-foot yellow cane, with a crook handle, gleaming and oiled. He handed the cane to Miss Harrod, with a little bow.

'Over the desk, girl,' she said, rising and flexing the cane between both fists. 'Skirt up, bum bare – you know the drill.'

Bending over the desktop, Sally lifted his skirt, baring his muscled ebony buttocks. The skirt rose at an angle, with its front balanced on the desktop, showing his naked cock beneath.

'Legs apart,' Miss Harrod commanded.

He obeyed; Belinda gasped at his massive black balls, dangling between quivering thighs, and the huge bare-shaven cock, stiff under his belly, its prepuce stretched fully back to reveal the shining, swollen helmet, and its ebony shaft pocked with lumps from the jingle balls.

That cock begs to be wanked. Or to mount me, and rip my bumhole to shreds . . .

With a slither of stockings, Belinda crossed her legs tight to stem the gush of come from her pulsing cunt, as her clitty throbbed, poking long and stiff into the cloth of her panties. The headmistress lifted her cane, her arm whirling. *Vip*! *Vip*! The wood laid two livid crimson stripes across the boy's naked buttocks. The cheeks clenched, and he gasped, but did not tremble. *Vip*! A third cut took him aslant. *Vip*! *Vip*! Two cuts sliced his haunches. Sally's legs began to shiver, and his chest pumped, with his breath rasping hoarse, and the bum cheeks clenching hard, but only at the cane's impact, and not before. *Vip*! *Vip*!

'Ahh ...' he gasped softly, with a mist of tears at his eyes, and his throat swallowing violently.

Vip! *Vip*!

'Uhh ...'

His cock jerked at every stroke, the helmet slapping his tensed belly, with his skirtlet bouncing prettily over his naked, rippling back. Belinda's panties were soaking; she longed for a wank. *Vip*! *Vip*! Sally's buttocks were squirming, now, in a fast, clenching rhythm.

'And twelve,' panted Miss Harrod.

Vip!

'Ahh ...' gasped the caned boy, in a long, anguished exhalation, his flogged bum twitching, with dark crimson stripes blistering his satin black skin.

'That will be all, girl,' she said, regaining her seat. 'Gracious, my tea will get cold.'

His lips wrinkled in a pout; the boy smoothed down his skirtlet over his glowing bum. Without warning, he swooped to the floor, kneeled at Miss Harrod's feet and began to lick the soles of her shoes, then the toes and uppers, with his tongue rasping on her nylon stockings. His massive cock swayed, still erect, beneath his frilly skirtlet. Miss Harrod flushed, and, after several seconds, told him to rise.

'Don't forget you have classes this afternoon,' she scolded.

He slipped out the door, and she sighed.

'The dear boy has a pash for me, you see. The more I whip him the more he swoons. Aren't males the strangest creatures? It was the same at Gishington. The headmaster deputised me to whop miscreants – bare bum, of course –

and, no matter how hard I laid on the cane, it never stopped them reoffending. Then, they would get disgracefully excited, and, as matron, it was my duty to . . . do something. You know.'

'You don't mean . . .?'

'Yes,' said Miss Harrod. 'I would relieve their tension, and rather enjoyed it. A girl has such a glorious feeling of power, when she's . . . wanking off a spunky boy. There was one – Quince, I think – who positively begged me to thrash him. I always had to tame him, and I was astonished how much cream his ballocks could produce.'

'Isn't it a bit unfair, leaving Sally in such obvious engorgement?' Belinda murmured, sipping her tea.

'That's part of his punishment,' replied Miss Harrod, frowning, 'although, if I know him, he'll probably lower some girl's knickers – doubtless that hussy Wunu's. The girls are all far too precocious, and that monstrous organ – well, you can imagine the effect on a hot young slut.'

'How well do you know him, miss?' Belinda asked slyly.

Miss Harrod flushed. 'Exactly what do you mean?' she snapped.

'You said he'd had half the girls, and half the mistresses, and he is a juicy young spunk, so I wondered if . . . I mean, I should perfectly understand – in fact, I'd be awfully envious.'

Miss Harrod pursed her lips, then smiled icily. 'You are suggesting that I –' she gasped. 'I don't know whether to condemn or admire your appalling cheek – as if you are demanding to be lashed.'

'Oh, no, miss.'

She crossed her red nylons, and peered over her spectacles at Belinda's jutting breasts, then picked up her cane and stroked it.

'I not sure I shan't award you a beating. Have to nip insubordination in the bud, *pour encourager les autres*. You do see my point of view.'

'Why, yes, miss,' Belinda replied meekly. 'I'm dreadfully sorry – I mean, if I've offended –'

'You don't mind baring up . . . so soon?'

Belinda shrugged. 'If I'm to use the cane, I must prove I can take it.'

'Well, that's settled. You'll take a dusting. Let's have another cup of tea first, eh?'

They sipped daintily, until Belinda drained her cup, and stood.

'Shall I bare up now, miss?'

'Why not. Over the desktop?'

Belinda bent over the desk, lifted her tan uniforrm skirt and rolled down her white silk panties. Her naked bottom was framed by her white sussies and garter straps over her cream stockings. She parted her legs, stretching the panties to a bridge, and thrust up her buttocks, the pendant cunt lips swollen between her thighs.

'A dozen all right?' said Miss Harrod.

'Perfectly, miss.'

'I won't lay it on too hard. But, by the marks on your bum, I'd say you've been beaten not long ago.'

'Yes, miss. I'd prefer not to –'

'I quite understand.'

'Thank you, miss. It's just that I am one of those girls who sort of – well, I often find I deserve a bare-beating.'

'You don't mean you like it?' murmured Miss Harrod, raising her rod.

'No, miss! I hate it. The pain is so awful.'

'But you make sure you earn it.'

'May I speak frankly? It may sound silly, but I think, somehow, I crave the shame of punishment,' whispered Belinda, her bottom tensed.

Miss Harrod stroked Belinda's upturned globes with cool fingertips. 'My, you have got a lovely pneumatic croup. Your bumskin's smooth as silk. It's so . . . big and firm and rounded, yet your waist is so deliciously narrow. So you relish your whackings? Good! Let's play bouncy bum.'

Vip! The first stroke lashed Belinda squarely in mid-fesse. Her buttocks clenched and she gasped. *Vip*! The second wealed her underfesse, just above the thighs. *Vip*! A third, to top buttock. *Vip*! A fourth, to the backs of her thighs, below the fesses. Tears moistened Belinda's eyes, and her throat gulped, as her breasts heaved violently and her bum cheeks clenched, with her cleft a tight crevasse. Her breath came in hoarse, anguished pants.

'Ooh . . .' she groaned. 'That's tight, miss.'

'But your bum's practically still! Go on, Belinda, squirm,' said Miss Harrod. 'I want to see those juicy pears wriggling and clenching, as they redden. Keeping still is for boys.'

'I was taught to keep a stiff upper lip, miss,' Belinda gasped.

'Lip, yes –'

Vip!

'Ouch! Ooh!'

'– not bottom.'

Vip!

'Oh! Gosh! My bum's on fire, miss.'

In addition to her tight clenching of the bum cleft, Belinda's flogged buttocks squirmed in a rolling motion, mashing the blistered globes into folds and trenches of reddened flesh. Her legs quivered, rigid and straight behind her. Miss Harrod paused, breasts heaving, to brush a strand of hair from her flushed face.

'Well!' she panted. 'Six down, miss, and six to go.'

'Oh,' Belinda whimpered, 'how I wish it was over.'

'Do you?'

'Uhh . . . it hurts so . . .' Belinda sobbed.

'My, your croup's lovely and hot,' said Miss Harrod, stroking her whipped nates, 'and the weals are a delicious fruity red. You're about the best bum I've caned.'

Vip!

'Ooh! Ahh!'

'Describe your feelings when you are caned. I'm curious why you crave beating.'

'Oh, it's the feeling of being used, humiliated, like an animal. Especially when – when a male canes me. I'm his thing, his chattel, to use as he pleases. It's such a giddy pleasure, to bear pain for a master.'

Vip!

'Ouch! Ooh!'

Belinda's reddened bare fesses wriggled helplessly, the welts darkening to crimson and surmounted by swelling pale blisters.

'What else must you bear, Belinda, when that lovely bum is reddened by a male's cane? Disgraceful gropings, I expect.'

'Sometimes more . . . he biffs me, miss.'

'In your twat?'

'Mostly elsewhere.'

'You take bumming? Why, you vile girl –'

Vip! The cane stroked Belinda in an uppercut to her arse cleft, lashing wetly between her cunt lips and on the anus bud.

'Ohh! Ahh!' Belinda shrieked, her arse squirming frantically, legs shuddering, and with droplets of come spraying from her spurting cunt. 'Oh, miss, that's cruel.'

There was a swish of clothing; she twisted her head to look at Miss Harrod through tear-blurred eyes, and gasped, as she saw the headmistress bare-breasted, big pink nipples erect, with her green skirt raised, and her fingers in her wet panties.

'Head forwards, miss,' panted the masturbating headmistress. 'We're all girls here.'

Vip! Belinda's naked buttocks jerked, at the slap of wood on her sweaty skin.

'Ooh!' she whimpered, as waves of pain rippled through the flesh beneath her cane blisters.

'It's this damned heat!' Miss Harrod gasped. 'Surely you understand. Girls need a tup or a wank.'

Vip!

'Ahh! Yes, miss. Or a tickling on the bum. Can't you see how wet my twat is? I'm so ashamed.'

Vip!

'Oh! Oh! Ouch!'

Belinda's juicing cunt sprayed come, staining her cream stockings dark.

'Bold vixen. That's your twelve, but hold position. No rubbing.'

Miss Harrod's nylons slithered wetly, as she crouched with her face between Belinda's thighs. Belinda gasped shrilly, as the tongue probed her gushing slit, poking the juicy flesh, while licking Belinda's throbbing erect nubbin.

'I've never tasted a nub so big,' murmured Miss Harrod, her voice muffled by Belinda's skirt and her fleshy wet cunt folds.

'Ooh!' Belinda groaned, as the headmistress took her throbbing clit in her mouth, and began to suck, pressing her lips on the extruded clitty shaft, while her tongue flicked the glans of the nubbin.

Come spurted from Belinda's writhing cunt, and Miss Harrod made slurping noises, as she drank the hot liquid.

'It's lovely to frig!' gasped the headmistress, as her fingers poked her own cunt, wetting her panties and skirt.

She rubbed her blonde tresses on Belinda's gash, soaking the hairs in come, then squeezed them to drip come onto her bare breasts. 'Such a heavy comer,' she panted, rubbing Belinda's juice into her nipples. 'Lovely come, for my nips. Oh, this heat makes a girl so fruity.'

'Yes, miss, do me . . .' Belinda moaned.

Miss Harrod's palm cupped a wealed fesse, and Belinda winced, whimpering, as her nails raked the rubbery cane blisters. A finger delved into her anus, then another, and began to fingerfuck Belinda's rectum. Belinda squirmed, squeezing the fingers with her anal sphincter, as her belly and spine fluttered.

'Gosh, miss, I'm coming . . .' she whimpered.

'Flogging excites you, slut,' hissed Miss Harrod, masturbating vigorously, as her tongue squelched the swollen wet folds of Belinda's cunt. 'Admit it.'

'Oh, yes, miss. I love to have my bum smacked. There! I'm coming – oh! Oh! Oh! Ooh!'

'Urrgh . . .' gasped Miss Harrod, drinking Belinda's come, as both females spasmed.

With a plop, as her lips disengaged from Belinda's gash, Miss Harrod rose. She turned to pull up her come-soaked panties, and Belinda gasped, glimpsing the full, hard orbs of the woman's naked bottom. Both fesses were striated with old canestreaks.

'Do you like my titties, Miss Beaucul?' she asked coyly, tweaking her stiff nipples.

'Yes, miss, they're lovely,' Belinda gasped. 'So is your bottom.'

'Why, thank you! How sweet. I am so glad we understand each other,' the headmistress purred, licking her lips. 'I know I caned you for suggesting it, but, between us girls, Sally's conquests do include me.'

The perfume of the girls mingled with the scent of bougainvillea, its blossom bright amid jacaranda and palm trees, swaying against a panorama of sparkling blue sea, a mile away. Belinda wiped her brow, gazing at the rows of ebony schoolmaids, immaculate in short blue pleated skirts, bare-legged and with white blouses and ankle socks above gleaming polished black shoes. These eighteen-year-olds bulged in their clinging uniforms, always too small; most did without bras – often knickers, too, as Belinda knew from the daily experience of spanking an errant bare bottom – and breathed the smoky sensuality of Africa.

Their breasts were awfully large for their age, many of them with hard, conic teats like little volcanos, topped with the big plum-sized domes of their nipples; others with ripely jutting, curving teat gourds, equal to Belinda's own. Their bottoms swelled from narrow waists into big firm melons, swaying and shivering adorably with their sultry, long-legged gait, the big ebony fesses wickedly inviting caress or penetration. The girls knew that uniforms and grammar books were a pretty conceit; beneath, they were fragrant female meat, naked for the tupping.

These girls know what they are for.

Dominating every classroom, the punishment cabinet shone with polished glass and, inside, a gleaming array of canes and whips. The mistress wore the punishment key around her neck, and for her first few days Belinda avoided using it. Miss Harrod was right, of course – the pupils expected chastisement in every class, and seemed restless, until the crack of palm or leather had reddened at least one bare bottom. The boys, loose-limbed and arrogant, swaggered, baring up with pride – the handful of Europeans adopting the manners of their African comrades – as most of them sported massive erections, which Belinda, at first, pretended not to notice. A brisk spanking of thirty smacks reddened the most ebony bottom, with a theatrical display of squirming, which could not fail to stimulate Belinda, especially when the African boys returned to their desks with robes undone to show off their engorged sex organs. Many of them jingled with the tender, gash-moistening sound of bells.

The girls were a different matter. They bared up with sullen, silent defiance, sneering, as Belinda spanked the firm, slightly moist, ebony buttocks, parted slightly, to show the wriggling arse cleft, and fragrant with the smoky perfume of a girl's underparts. The black quim lips hung, full and firm, between delicately quivering thighs, as Belinda spanked, with the anal pucker wrinkling and pouting, distinguished from the satin smooth ebony of the fesses only by its crinkly whorls of dark, tender skin.

As her palm smacked the firm ebony buttock meat, Belinda wanted to let it rest there, caress the smooth flesh and stroke the cleft down to the moist quim and anus; tickle the girl and press her own mouth and nose to that succulent bottom, then penetrate her intimate wet holes, and really make her wriggle, until the girl came, splashing come on Belinda's face and breasts. The girls prided themselves on not clenching or squirming too much, and some did not even clench at all, no matter how crimson their dark bottoms glowed. The parted bare buttocks seemed to float, merely shivering at Belinda's hard smacks.

'You have to whip them, Belinda,' said April Bitter, Belinda's best friend among the staff, and the senior PT mistress, a hard-muscled southern girl from Derby. 'The sjambok is terrific exercise, you know. But use the cane at least.'

Among her duties, Belinda was assistant girls' PT mistress, which she didn't mind, as April did all the work. Belinda's job was mostly to blow the whistle at the girls sweating in skimpy tops and shorties, climbing wall bars, vaulting the horse or doing cruel sets of press-ups and sit-ups, while April bounced around the gym, cane flapping at her waist. Her cane got frequent use, a lazy or sullen girl being ordered to continue the class in the full nude, after April had caned her a dozen on the bare bum, pumping, as the girl went through agonising press-ups. April liked to finish her beatings with a cut between the legs, to lash the bumcleft and gash, which always made the girl squeal – otherwise, she confided, a caning wasn't really punishment.

After classes, April and Belinda sunbathed in the nude, in April's secret spot on the roof, with glasses of cold sherbet. The first time, it seemed the most natural thing in the world for the two sweating girls to masturbate together, at April's suggestion of hygienic exercise; briskly, they wanked each other off, thighs raised, quim lips spread and hands on gashes, without kissing or bub-touching, or anything soppy, their conversation interrupted only by an occasional 'ooh' or 'ahh'. April's body, rippling with muscle, was completely shaven, with a cunt hillock almost as big as Belinda's, but a clitty of normal size, until erect. Kissed nude by the sun, as April's deft fingers wanked her, Belinda found her body quickly golden.

Although there was no need to venture into Berbera, as all their needs were met in the sprawling, dusty school compound, with vendors of cosmetics, underwear or sweets permitted to hawk within the school yard, nevertheless Belinda gladly accompanied April on forays into Berbera's nightlife – to the Empire Club, where they drank pink gin with British officers, or the Café de la Lune, where Egyptian belly-dancers writhed, almost nude, and April flirted outrageously with French foreign legionnaires from neighbouring Djibouti. They were real spunks, and generous with drinks, but, when Belinda danced with them, were ardent, stiff-tooled gropers.

The most blatant was 'Robespierre' – his *nom de guerre* – a lean, lustful officer, who let slip that his real name was Count Scazza. His hands were under Belinda's skirt, caressing her bare buttocks, and his erection pressed to her groin, as they swayed on the dance floor. Belinda blurted that she knew Jeremy Quince, at which Scazza slipped his fingers into her cunt, and began, outrageously, to masturbate her.

'Mm . . .' Belinda gasped.

'Cher Jeremy didn't stay long – I don't know what's become of him – but he mentioned you,' he whispered, pumping his fingers in her soaking slit. 'You are the sort of girl I need, for my camp brothel.' He felt Belinda tense. 'I mean as house mistress, keeping the girls in order, with whips. You would have your own African servant boys, fine frocks, champagne and a two-litre Peugeot.'

'I couldn't,' Belinda whimpered. 'I'm under conrtract to HM Forces.'

His fingers tweaked her extruded throbbing clitty.

'Ooh . . . don't.'

'Why, with that giant nub, you are almost an africaine,' he murmured. 'Come and work for the legion. Think of it, your own naked boyslaves, with enormous cocks, and juicy bare culs for your whip.'

'You flatter me, sir, with your foreign wiles,' Belinda gasped, as his fingers slopped in the come gushing from her cunt and soaking her panties. 'I'll bet you finger all the girls' twats. Well, I know what your sort needs.'

Her fingers slipped under his waistband, found the hard, throbbing tool and began to rub his glans. He bit her ear, frotting her slit, while she rubbed his glans and cockshaft, wanking him off to a massive spurt. As his cream poured over her fingers, Belinda's wanked cunt spurted in a trembling orgasm.

'Ooh! That's your lot, sir,' she gasped.

'You divine English maiden, I know you will work for me, one day!' he crowed.

He opened his gold cigarette case, and she helped herself to a virginia. Belinda sucked smoke, exhaling flamboyantly.

'Mm . . . I thought you'd smoke smelly French cigs,' she said.

'Ah no,' Scazza replied. '*Je ne fume que des blondes.*'

'That sounds rude,' she said, giggling.

'It means, "I only suck blondes."'

* * *

Belinda found herself masturbating vigorously, two or three times a night, soaking her chaste bed in come.

'You need a regular spunk,' April drawled, puffing on her Lucky Strike. 'Otherwise you'll go potty. Not Scazza – he letches all the girls, but when he's finished with one girlslave, whipped and buggered rotten, then she's in the brothel, tooled by a dozen bucks a day. Our male colleagues are only interested in African girls, so pick one of the not too awful African boys – they're best for cock, especially ones with jingle balls. You can sneak them up to your room – we all do, even Miss Horrid.'

She swigged her cocktail, with a quizzical glance at Belinda. 'Or a girl, if you prefer. Choose the juiciest bum as you thrash them. I do like our diddling sessions, but we're busy girls, so I expect you're wanking off by yourself quite a lot. I know I did, at first. '

'Well, yes,' Belinda admitted. 'This heat –'

'Get yourself a juicy spunk, for twatfill – or a succulent girl, with a strong tongue. Of course, it doesn't hurt to wank off as well. Jessica Twobbs wanked five or six times a day, and Sally was tooling her. She disappeared, though, a complete mystery. They say she scarpered back to Blighty, but who knows?'

It was beastly hot in the classroom, despite the silently whirling ceiling fan. It was her third week, the last class of the afternoon, and it had to be done. The girls were effervescent – Belinda fingered the punishment key.

'Wunu! Up here at once,' she rapped.

It would be the sensuous Wunu who cheeked her the worst. The girl slouched towards her, licking her lips.

'Another spanking, miss?' she purred.

'No,' Belinda said. 'You've earned a caning.'

Wunu made a moue but, with a silent flourish, proudly raised her blue skirt and lowered her dazzling white panties. Her full ebony buttock pears shone at Belinda, who could see her own blurred reflection in the girl's gleaming bumskin. She inhaled the musky perfume of Wunu's anus and cunt, with the gash flaps full and pendant. Has Sally's cock been inside her? With trembling fingers, Belinda unlocked the punishment cabinet, and selected the hardest, whippiest cane on the rack, a fearsome three-footer in dark rattan.

'Now, I know this is the first time –' she began.

'Please, miss,' Wunu interrupted scornfully, 'I'm ready if you are.'

The cheeky so-and-so!

The class hushed, as a furious Belinda commenced the girl's flogging. *Vip*! The cane lashed a deep red weal on her liquorice buttocks. *Vip*! *Vip*! Her cheeks clenched only slightly, but her upper body shivered, and her breasts began to heave. Wunu's lips trembled, and her eyelids blinked rapidly. *Vip*! *Vip*! By the fifth stroke, her bottom was squirming and her legs quivering, rigid behind her. Wunu's breath came in hoarse pants, her nostrils flaring, as they frantically sucked air. *Vip*! *Vip*!

'Ahh . . .' she gasped, at the seventh cut.

Belinda ordered her to be silent. *Vip*! *Vip*! By the ninth, the naked black buttocks were glowing with crimson stripes, and Belinda gasped hard, as her panties filled with come. Weals on an English girl's pale bottom were like the marks of a raptor, but on Wunu's African fesses, crimson weals blossomed coyly, like flowers in the dark succulent earth. Between the clenching arse cheeks, Wunu's gash glistened with cunt dew. *Vip*! *Vip*!

'Uhh . . .' the girl groaned.

The class was silent, staring wide-eyed at the girl's wriggling bare. *Vip*! Belinda delivered the final stroke with both hands on the cane, and sliced a deep welt across the existing blisters.

'Ooh!' Wunu whimpered, her flogged bottom jerking and wriggling frantically, with droplets of come spraying from her flapping cooze.

Panting, Belinda said her beating was complete. Belinda's stockings squished, as she walked, with come soaking her panties and bare thighs. The rest of the lesson was peaceful, but Belinda was awfully itchy, and dying for a wank. At the bell, she scooped her papers, and fled to her room, where she lowered her panties and squatted on her porcelain chamber pot, gasping in relief, as she pissed luxuriously. After stripping off the panties, she lay on her bed, skirt up and legs spread wide. Her fingers slid down her bare belly to her juicing cunt, with the clitty stretched in full erection, and she began to masturbate. Her fingers were squelching in her copiously flowing come, and she was breathing hoarsely, when there was a knock on the door.

'It is I, miss – Wunu,' cooed the girl's voice.

Belinda leaped to her feet, smoothing down her skirt, and opened the door, brushing back moist tresses from her flushed brow. Wunu proffered a bowl of flowers.

'For you, miss,' she said.

'Lupins,' said Belinda. 'My favourite! Thank you, Wunu – but why? Won't you come in?'

Wunu sat on the bed, decorously removing Belinda's come-slimed panties, thrown there. She held them up, her lips pursed.

'Oh,' blurted Belinda, 'just throw them . . . it's so hot . . . sweat, you know.'

Wunu rubbed the oily gusset between her fingers, before placing the panties aside, then gravely accepted a glass of lemonade.

'I wanted to apologise for my naughtiness in class,' she murmured.

'There's really no need,' Belinda said. 'It is I who should apologise for having flogged you so hard. But I had to set an example, Wunu.'

'I quite understand,' said the black girl. 'I am very naughty, and need regular beating, just as we girls are whipped at home. We have a saying, "the rod speaks for the heart", and I felt that your rod spoke to me, miss.'

'I don't quite –'

Wunu gestured to the wet panties. 'You must have seen my twat moisten, as my bottom reddened,' she purred. 'I think you felt the same. Were you masturbating just now, miss?'

'I say,' blurted Belinda, reddening, 'that's a bit – well, darn it, yes, I was.'

'Thinking of my bared bottom?'

Belinda gulped. 'Yes,' she whispered. 'I was thinking I'd like to do more than beat you.'

'Then we do feel the same,' said Wunu, moving closer to Belinda on the bed.

12

Blue with Welts

Wunu's hand stroked Belinda's thigh, her fingers moving softly under the skirt, towards the naked cunt. She penetrated Belinda's wet gash, parting the lips with a squelching sound, then clasped Belinda's extruded clitty between thumb and palm, and reamed the throbbing nub.

'Ah! Belinda gasped. 'It's so good . . . oh! Ohh!' Belinda came, almost at once. 'Oh! Ooh! That's never happened before,' she panted. 'Oh, Wunu . . .'

She embraced Wunu's buttocks, fumbling under the skirt and knickers, until her palm clasped the wealed, ribbed bare, still hot from the flogging.

'You poor thing,' she murmured. 'I was awfully cruel.'

'Not cruel enough, miss,' purred Wunu. 'At home, a girl's stripes show how she is loved. A wife demands her husband's whip, to make her wet for his tool.'

Belinda stripped off her skirt and blouse, while watching the ebony girl coolly unhooking her bra, and flicking open her blouse buttons, before slipping out of her knickers and pleated school skirt. The two girls sat, kissing, tongues deep in their mouths, wearing only their stockings and sussies. Thighs enlaced, each masturbated the other's gushing cunt, with come-slopped fingers, while their naked breasts rubbed together, at the stiff points of the nipples.

'Gosh, that's so nice,' Belinda panted.

Wunu's tongue darted to her throat.

'Phew!' gasped Belinda. 'I'm so giddy. Shift up a little – put your thighs across mine. Let me get your bubbies in my mouth – don't stop diddling my clitty – yes!'

With her fingers stabbing the ebony girl's streaming pouch, she tongued Wunu's stiff chocolate nipples, flicking the swollen buds with her tongue, and nuzzling her nose in the firm bare breastflesh, softly quivering. Both giggled, as Belinda hooked Wunu's frilly white suspender belt with her thumb, and snapped it against her belly. They rolled off their come-wet stockings, and entwined their naked legs, cupping come from their gushing slits, then smearing it on their bottoms, or shaven quim hillocks. Wunu bent her leg, and thrust her toes into Belinda's mouth.

'Mm, that's lovely,' Belinda gasped, sucking the toes. 'Am I tickling you?'

'That's the point, miss,' said Wunu. 'Let me suck yours.'

'They're a bit cheesy.'

'That, too, is the point.'

Their feet in each other's mouth, the girls sucked toes and licked soles and ankles, while their fingers poked wet pink slits. Wunu penetrated Belinda's anus with two come-slimed fingers, and began to ream her rectum, making Belinda's buttocks squirm.

'Gosh, Wunu,' Belinda gasped. 'I so love it there! Please, won't you –'

'Yes, miss? Anything.'

'Won't you please whip my bum?'

'Spank you, miss?' said Wunu, licking Belinda's drool from her lips.

'No, no – wait –' Belinda scrambled in her luggage, and presented Wunu with her oiled, shiny tawse. 'A keepsake from England,' she said. 'They're rather special.'

Wunu stroked the supple leather tongues. 'I might hurt you very badly, miss, with these.'

'Yes – please – it's what I want. Thrash my bare, Wunu, till I squeal. If only you understood . . . when the vicar at Bolton-le-Sands caned my bare, I always got a lovely cream tea afterwards, with Eccles cakes and blancmange and everything. Oh, please, whip my naked bottom.'

She plunged her face in her pillow, bare tiptoes on the floor, and buttocks thrust high.

'But I do understand, miss,' Wunu purred, taking her whipping stance over Belinda's croup.

Her toe parted Belinda's arse cheeks, tickling the anus and cleft, before penetrating the wet gash. Belinda gasped, wriggling her cunt against Wunu's probing foot.

'Ooh!' she shrilled, as the toes poked her clitty. 'I'm going to come again, any second.'

The toe withdrew. The twin tongues lashed Belinda hard, across the bare, and she gasped, clenching her fesses. Belinda's bare fesses blossomed red, as she squirmed, gasping.

'Ouch!' she cried. 'That hurts, you beast. How many must I take?'

'How many can you take?'

'Oh . . . thirty, I'm sure.'

'Then I'll give you more,' Wunu purred.

Thwap! Wunu's hard conic breasts bounced, beaded with sweat, as she flogged Belinda's squirming bare. The coverlet darkened, under Belinda's writhing cunt hillock, in a spreading stain of her come. *Thwap*! The hissing leather tongues blistered the full expanse of Belinda's bare, raising harsh puffy crimson weals from thigh to top bum. *Thwap*! *Thwap*!

'Ooh! You're cruel . . . harder, please . . .'

Thwap! *Thwap*!

'Ooh!'

The tongues licked Belinda's quivering arse cleft, slapping the pendant lips of her swollen gash. *Thwap*! *Thwap*! The tongues' tips thrashed her extruded, erect clitty.

'Oh! My twat! Ahh! Gosh, that hurts! I'm going to come again –'

Thwap! *Thwap*!

'Yes . . . oh! Oh! Ohh!'

Belinda writhed in orgasm, as the leather flogged her crimson, squirming buttocks, her arse cleft a deep red gash, glazed with the come spurting from her twitching cunt flaps. Feet in fencer's stance, thighs and belly rippling as she twirled, and the tawse tongues flashing in the afternoon sun, Wunu masturbated her shiny shaven cunt, with gleaming rivulets of come streaking her ebony thighs. She whipped the whimpering Belinda past thirty, then past forty lashes, bringing her off twice more.

'More ... harder ...' Belinda moaned. 'I need it so badly ...'

'You are a very demanding bitch,' Wunu panted, wanking her hugely stiff clit, and stabbing the pink, glistening flesh of her pouch, framed by swollen black cunt lips, shiny with come. 'Your nub is as big as mine, bitch. Why, you are almost African.'

She flogged Belinda past sixty, licking haunches, thigh backs and quim, until Belinda's naked bottom was a squirming glow of red and purple bruises. After a final, jarring lash to Belinda's gushing cunt, Wunu jabbed three fingers into Belinda's pouch, curving her fingers past the pubic bone, and pressing hard.

'Oh! Ooh!' Belinda whimpered. 'Ooh, I'm coming ... ah! It's so ... good ... yes!'

Suddenly, a clear stream of liquid spurted from her cunt, splashing Wunu's breasts and belly.

'Oh, I'm sorry, I didn't mean to pee –'

Wunu lifted her onto the bed, and squatted with her cunt over Belinda's face. 'You didn't. The best come is squirting your waters,' Wunu panted. 'A big-nubbed African girl strokes her clit for ordinary comes, but her magic spot for a waterfall, a double come. Now, lick me, bitch. Take my nub in your mouth, and suck me off.'

She sat on Belinda's face, squashing her nose and mouth with her meaty black buttocks. As Belinda, clasping Wunu's bare, sucked the hard pink tube of the African girl's clitty, Wunu frigged her own slit.

'Uh ... uh ... yes,' Wunu panted, as her belly fluttered in climax, and come spurted from her gash into Belinda's mouth. 'Yes!'

A torrent of clear, fragrant liquid spurted from her quim lips, soaking Belinda's eyes and hair.

'Ooh ... ooh ...'

Wunu's voice shrilled in breathless ululation, as she wanked her spurting cunt, and tweaked her swollen brown nipples, while her buttocks writhed, crushing Belinda's come-glazed face.

Fingernails scratched Belinda's door, which promptly opened, admitting Sally, clad only in his frilly maid's skirtlet. His eyes widened, and his sullen pout turned to a sneer.

'Miss Harrod invites you to tea, Miss Beaucul,' he said. He sprang forwards, and wrenched Belinda's hair, making her squeal. 'But I see you're otherwise engaged,' he snarled, 'diddling my slut.'

'Ouch! You're hurting me,' Belinda gasped. 'Let go, you beastly whelp, or I'll cane you.'

At the male's command, Wunu rose, gripping Belinda's nipples, and pulling her over, while Sally slammed Belinda's face into her come-wet pillow. His nails clawed the welts in her whipped bottom, and Belinda squealed. Twisting her head, with Wunu's foot pinioning her neck, she saw Sally doff his skirtlet, and reveal his ebony cock, lumpy with bells, and shining stiff.

'Please, no!' she whimpered, before Wunu squashed her head to the pillow.

Belinda's body threshed, with her buttocks heaving, as Sally spread the cheeks and nuzzled her anus with his cock. She let out a muffled shriek, as his cock penetrated her anus, plunging to fill her rectum, with his glans ramming her colon.

'Urrgh!' Belinda groaned, her buttocks writhing.

Sally's hips slapped her wealed arse skin, as he began to bugger her with merciless, powerful stabs. Impaled on his huge knobbed cock, Belinda sobbed, with Wunu pinioning her wrists painfully up her back.

'Ooh!' she squealed, from her pillow. 'You're ripping my bumhole!'

The knobs on Sally's cock rasped Belinda's tender anal elastic, as he pumped with rapid, jerking motions, his cock, slimed with her copious arse grease, sliding fully from her hole, before plunging again, to his balls, so that his peehole slapped the tender opening of her sigmoid colon. Belinda's nude body, slippery with sweat and come, wriggled helplessly, as she whimpered under her buggery. Sally enculed her for minutes, and Belinda's choking squeals grew softer, her buttocks squeezing the massive cock and balls impaling her, so that Sally panted at each withdrawal of his tool from her clutching anus.

'You're game, bitch,' he gasped. 'Suck my tool with your tight little whore's arsehole.'

'No!' groaned Belinda. 'You're horrid!'

Smack! Smack! The boy slapped her squirming buttocks.

'Ooh! You're vile,' she moaned. 'Oh, yes, damn you, do me, Sally, do me harder! Spank my bare! Bugger my bum till I come! I need it so badly.'

Come sprayed from her squelching gash flaps, as her thighs flailed, awash in the oily cunt juice. Wunu, pinioning her victim, wanked her own cunt, with her stiff clitty bobbing, a baby marrow between her masturbating fingers, slopped with her copious come, which dripped onto Belinda's hair.

'Mm! Oh! You're as good as Amur,' Belinda gasped. 'Bugger my hole, bugger me . . . yes! Oh! Oh! Ahh!'

Come spurted from her cunt, as she whimpered in orgasm; with a sucking plop, Sally pulled his cock from her anus. Wunu released Belinda, and Belinda stared through her tears at the monstrous cock, shining with her arse grease.

'I want your cream . . .' she moaned, drool trickling from her lips.

Sally seized her bubs, pinching the nipples hard, and thrust his cock between them.

'Jelly me, bitch,' he commanded.

Belinda's naked breasts squashed his cock, rubbing the balls and shaft, with her stiff nipples flicking his glans and peehole. The squatting Wunu's cunt gaped over her face, with Wunu masturbating vigorously and squirting come into Belinda's eyes. Sally gasped, as Belinda's teat jellies mashed his cock, until a bead of spunk appeared at his peehole.

'Ah! Ahh!' Wunu panted, fingers pounding her cunt, as a fountain of clear ejaculate, mixed with come, jetted from her gash, into Belinda's mouth.

From Sally's cock spurted a powerful stream of spunk, blending with Wunu's ejaculate, to fill Belinda's mouth, with Belinda gurgling, as she swallowed the mingled fluids. As his cock bucked and spurted, she rubbed the neck of his glans with her nipples, squeezing her bubs hard against his stiff tool, so that he panted hoarsely. Spunk bubbled from Belinda's lips, to smear her titties, and Wunu bent to lick Belinda's breasts clean of spunk, biting her nipples hard, as Sally's cock softened, and slid down Belinda's belly. Belinda's fingers darted to her sopping gash, and, plunging them in the drooling cunt-slime, she wanked herself in a few deft strokes to another orgasm. Thumb mashing her clitty, and fingers bent back above her pube bone, she pressed her magic spot, and squealed, as a fountain of clear ejaculate erupted from her gash into Wunu's face.

'Oh, Wunu,' Belinda gasped. 'What a lovely spurt! Such lovely, horrid pain from his jingle balls, as if he was tearing my bum to bits.'

'Better than Amur, miss?' spat Wunu.

'Well, nearly as good . . . but why . . .?

'I'm Sally's slut, but Amur is my husband, bitch,' the eighteen-year-old girl snarled, slapping Belinda's cheek.

'Where is that dratted girl?' Miss Harrod's voice wafted from the corridor. After a clatter of footsteps, and a perfunctory knock, the door opened, and the headmistress entered, to gaze on three nude bodies enlaced with Wunu sucking Sally's cock, while punching Belinda's breasts, and slapping her face.

'Miss Beaucul!' she gasped. 'Are you all right? Sally – you vile girl! Wunu, seize her ballocks!'

As her lips released Sally's tool, Wunu grasped the boy's balls, and he moaned, helpless to escape.

'Make her stand – that's right – now bend her over, with her beastly bum bared. She must have punishment at once. You see, Miss Beaucul, how hot-blooded these young people are. Why, your bottom is bruised! Did Sally –'

'But you remember, miss,' blurted Belinda, blushing hotly, 'you disciplined me –'

'Surely not quite so vividly?'

'I – I sometimes practise on my own bottom,' Belinda said.

'Very well. But Sally – in the nude – surely –'

'Really, it was nothing, miss.'

'So, Sally attempted – the swine must learn a lesson. You shall flog her, Miss Beaucul.'

'Wunu and I stripped for comfort, in this heat,' Belinda said, 'then Sally did, too. A harmless spanking game may have got out of hand. I was the guilty one, showing off my new tawse.'

Miss Harrod threw up her hands, glaring at Belinda.

'Enough, miss,' she rapped. 'I know an English girl isn't to blame when she's full of juice, and sees such a monstrous pole, lusting to penetrate an innocent gel's hot, wet – well, even I have felt –' Her red-nyloned legs trembled, with a seep of moisture visible on the upper stockings. 'Oh! Whip the whelp raw!'

Sally gasped, as Wunu clamped his balls. His gleaming ebony buttocks quivered, upthrust. Belinda licked her lips, while rubbing her own smarting bottom. Wunu's hand was thrust between the thighs, from behind, clutching the balls, while Sally's massive knobbed cock, drooling with Wunu's saliva, quivered stiff against his belly. Belinda picked up her tawse.

'Crupper's of Kirkudbright, if I'm not mistaken,' said Miss Harrod.

'Why, yes.'

'They also make the finest sjamboks. Now, I quite understand your wish to be undraped, in this heat,' said Miss Harrod, mopping her brow.

The sunbeams, even through gossamer curtains, were harsh, and Miss Harrod's thin blouse stuck to her body, showing her breasts quivering in their brassiere, with the nipples broad, erect cupolas.

'Do please remain at ease, for Sally's beating. We are all modern girls, aren't we? In fact, I myself may take the liberty –' Trembling, with forced nonchalance, she lowered her green skirt, and unbuttoned her blouse. Standing in red nylon suspenders and stockings, with matching bra, she casually unhooked her bra, and let her breasts spring free, trembling tightly, with the nipple domes glazed and stiff.

'That's better,' she said, and unhooked her garter straps.

The red suspender belt was unhooked, and then she rolled down her panties, revealing her plump, shaven cunt hillock, shiny above the moist pink slit. She rolled off her stockings, and stood in the nude, smacking her bare buttocks, imprinted with her tight panties, and mauve with faded spanking bruises.

'There! All girls together,' she chirped. 'And all bare twats! Now let's punish this one.' She pointed at Sally, whose shaven cock strained, fully erect, above his belly button, while Wunu's palm imprisoned his balls.

Wunu withdrew her hand from his arse cleft, baring his buttocks for whipping, and at once resumed her ball clasp under his belly. Feet well apart, Belinda raised her tawse, and lashed the tongues across Sally's bottom. *Vap*! He gasped, clenching his fesses, as a vivid red stripe marked him. *Vap*! The second deepened the same weal, and his buttocks quivered. *Vap*! Sally's legs jerked straight, and trembled, as his flogged bare clenched and began to squirm; Belinda waited until the buttocks relaxed, then whipped him again, on full fesse. *Vap*! *Vap*! Her whipping continued, with the tawse lashing the quivering arse globes from top to bottom, his squirms wrenching his balls against Wunu's imprisoning grasp. *Vap*!

'Ooh . . .' he groaned, at the fifteenth stroke, his bum writhing fiercely.

His eyes were moist with tears, yet his cock still throbbed stiff in Wunu's fingers. Belinda panted, her bubbies flapping as she flogged the gasping boy, and sweat running in the cleft of her breasts, down her belly to her quim, which seeped come over her rippling thighs. Miss Harrod stood akimbo, eyes fixed on the flogged arse globes and her quim lips dribbling a froth of come. Wunu's fingers were rubbing her ebony slit, showing flashes of wet pink gash meat, and her thumb tweaking her erect clitty, extruded well outside the swollen flaps. With an impish smile, she masturbated openly, staring at Miss Harrod, who blushed.

'Girls will be girls,' she murmured, as her own fingers poked her dripping gash and she, too, began a vigorous frig. 'You may take Sally to thirty, Miss Beaucul.'

Vap! The flogged bum wriggled violently, with Sally's breath a hoarse rasp, and little gasps from his throat, as the leather striped his bare. Belinda's cunt spewed come; Wunu and Miss Harrod masturbated vigorously, as they ogled the crimson welts on the boy's arse, and, panting, Belinda slid her own fingers into her pouch, and began to wank off, as she whipped. She took him to thirty, then beyond, without comment from the headmistress. Forty strokes, then fifty. The three wanking girls sighed, panting, as come spurted from their pulsing cunts. *Vap*!

'Ohh! Miss, that's far more than thirty,' Sally squealed.

'Silence, whelp,' Belinda snapped.

Vap! *Vap*!

'Ooh!'

'Yes,' moaned Miss Harrod. 'Whip hard, make that naughty bum blush.'

Vap!

'Yes!'

Vap!

'Yes!'

Vap!

'Ooh! Oh! Oh! I'm coming ... ohh ...' panted Miss Harrod, as her belly convulsed in orgasm, and come spurted from her wanked cunt.

Wunu's rapid panting indicated her climax, with her fingers feverishly caressing the boy's trapped balls, and, as Belinda dealt a vicious stroke to his top buttock, rewarded by Sally's shrill whine of agony, her own cunt exploded in a trembling spasm.

Sally turned his tear-streaked face. 'Miss Harrod, that wasn't fair,' he said. 'She gave me over sixty.'

'You deserved them,' snarled Belinda.

Miss Harrod's face darkened. 'You were beastly cruel,' she gasped. 'You, and your lustful slut ... oh, poor Sally, how can I make up for it?'

She kneeled, and slid her face under his belly, getting the

glans in her mouth, and beginning to suck powerfully on his erect cock. Her bare bum wobbled, thrust high, as she fellated the huge cock, sliding her lips to his balls, and then returning up the cockshaft to the glans, where she licked his corona and peehole, before plunging again down the drool-slimed knobbed tool.

'Oh, my precious,' she gasped, sucking his ebony bell end. 'Can you ever forgive me? I so deserve punishment.'

Rolling onto his back, Sally pulled Miss Harrod's hair, clamping her face to his groin. 'You sluts,' he drawled. 'Punish her.'

Wunu seized the tawse, and began to whip Miss Harrod's bare buttocks, which bobbed, squirming, as the headmistress fellated her boymaid.

Vap! *Vap*!

'Ooh!' squealed Miss Harrod. 'Stop!'

Sally held her down by her wrenched hair, and ordered her to suck him in silence. As Miss Harrod snuffled, fellating Sally, Wunu flogged her quivering nates, blotching rapidly with a lattice of crimson tawse stripes.

'Oh! It hurts!' blurted Miss Harrod.

Vap! *Vap*!

'Ooh! Ouch! Yes, I need thrashing. Make my bum squirm, girl, whip me raw.'

Vap! *Vap*!

'Yes!'

Come spurted from her twitching cunt, sliming her thighs. At twelve strokes, Belinda took the tawse, and continued the beating, while Wunu unashamedly wanked off, watching Miss Harrod's buttocks wriggling, as the headmistress slurpily tongued Sally's cock. Changing on the dozen, the girls flogged their superior's bottom to over fifty strokes. Miss Harrod's hand scrambled between her spurting gash flaps, as she masturbated her clitty under the savage tawsing. *Vap*! *Vap*!

'Oh! Yes, whip me! It's been so long since I felt Count Scazza's crop – whip me to the bone, gels.'

'You – the count?' Belinda hissed. 'Why, you shameless trollop.'

Vap! *Vap*!

'Ooh! Yes! I'm a naughty girl. Whip me till I come –'

'I'll make you come, a real woman's way,' snarled Sally, wrenching her head from his cock.

'Oh, beloved Sally . . .' she moaned, drool trickling from her lips.

Pushing Belinda aside, he sprang behind, and mounted her. His cock plunged savagely into her anus, and, with a single thrust, penetrated her rectum, right to his balls.

'Ooh! No! please,' whimpered Miss Harrod, as he began to bugger her. 'You're hurting me!'

Sweat sprayed from his rippling body, as, teeth bared in a snarl, he slapped his hips against Miss Harrod's writhing bare bum. Cock squelching loudly in her arse grease, he slammed his bell end to her colon, and the buggered woman gasped, her teats heaving, and her face wrinkled in agony. Wunu kneeled, and began to tongue Belinda's gushing cunt, before pulling her to the bed, where the two girls lay clasped, faces to cunts, and gamahuched, with loud slurpings at their quims.

'If you were my slut, at the oasis,' Sally panted, 'I'd hang you upside down and flog your cunt to jelly, bitch.'

'Oh! Yes, I deserve it,' gurgled the buggered headmistress. 'That's so good; that's sinfully nice. Split me in two with your cock, Sally. I'm sorry I called you a girl! Fuck me with that pole! Biff me hard! Gosh, those knobs on your cock are so ripping – not even Scazza tools like this.'

Belinda cupped Wunu's squirming buttocks in her palms, pressing the girl's belly to her face, and French kissed the wet ebony cunt like a mouth. She whimpered, panting, as Wunu's tongue stabbed her wombneck, and her nose flicked Belinda's erect clitty, throbbing outside her gash lips. Wunu's long nubbin was in Belinda's mouth, and she sucked it like a lollipop, with Wunu's bum and belly squirming violently, as come poured from her slit, into Belinda's throat. Wunu sucked loudly, as she swallowed Belinda's spurting come; the two girls whimpered into each other's cunt, as they convulsed in orgasm.

'Oh! Oh! Yes . . . ooh!' sobbed Miss Harrod.

Belinda turned to see creamy spunk bubbling from her bumhole, as Sally's balls hammered her anal opening and ejaculated their load into her colon. Sneering, Sally withdrew his dripping cock with a loud plop, and wiped it on Miss Harrod's hair.

'Well!' she gasped, uncoiling from her crouch.

Wunu's crooked fingers slipped into Belinda's cunt, found her bone and pressed hard.

'Ahh . . .' cried Belinda, convulsing, in further climax, as a long jet of clear fluid spurted from her cunt, and splashed Miss Harrod full in the face.

Belinda's ejaculate dripped from Miss Harrod's chin, and the peaks of her quivering bare breasts. The headmistress's face was livid.

'Insolence, Miss Beaucul?' she hissed.

'You cheeked the head, you rotten bitch,' hissed Wunu, and kicked Belinda between her legs.

'Ooh!' Belinda howled, as Wunu's toes penetrated her cunt.

Sally began to kick her bare bubbies, mashing the teats with hard slams, while Wunu kicked her cunt and buttocks, clawing her pouch flesh and anus bud with her toenails.

'Oh! Ouch! Stop!' Belinda wailed, squirming, under the thudding bare feet of her tormentors.

Wunu dragged her by the hair, and began to slap her face, while she kicked her titties and gash, and Sally kicked her bottom. Miss Harrod watched, licking her lips, for several minutes, until she stilled the beating with an imperious wave.

'For your insolence, you shall be flogged with the sjambok, Miss Beaucul, after supper tomorrow,' she said.

'Not before the school, miss?' sobbed Belinda, rubbing her bruised bum and gash.

'Certainly not. Your whipping shall be before the staff, in the gym, by your friend Miss Bitter.'

After a restless night, when even two powerful frigs did not bring sleep, and a nervous day in the classroom, Belinda found herself without appetite for supper. Her friends on the staff edged away from her with embarrassed smiles, and she toyed listlessly with her soup. She had her copy of the school rules, indeed draconian. They specified when punishment was due, for almost any infraction, but were vague on the limits of the punishments themselves, leaving the duration, instrument, and number of strokes 'to mistress's discretion'. All whippings must be on the bare, generally the buttocks – or, in special cases, 'up to one hundred lashes on the full naked body'. Belinda shivered at a tap on her shoulder.

'It's time, Belinda,' said April Bitter, splendid in shiny white gym kit of short pleated skirt, fluffy ankle socks and tight blouse, barely constraining her breasts. She held a coiled sjambok under her arm.

'So soon? Oh, yes, of course,' Belinda blurted. 'My, you look hearty.'

'Always hearty for a flogging, girl,' said April, licking her lips. 'Nothing personal, mind.'

Belinda followed April out of the staff dining room, eyed furtively by her colleagues. They entered the deserted gym, where a row of benches faced the centre floor. April began to adjust ceiling rings and pulleys.

'Have to wait until the sightseers arrive, Belinda,' she said. 'Rotten luck, I know – this lustful heat ruins us all – but I can't pretend I won't enjoy whipping you.'

'Oh, April . . .' Belinda wailed.

'You've a bum to die for, girl, that just begs for stripes,' April said. 'And you'll be strung naked – I am looking forward to that fabulous bod wriggling. Tell you what, we could go to the Café de la Lune for a drink afterwards, if you feel up to it. Scazza will love groping your welts. See this lovely tongue?' She caressed her whip. 'It's a good long wraparound. So, when I flog your back or bum, I can curl her round that tiny waist, and lash your front. Ever been twat-whipped, Belinda?'

'Not really – only on my buttocks,' Belinda blurted. 'I'm more scared than I've ever been. What can it be like to have my bare back flogged?'

She began to cry, as Miss Harrod led in the staff members, who sheepishly nodded to Belinda, before taking their seats. Miss Harrod ordered Belinda to stand within a chalked circle, under the roped ceiling rings, and asked her formally if she was aware what brought her here.

'Yes, miss,' Belinda snuffled. 'Gross insolence to the school principal.'

'Is there any reason why you should not receive fifty lashes of the whip, on your naked body?'

Belinda gulped. 'N–no, miss.'

'Then, you will please strip to the full bare.'

Scarlet with shame, Belinda undid her blouse buttons and stripped to her bra, which she unhooked, letting her breasts spring bare. April carefully folded her garments in a pile on a vaulting horse. Next, she unfastened her skirt, then her suspender belt and garter straps, and slid her panties down, stepping out of them as gracefully as possible to let her naked quim shine in the harsh white light.

Thank goodness I shaved my hillock this morning. It would be awful to be whipped hairy.

She slipped off her shoes, then rolled down each stocking, handing them to April, who wrinkled her nose, and finally stood in the nude before the staff, fidgeting and licking their lips.

'Stand to attention, Miss Beaucul,' rapped the headmistress.

Belinda obeyed, her bum and bubbies shivering, despite the sweat dripping from her chin and nipples. And there was other moisture . . .

Oh, no . . . I'm wet between my legs.

Paraded nude for whipping before those lustful eyes, Belinda felt her cunt juicing, the more so, as Miss Harrod issued intructions for her binding; she was no longer a girl, merely naked female meat for correction. She raised her arms, allowing April to rope her wrists to two dangling rings, which she then pulled tight, lifting Belinda onto tiptoes. A four-foot hobble pole was strapped to her ankles, forcing her legs wide, and the ends of the hobble screwed into stone barbell rests. Miss Moggach, the matron, stepped forwards, eyes opaque and stern behind her glasses, and donned rubber gloves, before prodding Belinda's titties, buttocks and belly, then applying her stethoscope to her breast. Two rubbered fingers slipped into Belinda's pouch, and probed the squashy slit. Miss Moggach lifted her fingers, glistening with Belinda's cunt dew.

'I pronounce the subject fit to receive punishment,' she intoned. 'Be it noted that the subject betrays excitation in her private parts.'

Belinda was scarlet, mortified with her visible shame, yet it was true – as her body trembled before the awful prospect of a full bare-body whipping, her quim dripped come over her thighs, for all to see. April bunched Belinda's hair, and secured it with a rubber band in a pony-tail, then placed a black cotton hood, without eyelets, over her head. Belinda quivered, naked, blindfold and helpless to move, with her arms and legs painfully stretched, and Miss Harrod decreed punishment could begin.

Panting, her breath hot under her hood, Belinda clenched her buttocks, and tightened her back muscles, as the whip whistled. *Thwap*! A streak of whipfire seared her back, just beneath her shoulder blades, the force of the stroke jolting her forwards, and wrenching her wrists and ankles in their ropes. She gasped audibly beneath her hood, as her buttocks slammed tight, in automatic reaction, although her bottom was as yet unwhipped. *Thwap*!

'Uhh . . .' she groaned, as the whip took her high on the shoulders, just below her nape.

Thwap!

'Ahh!'

The whip sliced her ribs, then snaked round, to lash her erect nipples. *Thwap*! The whip slapped her bubbies.

'Oh! Ohh!' Belinda sobbed, her whipped bubs bouncing against her ribcage.

April flogged Belinda's back to ten strokes, with Belinda jerking and wriggling in her bonds, sobbing beneath her hood at the fire that burned her bare back. *Thwap*!

'Ooh!' she shrieked, as the eleventh lashed her buttocks.

Thwap!

'Oh! Ah!'

Her bottom clenched tight, and she began to squirm, rolling the fesses vainly to try and dissipate the smarting agony. *Thwap*! Tears glazed her cheeks, as her gorge rose at every dreadful whipstroke, searing her naked skin. *Thwap*!

'Ahh!'

Her body danced, rattling her hobble bar, and the gymnastic rings tethering her wrists. *Thwap*! Belinda whimpered, her titties heaving with loud, choking sobs, and her buttocks squirming frantically, as the whip licked her haunches, and curled round to lash her cunt hillock.

'Oh! Oh! No, please . . .' she groaned.

Thwap!

'Ahh!'

Thwap!

'Ooh!

The heavy sjambok stung her buttocks as fearfully as a cane, but with a far greater thud, knocking her cunt basin forwards, and welting her bare nates wider, with a greater smart than even a cane's searing bite. After ten lashes to the buttocks, April paused, panting, to caress Belinda's fesses and gushing cooze, until Miss Harrod ordered her to proceed, on pain of her own whipping.

'I'm sorry, girl,' she whispered. 'Drinks are on me, at the Café de la Lune, and I'll make Scazza give you a decent tooling.'

'Don't be sorry, April,' Belinda moaned. 'I hope you're as wet as I am.'

For the twenty-first stroke, April again whipped her shoulders, followed by several stingers to the back, varying her aim, so that Belinda's whole bare upper back smarted with crisscrossed weals. The flogging continued thereafter with lashes at random to back or croup. Neither portion had a chance for the smarting to fade, before its next lashing. Belinda's head drooped, her eyes awash in tears, only to be jerked up by each new whipstroke, when her body would stiffen, arms and legs rigid, and flogged portion writhing. *Thwap*! *Thwap*!

'Oh! Uh . . . please, I can't take any more!'

Thwap! *Thwap*!

'Mm! Urrgh!'

Her gasps sucked the cotton hood into her mouth, and she had to spit it out, soaked in her own drool, to whimper, as her whipped flesh squirmed. Her head shook wildly, as the strokes mounted, yet her cunt continued to ooze come down her wriggling thighs. *Thwap*!

'Ooh! Ahh!'

The thirty-fifth snaked between her legs to whip her quim full on. *Thwap*!

'Ohh! No!' Belinda squealed, as a jet of piss streamed from her wriggling gash, and splashed on the polished wooden floorboards.

'Ten more strokes for that disgrace,' snapped Miss Harrod.

'No! please . . . ooh!'

Thwap! The whip slapped her again in the arse cleft, with the tip catching her extruded, throbbing clitty. Come spurted from Belinda's flogged gash. *Thwap*!

'Oh! Oh! That's not fair . . . ahh!'

Thwap! April whipped Belinda once more between the legs, before switching to backstrokes and teat wraparounds. Belinda no longer tried to suppress her screams of agony or stifle the frenzied, doll-like squirming of her tortured bare body. Piss and come dribbled from her flapping cooze, sliming her thighs and feet. *Thwap*! *Thwap*! The beating mercilessly went on, past the fifty, with Belinda's pain-wracked body whimpering, blubbing and pissing, blue with welts. Her belly fluttered, her whipped clit tingling, as come drooled from her open flogged gash.

Oh! I'm going to come . . . the shame . . .

Suddenly, the door crashed open, with a babble of African voices and jingling cock bells.

'What is the meaning – ooh!' Miss Harrod squealed, as a whiplash silenced her.

Belinda's bonds were cut, her body shouldered, and she

was carried, whimpering, into the hot night air, to be hurled into a vehicle, whose motor was running. The vehicle, some kind of open-top jeep, lurched and took off, racing through the darkened streets of Berbera, and then Belinda smelled the sea, then the dry acrid whiff of the desert, with clouds of dust and sand choking her, under her hood.

'Who are you?' she wailed. 'Where are we going?'

'Shut up, bitch,' snarled a girl's voice. 'We are rescuing you. The prince is coming home, and we must offer him the choicest girlmeat.'

Belinda smelled the smoky flesh of Wunu, then Sally. Before she could speak, she was thrust forwards, over the side of the jeep, with the metal edge cutting into her bare titties.

'I deserve one last poke, bitch, before cousin Amur gets you as his slave,' hissed Sally. 'Wunu can wank off, as she watches your bum squirm.'

Breasts bouncing on the scorching metal, Belinda shrieked, as Sally's stiff cock penetrated her anus. She came almost at once, squealing in orgasm, as he filled her rectum and slammed her sigmoid colon, beginning a fierce buggery that had Belinda squirming, as she hung over the jeep's side, with sand spraying her flapping teats. When Sally's hot spunk squirted into her colon, she orgasmed once more.

'You bastard, Sally,' she gasped, as she slumped back into the jeep. 'I needed that.'

Wunu's lips pressed to her cunt, and tongued her for long minutes to another come, while Wunu panted in pleasure at her own frig. Then, she spanked Belinda's wealed bottom, and Belinda squirmed, wanking and whimpering, until she smelled water, flowers and fruit, with the sound of fountains and the swishing of palms. The jeep stopped, amid a flurry of girls' voices, and Sally carried Belinda into a tent, dumping her on a crackly straw palliasse.

'New slave, nurse,' he said.

'Well, let's take a look at her. Gosh, she's taken quite a

lacing, but she'll be all right when we get the red mud on her. Seems a pneumatic bitch, whoever she is.'

Belinda shook her head, sobbing and groaning, as her hood was ripped off.

'Clarice!' she gasped.

13

Mudslave

'Stick your bottoms up higher, you filthy slaves,' rasped Clarice, 'otherwise, no breakfast.'

A dozen nude, freshly thrashed girls, obeyed, eyes wide. The nurse's sjambok swished above their buttocks, while the guard girls, rippling with ebony muscle and naked, but for thong boots and thin gold G-strings, cradled their canes, their eyes sullen with menace. Clarice sweated in her whites and blues, with white rubber bootees. Beyond the prince's yard, beneath the lush canopy of date palms and jacaranda trees, naked girlslaves carried baskets of fruit to market; young male nobles swaggered, cock balls jingling under crimson robes; lush-skirted mistresses sauntered, bare to the waist, their painted nipples pierced with golden hoops, leading their naked boyslaves by ball-chains or foreskin-rings.

Noble ladies wore their skirts rear-slit, with bare fesses waggling before their boyslaves' erect cocks; nude ebony girls, chained at the waist, under a guard's whip, chanted, on their way to pick vanilla pods. Derelict tanks and armoured cars slouched in the red mud, their flanks festooned with flowers, and sometimes echoing with the sobs of a scourged prisoner, sweating in bondage. The desert air and azure sky were fresh with the scent of fountains and pools. Shimmering at the centre of the oasis, the great lake gleamed silver-blue, splashed with the nude ebony bodies of early-morning swimmers.

Wincing at the surgical speculum holding her anus wide, Belinda thrust her bottom high, her breath hot on the gaping speculumed anus of the girl next in the circle. Steam wafted from an abandoned Panhard armoured car, where cookpots bubbled. Two apron slaves, their naked bodies glistening with red mud under white rubber aprons, wheeled a cauldron of mealie porage towards Clarice, who brushed a tress back beneath her nurse's cap, before lifting a rubber syringe, over the twelve crouching girlslaves.

She filled the syringe with the glutinous brown mess, and injected each girl, filling her rectum, until the porage dripped from her anus. When each hole had its cargo, she ordered them to strain and eat. Belinda glued her lips to the anus of the ebony girl in front, and began to suck the food, while heaving, to eject her own filling of porage into the mouth behind her. At Clarice's footsteps, she tensed. Slap! Clarice's bootee slapped her pendant breasts, making her choke on her porage.

'Bum up, and force, Miss Beaucul,' sneered the nurse. 'If there's one drip of porage left in your hole, at enema time –'

She kicked Belinda's teats twice more, whistling softly, as tears sprang to Belinda's eyes. Then, Belinda's body jerked, and she spluttered porage, as Clarice aimed a kick between her legs, slapping her dangling clitty, bulging in its coil of thin gold wire.

'Uhh!' she gasped. She did not speak, or look up at the nurse.

'That beastly priapiscus is soft, bitch,' snapped Clarice. 'It had better stiffen up for frottage – I want a full pot from you today. You slimy toad, you don't know how lucky you are to have such a nub – positively grotesque! – otherwise, a slut like you could never be the prince's mudslave, let alone compete for prime slave. Did you fill your wanking sponge last night?'

Belinda nodded, still slurping her porage, scented with the black girl's arse grease.

'I hope you're lying,' said Clarice, cracking her whip inches from Belinda's bare. 'Then I can give you extra lashes.'

Sobbing, Belinda swallowed the rest of her porage, while straining to empty her own rectum of the greasy mess. It was like this every day – the merciless routine of training, breaking her will, to fashion her as a pleasure girl, submissive to any lash or any caress, and hardened by torments from the other girlslaves. The dormitory guards punished any word illicitly spoken, but sat, idly masturbating under their jingling gold G-strings, as the naked girls gamahuched, spanked, tortured or frigged each other.

That first night, her bruises healed by immersion in hot mud pools, and with red mud and camel butter coating her body, Belinda was delivered naked to the dormitory, powerfully scented with girlsweat. Bright eyes followed her in the darkness, as she lay on her stiff palliasse, and then nude ebony bodies crushed her in a pile, drowning her squeals. Her face was squashed under bottoms and cunts, filling her mouth with girl come, with her slit invaded by eager lips and tongues; between tribadic embraces, the girls turned her over, for spanking.

The enforced silence, broken only by slaps and gasps, made their slippery, desperate caresses the more precious; Belinda surrendered to the pain of spanking, pinching, clawing frottage and the lustful passion of her new sisters in submission. Lips kissed nipples, fingers poked juicing cunts, toes filled eagerly sucking mouths, tongues probed squirming, arse-greased bumholes. The sole European, Belinda shuddered, gasping, as the ebony girls, shining with sweat, sucked her trembling clitty, biting and chewing the stiff nub, and flicking it with wet slurping tongues, while her pinched titties and bumhole writhed. Her gasps of orgasm, crushed under slimy nude bodies, were loud and genuine, and Belinda was quickly accepted into the nightly wanking games.

A girlslave was issued with a stiff leather dildo, like a policeman's baton, optionally worn from a waiststring, and a daily wanking sponge, which she had to fill with come every night. The dildos, spoils of war, had Armamento Femminile Igienico Italiano embossed in gold, well worn by frotting. The come, squirted into vials, was stored for the nobles to drink. At intervals during their day, Clarice imprisoned the girls in the frotting hobble;

they sat, thighs spread and ankles imprisoned, fucking themselves with their dildos, and tweaking their clitties, to fill their come pots from their wanked cunts.

Every morning, roused from their palliasses, the girlslaves scampered naked to the lake, where they bathed; dripping, they stood still, while the guards lashed their wet bottoms twenty strokes with wide, knobbly tawse, of Michelin rubber. After this crude whipping, they took breakfast of porage from the anus; then repaired to the latrines, to squat for a communal dung, followed by a hot mud enema, painfully delivered by rubber hosepipe, and a final evacuation. Then, the girls anointed each other with mud and camel butter, until their nude bodies shone red.

Amid exercises, games, punishments and frottage, were luncheon, of raw fish and vegetables, slurped as at breakfast, but from the cunt; supper of tea and scones, eaten at high table, in ladylike deportment, with whipstrokes for any back not ramrod straight, and, finally, evening dunging. Any girl needing to evacuate during the day pissed in another's mouth, while dungs had to be held in on pain of scourging. At any passing noble's crooked finger, a girlslave must kneel at once, and tongue his cock to spunk, swallowing every drop; or present her buttocks for anal penetration.

Failure to please Clarice meant formal punishment after supper, with few girls spared a back-whipping, bottom-caning or a 'teat-and-twat' on the breasts and cunt, with quim lips pegged open to expose the clitty and slit flesh. Otherwise, there were punishments of simple bondage, like the crab: trussing in ropes, with thumb stocks, spine bent backwards, and mousetraps clamping the nipples and clitoris. Whippings were often given by the girlslaves themselves, with the miscreant strung, but Clarice herself always flogged Belinda, strung, horsed or in spiked rubber bondage, gagged with Clarice's soiled panties.

On the avenue to the lake, the trees were hung with cages, containing naked pleasure girls, available free, for boyslaves, who climbed the tree and entered the cage, to tup the whimpering girl in public view. Clarice liked to lock her girls in those cages, not for fucking – the prince's slaves were reserved for the nobility, with miscreant tuppers, male or female, punished by a month's daily scourging, and buggery with a basalt dildo – but for public shame. Limbs and teats bound, with toes in their mouths and cunts open, the girls had to piss and dung through the cage bars. Once, groaning and sobbing in her caged bondage, Belinda narrowly missed pissing on Wunu, bare-breasted, her naked bottom winking from her split silk robe, and followed by an erect boyslave.

Frequently, the girls served at 'noble teatime'. Heads hooded, they bent over a rail, exposing their bottoms for anal penetration by any noble, with most girls enduring several buggeries. Beneath their cunts stood come pots, which the bum-fucked girls strove to fill, wanking their clits, as jingling cocks rammed their rectums. All this was endured without even the consolation of a smoke, forbidden, on pain of exile – never alone, the girls had no chance to sneak one, anyway – although, as a pleasure exercise, they learned to smoke cigarettes with their cunts. As she worked her sphincter, puffing smoke from her quim, and longing for a quick drag, Belinda noticed the cigs were Scazza's brand.

'Remember, sluts,' Clarice would drawl, 'you are nothing but pleasure animals, vessels for the spunk of men and skins for their whipping. I myself gained appointment as the prince's nurse, by offering every hole and swelling of my body to his pleasure.'

Agonising exercises made the girls' bodies supple, to assume every lustful contortion, and girls' clitties were measured daily to gauge their growth, bound in stimulating wire sheaths. They performed clitoral traction, masturbating their nubs up and down, while squeezing hard, and one girl, a wiry Nubian, with hard conic teats, and a huge, pneumatic bottom, amazed even Clarice, because she could contort herself to lick the tip of her own nubbin. According to Clarice, African clits of over two inches were not unusual, and favoured by the prince. But where was Amur? As the weeks passed, Belinda's body toughened, and, under punishing masturbation, her clitty did seem to be growing. She longed to feel her prince's cock in her anus – she knew he would choose her as prime slave.

Several times daily, the girls replenished their coating of mud, and bathed in viscous mud pools, where a favourite punishment was total inhumation. Belinda shuddered, at her first live burial – the clammy feeling of the mud, like quicksand, closing over her bound, naked body; the agonising bite of the ropes, pinioning her limbs; the awful taste of mud, and its cold heaviness in her stomach, as, gasping for air, she frantically ate her way to the surface.

In this, as in all contests, the girlslaves were fiercely competitive, winning the right to piercings of their flesh, and pins, rings or studs inserted into their bodies. After weeks of training, Belinda was a champion at live burial, with numerous metal studs on teat, thigh, perineum, toe and gash flap. She looked forward to her inhumations, and meals of mud, although satisfying a girl's stomach-craving for mud was – so unfair! – a whipping offence at any other time.

The girlslaves practised their sensuous art on noble males who were of age, but not yet permitted buggery. Like the others, Belinda sucked their cocks, and swallowed copious spunk, while wanking herself off into the omnipresent come pot; pumped her thighs, goosing, to rub stiff tools to spunk; wanked cocks with her titties, armpits, toes, or hair – called a 'Rapunzel'. Belinda became adept at the art of pygisma, bringing cocks to spunk by trapping the glans between her squirming, squeezing bum flans, and milking them of spunk, to spurt over her anus bud.

The spunk was kept in spunk pots, and when Clarice bathed, in an old Hotchkiss tank turret, the girls mixed a lotion of spunk and their own come to rub into Clarice's nude body, while they took turns to wank her clitty, and fuck her with their dildos. She never looked her tribadists in the eye, not even Belinda, whose gamahuching services she required the most. Otherwise, Clarice seemed to abjure masturbation, even at the mud-wrestling matches, attended by numerous noble ladies, who made no secret of openly diddling, as the nude girls grappled in the sloppy red dirt.

In their wrestling league, each girlslave had to fight all the rest, and Belinda quickly excelled. From the league sprang a tournament, and Belinda reached the final, against the supple Nubian. Count Scazza and a host of brawny legionnaires were in the audience, as well as Wunu and Sally, all sipping girl-come cocktails, and sucking on vanilla pods. There were no rules – any kicking, gouging or twisting was allowed, until one girl submitted.

The Nubian sprang at Belinda first, getting her in a headlock and forcing her head under the mud, where Belinda gurgled, bubbling helplessly and her limbs threshing, as the Nubian kicked her in the cunt and bubbies. Slamming her head against the girl's thighs, Belinda found her cooze, and bit savagely on the extruded nubbin, toppling the lithe ebony girl; after rising, Belinda straddled her, punching her teats and clawing in her cunt, with her nails raking the girl's clitty, and scratching hard inside the pouch, as the girl writhed, shrieking helplessly, her face plastered by dirt. The girl shrieked, as Belinda pissed hard on her face, and, as Belinda kneed her repeatedly in the groin, the Nubian pissed, loosing a cargo of dungs over Belinda's thigh, into the mud.

Belinda saw Wunu kneeling before Count Scazza, and sucking his cock. Wunu masturbated, with her bum bare and sumptuous dress piled daintily on her bobbing back, while Sally buggered her. Where was Amur? Legionnaires were serviced by common girlslaves, by mouth, armpit, toes, squeezed bubbies and bottoms upthrust for pygisma or full anal penetration.

At last, Belinda immersed her opponent in the frothing slime of mud and dung, then pulled her hair down to her crotch, forcing the girl's face into her own cunt. The girl groaned, dunging copiously; Belinda got her in a thigh lock, around the neck and bum, and plunged the pinioned girl deep below the mud, with only her feet sticking up, which Belinda bit savagely. After over a minute's immersion, she let the girl surface, and freed her face from her cunt; the dung-splattered girl sobbed submission to rapturous applause.

Still slopped in mud, the loser had to take an on-the-spot whipping from Belinda, with Clarice's own sjambok, sullenly yielded; she writhed, shrieking, in the mud, as Belinda stood over her, lashing her with the leather tongue, before signalling the end of the beating with another steaming piss, all over her wealed body. For this triumph, Belinda received her first teat-piercing. She thrust her heaving bare breasts at Clarice, who needled her nipples – Belinda, eyes shut, suppressing her squeal of pain – and smiled, as she felt heavy gold hoops dangling from her breasts.

As their training progressed, the girlslaves collected such trophies – cunt, toe and nipple rings, nubbin studs, and anal or clit rings – until Belinda's body proudly jingled with her mass of metal. Whenever she glimpsed herself in water, she saw a proud, African warrior slave, dripping gold, massive titties and muscles rippling under their slimy mud coating, and her clitty poking generously from her cunt flaps, the whole twat swollen by constant masturbation. With the other adorned girlslaves, she marched proudly, titties and cunt jangling.

There were also some amusing punishments, like the mousehole. The trussed victim crouched, with her buttocks clamped apart and her anus opened by a speculum. Her rectum was filled with cheese, and mice released to burrow into her for the food, while she shrieked and wriggled, and all the girls laughed. Belinda suffered this punishment, but with her head immersed in a bowl of mud, and, after the mice, Clarice released a little grass snake to chase them. Belinda gurgled, under the mud, as the snake's tongue flicked her sigmoid colon, and her tripes seemed to explode with hideous tickling pain.

Nude combats, on which the girls bet food or spankings, took place in the dungeon: each girl hung by hooked armpits from the ceiling, bound in ropes and chains, with her titties clamped in suspension, and padded hooks in her cunt and anus. Pushed forwards, the girls swung together to clash with fierce gouging and biting, the aim being to dislodge the opponent from her hooks and teat clamps, and send her plunging. There was no submission, and the audience gleefully applauded the tortures inflicted on the pinioned loser, helplessly hanging by her titties and armpits, until the victress deigned to topple her bruised, kicked and bitten body to earth.

Otherwise, the daily punishments were orthodox floggings. Always for some miscreance of Clarice's invention, Belinda raised her arms to be strung by the wrists, then, suspended and wriggling, endured thirty or forty whipstrokes on her bare back and croup; or, gagged and bound, over a horse, she crouched, buttocks up, for a 'school caning' of several dozen. All the girlslaves were flogged, but Belinda most cruelly and most often.

If the girls had bared up bravely, Clarice announced a 'dorm feast'. Giggling, the girls would part their thighs for their cunts to be filled with vanilla, cake and ice cream, and masturbate vigorously, as each girl took her turn to gobble the treats, from a cunt slimed with come. For an extra-special treat, she permitted the girls to fill their slits with mud, and feast from each other.

One evening, Clarice summoned Belinda outside under a full moon, and handed her a thin, whippy cane, with a crook handle.

'Back to school, miss?' Belinda said.

'Something like that,' Clarice replied. 'A prince's slave must be adept at dominance as well as submission.'

'Clarice,' Belinda blurted, 'why are you so cruel to me? Such beastly floggings, and ... eating porage from girls' bums, and ... you know.'

'Why is any girl cruel to another?' Clarice spat. 'The prince wanted you trained for him. But he shan't have you. He shall have me.'

They came to a ruined Renault tank, with its tracks covering a hole, leading underground. They squeezed past the tank tracks down wooden steps to a candlelit dungeon, equipped with flogging stools and horses, wrist rings, ankle chains, stocks, numerous hobbles, even a rack and gibbet, amid the perfume of fresh flowers. A dozen nude slaves lay indolent on velvet cushions, supervised by six bewhipped guard girls, black bodies glowing in their glittering gold G-strings.

'They're all Europeans,' Belinda gasped.

'These are the night slaves,' Clarice said. 'They collect rubbish, clean latrines and scavenge. Others live in the treetops, out of sight. All are volunteers.'

'But why?'

'You'll see. Select any two, and cane them.'

'What? But –'

Seeing Belinda's school cane, the slaves crouched, imploring her to flog them. All the males had erect cocks, while the females parted their thighs and wanked, showing dripping coozes, with their nipples and quim lips individually squeezed in heavy metal clamps.

'Please, miss, I've been so naughty.'

'My bum's aching to be caned, miss.'

'Jeremy!' gasped Belinda.

Jeremy Quince, cock stiff, beamed. 'Yes, mistress,' he blurted. 'Thrash my bare raw, I beg you. It's what I've really always craved.'

'Me, first, mistress!' cried a girl. 'You must tan my bum. I need it so badly.'

'That slut is Jessica Twobbs,' sneered Clarice. 'She learned her flagellance at St Cloud's, but giving it didn't suit the bitch.'

'Ladies first. Bare up, miss,' said Belinda to the pale English girl.

With a squeak of joy, Jessica crouched, presenting her naked fesses to Belinda's cane. 'I've been so naughty, mistress,' she murmured dreamily. 'My bum needs beating.'

'Miss Twobbs – Jessica – how could you choose this?' Belinda blurted.

'How could I choose anything else?'

Her nude body rippling red with mud, nipple rings clinking and cooze studs gleaming, Belinda raised her cane. She lashed the girl's pale bare buttocks, leaving a long pink stripe, and Jessica clenched, exhaling sharply.

'Ouch!'

Belinda began to cane methodically, lacing the whole expanse of bare bumflesh, in addition to the thigh tops and haunches, with Jessica's croup squirming, as her gasps of pain quickened.

The buttocks shuddered, and Jessica gasped, gurgling with pleasure, as the cane whipped her quivering fesses to crimson. Come sprayed from her writhing, pendant cunt flaps, over her thighs. Watching one nude girl cane another, the female slaves wanked off, squirting copious come from their diddled cunts, and even the G-stringed guards began a lazy frottage, while Clarice, red-faced, stood aloof. Jeremy, cock stiff, trembled, his tongue hanging out, and drooled.

'Stripe her, mistress, stripe the bitch,' he crooned.

'Insolent pig,' spat a guard girl, and lashed Jeremy's arse.

'Ooh!' he squealed.

The guards trampled his threshing body, with one girl's foot squashing his face, another's foot tweaking his balls, and the others kicking. His stiff cock bobbed between stamping feet.

'Yes, oh yes!' he groaned. 'Crush me, ladies.'

The girl squashing his face let him sniff and lick her toes, then removed her foot and dropped to his head, squatting heavily on him, so that her naked buttocks crushed his face. A bubble of piss spurted from her cooze, splashing her thighs and running over the captive's face, while Jeremy gurgled, swallowing the girl's golden fluid. With one guard's toes clamping his balls, another girl kicked the glans of his erect cock.

'Oh! Uh!' he moaned, his voice muffled by his queen's buttocks, as a droplet of cream appeared at his peehole. 'Don't stop.'

The girl kicked his bell end, with the other shrimping his balls, as his tool bucked, spraying copious jets of spunk over the bare feet of his tormentresses.

'Filthy swine,' hissed one guard, wiping her spunked toes in Jessica's hair. 'Miss Clarice, please tell your girlslave to punish the pig.'

The other girl thrust her slimy toes in Jessica's mouth, and ordered her to lick them clean. Her bottom squirming under Belinda's cane, Jessica obeyed, swallowing the spunk licked from the black girl's toes. Her own thighs glistened with come, oozing from her cunt. *Vip*!

'That's forty,' Belinda panted.

The guard slapped a rubber harness round Jeremy's balls, tightened it and pulled him up to a crouch. Jeremy's upthrust bare faced Belinda. *Vip*! She lashed his fesses, and he gasped. *Vip*!

'Ooh! That's tight, miss.'

'Silence, worm,' Belinda hissed. 'This is no game. I'll make you suffer.'

Belinda's cane flashed, a blur, as she flogged the whimpering male's buttocks. Sweat poured from her, her lips frothed with drool and her thighs slithered in the come sluicing from her cunt, as she ribboned his wriggling bare arse. Unable to escape the strokes, with his tight ball harness, Jeremy squealed, squirmed and sobbed, until, at the seventieth canestroke, Clarice stayed Belinda's caning arm. Jeremy looked up.

'Thank you, mistress,' he sobbed. 'Old "Groggy" Garstang was right, there is no pleasure like a lady's thrashing.'

'What?' Belinda gasped.

'Truth is, the navy sent him home as wounded, only because the African gels flogged his bum so raw. How we chaps long for a truly cruel mistress, like you!'

Belinda was still panting, as she followed Clarice up the steps.

'Having doubts?' said Clarice.

'Please?'

'About being a slave. You gave those two toads a rare pounding. Do you really want to be submissive, like Jessica, or be a whipper? Scazza could use your disciplinary talents, Miss Beaucul, in the legion brothel.'

'I don't know,' Belinda sighed.

The warm night air caressed her body, glistening under starlight. Clarice scooped two handfuls of mud, and the girls eyed each other guiltily, as they munched.

'Cigarette?' said Clarice, proffering a Gold Flake.
'Gosh, thanks,' said Belinda.
They lit up and puffed.
'You juiced as you whipped them,' Clarice accused.
'Yes, I did.'
'You love power. You wanted to masturbate.'
'Oh . . . yes. Stop it, Clarice.'
Pouting, Clarice kicked the red earth. 'Dash it, Belinda, you know how jealous I am of you – of your bum, and that superhuman clitty. Let's wank off, just you and me.'
Cigarette dangling, Clarice stripped off her nurse's uniform, hanging each garment neatly from the tank's gun barrel. Naked, she embraced Belinda, pressing her breasts against her nipple rings, and the girls sank to the dirt, stroking bottoms, with lips and cunts squelching in mud-slimed kisses. Belinda gasped, as Clarice's fingers entered her slit, and began to wank her throbbing nubbin. She penetrated Clarice's anus, and poked vigorously, while rubbing Clarice's clitty with her thigh.
'Gosh, Clarice, it's so good,' she moaned. 'We shouldn't be enemies.'
'Yes, we should,' gasped Clarice, and stubbed her cigarette to sizzle on Belinda's wet cooze.
'Ouch!' Belinda yelped. 'That's beastly!'
Clarice overturned Belinda, straddling her, with her mouth clamped on Belinda's cunt, and her own cooze pumping in Belinda's face, showering Belinda with come. With both girls thoroughly slimed in mud, sweat and cunt juice, Clarice's mouth fastened on Belinda's engorged clitty to suck and chew the trembling stiff nub. Belinda sucked Clarice's juicing pouch flaps, swallowing the copious come that poured from the nurse's cunt. Her belly heaved, trapped by Clarice's squirming titties, as her gash sluiced come, and she shivered, at her approaching orgasm.
'Mm . . .' she gasped, as Clarice pulled her nipple rings, crushing Belinda's mouth with her cunt, and stabbing her soaked slit with her tongue. 'Mm . . . mm!'
They writhed in mutual orgasm, until a light shone on their slippery, squirming bodies, and ebony hands pulled

Clarice off Belinda by the hair. *Vip*! A cane slapped Clarice's breasts.

'Ooh!' Clarice squealed. 'Let me go! Don't you know who I am?'

The whip struck her between the legs.

'Ooh!'

'Silence, slut,' snarled the guard.

There were two guard girls, and one helped Belinda to her feet.

'I'm so sorry, miss,' she purred. 'Waylaid by a filthy tree slave? And you a prince's girl.'

'No, no . . .' blurted Belinda, but the guards were already strapping Clarice astride the tank's gun barrel, her ankles roped together, beneath her, obliging her to lean forwards for balance on the metal tube.

'You have the right to punish your assailant, miss,' said the guard, curtsying and proffering her whip.

Belinda stared at Clarice's bare, unblemished buttocks, her pleading eyes and the tears glazing her face. She licked her lips and raised the quirt, a short affair of three hard rubber thongs. Pink stripes sprang to Clarice's whipped bumskin, and the girl gasped, her gushing cunt oiling the gun barrel with come.

'Oh! Belinda, please!'

Clarice's wealed buttocks wriggled frantically.

'Ouch! Ah! Belinda, for heaven's sake, tell them the truth,' Clarice whimpered.

'Silence, you filthy slut,' Belinda hissed. 'There's only room for one English girl in Amur's hareem.'

'Ha!' spat Clarice. 'Amur's returning tomorrow, Belinda. He'll choose me!'

'Then we must fight,' Belinda hissed.

Vap! *Vap*!

'Ahh!'

'Or, wank for it,' Belinda sneered. 'Juiciest girl wins.'

'That's absurd. I'll arrange combat tomorrow.'

Vap! *Vap*!

'Oh! Stop!'

'Not a chance, bitch,' Belinda replied. 'You're right – I do like dominance.'

Belinda flogged the weeping, squirming girl to forty strokes, then cast down her whip, took her dildo from her waistband, and spanked Clarice's raw red buttocks with the leather baton. After two dozen lashes, she pushed the dildo into Clarice's anus and buggered her fiercely, until Clarice's cries of pain became whimpers and gasps of ecstasy, and her come sluiced the gun barrel. Belinda buggered her to orgasm, then allowed the guard to complete Clarice's punishment. She padded back to the girlslaves' dorm, with Clarice's shrieks filling the night's warm air. After gamahuching three eager girls, she sought the Nubian, with whom she spent the night, masturbating in slippery, whispering embrace.

Breakfast in the morning was, unusually, taken at table. The sullen Clarice instructed Belinda to prepare for their combat, before Amur and his whole people. All the girlslaves anointed themselves in red mud, close-shaved their quims and polished their body metal to brightness, before they followed Belinda and Clarice, escorted by guards, to the lakeside. Clarice, like Belinda, was nude, the layers of mud failing to conceal her whipweals from the night before – perhaps on purpose, for Clarice wiggled her striped bottom, as proudly as any prince's slave. Amur sat enthroned, wearing crimson robes, with his guests beside him: Count Scazza and his officers. They sucked vanilla pods and drank champagne, served with girl come, poured from come pots by scampering bare apron slaves. Jeremy, Jessica and the other night slaves stood by a pool of solid mud, holding shovels.

Belinda and Clarice faced off on either side of the mud pool, then, on Amur's signal, dived in. They grappled, biting and gouging, while the slaves showered them with mud, so that, as soon as either girl rose for air, she was at once inhumed. They clawed at each other's cunt, to scratch clitties and pouch flesh, raked fingernails over nipples and anus, wrenched and gouged tortured titties. Belinda shrieked often, as Clarice tore at her nipple rings or cunt studs, with Clarice howling, as Belinda's metal scraped her flesh. After several minutes, Belinda got Clarice's head in an armlock, and held her under, with her toes in the girl's cunt, kicking and tearing at her wombneck.

'Eat dirt, you bitch,' she snarled, as Clarice's body threshed under the mud.

At last, Clarice went limp, and Belinda hauled herself out of the mud, dragging Clarice by the hair. As they heaved, gasping, on dry earth, Clarice kicked Belinda savagely in the quim.

'Fucking bitch!' snarled Belinda, and wrenched Clarice's hair once more under the mud, holding her head down, while she viciously spanked Clarice's squirming bottom.

'She's very dominant, that girl,' said Count Scazza, sipping champagne and come, 'just what I need for my Centre of Carnal Comfort.'

'Dominant, yes,' mused Amur. 'Granted, her rectum is succulent, but a true slave must be submissive.'

Belinda ceased spanking, and dragged Clarice from the mud. 'Spank me, Clarice,' she gasped. 'My bum's yours to hurt.'

Leering, Clarice shook her head, and presented her own bum, dripping mud, and heavy with bruises, for further spanking.

'You asked for it, fucking bitch,' Belinda hissed.

Belinda sat on her, spanking her bottom, and grinding her face in the mud; then threw herself on the whimpering girl, and bit her buttocks, thighs, belly and teats, until Clarice's wriggling body was a mass of raw red teethmarks. She delivered savage bites to Clarice's come-spewing muddy cunt, yet Clarice, howling in pain, refused to submit.

Amur ordered a second round. Both dripping girls were fastened naked in body stocks, hinged wooden blocks whose centre holes imprisoned the girls' waists, with their buttocks upthrust, ankles hobbled wide apart and hands clamped by thumb stocks, stretching their arms and torsos. Two G-stringed guards kneeled beneath their cunts, tickling their clitties with feathers, while two caned their buttocks with rattan rods and two whipped their wrenched backs with leather scourges of six knotted thongs.

The girls gasped, bums squirming, as their helpless bodies were wealed and come flowed from their tickled cunts into come pots. Their moans were stifled by stiff ebony cocks, thrust into their gaping mouths, and which they sucked to climax, swallowing every drop of spunk. At intervals, their bum-caning paused, for jingling noble cocks to penetrate their bumholes in vigorous buggery, while their cunts sluiced come, tinkling into the pots.

Belinda wept, moaning, over the tool fucking her mouth, as cock after cock split her rectum. She groaned her reply to Count Scazza's polite greeting, as his legionnaires lowered their shorts, to bugger both girls' dripping bumholes. Scazza himself tooled Clarice's anus for several minutes, without spunking, then withdrew his slimed cock, and fiercely buggered Belinda, hips slapping her shuddering buttocks, as his cock squelched in her arse grease, while his glans tupped her sigmoid colon. He whispered that she should accept his job offer.

'Then, I could suck your blonde English arsehole every day.'

'No ... no ...' gasped Belinda. 'Oh, you brute, I'm going to come!'

He spurted hot spunk to her colon, and she gasped and whimpered aloud, in orgasm, as Amur raised an approving eyebrow.

'Hmm ... submissive,' he murmured.

Clarice orgasmed, too; after an hour's buggery and whipping, their come pots stood equal, each brimming with cunt fluid.

'A tie,' said Amur. 'Let them diddle for it.'

Released from the stocks, they squatted before him, each girl wanking her cunt, with her come pouring into a new pot between her thighs. The pots filled equally – another tie! – until Belinda sprang up, then flung herself in the mud, rolling herself in a ball. The audience gasped.

Can I do it? I'm almost there ... I must! Remember what the Nubian taught me ...

Her head was between her thighs, her ankles behind her head, spine curled in the fiercest girlslave contortion.

Before her eyes, her cunt glistened with juice, and the extruded clitty pulsed, like the pistil of a succulent flower. Her mouth opened wide – there was a delighted roar from the watchers – her lips closed on her throbbing clit, her priapiscus, and squashed into her swollen wet cunt lips. With loud slurping noises, Belinda sucked her own cunt, kissing her quim like the mouth of a lover. Her priapiscus tingled between her tongue and palate, as her mouth filled with her come, until she sucked and tongued herself to double orgasm, with a vigorous clear spout of ejaculate splashing Amur's feet; smiling, Amur applauded. Clarice began to cry.

Belinda uncoiled, sprang to Amur's throne, and kneeled, parting his robes to seize his stiff bare cock between her lips. Her mouth full of her own come, she sucked the massive, jingling tool, without spilling a drop of her come. Amur grunted, holding her hair to him, and spunked into her come-filled mouth; Belinda swallowed every drop of his spunk and her own juice, before releasing his cock.

'Sir, whip me for my insolence,' she pleaded. 'Whip me and bugger me and bury me in dirt. Make me suck your cock, as your abject mudslave.'

Amur conferred with Count Scazza. 'Submissive Belinda is my prime slave,' he intoned, 'for as long as she shall please me. Miss Clarice shall take up Count Scazza's post with the legion.'

Clarice licked her lips at Scazza.

'I shall make sure I always please you,' Belinda gasped to Amur, 'as long as my bumhole is ripe for your tool, and my bottom is bare for your whip.'

Count Scazza pushed two cigarettes into Belinda's cunt, and lit them. 'The come of the lady makes a cooler smoke,' he said to Amur.

Belinda sucked with her belly, to puff luxuriant smoke from her gash lips, then transferred one cigarette, slimed with her come, to Amur's mouth, taking the other for herself, and drawing deep. Amur lifted her to sit on his lap, with her naked buttocks squirming over his stiffening cock.

'Make me eat mud, cane me, make me lick the twats of girlslaves,' she purred, her titties heaving under his squashing fingers, cigarette bobbing at her lips and her buttocks squirming in pygisma, frotting his tool to hardness. 'Anything, for your male pleasure.'

'Tomorrow,' he said, 'I shall whip you naked, hung upside down.'

'Publicly?' she gasped, eyes bright. 'My shame seen by everyone?'

'Of course.'

'Gosh,' said Jessica Twobbs to Jeremy, 'slavery games are fun, but within limits. What modern girl could possibly want that?'

'What modern girl could want anything else?' retorted Belinda, as she pleasured her master.